AN UNSAFE PAIR OF HANDS

Chris Dolley

Book View Café

AN UNSAFE PAIR OF HANDS

Published by Book View Café

Book View Café Publishing Cooperative
P.O. Box 1624
Cedar Crest, NM 87008-1624

www.bookviewcafe.com

ISBN 13: 978-1-61138-396-6

Cover art © Gail Johnson - Fotolia.com
Cover design by Chris Dolley

First printing, July 2014
First digital edition, July 2011

Books by Chris Dolley

Resonance

Shift

French Fried

What Ho, Automata

Medium Dead

Magical Crimes

International Kittens of Mystery

How Possession Can Help You Lose Weight

CHAPTER ONE

The woman's body lay face down inside the ancient stone circle, her long pale coat almost glowing in the early morning gloom. What colour was it? White? Yellow? DCI Shand moved closer, stopping at the edge of the circle. As the first detective at the scene, he had to take his time to observe and appraise.

His eyes were drawn to the woman. He'd never seen a dead body before. Not in the field. He'd lectured about them, he'd studied countless pictures, he'd taken raw recruits through every nuance of crime scene protocol. But that was all theory. This was the real thing. Only his second day in CID and already he had his first murder.

And it had to be murder. The way she lay there – arms down by her side, legs straight, clothes unruffled, her head turned slightly to one side so that her left cheek was resting on the grass. She'd been arranged. Was her head pointing towards the rising sun?

He looked up at the heavy blanket of cloud – no help there, not even the merest hint of where the sun might be. Perhaps he was being influenced by the situation. Everything about the location screamed ritual. A body laid out inside a stone circle. It had to be significant, didn't it?

But if so, shouldn't she be at its centre? Why position her to one side?

He ran his eye around the stones – more than a dozen of them, irregularly shaped, equally spaced, their heights ranging from four to six feet. The circle stretched to maybe forty feet in diameter. The body was about ten feet from the far side.

He shivered. There was something eerie about the scene. Everything so quiet. Nothing moving for miles around. The stones crowded around the body like silent mourners. The far side of the valley patchworked in shades of twilight grey, mist and smoke rising up from the valley floor. The smell of autumn everywhere – damp rotting leaves and wood smoke.

He looked across the field towards the road on his left. Was that the way she'd come? Up the winding road from the village on foot? Or had someone driven her here, pulled off onto that chalk track, and dumped her?

He turned back to the circle. He could see the slight outline of footprints on the grass, little more than rectangles written in the dew. They scuffed a braided path between the outer stones and the body. One set of tracks would belong to the girl who'd found her, another to the uniformed officer who'd called it in. Maybe they'd get lucky and find a third, but he doubted it. The dew was light, and probably formed only a few hours before dawn.

He shivered again, pulling his jacket tighter in a vain attempt to keep out the cold. Where was SOCO? He'd expected the Scene of Crimes team to be on site when he arrived, handing out gloves and white coats, and sealing off the crime scene.

He shouted to the lone policeman who was over on the chalk track talking to the girl who'd found the body. "Scene of Crimes *are* on their way, aren't they?"

"Yes, sir. They should be here any minute."

Shand checked his watch, shuffled his feet, peered at the road, listened. He'd never been any good at waiting. There was a dead body yards away, valuable time ebbing away...

He stared at the body. What if she wasn't dead? The girl had probably never seen a dead body before. The constable was barely out of his teens. Wouldn't it be judicious to have a look himself?

He pulled on a pair of latex gloves and entered the circle, tracing a path well away from the footprints, each step slow and deliberate, his head bent scanning the ground. Whatever happened he was *not* going to compromise the crime scene.

A yard away now. He could see a darkened patch of matted hair on the back of the woman's head. It didn't look fresh. And, looking closer, her body appeared to be laid out on a slight mound. Was that why they'd chosen this site? Was it some kind of altar?

He bent down to touch the woman's neck. No pulse that he could feel through the gloves. He checked her fingers, applying the slightest of pressure. They were stiff. Rigor had set in. He tried the wrist. Rigor there too. And at the elbow, though not the shoulder. Five to nine hours, by his somewhat rusty reckoning, which made time of death somewhere between eleven and four last night.

He took another look at the woman's fingers. The nails were manicured. No cracks, no blood, no signs of defensive wounds. And nothing obvious under the nails.

No signs of sexual interference either. The hemline of the woman's coat ran arrow-straight along the backs of her knees. And her coat was spotless. No blood, no dirt or grass stains, barely even a crease. It could have come straight from a shop window.

He leaned farther over the body to examine her face. Late thirties, early forties. No bruising, no cuts, make-up unsmudged. And her eyes were closed. The killer, perhaps? Someone who didn't want the victim to stare at them while they arranged the body?

The sound of a car broke his concentration – the first real noise he'd heard for minutes. He looked up. Three cars had pulled off the road, and were bumping along the rough chalk track that passed within thirty yards of the circle. Shand rose quickly. What had he been thinking? He should have blocked the track off, had a word with the constable about finding an alternative car park while he determined the extent of the crime scene.

"Hey," he shouted.

That's when it happened. Something tightened around his right ankle. Something that felt like fingers and gripped like a hand. He jumped, a startled cry rising from his throat, but the fingers held firm. He looked down, panic-stricken. The woman had to be dead, he'd felt the rigor in her hands!

Time froze. He stared in disbelief. A hand had risen out of the ground beneath the body. At first he couldn't take it in. He felt slow and befuddled. Where had the hand come from?

And then time catapulted the scene into needle-sharp clarity. There was someone alive down there. Someone buried beneath the corpse.

"Quick!" he shouted, waving frantically at the newcomers,

his voice unnaturally shrill. “Over here! They’re buried alive!”

He bent down, broke the person’s grip, pulled back their fingers, wanting to squeeze that hand, give comfort, but not having the time. “We’re coming,” he said, throwing himself to the ground. “Hang on!”

And then he was digging, scrabbling wildly at the earth. How long had they been down there? How could they breathe?

He freed the hand to the elbow. Pulled hard. The body wouldn’t budge. He shouted to the others to hurry. Car doors slammed, people ran. “Help me move the corpse!” He thrust his hands under the dead woman’s shoulders, swung her off the mound, then dived back, ripping at the clods of turf that covered the grave.

Turf flew in all directions - and dirt - everyone on hands and knees, clawing at the ground. No shovels, no tools, no time. The earth soft to the touch. Another hand discovered, an arm, a leg. Soft flesh, feet kicking wildly, a frantic search for a face. Shand’s fingers found something smooth and flat - a box? The person’s head was encased in a cardboard box!

He swept the soil back, fast choppy strokes, dug his hands down and along the sides. People were pulling from the other side, easing the person out by the legs. A head appeared. A woman, middle-aged, red-faced and gasping.

But alive.

CHAPTER TWO

The police doctor examined the woman while Shand took a few seconds to recover. He was shaking. How had the woman survived for so long? There wouldn't have been enough air in that box. She should have been dead.

He took another look at the box, sliding his hand across the top. There was a hole, the size of a pea. Had there been a tube? Had he pulled it out in his rush to dig her free?

He found the tube buried amongst the pile of strewn turfs. It looked like a siphon - clear plastic and flexible. He bagged it, then hurried back to the woman.

She was in shock, her body still heaving between ragged breaths, tears carving channels down her dirt-stained face.

"I've given her something," said the doctor. "She's cold and terrified, but I can't find any injuries. The ambulance'll be here soon."

One of the police constables removed his jacket and placed it delicately around the woman's shoulders. She shivered, hunched up, her thin hands pulling the jacket tighter. She had to be in her late fifties. Maybe older. The doctor gently massaged her back and arms.

Shand squatted next to her.

"What's your name?" he asked softly.

She didn't appear to register his existence. Her eyes flitted vacantly over him.

"Cold," she said. "So cold." Her lower lip trembled.

Shand pulled off his gloves and wrapped her left hand in his. It was like ice. "Can you tell me what happened?"

Her focus began to wander again. She looked at her hands, the circle, the cars, then back at Shand. "Where's George?" she asked.

"Who's George?"

She didn't answer. She looked confused. "Who are you?"

"I'm Detective Chief Inspector Shand. Who's George?"

"My husband, of course," she said, breaking into a smile. "He's..." She stopped mid-sentence, her smile fading as her eyes widened. "No," she cried, then louder, "No!"

"What is it?" Shand asked.

She struggled, pulling away. "You've got to save him. You've got to!"

"I will," said Shand. "Where is he? What's happened to him?"

Her hands flew to her mouth, her face crumpled. "George," she wailed. "George!"

Shand turned away in frustration. One person dead, one buried alive and now George. Wherever *he* was.

He looked back at the sobbing woman. It could be hours before she made any sense.

He stood up. Where was the girl who'd found the body? His eyes flicked over the growing number of onlookers. Another five cars must have arrived since they'd pulled the woman out.

"Does anyone know this woman," he shouted. "Anyone know who George is?"

A hand went up to his left. A teenage boy stepped forward.

"Helena Benson. George's her husband."

Shand ran towards the teenager. "Where do they live?"

"Ivy Cottage. It's the first house on the right as you go down into the village."

"Thank you."

He was away and running. First towards his car, but it was blocked in. Shit! Cars front and back and nowhere to turn – a barbed wire fence on one side of the track, a ditch on the other. He looked back towards the road, more cars arriving by the second. He sprinted to the entrance, and flagged down a police car just as it turned into the track.

"DCI Shand," he said, breathing hard. "Back the car up. You're taking me into Athelcott. Now!"

He got in. The young police constable threw the car into reverse, loose chippings flying as it bounced back off the track. The car rocked to a stop, then flew forward, tyres squealing.

"It's the first house on the right. Ivy Cottage," said Shand.

The car raced down the hill, the road curving to the right and sinking between high banks and hedges. Shand clung to his seat, no time to belt up, his left shoulder pressed tight against the door as the car flew around the bend. He peered ahead, straining to see through the mist and hedgerows. The road swung left, Shand slid with it, gripping the seat with all his strength to keep him from colliding with the driver. Then there it was, a thatched roof on the right. A break in the hedge. A gate. 'Ivy Cottage' written in wrought iron to the side of the porch.

He had the passenger door open before the car stopped. "Follow me," he said, running around the front of the car. "Don't touch anything. We're looking for a George Benson. He might be hurt."

He slowed at the gate, his heart racing, not knowing if he was going to find a blood bath or a garden full of graves. He took a deep breath and drank in the scene. The gate was open. Was that significant? He walked through. A small front garden; cottage style – perennials and shrubs – a flagstone path to a trellis-framed porch. The front door ajar.

A bad feeling. He edged towards the doorway, glanced down at his shoes. His training told him to take them off. They were wet and covered in dirt from the circle. He'd contaminate the scene. His heart told him different. George could be bleeding to death inside. His first priority was to preserve life.

He quickly scraped the soles of his shoes against the edge of the stone step, rested the tip of his left elbow on the solid oak door and pushed. The door creaked open. It was dark inside. Low ceilings, huge beams, drawn curtains. And a rich smell. One he couldn't place. Almost like pipe tobacco, but not. Was it the oak beams?

He called out. "Hello? Mr. Benson?"

No answer. Shand flipped on the lights. The front door had opened straight onto the living room – nut-brown beams, period furniture, inglenook fireplace, knick-knacks everywhere.

"You try upstairs," said Shand, ducking under the central beam towards the back of the room. He wondered how tall

George was. The clearance couldn't have been more than five ten.

He checked behind the sofa, along the back wall. No sign of a struggle, no body, no bloodstains. Heavy footsteps reverberated overhead, the central lampshade shook in sympathy. Not a house someone could move about quietly in. He stepped into the kitchen. And stopped. The back door was ajar. Another bad feeling. He called out again. "George!" The sounds from upstairs stopped for a few seconds. No one replied.

Shand went outside. The back garden was huge – extensive lawns, fruit trees, vegetable garden, shrubs, a stone outbuilding. But no sign of George.

He stood for a few moments, scanning the lawn for any signs of recent disturbance, half-expecting to see a line of newly-formed graves.

Nothing.

He turned back inside. There was washing up in the sink. A single plate and a cup. One person?

Another door led off the kitchen into a back corridor. He took it, following it around to a downstairs bedroom. The bed was made. A slightly musty smell hung on the air. A spare bedroom?

A sound from the other side of the wall made him stop. He froze instantly, tilted his head to one side and listened. There it was again. A scraping sound coming from the living room. Not his colleague. He could still hear the creaks and heavy feet from upstairs.

Shand moved swiftly back along the corridor, up on the balls of his feet, treading as lightly as he could into the kitchen, across the quarry-tiled floor, pausing by the entrance to the living room. A floorboard creaked a few feet away. Shand pulled back and pressed himself flat against the interior wall. He could see the shadow now. An outline of a person caught by the living room light and projected onto the kitchen floor. Someone was standing on the other side of the doorway. Shand waited. A thousand thoughts running through his mind. Was this the killer, was he armed, should he call for assistance? Fifteen years behind a desk hadn't prepared him for this. He'd never tackled a suspect in his life.

He swallowed hard and braced himself. Another creak, the shadow shuffled slightly, but still no closer to the door. Footsteps from above, the sound magnified in the tense silence. Should he wait for the PC to come down? Should he shout a warning? What if the officer ran downstairs into a hail of bullets?

He closed his eyes for a second. He had to take control. He was letting his imagination conjure gunmen out of shadows. Anyone could be in that doorway. A colleague, a neighbour, George. He was being ridiculous.

"Police!" he said, forcing his voice to resonate a confidence and authority he didn't possess. "Step away from the door."

The shadow jumped back. The footsteps overhead stopped. Shand took a deep breath and stepped into the doorway.

CHAPTER THREE

A middle-aged man stared back at him, eyes bulging in shock. A man in his fifties, slightly overweight, receding grey hair and a salt and pepper moustache.

"Who are you?" the man said, his voice trembling. "Where's my wife?"

Shand relaxed. "George Benson?"

The man nodded. A thundering of feet on the stairs announced the arrival of the constable.

"Nothing upstairs, sir," he said, eyeing George suspiciously.

Shand ignored him, keeping his eyes on George. "Detective Chief Inspector Shand," he said, producing his warrant card, "I think you should sit down, Mr. Benson."

George Benson swallowed hard and pulled out a chair from beneath a heavy oak table. He looked terrified. His hands were shaking.

"Your wife's fine, Mr. Benson. When ... when was the last time you saw her?"

George rose from the chair. "Has something happened to Helena? Where is she?"

Shand placed a hand on the man's shoulder and gently coaxed him back down. "She's fine," he repeated. "You'll be able to see her soon, but I need to ask a few questions first, okay?"

George let out a deep breath and nodded. "You're sure she's all right?"

"Positive," said Shand. "Now, when was the last time you saw her?"

George looked like several large weights had been lifted from his chest. "Yesterday evening," he said. "About seven thirty. I spent the evening over at Sherminster. On a stag night."

He smiled nervously, and looked down at the table.

"You stayed out all night?"

"Yes. Helena thought it best. In case I drank too much. Which I didn't. I just drove back now." Another nervous smile then, "perfectly sober," added as an afterthought.

"Did your wife have any plans for yesterday evening?"

"I don't think so. Other than a quiet night in."

"On her own?"

"Yes, there was a film she wanted to watch."

Was it Shand's imagination or was there something strange about George's demeanour. A nervous excitement. A forced bonhomie. Or was that a typical stress reaction? Shand's experience of interviewing shaken relatives was zero.

"Did you phone your wife last night?" he asked.

"No, she'd have been in bed by eleven. I wouldn't want to wake her."

Shand paused for a second. "Have you or your wife any enemies, Mr. Benson?"

"No, of course not."

The answer came too quickly. Shand tried again. "This is very important, Mr. Benson. Can you think of anyone who might want to hurt your wife?"

"She's hurt?" He started to rise again. Shand eased him back down.

"She's fine now," he said and then paused, searching for the right words. Were there any right words? "There's no easy way to say this but ... someone buried your wife alive at the stone circle..."

"What?" George's eyes widened in shock. He swallowed hard. "All those cars? You mean ... that was Helena?"

"She's shaken up but the doctor found no other injuries. They'll be taking her to hospital for a check-up. Just precautionary. I'll arrange for a car to take you to see her."

Shand stayed at the cottage after the PC and George Benson left for the hospital. Scene of Crimes would be tied up at the circle for several hours, someone had to check the house.

And he needed to make a phone call.

He tried her mobile first. No answer. Same as last night. She must have switched it off, though why she'd switch the thing off the weekend her new system was going live he couldn't begin to think. It made no sense.

But then nothing had all week.

He tried her office.

"Can I speak to Anne," he asked.

"Who shall I say's calling?" The voice was young, female and unfamiliar.

"Her husband."

"Oh, you must be Gabriel! I'll see if I can find her."

Peter Shand was too shocked to reply. His biggest fear had just been given a name. Gabriel.

A year ago he would have laughed it off. A new girl getting his name wrong. A silly mistake. But now...

There was a muffled conversation on the other end of the line. He strained to make it out, but the phone suddenly went dead – someone must have pushed the mute button.

Shand closed his eyes. His heart was racing, his mouth drying up. Did he really want to continue this call?

The girl's voice came back on the line – nervous and apologetic. "I'm so sorry," she said. "She's tied up in a meeting. I'll tell her you called."

Click. The phone went dead. A little piece of Shand died along with it. He hadn't spoken to Anne since he'd left London on Thursday night to take up his new job. It was now Saturday. He'd rung several times yesterday only to be told she was in a meeting, or at lunch, or 'just stepped out.' He'd rung their flat every hour last night until two. Had she been with this Gabriel? Who the hell *was* Gabriel?

He told himself he was being stupid. There was no Gabriel. She was busy, that's all. She had a high-pressure job and a new system to put live. That's why she'd been distracted all month. That and the prospective move. He'd known she wasn't as enthusiastic about moving to the country as he was, but he'd thought she'd come round. It was only for a year, after all. Just enough time to clock up the required operational experience so he could put in for promotion. They'd talked about it for years.

But not recently.

Maybe *he* should commute? Keep the London flat, and rent somewhere local. It would cost more. Leasing out their London flat would have more than paid for a house down here. They could have rented a cottage like this with a garden and...

Maybe they still could? Even Anne couldn't resist a place like this. He'd arrange a house-hunting trip when she came down next weekend. Line up a stack of dream cottages with honeysuckle around the door and eyebrow windows poking out from under golden thatch.

He tried to hold onto that thought. But soon found others nudging it aside. What if she didn't come down? What if she decided that even a year in Wessex was too much, that *he* was too much, that...

Deja vu with a vengeance. The same thoughts, the same arguments had kept him awake most of the previous night.

And to cap everything he was now in charge of a murder case. The very thing he'd been sent to Wessex to avoid. 'I'll find you a billet in the quietest, most crime-free corner of the country,' his boss at the Inspectorate had told him. 'One year as a DCI in the sticks and you'll be back on fast track. Chief constable within ten years.'

And now he was treading water at the deep end. No time to ease himself into the job at all – sink or swim, sink or swim.

Time to search the place. Instinctively his hand went to his pocket in search of the spare pair of latex gloves he'd packed this morning – just to be on the safe side in case SOCO was late arriving. The pair he'd already used and left discarded at the circle. He closed his eyes. How many spare packs of gloves does a person need! Was this what life in the sticks was going to be like? Bring your own forensic kit in case SOCO was busy elsewhere dusting down tractors?

He found a handkerchief and removed his shoes. A bit late but it eased his conscience. He'd spread enough dirt over crime scenes in the last thirty minutes to fill several buckets. Then he started to walk the rooms, slowly and methodically, looking for anything that might shed the slightest light on what had happened the previous night.

He found nothing. No sign of a struggle, no sign of

anything missing or out of place. No messages on the answerphone. No computer, so no emails. And the only correspondence he found were bills or letters from friends and family. Nothing.

Except for two open doors and a woman buried alive in a nearby stone circle.

And a murder.

Which is where the case confused the hell out of him. What did he have - a murder *and* an abduction? Why would anyone go to all the trouble of digging a grave and setting up breathing apparatus for one victim, but simply kill the other? Was their original plan to bury both victims, but the digging took longer than expected and they gave up?

Or was there a struggle? One of the women tried to escape and was hit too hard? The kidnappers then panicked and ran off.

And what was the connection between the two women? Mother and daughter, sisters? Shand kicked himself. He should have asked George. What had he been thinking? He hurried back to the living room. The display cabinet against the back wall had been covered in photographs. Maybe...

He went along the line, scanning every face, dredging back the image of the dead woman at the circle and trying to find a twin. He wasn't sure. Some of the pictures were old - young girls playing by the sea, could one of those have grown up into the thirtysomething blonde woman at the circle?

He stopped. He was wasting time. They might have identified the dead woman by now. He should be back at the circle.

He dug out the list of phone numbers he'd made the day before. Members of his team. Names and numbers he could barely attach a face to yet. One of them must have arrived at the circle by now.

He rang his sergeant first, Bob Taylor, a local man if he remembered correctly. A West Country burr answered on the third ring, "Hello."

"Shand here. I'm at the Benson house. Any ID on the dead woman yet?"

"Yes, the girl who found the body identified her as Annabel Marchant. Moved into the village a couple of years back."

"Any connection between her and the Bensons?"

"Not that I know of. I haven't talked to the girl myself, though Marc says she knows both families."

Marc? Shand was thrown for a second, then glanced down at the list in his hand. Marcus Ashenden, detective constable, the youngest member of his team.

"Ok, I've finished here," said Shand. "Can someone drive down from the circle and pick me up? And we'll need a uniform to secure the cottage until we can get SOCO down here."

Bob Taylor was waiting for Shand by the entrance to the track. Most of the cars were parked along the roadside now, but Shand noticed his car was still blocked in by the circle.

"Doctor's just left, sir," said Taylor. "She reckons around 12:45 last night for the time of death, give or take an hour or so. Cause of death our old favourite, the blunt instrument. More than one blow. Struck from behind, no obvious defensive wounds."

"Any sign of a murder weapon?"

"Not that I've heard. Though SOCO says he wants to see you. If I were you, I'd give him another minute. He's not best pleased."

Shand glanced over at the four figures dressed in Scene of Crimes white. "Which one's SOCO?"

"The surly one."

Shand walked over to the circle. Four white shapes stood within like druids on a midsummer morning. Shand stayed back, looking between the stones, surveying the carnage now the early morning gloom had lifted.

It looked a mess. The grave half dug, piles of earth and turfs strewn haphazardly around the circle. Countless boot prints and scuffs added to the scene. At least the body had been taken away - one less reminder of his destruction of the crime scene.

But what else could he have done? The woman had been buried beneath the crime scene. He didn't know if she had seconds or minutes to live. All he knew was that he had to get her out. Could he have done it another way? Could he have dug in from the side and dragged her out that way?

He dismissed the idea. They'd had no tools, only bare hands. There'd been no time to plan an excavation.

But still something nagged at the back of his mind. A feeling of failure. The moment Helena Benson had grabbed his ankle, he'd lost control. And in that instant, all his training deserted him.

One of the white figures approached. A moon of a face surrounded by sterile plastic. "Are you Shand?" he asked in a broad Scottish accent.

"Yes, I'm sorry about the crime scene."

"I suppose you didn't stop to take a photograph first?"

Shand winced. He hadn't thought of that. Should he have carried a camera with him? Could he have reached into a pocket and casually taken a few snaps while the woman's hand clung to his ankle?

"I didn't have a camera," he said.

The Scene of Crimes Officer continued to look at him. Shand tried to read what he was thinking, feeling like a child brought before the headmaster, unsure if it was detention or the cane.

"No reason why you should, I suppose," said SOCO, now looking away and gesticulating at the grave. "The constable who found her says the dead woman was lying over the grave there. Is that right?"

"Exactly," said Shand. "Her body covered the mound with her head pointing towards the road. She'd been placed there."

"What makes you think that?"

"Because the body was lying unnaturally. She was lying on her stomach, her head turned slightly, resting on her right cheek. Her arms were down by her side, and her legs straight. Almost as though she was standing to attention."

"And her clothes? Were they pulled up at all?"

"No. Her coat covered her to her knees and the hemline was straight. And both shoes were still on. It looked as though she'd been carefully arranged."

Something that Shand hadn't appreciated before. The body *had* been carefully arranged. The killer had had time. They hadn't been interrupted or panicking. They'd *deliberately* placed the body where it would be found. They *wanted* it to be found.

But if so, why? Burying a body was all about concealment. You bury someone you don't want found. You don't put a marker on the top that no one can ignore. It didn't make sense and yet ... there was obviously a mind at work here. He could see the planning and the effort. Someone had taken the time to dig out a grave, cobble together a rudimentary breathing apparatus, and even replace all the turfs. It must have taken a good half-hour. And premeditation, they had to have brought the box and siphon with them.

Or had they taken them from the Benson's cottage?

"Is there anything written on the box?" Shand asked.

"There's some lettering. Cans of peaches, I think. I doubt our friend has left any fingerprints, but we should be able trace the store it came from."

Which would probably be a hypermarket with a million customers, thought Shand. Or a local supermarket frequented by the Bensons.

"We have found some duct tape though. Two pieces, one about sixty centimetres, the other ninety-five. Both partly buried in the grave infill. Might have been used to secure one or other of the victims. We're sifting for more."

"Good," said Shand. This was more encouraging. The more they found the more chances of finding something they could match. Tape had to be cut. And a cut could be traced back to the knife or scissors that made it.

"Bob," said Shand, jogging over to where his sergeant was standing holding a clipboard. "Where's the girl who found the body?"

Taylor peered over his shoulder, then pointed to a young dark-haired girl, late teens, standing by the fence. "Lisa Budd," he said. "She was walking her dog when she saw the body. Recognised the woman and called the police."

"What time did she say she found the body?"

Taylor reached into his pocket and produced a notebook. "Let me see. Just after seven. The 999 call was logged at 7:09."

"Did she see anyone hanging around the circle? Any traffic on the road."

"No one hanging around the circle. I didn't ask about

cars."

"Okay, thanks. Are you arranging the house-to-house?"

"About to start in ten minutes. We're getting another dozen uniforms over from HQ."

"Great, start from the victims' homes and work out from there. Has anyone informed Mrs. Marchant's next of kin?"

"Not yet. We were waiting for you."

Another job he wasn't looking forward to.

"There's a husband - Gabriel - and a teenage daughter-"

"Gabriel?" said Shand.

"Yes, Gabriel Marchant. Do you ... know him?"

Shand shook his head, feeling stupid, wondering why after forty years of never meeting a single Gabriel he was suddenly beset by them. It wasn't that common a name surely?

"Sir?"

"What? Sorry, you were saying, sergeant..."

"Daughter's away at University somewhere, but the husband should be home."

Shand scanned the small crowd that had gathered around the entrance to the track. Why wasn't the husband at the line of tape shouting to be let through? News would travel fast in a small place like this. If Anne had been missing since midnight he'd...

Shand squashed that line of thought. She'd been as good as missing since Thursday.

"Has anyone checked to see if he reported her missing at all?"

"I'll do that now, sir."

"Oh and, Bob," he said, throwing his sergeant his keys. "Get someone to unblock my car."

Shand walked over to the girl by the fence. She looked bored. And cold, her arms were wrapped tightly around herself. She yawned as Shand approached.

"Lisa Budd? I'm Detective Chief Inspector Shand. I expect you want to get off home."

"Yeah. Can I go now?"

"A few questions first. Won't take long."

The girl grimaced.

"Did you see anyone when you were on your walk this

morning?"

The girl shook her head. "No. I already told the other one. I didn't see anything."

"What about traffic. Any cars on the road?"

"No!"

"What about yesterday evening?"

"What *about* yesterday evening?" Her voice rose defensively. She glared at Shand and shuffled her weight onto her other foot.

"I wondered if you might have seen anything unusual last night. When you came home."

"I stayed in last night. Didn't see a thing."

Shand stared at her, wondering why she was so antagonistic. Was it him? His job? The questions? He'd never understood teenagers. He had no kids of his own and had never been a teenager himself. He'd been so busy focussing on his grades, exams and career path that he'd skipped from child to adult in a matter of months.

He tried a lighter approach. "When I was your age, I didn't stay in on Friday nights."

Lisa shrugged. "I've had a lot of late nights recently. I needed a night in."

"Do you know the Marchants well?"

The girl snorted. "They're incomers. I'm an ignorant local."

And never the twain shall meet, thought Shand. "What about the Bensons? Are they incomers too?"

The girl's face warmed. "No, they've lived here for years. Mrs. Benson was born in the village."

"Were they friends of the Marchants?"

The girl shrugged. "Doubt it. Most of the Marchant's friends come from London. You see 'em at the weekends, parading through the village in their designer clothes, laughing at us yokels."

She ended the sentence with a sneer.

"You don't like the Marchants?"

She shrugged. "It's them that don't like us."

"What about the Bensons, do people like them?"

Back came the smile. "Everyone likes George. And Helena too."

"No arguments? Village disputes? Quarrels with

neighbours?"

The girl shook her head. "Nothing at all."

Shand let her leave. He'd hoped to find a connection between the two women. Was it possible that the murder and the abduction weren't linked?

The Marchant's house was on the other side of the village, a long stone-built property that looked like three terraced houses knocked into one. It had been renovated extensively. New windows, new roof and a landscaped garden at the front. Everything immaculate.

Shand opened the double gate to the side of the property, and walked around to the front door, glancing in the windows as he passed. Some of the downstairs curtains were drawn, and the outside light was still on.

He rang the doorbell, steeling himself for a messy encounter with a grieving husband. He'd brought along a WPC for support, his own as much the husband's.

He waited, thoughts flashing through his mind. Was he standing on the doorstep of a grieving spouse or a prime suspect? No missing person report had been filed. Not according to Bob Taylor. And none of the local stations had any record of anyone enquiring about her.

Was that significant?

The stats-loving part of Shand's brain kicked in. He'd helped compile so many reports on crime statistics, he knew the numbers off by heart. In the old days, husbands were always the first to be suspected whenever a wife was murdered. But nowadays, society had changed. Easy divorce, drugs and a diminishing respect for human life. Today, only 20% of murders were committed by family members, 40% by acquaintances and 40% by strangers. But did those figures apply to a small rural village like Athelcott? Had drugs and violence spread this far from the cities? Or was he looking at an old fashioned crime, where victim and murderer lived under the same roof?

Seconds passed. He rocked back and forth on the balls of his feet, looked up and down the lane. The house-to-house had begun. Police cars dotted throughout the village, lines of men and women knocking on doors.

He rang again. The WPC leaned towards the window on

the right and peered inside, shading her eyes with her hand against the glare. "I don't think anyone's in," she said.

Shand tried the door. It was locked. Double locked from what he could see – a Yale and a dead bolt. And an alarm, he noticed the bright yellow box protruding from the wall just below the gutter.

"Try around the back," he told the WPC.

Shand took the front of the house, peering in the windows one by one. Nothing looked out of place inside. Every room looked liked a page from a glossy magazine. Would they have a cleaner? Shand couldn't see a woman with Annabel Marchant's manicured hands looking after a place this size. It would have to be someone in the village. Maybe they'd have a key?

"Nothing round the back, sir," said the WPC, appearing by the corner of the house. "The back door and both French windows are locked."

They checked the garage next. A modern two-car garage, built in artificial stone. Shand looked through a side window. Only one car inside. A yellow Mazda MX-5. Had the husband fled? Or hadn't he been at home?

Shand stood by the front door, unsure how to proceed. He wanted to break in, impatient to keep the investigation moving forward. But he'd done enough damage at the stone circle, and didn't want to prejudice the case with an illegal search.

The neighbours either side weren't much help. They confirmed the daughter was away at University, and that was about it. Gabriel Marchant might be in London, or he might not.

"London?"

"Yes," said a neighbour. "He works for some big London company, but I've no idea who, or what he does there."

Shand had difficulty nudging his inner jealous husband past the fact that both Gabriel and Anne worked in London. London's workforce may be counted in the millions, but how many were Gabriels?

"Did Mr. Marchant work in IT?" he asked. "Was his office in the City?"

No one knew. They didn't know his telephone number

either. And no one had a spare key. Not even the cleaner.

"Mrs. Marchant doesn't believe in giving out keys to the likes of us. She makes Ruthie ring the doorbell and wait. Some mornings she's standing on the step for ten minutes. Even in the rain."

But at least they provided a name of a friend in the village who might know how to reach the husband. As for Mrs. Marchant, no one had seen her since yesterday afternoon - she'd been seen deadheading roses in the back garden - and as for last night, no one had seen or heard anything unusual at all.

Shand hoped his team were having better luck elsewhere. He could feel the investigation stalling. Time was critical in a murder investigation. Especially in a case where there was no obvious motive or witness.

Which was when he remembered Helena Benson. Maybe she'd make more sense now.

CHAPTER FOUR

Helena Benson was sitting up, and apparently lucid. Her husband, George, sat by her hospital bed, holding her hand.

"I was on the phone," she said, "when there was a knock at the door."

"What time was this?" asked Shand.

"Late. Maybe ten, ten thirty? No, wait, it..." She closed her eyes and frowned. George hovered closer, concerned. After a moment or two, Helena opened her eyes and smiled apologetically. "You'll have to forgive me, inspector. My mind's fuddled. I know I was watching a film last night, but for the life of me I can't remember when it finished."

"That's all right," said Shand. "We can check the listings."

"Can you?" she said. "It was on BBC One. I'd waited for the film to finish before phoning Ursula. I wanted to talk to her about next week's parish council meeting."

"Ursula?" asked Shand.

"Ursula Montacute. She's the chairwoman - or 'chair' as I think they prefer to call it nowadays - of the parish council. There's a meeting on Wednesday."

Shand was amazed at how bright Helena appeared. She smiled, she chatted. It was hard to recognise her as the same woman he'd pulled out of the ground a few hours earlier.

"Where was I?" she asked, confused.

And in that second, back came the frailty, an uncertainty in her eye.

"You were on the phone," said Shand, "when there was a knock at the door."

"That's right. Well, I thought it must be important. Neighbours don't knock on one another's doors late at night without a good reason. So I told Ursula I'd ring tomorrow." She paused, a slight look of confusion clouding her face. "That's today, isn't it? Is it Saturday?" Her lower lip trembled as she looked to her husband for confirmation.

"It is Saturday, dear," he said, patting her hand.

Shand wondered how long she thought she'd been buried. He couldn't imagine being buried alive for five minutes let alone several hours.

"So you went to the door?" he prompted.

"Yes, but no one was there. I remember calling out." Helena paused, her eyes unfocussed.

"And?" asked Shand.

Her eyes snapped back into focus. "What? Oh, I ... I stepped outside to look. I..." She took a deep breath and looked at her husband. "Someone grabbed me from behind. I couldn't see their face. I tried to call for help, but they put a hand over my mouth. I tried to fight back. I really did." Her lower lip quivered. "But there were two of them."

"It's all right, dear," said George, "It's over now."

Helena sniffed back a tear and continued. "They dragged me back into the house. I didn't know what was going to happen. You hear so many terrible stories – robbery and," she lowered her voice, "you know."

George swallowed hard. "You weren't..."

"No," said Helena. "They told me if I calmed down and stopped struggling, it'd be all right. No one would get hurt if I did as I was told."

"Did you recognise these men?" asked Shand.

"No," said Helena, wiping away a tear. "They were wearing masks."

"What about their hands, were they wearing gloves?"

Helena shrugged. "I can't remember."

"When that hand covered your mouth, what could you feel? Did it feel like a bare hand or what?"

She thought for a while. "Leather, I could definitely smell leather."

"Leather gloves?" asked Shand needing the confirmation.

"Yes, leather gloves."

"What about their accents? Were they local?"

Another long pause as her brow furrowed in thought. "No, they had London accents. I'm sure of it. Working class

London accents."

"What about their heights or ages? Were they big men, young, old?"

Helena smiled weakly. "I'm afraid I'm a terrible witness, inspector. I'd say they were both bigger and stockier than George, but as for their ages ... they could have been in their twenties or thirties or even forties. I think one was older than the other. But that might just be because he seemed to be in charge."

"Did they have to duck much to walk under the beams?"

"I couldn't tell. They put sticky tape over my eyes. And my mouth and wrists. They bound my wrists together behind my back."

"They wore masks, *and* they taped your eyes?"

"Yes, the older one said it was for my own good. If I didn't see anything, I couldn't testify. They'd let me live."

She looked at George again, they squeezed each other's hands.

Shand wondered why they had to tape Helena's eyes. Were they going to do something that they didn't want her to see?

"What happened next?" he asked.

"I think one of them went out the kitchen door. I heard it creak. I don't know what the other did, but I heard him walking around the house."

"Did he go upstairs?"

"No, but I think he went into the spare bedroom and George's study."

"How long did this go on for?"

"Not long. The younger one came back and told me to get up. Next thing I knew I was being pushed in the back and steered towards the front door. One went out, said it was clear, then I was bundled into the back of a car."

"Had you seen the car earlier when you opened the door?"

"No." She paused and looked confused. "But it must have been there, mustn't it?" She shook her head. "I'm sorry inspector. I can't remember. I wasn't looking for a car."

"It doesn't matter, Mrs. Benson. You're doing very well to remember as much as you have."

"Yes, dear," said George. "You're doing splendidly."

"Did you form any impression of the car they put you into?"

Helena looked at him blankly.

"Were you in the front or the back of the car?"

"I'm not sure."

"Was the driver in front or was he beside you?"

"In front. The other one got in beside me."

"Now, can you remember if there was a rear door or did you have to climb in from the front?"

"A rear door," said Helena. "There must have been. They opened the door and I slid in. And now I think about it, the seats were very slippery – like leather – and well sprung. Very roomy, I think. A big car."

Excellent, thought Shand. Large four-door, leather seats.

"Oh," said Helena, suddenly snatching her hand away from her husband and clasping her face with both hands. "There's something else. I found something. I remember now. It was wedged in the crack at the back of the seat. My fingers brushed over it. Something hard and about two inches square. I put it in my pocket. I thought it might be a clue."

"Helena!" chided George. "You shouldn't have done that. What if they'd seen?" He turned to Shand. "My wife reads far too many detective novels, chief inspector."

"They didn't see, darling. I was careful, and I had my hands behind my back."

"Excuse me," said Shand, looking around the room for Helena's clothes. "Which pocket?"

"My skirt. With my hands tied behind my back, it was the only pocket I could reach."

Shand tore open a pack of surgical gloves – he'd borrowed two packs from the ward sister the moment he'd arrived – pulled on the gloves, then fetched Helena's skirt from the table. He found a book of matches in the right pocket. It was shiny black with a name embossed in gold on the front – *Gulliver's, Hanover Lane, London.*

He opened it carefully, two matches were left. He prayed for a scrawled name or message, but his luck ran out. The inside was blank.

"Is it any help, inspector?" asked Helena.

"I hope so," said Shand, depositing the matchbook into

his last evidence bag. And wondering if the ward sister had any spare freezer bags he could borrow.

He hurried to the door and handed the bag to the constable outside.

"I want this sent over to Forensics. And put a request into the Met. I want to know everything about a place called Gulliver's in Hanover Lane. If it's a club, I want membership and employee lists. If it's a pub, I want to know who drinks there. Everything they've got, understand?"

Shand returned with a spring in his step. At last he was getting somewhere. If he was lucky there'd be prints, luckier still Gulliver's would be an underworld haunt under surveillance by the Met.

"Now, Mrs. Benson. Any idea how long you were in the car? Were you driven straight to the circle, or was there a detour?"

Helena considered the question for a second. "I think they drove straight to the circle. I remember hearing the crackle of gravel under the tyres. I thought we were turning into someone's drive."

"Then what happened?"

"They left me in the car," said Helena, pausing between sentences, "I could hear someone digging in the distance. I thought they were digging something up. It went on for such a long time."

"This digging," said Shand. "Presumably they had a spade. Did they have it in the car? Could you tell at all?"

Helena looked blankly for a second. "It might have been in the boot. I remember hearing the boot slam shortly after we stopped."

"Are you sure it was a boot and not, say, the rear door of a hatchback?"

Helena looked confused. "How would I know?"

"Did you feel a rush of air as the boot slammed?"

"No."

Another piece in the jigsaw, thought Shand. Large four-door *saloon* with leather interior.

"And then what happened," he asked, gesturing for her to continue. "You were in the car..."

"I thought about trying to escape," said Helena staring unfocussed into the distance, "but I couldn't tell if I was being watched. And I kept thinking that it had to end soon because it had all been a dreadful mistake. It had to be. They'd taken the wrong person.

"Then they took me outside and walked me over to the circle. They told me not to worry. That nobody would be hurt if I did what they said. Then I was lifted off my feet and lowered into the hole. They peeled off the tape. I remember how it stung. My eyes watered. I couldn't see where I was. They told me to lie down. And then a box went over my head. I didn't know what was happening. I..."

"It's all right, dear," said George. "Take your time. The chief inspector doesn't mind waiting."

Helena took a deep breath and continued. "They said it wouldn't be long, and that someone would be along soon to let me out. Then they explained about the breathing tube, and how it would be safe."

She turned to her husband. "I panicked," she said, her voice faltering. "I tried to get up, but they held me down. They were getting angry. I could feel it. Then," she paused and turned to Shand. "Then I thought about it. George's a bank manager. I'd heard of cases where gangs take the manager and his family hostage, and force the husband to open the vault. It was the only thing that made sense. They must have George somewhere. Maybe at the bank already. And unless he helped them, they'd not tell anyone where I was."

Shand turned to George. "You're a bank manager?"

"Yes, but," he looked flustered. "No one took me hostage, chief inspector. I can assure you."

"I don't remember much of what happened next," said Helena, dragging Shand's attention back from her husband. "I was terrified for George." She smiled warmly at her husband, and stroked his hand.

"Did you hear anything at all while you were down there?" asked Shand. "Did you hear the car driving off?"

"I'm sorry, inspector. When the soil was piled on top of me, I panicked and lost the breathing tube. Everything was black and..." her lower lip quivered. "I couldn't use my hands. I had to feel for it with my tongue, and pull it down with my teeth ... after that I went rigid. I daren't move or cry out or anything. All I could hear was the blood pumping in my ears. I stayed like that for hours. Or maybe I passed out."

George leaned over, pulled his wife towards him, and held her.

Shand waited, wondering how – or if – he would have coped under similar circumstances.

"Can you think of any reason why Annabel Marchant would be at the circle?" asked Shand.

George relaxed his grip on his wife. Helena looked surprised. "Annabel was at the circle?"

"Was she a friend of yours?" asked Shand.

"No, not particularly. Why do you ask?"

Shand pressed on. "Was she in the habit of going for walks past your house at night? Maybe up to the circle?"

"No, inspector. At least I don't think so. Did she, George?"

"Not that I ever saw."

"I know this is difficult for you, Mrs. Benson, but think very carefully. Can you remember hearing anything, anything at all, while you were buried?"

She glanced at her husband. "I ... I don't know."

"What about voices? Did you hear anyone talking at all?"

Helena was silent for several seconds, then her eyes widened. "Yes," she said. "I *did* hear a voice. At the end. I wanted to cry out, but I daren't let go of the tube. So I tried to move my hands, but they wouldn't move. I thought I was paralysed. I was losing feeling in my legs. My back ached. But I managed to wiggle the fingers of one hand, then I pushed and pushed, I felt air and something else, and I grabbed it."

"That was me," said Shand. "You grabbed my ankle." Something Shand would never forget.

"That was you?" asked Helena surprised.

Shand nodded. "You're doing very well, Mrs. Benson. Now think, did you hear anything before that? Footsteps, an argument, a car?"

Helena shook her head, then lowered it. "To be honest, inspector, I don't know what I heard. I thought I heard worms slithering over the box. I thought I heard rats and spiders, and every horrible thing you could imagine." She started to cry. "I was down there for such a long time, inspector. A long, long time."

CHAPTER FIVE

Detective Chief Superintendent Wiggins appeared at the hospital room door.

"Shand? A word, please," he said, nodding towards the corridor.

Shand apologised to the Bensons, and followed his boss outside.

"Sir?" he said.

"How's it going, Shand?" Wiggins asked. "Second day on the job, and you catch your first murder case. Must be pretty daunting."

A knot tightened in Shand's stomach. Was he about to have the case taken off him? "Not really, sir," he said. "I like the challenge."

"Do you? Look, Shand, I won't beat about the bush. You know the staffing problems. I have three DIs on suspension, and a DCI on gardening leave. This corruption investigation has ripped the heart out of the department."

Shand waited for the 'but,' preparing his counter-argument for when it came. He'd never had a job taken off him in his life.

"Any other time," continued Wiggins, "I'd second a senior officer from one of the other divisions to take charge, but I haven't anyone free for a week. Everyone's overloaded as it is."

Shand fought back a smile. "I understand, sir, but I don't think it'll be a problem."

"You don't?"

"No, I'm confident I can clear this case." Shand looked the Chief Superintendent squarely in the eye. His years at the Inspectorate had taught him that appearance was everything. Look confident, act confident. He might not have the experience of running a murder enquiry, but he'd written the book on procedure. "I'm used to being thrown in at the deep end."

Wiggins held his gaze for several seconds before breaking into a smile. "Good man," he said, slapping Shand on the shoulder. "'A safe pair of hands,' isn't that what they called you at the Inspectorate?"

It was. When he'd first heard it, he'd been flattered - a recognition of his skills: his attention to detail, his ability to find the common ground between opposing factions, to anticipate problems before they occurred.

But lately it had begun to sound hollow. What was a safe pair of hands? Someone who never dropped the ball, never took risks, and always played it safe.

Something that didn't square with his inner picture of himself. Or, more accurately, the inner picture he'd held as a child. Then, he'd envisaged himself as a risk-taker, someone who'd never be satisfied with the mundane, someone who'd seize opportunities others couldn't even see.

Strange, thought Shand, how the older he became, the more his thoughts turned to his childhood, and the stronger those memories and feelings became. He could bring back the faces of old school friends he hadn't seen for thirty years, and yet struggle to recall the name of a colleague he'd known but five years ago.

"I've had a word with support services, Shand, so no worries there. They've agreed to make this case top priority, so you'll have all the forensic support you need. And if you don't, tell me and I'll give someone a bollocking. Okay?"

"Thank you, sir."

"And don't forget to keep the press sweet. I've set up a press conference in Sturton for four this afternoon. Should give you enough time to get your head around the case."

"Right," said Shand, suddenly realising that he'd never given a press conference in his life. He'd worked in the Inspectorate Press Office, he'd written press releases, he'd prepared senior officers for the occasional interview, but he'd never had to face the press himself.

"Our press officer will be there ten minutes before to take you through the ropes. Though, with your years in the press office I expect you could teach him a few things, eh Shand?"

Shand forced a smile and wondered how large the press conference would be. A few people he could handle, but what if it turned into a circus? Dead body in a stone circle, woman buried alive. It was bound to attract the tabloids, maybe even live TV, or the international media. He'd never dealt with the tabloids before. All his experience had been with the serious press, dry briefings of facts and figures, crime stats, trends, enquiries and reports.

Wiggins interrupted Shand's worried line of thought. "Oh, and Shand?"

"Yes, sir?"

"I'd change your trousers before the press conference."

Shand looked down at what had once been his best pair of trousers. Dirt and grass stains covered both knees, a souvenir from his frantic efforts to rescue Helena. He'd have to return to the hotel to change. Something else he'd have to fit in before four.

"Mr. Benson?" said Shand, leaning his head around the hospital room door. "Could I have a word? There's a few things I need to clear up."

"Of course," said George, reluctantly letting go of his wife's hand. "I won't be a minute, dear."

Shand found a quiet spot farther along the corridor.

"Has anyone been threatening you, Mr. Benson?"

George looked surprised. "No."

Shand watched him closely. George swallowed and looked away.

"Any name you give me will be handled in the strictest confidence. No one will ever know it came from you."

"I told you, chief inspector, no one has threatened either of us. We have no enemies."

"Someone abducted your wife, Mr. Benson, and buried her alive. That's no random act of violence. That's deliberate and targeted. Now, why would anyone do that?"

George shrugged. His breathing had quickened and his forehead had begun to glisten. Was it nerves or fear?

"Have you been told to keep quiet? We can protect you. Both of you. Just give me a name."

"There is no name. We have no enemies."

There was no conviction in his voice. He could barely look Shand in the eye.

"Where's your bank?" snapped Shand.

"My bank?"

"Yes, your bank, Mr. Benson. I want you to take me there now."

"I ... I can't. The keys are back at the house."

"You keep the keys to the bank at home?"

"Of course."

Suddenly Shand saw a reason for Helena's eyes being taped shut.

CHAPTER SIX

Shand rang the station at Sturton.

"Send a car to the Provincial Bank on Church Street. Tell them to look for anything unusual, maybe a robbery in progress. Monitor the situation, but exercise extreme caution. Assume anyone inside might be armed. Tell them to stay outside until I arrive with the manager."

He looked at George, watching for a response. George looked down at his feet.

"Is that a problem for you, George?" Shand pressed. "A police car outside the branch?"

"No," said George quietly.

"If someone told you not to involve the police, now's the time to say."

George shrugged, still not meeting Shand's eye. "No one told me anything, chief inspector. You're barking up the wrong tree."

Shand left Sherminster hospital and drove as fast as the country lanes would allow. Thirty miles of bends and slow tractors, rolling hills, patchwork fields, small woods and picturesque villages. George sat by his side, silently staring out the passenger-side window.

Shand tried to draw him out - in between dodging the oncoming traffic - but George stonewalled. He hadn't been threatened, and no one was robbing his bank.

"You know we'll check your alibi for last night?" said Shand. "If you weren't in Sherminster, now's the time to say."

"Check all you like, chief inspector. I have a dozen witnesses."

Shand glanced sideways at his passenger. The fear had gone, but the apprehension remained. It was everywhere – in his voice, his demeanour, the way he could barely look Shand in the eye.

"What time did your stag night break up?"

"About midnight. Maybe later. I can't remember exactly. Duncan and I took a taxi back to his place."

"Duncan?"

"An old friend. He lives in Sherminster so I arranged to stay overnight with him and his wife."

Shand swung out for the third time to see if the road was clear for overtaking. It wasn't.

Scenarios flew through his head, none of them making any sense. He could see the logic in taking a bank manager's wife hostage on a Friday night. Maybe even burying her to increase the pressure on her husband. But why didn't they take George? Had it been a miscalculation – they'd turned up on the one evening that George was away? Or was that part of their plan – to attack the Bensons when they were apart? To threaten George when all he could hear was his wife's screams at the other end of a phone line?

"We'll check your phone records, you know," said Shand, swinging out into traffic and accelerating hard. "Just say the word and we'll give you twenty-four hour protection. A safe house if you want. Any threats made against you are useless now."

George didn't say a word.

Miles passed. Several times Shand tried to tempt George with light conversation – anything to make him open up – asking directions at road junctions, the names of villages.

"What's that place there?" he asked as they passed what looked like an army camp.

"Nethercombe asylum camp," said George.

"Bet that's popular with the locals?"

George shrugged and looked away. Shand gave up.

Four miles later, they pulled up outside Ivy Cottage.

"Where do you keep the keys to the bank?" said Shand hurrying George out of the car.

"In the study."

"That's the room to the left?"

Shand was turning left at the door before George could

answer. It was the only room in the house that could be called a study. Bookshelves lined one wall, a couple of uncomfortable looking armchairs filled a bay window, and a desk lay in the gloom at the back.

Shand stepped aside for George to pass. He watched him walk over to the desk, unlock the top drawer and feel inside.

"Well," he said impatiently.

George smiled and produced a ring of keys. "See, chief inspector, they're all here."

Shand stood in silence for several seconds. He'd been so sure. It was the only explanation that had even begun to make sense.

He rang the station sergeant at Sturton.

"Any word from the bank?"

"I'll check."

Shand agonised as the seconds passed in silence. He could feel his right foot tapping anxiously on the floorboards. What was keeping them? Had there been a problem?

A voice crackled into coherence. "No sign of a break in at the bank, sir. Everything's locked and secure. Officers standing by."

"May I fetch Helena's clothes now?" asked George.

"What? Yes, go ahead." Shand was miles away. What if the gang had made an impression of George's key? They'd had ten hours. They could have made a copy, cleared out the vault, locked up after themselves and left.

He took the keys outside to examine them in the light. He couldn't see any wax or soap residue.

He sighed. Why was it that every time he thought he got a handle on this case the handle promptly vanished?

And why hadn't Anne rung? It was eleven fifteen. Two hours had passed since he'd called. Was the meeting still going on, or had she left for an early lunch with Gabriel?

CHAPTER SEVEN

Shand tapped on the police car window with his warrant card. "Anything to report?"

There wasn't. They'd checked the doors and windows of the bank, and walked around the back. Everything was secure.

"We listened at both doors. It's as quiet as the grave in there."

Shand waited on the steps, flanked by the two coppers as George struggled with the keys. Shand could almost smell the adrenaline. Four unarmed men about to walk into a potential bank robbery. Most of the Division twenty-five minutes away in Athelcott on house-to-house duty.

The heavy oak doors parted. George walked into the small entrance lobby, latched them open and disabled the alarm. Shand listened, not a sound from within. He traced the wires from the door to the alarm panel. Everything looked untouched. George went to push through the swing doors into the customer lobby, but Shand motioned for him to wait. He'd go first. Just in case.

He opened the door to the left a crack and peered inside. No sound, no movement. He pushed it farther. It was one of those old banks, more like a substantial house than a purpose built bank. Panelled walls, high ceilings, fancy cornices - probably Edwardian or late Victorian - the counter to ceiling glass wall the only sacrifice to the modern era. That and the ATM.

And it was small. Only three cashier positions. A small bank in a small market town. Would it carry enough cash to make all that effort worthwhile? Abduction, burial, murder?

Shand slid through, held the door open for the others,

then hurried to the counter. He peered through the glass into the back office. Desks, computers, cupboards. Everything neat and tidy.

George unlocked the panelled door from the customer lobby into the staff area. Shand followed. The floor was as tidy as the desks. No discarded wrappers from bundles of notes, or waste bins kicked over in someone's haste to get away.

"Where's the vault?" he whispered to George.

George pointed towards a door at the back. "I've got to get the keys first."

Shand waited while George unlocked a cupboard and took out two large keys. Shand's mood sunk. No one would waste time putting the vault keys back and locking them away.

But then who'd go to all the trouble of burying someone alive only to cover their grave with a dead body?

He followed George downstairs into a basement, along a corridor. Everything spotless; white walls, blue carpet. And at the end, a large metal door.

"Get it open," said Shand.

George took his time, inserting one key, then the other, turning them both, then placing both hands around the circular handle, a twist, a tug then...

Shand leaned forward, peering over George's shoulder. The heavy door swung back, lights flickered on inside. "Anything missing?" he asked.

Even as he said it his eyes alighted on the stack of notes on the far shelf. No one would have left that behind.

He kicked his heels in the corridor as George shuffled along the shelves of the small vault. Maybe they'd abandoned the robbery after killing Annabel? Didn't that make sense? They'd planned to have the entire weekend to rob the bank, then along comes Annabel and all plans go out the window. There's no time. They have to escape.

But that didn't accord with what he'd seen at the circle. They *had* had time. They'd stopped to arrange the body. Why? There was a wood fifty yards away. They could have hidden the body there. The chalk track even led into the wood, they could have driven down.

But they hadn't. Instead, they'd left the body where it couldn't be missed. Why? What was it that he was failing to see?

"Everything's here," said George in a quiet voice from the vault entrance. "I can't check the deposit boxes without the owner's keys, but none have been tampered with."

Shand didn't bother to look, if the safety deposit boxes had been a target they would have been drilled out. No one would have wasted time picking locks.

Unless...

A sudden idea. "Did the Marchant's have a safety deposit box?"

"No," said George. "I'm not sure where they banked, but it wasn't here."

Shand sighed. His one last throw. He looked at George, standing forlornly in the doorway to his vault, and felt even worse.

"I owe you an apology, Mr. Benson. I thought I knew what was happening here. I didn't. I'm sorry."

Shand arranged for George to be driven back to Sherminster hospital, then phoned Bob Taylor to find out how the house-to-house was progressing.

"Slowly," said Taylor. "Not everyone's at home and those that are, didn't see anything. But we have tracked down Annabel's husband. He's on his way home. Should be back at two."

Shand checked his watch.

"Is there a pub in the village?" he asked.

"The first thing we located, sir. The Royal Oak. It's on the village green, you can't miss it."

"Okay, I'll meet you there at one to discuss progress."

Shand returned to Athelcott, stopping at the stone circle first. SOCO was just leaving for the Benson's house. Still no murder weapon or anything that could in any way be described as a breakthrough. The duct tape had been sent away for analysis. Along with fifteen cigarette ends of assorted vintage.

"Doubt if any relate to the case, but it's worth a try," SOCO said. "As for tyre tracks, if someone had taped the track off this morning..."

"I know," said Shand. "I was just about to arrange it when ... you know."

"Too bad. The track itself wouldn't take much of an impression – it's rammed chalk – but the verges are soft. If they had as much trouble backing out as our lot did this morning we might have found something we could use."

Shand tried to convince himself that the gang hadn't left any tracks. The way they'd stopped to arrange the body, the way they'd replaced each turf, the way they'd worn gloves and masks at the Benson house. They were careful. They would have backed out slowly, keeping well away from any soft earth.

"I'd like a fingertip search of the area," asked SOCO. "If you've got the manpower. There's all the long grass between the stones and the track. And the track itself, plus the verges, all the way down to the road. You never know."

Shand agreed. He'd only have the extra numbers until the evening, might as well make use of them. There was still the murder weapon to be found. However careful the killers might be, they wouldn't risk having it found in their car. They'd have got rid of it somewhere.

"Which way is it to London from here?" he asked.

"Turn left at the mouth of the track. Take the Sherminster road for about seven miles until you hit the link road."

Shand wondered how many miles of ditches lay between Athelcott and the capital.

Shand accompanied SOCO back to Ivy Cottage and took him through Helena's account of events.

"I doubt you'll find any prints," said Shand. "But one of the men went out the back door. You might get lucky in the garden."

He then drove down to the village, turning right at the green – a triangular patch of rough meadow bounded by three roads. Cars were already lined up outside the Royal Oak, stretching back along the green. Shand pulled up at the back and got out.

Athelcott was not a picturesque village. It didn't have the neat rows of thatch, or the brightly painted cob, or the black and white quaintness of half-timbered cottages. It was more eclectic. A mishmash of styles and periods – a lot of stone, some rendering, some brick, a handful of thatch, some slate, a lot of red tile. And so many different styles and sizes –

from tiny terraced properties, to a sprawling Victorian rectory. The whole cobbled together over the centuries and strung out like a variegated ribbon along the roadsides.

He walked the village, traversing the three main roads. North to the Benson's, south to the Marchant's. Upper and Lower Street shared the east-west axis, separated by the green at one end and an infill of houses at the other.

Less than a hundred houses in all. Many expensive-looking, many far larger and more ostentatious than the Benson's. And yet Ivy Cottage had been targeted. If it wasn't because of George and his bank, why? Was it because of its proximity to the stone circle?

And why Annabel Marchant? It didn't feel like someone stumbling upon a crime in progress. She'd been arranged. Almost like a marker to bring everyone's attention to the body buried beneath. But why? Some sick mind trying to terrorise the village? Or did it have something to do with the circle itself? A cult?

It was at that point that Shand noticed something on the road. Writing. 'Free the Athelcott One,' chalked in large white letters across the road.

CHAPTER EIGHT

Shand pushed through the swing doors into the lounge bar of the Royal Oak. No sign of Taylor. He checked his watch. A few minutes to one.

He walked to the bar, glanced along the large array of beers and lagers, then noticed Taylor waving to him from the bar opposite.

"It's quieter in here," said Taylor when Shand joined him in the public bar. "The lounge is full of bloody journalists."

The two bars couldn't have been more different. The lounge was carpeted and decorated with horse brasses and all the tourist trimmings, while the public bar was stripped bare – lino floors, dartboard and ageing wooden furniture. A few locals eyed them suspiciously.

"Who's the Athelcott One?" asked Shand as he carried the drinks back to a table in the corner.

Taylor shrugged. "Someone like the Birmingham Six?"

"I saw it chalked on the road. 'Free the Athelcott One.' It was sprayed on the side of a garage as well."

"Kids most likely," said Taylor wiping the froth from his top lip.

Probably, thought Shand. Though worth checking. "Did the house-to-house turn anything up?"

"Besides the number for Gabriel Marchant's mobile, not a lot. Everyone seems to have had an early night last night. Even the pub closed on time. No one saw Mrs. Benson or any strange men."

"What about a car?" Shand told Taylor about the large four-door saloon. "It would have been parked outside the Benson house between ten and eleven."

"Two people saw George getting into his car about seven

thirty. That's it."

"They're sure it was George?"

"Positive. They're old friends and he waved."

"I don't suppose there are any CCTV cameras around here?"

Taylor laughed. "This is a village, sir. They don't even have street lights."

"What about speed cameras? There's a good chance the car came from London. Are there any speed cameras nearby?"

"Not within twenty miles."

"What about garages? They'd have CCTV. Any of those on the London road? They might have stopped for petrol or to clean up."

Even as he said it, Shand could see the improbability of the event. He wouldn't have stopped so close. Not if it had been him. He'd have put distance between himself and the crime and made sure there was no paper trail – the last thing he'd have wanted was a petrol receipt linking him to the scene.

"There's one about eight miles away," said Taylor. "But it closes at nine."

"What about the Marchants?" asked Shand. "Any witnesses to their whereabouts?"

Taylor leafed through his notebook. "Looks like Gabriel Marchant was in London all week. According to a family friend, a Miss Jacintha Maybury, one of the very few family friends we were able to locate. She saw Annabel yesterday morning and talked to her on the phone in the afternoon. Says she didn't notice anything odd about her behaviour. No problems in their marriage, no fears or threats. And no enemies who'd kill her."

"But she did have enemies?"

Taylor smiled. "Oh, yes. Both the Marchants did. But, according to Miss Maybury, there was never any violence. A bit of name calling here and there, and plenty of snubbing. Very petty, she said, and hardly likely to escalate to murder."

Shand wasn't so sure. He'd heard of disputes over the height of a garden hedge ending in murder.

"What about the Bensons? Any enemies there?"

"Not that we could find. Everyone likes them. Helena

Benson's on the parish council. George is the local bank manager. Pillars of the community."

Another dead-end. No enemies, no motive, no witnesses. Time was running out and it was looking more and more like a random killing.

"Is the house-to-house complete?"

"Mostly. Twelve of the houses were empty. According to the neighbours, eleven were second homes, the owners not seen for weeks. And the other was a family on holiday in Spain – they left last Saturday so they couldn't have seen anything either. And there's a handful," he counted them, "seven people who were out when we called. We'll be getting back to them tonight."

Shand's turn. He brought Taylor up to speed on his adventures with Helena, George and the bank.

"It doesn't mean that they didn't try to rob the bank," said Taylor. "Maybe their plan went wrong when George wasn't at home. So they winged it. Buried Helena as planned, then tried to ring George. After all, they had all weekend. But then along comes Annabel Marchant and everything goes haywire. She sees them, they kill her, panic and make a run for it."

Shand shook his head. "They stopped to arrange Annabel's body, they weren't panicking."

"Okay, so they stopped panicking, realised everything had gone to hell in a hand basket, and tried to make the most of it by making the murder look like something else."

"Like what?"

"Like a ritual."

Shand was unconvinced but, then again, did he have anything better?

"We need the phone records, Bob. If anyone phoned George last night I want to know. Might as well get the Marchant's records at the same time. How long would it take to drive to Sherminster at night?"

"From here? About forty-five minutes. Forty if you put your foot down."

Shand considered that for a moment, putting himself inside the heads of these would-be bank robbers. What would he do if he found that his intended mark was at a stag night forty-five minutes away? Would he wait for him to return or would he go after him?

DC Marcus Ashenden appeared at the table just as Shand was finishing his last sandwich. He reminded Shand of a puppy a friend of his had had. Bright eyes, boundless enthusiasm and a desire to please. That and an almost perpetual state of agitation. He'd noticed it the day before. The man couldn't sit still, if his feet weren't tapping, his eyes were darting around the room.

"I've got a message from SOCO, sir," he said breathlessly. "He wants to know when he can gain access to Mrs. Marchant's house?"

Shand checked the time. Quarter to. Marchant could arrive at any minute.

"Tell him any time from two, depending on when Mr. Marchant arrives."

"Will do, sir," said Ashenden, spinning on his heel to leave.

"Oh, and constable?" said Shand.

"Yes, sir?" said Ashenden spinning back.

"Find out all you can about the Athelcott One."

"The name that's chalked on the road?"

"That's the one."

Shand let Taylor walk on ahead when they left the pub, and called Anne. He was getting ready to ask if he could leave a message when she answered. "Anne Cromwell." She always used her maiden name at work.

"Hi, it's me," said Shand. "How's it going?"

It was a moment before she answered. A moment made longer by Shand's apprehension. So many of their phone conversations turned into silences punctuated by the all too infrequent word.

"Hello, Peter," she said. "Sorry, I couldn't get back to you earlier, but it's been crazy here. You know what it's like."

He didn't, but he'd have liked to. He blamed himself for not taking more interest in her work from the beginning, but he'd always been preoccupied with his own. The two of them sitting in the same room of an evening, ploughing through their respective documentation in companionable silence.

"Is it going well?" he asked.

"As well as ever. The users are refusing to sign off on the

acceptance test, and two of my programming team leaders haven't been seen since they went for a curry last night. If we go live on Monday, it'll be a miracle."

"You haven't been home then. Only I … I tried to ring last night."

Silence. Much longer this time.

"I was working late," she said, her voice clipped.

"Ah," said Shand, struggling to think of something to say. "I thought, maybe, we could go house-hunting next weekend."

More silence.

"Maybe," she said, "though it might be better to wait. After the weekend I'm having, I'll need to sleep for a week."

Shand's turn to hesitate. He didn't want to push, but he needed to know. "You're still coming down Friday night then?"

He waited, hardly daring to breathe.

"I'll see," she said. "Sorry, I've got to go now. Penny's waving at me from the conference room."

The line went dead.

CHAPTER NINE

Gabriel Marchant slammed his car door and marched towards the front step where Shand waited. He looked like a lawyer to Shand - sharp-eyed, sharp suit, and by the growing look of anger, probably sharp-tongued as well.

Anne would never have anything to do with him.

"What are all these people doing here?" Marchant snapped, a strand of hair detaching itself from his balding crown and covering an eye before being flicked back into place.

"They're waiting to conduct a search of your house. We have to-"

"*No one* is searching my house. You have no right."

"You object to us searching the house?"

"That's what 'no' usually means." He looked around. "Who's in charge here?"

"I am, sir. Detective Chief Inspector Shand. I'm sorry about your loss."

"Is that why all these people are massing outside my gates? To express their condolences?"

Shand was surprised at the man's belligerence. He'd expected a grieving husband. Or an oily gigolo.

"This is a potential crime scene, sir. There may be evidence inside which can lead to the arrest of your wife's killer."

"That," said Marchant, emphasising the word, "I highly doubt. You need to look elsewhere, chief inspector."

"We have looked elsewhere, sir. Now we want to look here."

"Tough. I'll answer your questions, but no one is searching this house without a warrant *and* my solicitor present."

"Then may I come inside to ask you these questions?"

Marchant looked in two minds.

"Do you really want me to conduct this interview in front of the whole village?" Shand asked.

Marchant glared to his left and right before reluctantly relenting. "*You* can come inside. Just you."

"I need my sergeant with me, sir. To take notes."

Marchant looked at Taylor like a father scrutinising a daughter's unsuitable boyfriend.

"Or we could go the station if you prefer," added Shand.

Marchant pushed past Shand and opened the front door, pausing to make sure both policemen wiped their feet before allowing them to follow him into the sitting room. Shand sat down, eyeing the decor – deep, richly coloured carpets, expensive wallpaper, furniture that looked as though it had never seen dust – and immediately became aware of his grass and soil-stained knees. He covered them with his hands.

Marchant remained standing. "First, chief inspector," he said, almost spitting out the words. "I'd like to issue a formal complaint. Reputation is everything in my business and when I heard today that someone had left a message at my office saying the police wanted to speak to me."

He stopped, almost as though he didn't trust himself to continue. Then took a deep breath. "I cannot, I absolutely can *not*, have any rumours of police investigations."

"What is your business, sir?" asked Taylor.

Marchant ignored him, continuing to glare at Shand.

"I'm sorry for any misunderstanding," said Shand, finding it difficult to reconcile Marchant's demeanour with that of a grieving husband. He hadn't mentioned Annabel once – not to ask to see her body, or enquire where she was, or even what had happened to her. He seemed more angry than distressed. Was that his way of dealing with grief? Or did he have no grief?

"Where do you work, sir," asked Shand.

"In the City," he said pouring himself a drink from a crystal decanter.

"Swindon?" asked Taylor.

Shand suppressed a smile. "And your occupation?"

"Senior Analyst, Mergers and Acquisitions. I'm an associate at Haversham and Glennie."

Shand watched him almost drain the glass in one swallow.

"Salisbury?" asked Taylor, persevering and putting on a look of mock-confusion as Marchant continued his refusal to acknowledge Taylor's existence.

"And you've been working there all week?" asked Shand.

"Yes. It's a high-pressure job, so weekend working is not unusual."

"Is it Bath, perhaps, sir?" asked Taylor.

Marchant snapped and turned on Taylor. "What *are* you talking about, you silly little man?"

"Tryin' to ascertain this city what you're big in, sir."

Shand could swear that Taylor's accent was thickening by the second, his esses had turned into zeds.

"London," Marchant sneered. "Shall I spell it for you?"

Shand stifled a smile and pressed on. "When was the last time you spoke to your wife?"

"Tuesday."

"Was she worried at all?"

"Only about her roses, chief inspector."

"Did she have any enemies?"

Marchant put down his glass. "Take your pick. The village is crawling with them. Have you heard of the character who goes around the village at night sabotaging incomer's gardens? The Moleman, they call him. The locals can't stand to see anything neat and tidy. This one digs holes in our lawns at night and pulls up flowers. Can you believe that!"

Shand could believe anything when it came to neighbours. He'd collated a report on neighbour related crimes once. The petty vindictiveness was mind-boggling.

"Do you know who the Moleman is?" he asked.

"I don't think you need to look much further than the tip next door. The son, Mark, is as dumb as they come. And his father..."

Marchant balled his fists, his anger rising. "Have you spoken to Bill Acomb, yet? He calls himself a farmer. The man has forty acres of wheat, seventy of beef and four acres of old vans. Take a look for yourself, chief inspector. They're scattered all over the place. It makes a gypsy encampment look like Buckingham Palace. And he has made our life hell."

He enunciated each word of that final sentence, filling every syllable with a deep heart-felt loathing.

"You would not believe the things he's done. Anything to make our lives a misery. He moved his manure heap next to our boundary fence. His idiot son leers at my wife and daughter whenever they leave the house. They run tractor engines in the yard for hours on end without reason. The noise and the diesel fumes make it impossible for us to sit outside. And then there's that chicken."

"Chicken?"

"Yes, chief inspector, the *chicken*. It crows at all hours of the night. And when we complained he moved his chicken house as close to our bedroom window as he could. So we took him to court and had his chicken impounded. He swore he'd get even. Ask anyone."

"Do you really think he'd kill to get even?"

"I wouldn't put anything past that man. He threatened us, chief inspector. In front of witnesses. It was in all the newspapers. And now my wife's dead."

For the first time a hint of an emotion other than anger swept across Gabriel Marchant's face. Shand watched him pour himself another drink. His hands shook, the crystal decanter clinked against the glass.

"Was your wife in the habit of visiting the stone circle?" asked Shand, softening his tone.

"No," said Marchant, more subdued now, staring into his glass. "We walked around it a few times when we first moved in. Why?"

"Can you think of any reason why she'd be up there at night?"

Marchant was surprised. He looked up. "She was at the circle?"

"Yes. Could she have been jogging past perhaps? Or walking?"

"My wife wouldn't walk anywhere at night. Not around here. It's pitch black."

"What kind of car does your wife drive?"

"A Mazda MX-5. Why? It hasn't been stolen, has it?"

"No, it's still in the garage."

Locked inside the garage, thought Shand. Was that

significant? He'd considered the possibility that Annabel Marchant had been driving past the circle when she'd seen something and stopped. But if so, and she'd been killed when she walked over, how had the car been returned to the garage? Were the killers that cool? Did they know where she lived?

Or was the locked garage proof that Annabel Marchant had not driven to her death?

"If your wife was driving late at night and saw something strange, would she stop?" asked Shand.

"Never," said Marchant. "You hear too many stories."

"What if it was someone she knew?"

Marchant put down his glass. "Who? Do you have someone in custody?"

"No," said Shand, but it was an interesting question – who would Annabel Marchant stop for? Her husband and daughter, presumably. But who else?

"Would your wife stop to help a stranger if she thought they were in trouble?"

Marchant shook his head. "Not at night. Not on her own. She might phone for help, but she wouldn't get out. Look, chief inspector, what exactly happened last night?"

The first time he'd asked.

"Would she stop to help Helena Benson?" asked Taylor, his accent back to normal.

"Helena Benson? What's *she* got to do with it?"

"She wasn't a particular friend of your wife's?" said Shand.

"God, no," said Marchant, confused. "We barely know the woman."

"Would your wife stop to help her if she saw she was in trouble?"

"Look, chief inspector, she wouldn't drive by if she saw her lying in the road, if that's what you mean."

"Helena Benson was abducted last night," said Shand, watching Marchant's reaction. "Two men took her from her home and buried her alive up at the circle. Your wife's body was found on top of her grave."

Marchant swallowed hard. "Good God," he said, reaching for another drink, then changing his mind.

"We're searching for a connection, Mr. Marchant. Now,

you said that your wife would have phoned for help?"

"Yes."

"She was in the habit of carrying a mobile phone?"

"She took it everywhere."

But where was it now? He didn't remember seeing one at the scene. And SOCO hadn't mentioned it.

"Where did your wife keep her phone?" he asked.

"In her handbag-"

"Could you ring the number now?" asked Shand, his excitement rising. There definitely had *not* been a handbag at the scene. Had the killers taken it with them? Or thrown it in a ditch with the murder weapon? They might be able to get a trace.

Marchant looked confused. "You want me to ring my wife's phone?"

"I want to know where your wife's phone is."

Other possibilities materialised. What if the phone was still in the house? Or in the car? What if Annabel had been abducted that evening too?

"Bob," said Shand, "Go out to the garage and listen. Her phone might be in the car."

Marchant rang as soon as Taylor left. Shand listened, slipping out into the hallway, the house silent, murmured conversation drifting in from outside. He cocked his head. Still no sound.

"Is it still ringing?" he asked Marchant.

"Yes."

Shand hurried to the front door and shouted over to Taylor, "Anything?"

Taylor shook his head. Shand went back inside. They'd be able to get a trace. He was sure of it. Maybe not a pinpoint trace, but to the nearest mast, a few square miles at most.

"You can stop now," said Shand. "Would your wife have left home without her phone?"

"I don't think so," said Marchant.

"I think it would be wise if you let my officers search your house now, Mr. Marchant."

Marchant rose to his feet. "I told you. I'm not having-"

"Sir, your wife's phone is missing. Probably her handbag too. I should imagine that means her keys and credit cards as well. It's very likely your wife's killers have been in this house. I need you to check for anything missing and I need access for my men."

Marchant looked torn, part of him looked ready for an argument while another part wanted to check his possessions.

"They broke into Helena Benson's house, sir," said Shand.

Marchant relented. "A limited search, chief inspector. But my study and my computers are out of bounds. Is that clear? My work is market sensitive. And don't tell me you'll make sure nothing gets leaked because I won't believe you. My lawyer will be here shortly."

"Did your wife have a computer?"

"I believe she had a laptop."

Shand passed the information along to Taylor and Scene of Crimes.

"Find Annabel's laptop and keep an eye on Marchant," he said, taking them aside. "He doesn't take anything off the property without it being checked first. And if you can, take a few photos of his study. Keep him sweet, but keep an eye on him."

The house filled up. Shand and Taylor followed Marchant through the house, checking for missing items or anything that could provide a clue as to why Annabel had left the house on Friday night. They found nothing. No note, no diary entry, no scribbled message on a kitchen calendar. And nothing on the answering machine either. The dishwasher was full, the sink empty. Everything was tidy, nothing to suggest that she'd left in a hurry or that anything had been taken.

"I have to ask you this," said Shand at the end. "But where were you last night?"

"At a restaurant," said Marchant.

"Can anyone confirm that?"

"I'll give you their names." He took out a business card and scribbled three names on the back complete with telephone numbers. "Colleagues from work, chief inspector. We were together until midnight. At *Henri's* in Covent Garden." He turned pointedly to Taylor. "And that's *not* in Swindon, sergeant."

"Much obliged, sir," said Taylor.

Marcus Ashenden was waiting for them outside. He looked pleased with himself.

"I've discovered who the Athelcott One is, sir."

"Who?" asked Shand.

"A chicken."

Shand saw another potential lead evaporate. "A chicken?" he said.

"Yes, sir, Bill Acomb's chicken. He's being held at a pound near Sturton while the court decides what to do with him. And you'll never guess who brought the action."

"We already know, Marc," said Taylor. "The Marchants. Which would make the animal in question a cockerel not a chicken. If you're going to live in the country, boy, you'd better get to know these technical terms."

Shand detached himself from the conversation and stared over at Lower Ash Farm. Was he really dealing with a fight between neighbours that had got out of hand? He didn't think so. Fights between neighbours tended to be settled on their properties with the bodies lying in the garden, not a half-mile away in a stone circle.

But who else had a motive? The mysterious bank robbers? That only worked if Annabel Marchant was an unlucky witness, but the more he learned about her, the less likely that option appeared. Her car was in the garage, her house locked up. She didn't like to walk through the village at night. How had she got to the circle?

And even if she had been driving past the circle and stopped to see what was going on, would her killers really have taken the time to return her car to the garage? It didn't ring true. The more he thought about it, the more convinced he became that Annabel Marchant had known her killer.

"Sir?" said Taylor.

"What?" said Shand.

"Is it worth taking a look at the neighbour while we're here?"

"I think it might," said Shand, "and Marcus, see what you can find out about these Moleman stories."

~

Lower Ash Farm was a complete contrast to the studied neatness of the Marchant's house. The front garden was a rutted yard edged by brambles and nettles entwined around islands of rusty metal, old machinery, rotting fence posts, discarded polythene and old tyres. Puddles in the yard shimmered oily rainbows. The farmhouse hadn't seen a lick of paint in years, an irregular tidemark of rising damp stained the grey rendered walls, and in the distance a succession of wooden and rusted corrugated iron outbuildings reminded Shand of a South African shantytown.

"You arrested 'im yet?" said a voice to Shand's right. "You been in there long enough."

A small weather-beaten man with a prominent red nose and a slight paunch emerged from a nearby barn. He was cleaning something black off his hands with an even blacker rag.

"Why should we do that, Mr. Acomb?" asked Shand.

"For killing 'is missus, of course. Terrible temper 'e has. And 'e don't like animals, you know. Which is 'ow they all start - them serial killers - ain't it? I was watching it on the telly the other night. They always start by torturing animals."

"Are you saying that Mr. Marchant tortured animals?" asked Shand, not sure whether to take Bill Acomb seriously. He had a glint in his eye and looked as though he was finding it hard not to grin.

"'E tortured me prize cock," said Acomb indignantly.

"The Athelcott One?" asked Taylor.

"That's 'im. Your boys 'ave 'im now. Locked up in a cell when all 'e did was do what comes natural."

"After you moved him as close to the Marchant's bedroom as you could," said Taylor.

"Maybe I did," said Bill Acomb, grinning. "But I wouldn't 'ave if they 'adn't started it. I was quite prepared to behave neighbourly until they started trotting out their orders. Trim that 'edge, move that muck heap, stop leaving mud on the road. Accused me of sheltering rats in me barns, they did. And me tractor was always too noisy or smelly."

"Townies," said Taylor.

"Too right," said Acomb. "The worse kind. Them that think they want to live in the country, but really want to live in a park where us yokels do nothing but keep the place tidy all day and look quaint."

"So when you threatened the Marchants, you didn't really

mean it?" asked Shand.

"Who said I threatened anyone?" snapped Acomb.

"I was told you threatened the Marchants in front of several witnesses."

"'E told you that, did he?" Bill Acomb darted a glance towards the Marchants house and cleared his throat. For one second Shand thought he was going to spit on the floor and prepared to step back. "All I said," continued Acomb in a slower more deliberate voice, "was I'd get even with 'em. And I will. In me own way, which don't include murdering nobody."

"And something which is entirely within the law, no doubt," said Taylor.

"Entirely," said Acomb. "Law-abiding family, us Acombs."

"You must see a lot of what goes on next door, Mr. Acomb," said Shand.

"I might," said Acomb.

"What about last night?"

"I already told your boys. I saw nothing."

"You didn't go out yesterday evening?"

"I might."

"And where might you have been," asked Taylor.

"Down the Oak."

"Until when?"

"Just after nine. Then I walked 'ome."

"A bit early for a Friday night?" said Taylor.

"I gets up early. I'm too old these days to go out drinking all hours."

"Did you look at the Marchant's house when you walked past?" asked Shand.

"I tries to look at it as little as possible. Used to be three families living in that 'ouse. Three 'ard-working local families. Until Mrs. Fancy Marchant moved in and knocked it into one gurt biggun."

"Was there a car outside? Any lights on inside the house?" pressed Shand.

"Yes and no," said Acomb, his eyes twinkling again. "Or should I say, no and yes."

Shand fought back a sudden inclination to throttle the farmer. He was tired, he'd barely slept, and he could feel a headache building up behind his eyes.

"Which is it, Mr. Acomb?"

"No to the car, but yes to the lights. But then that don't mean nothing. They always 'as the place lit up like a Christmas Tree. Some people don't 'ave to worry about bills."

"So she could have been in or out at nine o'clock when you walked by?"

"Could 'ave."

"Did she go out much at nights?"

"Not that I ever saw."

"What about in her car? Would you have heard her car if she'd used it last night?"

"Not me. I sleeps like a log. And when I'm not sleeping I'm watching the telly. Couldn't 'ear a tractor if someone drove one into me own yard."

Shand couldn't see anything more to be gained. He could see Bill Acomb dumping a trailer load of manure on the Marchant's front garden, but he couldn't see him killing anyone.

"What about your son, Mr. Acomb?" asked Shand. "Where was he last night?"

Bill Acomb shrugged.

"Where's he now?" asked Taylor.

"Out."

CHAPTER TEN

"Do you want me to check out the son," asked Taylor as they left.

"If you could," said Shand, looking at his watch. "I've got to get back for the PM."

Something he wasn't looking forward to. He'd attended three in the past, part of his forensics course. He'd found it hard to watch, even harder to blank his mind to the person on the slab, to see the cuts and the bruises, but not the living, breathing, human being that had had to endure them.

But he had to go - statistics again - *the attendance of the investigating officer at the post mortem significantly increases the probability of a murder being solved*. An unlikely statistic, Shand had always thought, but one he didn't feel confident enough to ignore. More likely it was non-attendance that was the significant factor - an indication that the investigating officer was too busy on other cases, or lacked the necessary commitment.

But Shand liked to play the percentages, so he went.

~

"Three wounds to the back of the head," said the pathologist, leaning over the body. "One on the right side, two on the left, one slightly higher than the other. The lower one struck first."

Shand stayed as far back as he could, coming forward only when invited and darting back as soon as he could. He'd already destroyed one crime scene. He couldn't face the thought of losing his lunch over the victim.

"You can see the slight overlap of the wounds. A flat-faced instrument, I'd say, maybe slightly curved."

Shand filed the information away, trying to use facts to block out the knowledge that this was Annabel Marchant, wife and mother. She was now the deceased, a statistic with three head wounds.

"And smooth," continued the pathologist. "Barely any debris in the wound. The dirt is post mortem, no sign of impaction."

Shand looked up at the ceiling and thought of smooth flat murder weapons. He saw the ceiling tiles, and thought of paving slabs, and cricket bats, and frying pans and spades.

"Could it have been a garden spade?" he asked.

"Possibly, I can't see any fragments of wood, or stone, or paint. Something metal, or a heavy plastic would fit."

"What about the force of the blows?"

"Substantial without being excessive. Business-like, I'd say, rather than frenzied. A strong women or a man. Or a teen for that matter - one with a fair amount of strength. From the pattern of the wounds, I'd say that the killer struck from behind with a sideways swing, two right-handed and one left. The second right-handed blow had a lower trajectory, probably because the victim was on the ground by then and her head was leaning forward. I don't think she could have been standing after the weight of the first blow.

"Would she have died instantly?"

"By the second or third blow. The third blow did the most damage."

Shand wondered about the significance of the right-handed and left-handed blows. Were there two killers? Or was the weapon being wielded two-handed? A garden spade, say, swung sideways from the right, then the left, then the right again.

"Any idea of the attacker's height?"

"Difficult to say with any degree of certainty. So much would depend on the angle of the victim's head. Was she looking up or down or straight ahead when she was hit? The blow appears to come from below, but that can be explained by the sideways swing." He demonstrated the attack holding an imaginary weapon in both hands. "The killer starts the swing at hip level and then brings it up and round - striking a glancing blow at the back of the victim's head."

"Are there any other wounds?" asked Shand. "Any sign she put up a struggle or tried to run?"

"No, I'd say your victim was surprised from behind. If

she'd been running and hit from behind I'd expect to see some damage or staining to the hands or nails when she fell. There's not even any soil under her fingernails and her knees are unscuffed."

Three blows, thought Shand, every one of them hitting the mark. No mistakes, no warning. Could someone do that in the dark? Or had there been light at the circle? They'd have needed light to bury Helena – torches, car headlights. Was it that that had caught Annabel Marchant's eye and made her stop?

Not if her husband was to be believed. She'd have driven past. Maybe phoned someone later and told them about the strange lights at the old stone circle.

Which was when another thought struck him. What if she'd phoned the wrong person? Someone who knew exactly what was happening up at the stone circle. Wouldn't that be a motive for murder?

He glanced at his watch. How long did it take to get phone records? He'd requested them hours ago.

"There'll be blood on the murder weapon," said the pathologist, bringing Shand back to the present. "Unless it's been cleaned, of course."

"Would the murderer have any blood on them?"

"Not if they were careful. But if they moved the body afterwards..."

"You think the body was moved?"

"Only from what I was told. She was laid out on an existing grave, wasn't she?"

"Yes, but what about lividity? Is there anything to suggest it was a while before the body was moved?"

"Lividity is consistent with her being moved very soon after death. Either that or she lay in the exact same position before being moved."

"What about time of death?"

"I see no reason to change the earlier estimate. 12:45, Saturday morning, give or take the usual hour."

Shand decided to leave. It was getting late and he had most of the information he needed. That and the gory business was about to start. The opening up and the examination of the internal organs. Something he didn't need to sit through. He'd leave it until later to find out what she'd had for her last meal.

"Leaving so soon?" asked the pathologist with a smile.

"Press conference," said Shand. "We try not to face the cameras with vomit down our shirts."

~

Shand was late and out of breath by the time he reached Sturton police station. Jimmy Scott from the Press Office had driven over from Sherminster HQ to brief him. He was waiting in the foyer tapping his watch. "Cutting it fine," he said between pursed lips.

Very fine. But then it hadn't been Shand's fault. The press had filled the small station car park. You couldn't move for large vans and satellite dishes. He'd had to circle the town square twice looking for a parking space. And he'd had to stop at a chemist on the way over to buy paracetamol when his head threatened to explode. Not to mention rushing back to his hotel room to change his suit.

Now he was hot, sweaty and waiting for the paracetamol to kick in.

Jimmy led him along a labyrinthine set of corridors, filling him in as they went.

"It's a full house. A very full house. TV, the nationals and a few overseas media. I've given them the basic handout. Names of victims, and the fact they were both locals. I've tried to play down the whole body on top of a grave aspect, but that's what they're all focussing on. That, and the stone circle. I think they want a serial-killing druid story."

Something that Shand hadn't considered. He wondered why. It made about as much sense as any other.

"Whatever you do," continued Jimmy, "watch out for Kevin Tresco. He's the local hack, works for the Echo. You know the corruption investigation? All the suspended DIs? Well he broke it. Now he thinks he's the next Bob Woodward. You know, Watergate? So watch him. He'll be out to impress the Fleet Street crowd, and won't care how he does it. Wouldn't put anything past him. So keep him sweet."

Keep him sweet. Words flying along a corridor. In a few minutes he was going to give his first ever press conference and he hadn't a clue what he was going to say. Something he'd been putting off all day, waiting for that one piece of evidence that would break the case and give him something to announce – *this* is what happened, *here's* what we're looking for. A simple statement delivered with confidence. A plea to the general public for assistance, and a big smile for the media.

But he didn't have that one piece of evidence. He didn't even know what kind of a crime he was investigating. A bank robbery/abduction gone wrong? A murdered witness? A wife murder? A dispute between neighbours? A ritual killing? Or even a serial-killing druid.

Tomorrow would be different. He was sure of it. If only the press conference could be delayed. There was the forensics on the book of matches to come back, the phone records, the club in London, Annabel's computer – once they cracked the password – maybe even tracing the location of Annabel's mobile phone.

Though that wasn't going to be as straightforward as he'd hoped. The phone company had got back to him while he'd been changing at the hotel, one leg in his spare trousers and hopping all over the floor. They'd traced the mast. A mast that covered nearly sixty square miles – encompassing one town and eleven villages, including Athelcott. If it had been a city they'd have triangulated it to an individual apartment, but this was rural Wessex and a single mast that served eight miles of link road, fifteen miles of major roads and countless minor ones.

And the phone had stopped transmitting – either the battery had died or someone had switched it off.

"How are you feeling," asked Jimmy. "You look a little stressed."

"Adrenaline," said Shand, feeling like a boxer being led to a bout he'd forgotten to train for.

~

The conference room was packed – people, cameras, cables, furry microphones on poles. And lights. The brightest lights he'd ever seen. The stage glowed like a rock concert.

Doubt and panic. He still had no idea what he was going to say. A man who prided himself on preparation and attention to detail, he felt naked and exposed. He should have allowed himself at least an hour to jot down some notes, work out what he was going to say. All that time wasted driving to the bank and back.

"Should be easy for you," said Jimmy. "What with your press office experience."

Shand forced a smile, masking his churning insides as he peered out from the wings. His spell at the Inspectorate press department hadn't prepared him for anything like this. His occasional meetings with journalists had been informal affairs – off the record briefings at pubs and dinner parties. This was a bear pit.

More doubt. Had he made effective use of police time? Eight hours into the investigation, countless man-hours expended and they were still collecting evidence. Had he misdirected the forensic teams? Shouldn't he have let them start analysing the data from the circle instead of insisting they search the Benson and Marchant houses first? That book of matches could have been important. Something he could have given to the press.

The press. They were growing restless. Four o'clock had come, gone and was probably decomposing somewhere on stage.

More panic. His reputation was on the line. Fifteen years of exemplary service about to be wagered on ten minutes of question and answer. Ten minutes which had to go well and be seen to go well. To show everyone, to show Anne, that he'd been right about the move to CID.

"They're waiting," said Jimmy. "Remember what I said about Tresco." He leaned forward to point him out. "He's the guy in front with the long straggly hair and the cheap suit."

Shand glanced at the reporter; a thin, sharp-featured man in his late twenties.

"Remember," said Jimmy. "Keep him sweet."

Shand walked out to a flurry of clicks and flashes, almost feeling his way along the stage, the lights were so bright. He took the middle chair of three behind a long table, the one with the microphone. The far chair was already taken. Someone he didn't recognise. Another press officer? The Chief Constable? Shand's mind blanked as he shook his hand. Jimmy settled into the other seat. Everyone sitting down, a room waiting, every face turned towards Shand.

He began, almost on autopilot, giving the basic details of

the case – the names, the village, the time frame, where everyone had been found. His mind drifted further ahead. What was he going to say next? What was he going to leave out? It was such a fine line: say too much and you tip off the killer, say too little and you miss the vital witness – the woman who saw the car or the handbag you omitted to mention.

He talked about the missing murder weapon. "We're looking for a garden spade. It may have been dumped from a car early this morning."

"Any idea where?" shouted one of the reporters

"Somewhere north of Athelcott."

"How far north?" asked another.

"Probably within ten miles," said Shand.

A sea of hands rose and fell. Everyone shouting questions at once, Shand looked from one side of the room to the other. He could feel the press conference slipping away from his control. Should he ignore the questions and press on with his statement? Did he have a statement?

"And we're looking for a handbag," said Shand, trying to retake the initiative. "Probably dumped from the same car."

"What kind of car?"

"A large four-door saloon with leather interior."

"What make?"

"We don't know."

"What colour?"

"We don't know."

"But it has got four doors?" asked Kevin Tresco.

"Yes, that's right."

"And presumably four wheels?"

Laughter. It was only a few people, but it totally threw Shand. Why were they laughing? This was a press conference about a murder. Tresco smirked from the front row, looking around at his colleagues, lapping up the attention. Shand swallowed, confused, desperately thinking of something to say.

Tresco didn't give him the time. As soon as the laughter died down, he was back. "You don't have much to go on do you, chief inspector? A man of your experience. Tell me, how much experience *do* you have?"

Shand hesitated. He was used to impressing people with

his CV. His Masters in Criminology, his time lecturing in the States, his years in Training Branch, his secondment to the Home Office, the Met, the Inspectorate of Police. He'd been a high-flyer all his career.

But now it sounded hollow. All theory and admin. That's what Tresco would see.

"I've been in the force for fifteen years."

"Mmm, impressive," said Tresco, looking down at his notes. "And how many of those years were in CID?"

Jimmy Scott reached over and took the microphone from Shand. "I don't think that question's relevant. Can we move on, please? Next question."

Tresco kept going. "How many murder cases have you been on, chief inspector?"

Shand opened his mouth to answer, but Jimmy cut in. "Kevin, this an open press conference, let someone else have a chance."

A reporter at the back repeated the question. "How many murder cases *have* you been on, chief inspector?"

Kevin Tresco leaned back in his chair, folded his arms and smirked.

Shand took the mike, his mouth suddenly dry, his palms oozing a cold sweat. "This is my first murder case," he said.

"Isn't this your first case ever, chief inspector?" said Tresco, now standing up. "In fact, isn't this only your second day on the job?" He turned to milk the reaction from the press corps. An excited buzz, a flurry of camera clicks. "What do you think of that, Mr. Shand? Do you think it right an outsider with no experience should run a local murder enquiry?"

Uproar. Shand suddenly felt very alone, the table elongating by the second taking his colleagues with it. The room doing the opposite - contracting - a sea of faces pushing closer. Open mouths, lights flashing, questions everywhere. Tresco in the front leading the chorus.

"I know what my readers think."

A sneer, a pointed finger, that irritating laugh.

"Have you got one single lead?"

Everyone was watching. His own people in the wings, countless viewers at home, Anne. His career was incinerating before his eyes.

He had to say something, do something. The schoolboy in him wanted to get back at Tresco, wipe the smile off his face. Destroy him with one withering remark.

Another voice. One from memory. What was it his old boss at the Press Office used to tell him? *If you want to kill a story, give them a better one. Something they want to hear.* He glanced down at the table. Saw the folded newspaper. Bold headlines – Asylum Seeker Row Deepens. He remembered the camp a few miles outside Athelcott. The barracks, the high fences.

And then he was talking, the words coming out of his mouth before he'd had time to think.

"We do have one very important lead."

The room quietened. Shand continued, his voice emotionless. "We're investigating a link between the murder and local asylum seekers."

The room erupted. Shand was almost blinded in the flash of cameras. Questions came at him from all sides. *Do you have anyone in custody? A name, a nationality. Are they Muslims?*

Shand held up his hands, then leaned farther into the microphone. "Obviously I can't go into details at this juncture. But it is a very promising lead."

"Is an arrest imminent?"

Shand smiled and got up. He wanted to leave as quickly as possible. He shuffled behind the seats, nodding to various people, shaking hands and speaking meaningless words that he instantly forgot.

By the time he reached the wings, he was in a cold-sweat daze.

CHAPTER ELEVEN

"What asylum seeker lead?" asked Taylor, suddenly appearing in the cloakroom mirror. Shand closed his eyes and cupped another handful of cold water over his face. What had he done?

Besides destroying his career, that is. He'd lied to the press in front of a million witnesses. He'd jeopardised a murder case. And probably made life even worse for tens of thousands of asylum seekers who'd have to wake up to another wave of migrant bashing headlines.

And all for what? A playground argument with a local journalist. What had he been thinking?

Easy answer. He hadn't. He'd been reacting to events when he should have been leading them.

Shand grabbed a paper towel and dabbed at his face. Taylor was still there. Waiting.

"An anonymous tip off," lied Shand.

"Who to?" asked Taylor. "None of the boys on the desk heard anything."

"They wouldn't have," said Shand, digging himself deeper. "I took the call."

"Oh."

Shand pushed through the cloakroom door into the corridor, glad to get out.

And ran straight into Chief Superintendent Wiggins.

"Shand!" he boomed. "I've been looking all over for you. Where have you been hiding?"

Somewhere not as private as he'd hoped, thought Shand, dreading what was about to happen next. Was he going to be taken off the case?

Wiggins raised his hand and for one horrible second, as

the hand arced towards him, Shand thought he was going to be struck. He flinched, he couldn't help it. Then the hand slapped him on the shoulder.

"Have to hand it to you, Shand," said Wiggins. "The way you played Tresco. He really thought he had you. Even I did. But then you pulled that asylum seeker lead out of the hat and his jaw nearly hit the floor. Masterful, Shand. Truly masterful."

Shand smiled, not daring to say anything. How long could he keep the deception going?

He extricated himself as quickly as he could, thanked Wiggins, looked at his watch and hurried off in the other direction. He had to get the investigation back on track, bury the bogus asylum seeker lead, and prioritise the real leads.

Taylor followed. "Where you going?" he asked.

"Back to my office," said Shand. "I need to collate all the information we've gathered so far."

"You're not going to the asylum camp?"

Shand stopped dead, his eyeballs furrowing into his brow. "Of course," he said, thinking quickly. "I was just going via my office to pick up my personal organiser."

Shand smiled to himself. If he ever got through this day, he'd find so much tangled web around his legs he'd never get his trousers off.

~

Taylor drove. Shand sat in the passenger seat planning ahead. He'd go through the motions at the asylum camp. Interview whoever was in charge and slowly bury the lead. Anonymous hoaxer, we get them all the time. Then he'd have a day to find a real lead before the papers started clamouring for another statement.

It might work.

"So this anonymous caller asked for you personally?" said Taylor.

Shand pretended to be engrossed in a sheaf of scribbled notes.

"The tip off," repeated Taylor. "The caller asked for you personally?"

"I don't know,' said Shand, feigning indifference, "I just took the call."

"In your office?"

"No, on my mobile."

"So they had your number?"

Shand was beginning to wonder if Taylor had his number too. "How did you get on with Bill Acomb's son?" he asked.

There was a pause before Taylor answered. Shand waited, keeping his head down in his notes.

"Couldn't track him down," said Taylor. "But I asked around and he's got a bit of form – two drunk and disorderlies from two years back. Handy with his fists and doesn't need much provocation."

"Anything recent?"

"Not that I could find. His name doesn't come up on any searches. No criminal associations. Maybe he's grown up. He's twenty-one now and has a steady job on his father's farm."

"What about Friday night? Anyone see him at all?"

"No. Which might be significant. According to the landlord, he spends most nights down the Oak."

~

The asylum camp was four miles outside Athelcott on the London road. It looked like an army camp – high perimeter fence, sprawling single story buildings, wide expanses of grass and asphalt. Only the groups of irregularly dressed adults and bands of playing children gave the game away.

Shand and Taylor were stopped at the gate, then directed to a parking bay where they were met and escorted to the director's office. Groups of people watched them all the way, no one saying a word.

"I'm curious, chief inspector," said the Director after Shand had made the introductions. "How did you know that Marius Lupescu was missing?"

CHAPTER TWELVE

"Someone's missing?" said Shand, before he'd had time to think – a situation that was becoming far too frequent.

"Yes, since this morning. Well, maybe before that. We only take a head count at breakfast."

"Did you report this to the police?" asked Taylor.

"It's not general policy, sergeant. This is not a secure centre. None of our guests here have committed any crimes. We're a collection centre really."

"With ten foot high fences and barbed wire?"

"That came with the army camp, I'm afraid. We try and play down the detention centre aspect."

The Director looked like an army officer. A neat, prim little man with a pencil moustache and slicked back hair.

"So people can come and go as they please?" asked Taylor.

"Not exactly. Everyone's supposed to stay inside the camp. But we try and be flexible. There's a limit to what we can provide inside the camp, and we don't want any riots."

Shand kept quiet, content to let Taylor take the lead. He'd let the interview proceed, go through the motions, then leave as quickly as possible. The chance of this disappearance being linked to a murder four miles away was negligible. But it did provide his fabrication with a touch of credibility. Who knows, thought Shand, maybe fortune did favour the brave.

"So you let people out now and then?" asked Taylor.

"We bus the children to the local school at Nethercombe and some of the adults are taken to English classes in Sturton. They're not supervised all the time and sometimes fewer come back than we send out. But it's usually a misunderstanding. They make their own way back eventually.

Free food and a bed for the night is not something to be given up lightly, sergeant."

"Don't they want to escape?" asked Taylor. "I thought that's what they did. Run off to the cities and disappear so they can't be sent home."

"So the media would have us believe, sergeant. But this facility is for those that have been fast-tracked as most likely to be granted asylum. They have no reason to run. Other than a quite natural fear of confinement and, for some, an ingrained distrust of authority."

"Do people often miss roll call?" asked Shand, deciding it would be more suspicious if he didn't ask at least one question.

"Occasionally. But they usually return the next day. Chastened and sometimes a little frightened. If someone was missing for three days, we'd contact the authorities, but that hasn't happened yet."

"Does the camp have any links with Athelcott?"

"Not that I can think of. The children go to school at Nethercombe. There may be some children from Athelcott attending, but you'd have to check."

"Do the names Helena Benson or Annabel Marchant mean anything to you?"

"No, not at all."

Shand smiled and held out his hand. "I don't think we need to take up any more of your time. If Marius is still missing next week, give us a call."

"Yes, of course. I'm still curious, chief inspector, how did you find out about our missing man?"

"An anonymous tip-off," said Taylor. "Straight to the chief inspector's mobile."

~

"You're not pursuing this?" asked Taylor as they walked to the car.

"Not tonight," said Shand. "There's a few things we need to do in Athelcott first."

A television van pulled up outside the gates as Shand and Taylor left. The first of many, thought Shand as he slipped lower in the passenger seat.

They drove to the circle first. Shand wanted to see the

fingertip search for himself. He watched from the road as lines of uniformed policemen crawled and combed through the rough grass along the track edge. He talked with the sergeant in charge. Nothing much to report. Drink cans, food wrappers, cigarette packets, assorted scraps of paper and plastic.

"Oh and we found some spent shot gun cartridges up by the entrance to the wood."

Shand looked up from the pile of plastic evidence bags. "Shot gun cartridges?"

"Probably someone shooting pigeons," said Taylor.

"That's what we thought," continued the sergeant. "Or rooks, you can see a few nests in the higher branches."

Then they drove back down the London road, Shand wanted to retrace the probable escape route while it was still light. They might get lucky. It was about time they did.

They crawled along the country lanes, Taylor keeping the speed below twenty, both men checking their side of the road. They stopped at every lay-by and rubbish bin, at every suspicious pile of debris lying in a ditch or flapping piece of fabric caught in a hedge.

No handbag. No garden spade. No flat, smooth metal object. No mobile phone. By the time they returned to Athelcott it was dark.

"Who haven't we seen?" said Shand, picking up Taylor's list - people who'd been out when the house-to-house had called. There were seven names. Shand decided to take them in order, starting at one end of the village and working his way along.

On the sixth name, they struck lucky.

"I saw her, you know?" said the old man. A Mr. Derek Wootton according to Taylor's notes. He was sitting in a battered armchair in front of an open log fire as his daughter fussed around him.

"You saw Mrs. Marchant?" asked Shand.

"That's right. I was only talking about it five minutes ago to our Ruthie. 'No!' she said, 'you must have been the last one to see her alive.' And I bet I was, you know?"

"What time did you see her?"

"Six minutes past twelve exactly," he said, enunciating each word. "And I knows that for a fact 'cos I looked over at my alarm clock and I remember thinking to myself, 'where's she going at this time o' night?'"

Shand could barely get the next question out quick enough. "Where did you see her?"

"I'll show you if you like." His arms strained as he pushed himself out of the armchair. "I was up at the bedroom window." He walked over to what Shand had assumed was a cupboard door and opened it. Inside was the narrowest and steepest staircase Shand had ever seen. There was barely headroom at the bottom and the stairs turned immediately alongside the back wall.

Shand and Taylor followed the old man up the stairs and along a sloping corridor into a small bedroom overlooking the street. There was a digital alarm clock by the bed. Shand checked it against his watch. It was correct.

"I had to get up," said Mr. Wootton. "'Cos the moon was in my eyes. So I went over to draw the curtains and that's when I saw her. Down there."

He pointed to the other side of the road. "She was on her way to the green."

"You're sure it was Mrs. Marchant?" asked Shand, shading the glare of the hall light on the window with his right hand as he tried to make sense out of the grey shapes below.

"Positive," said Mr. Wootton. "She had on that long coat of hers. And the moon was that bright it was like daylight out there."

"It was a full moon last night?" asked Shand, surprised that he hadn't checked. He'd assumed it had been overcast. It had been when he'd left the hotel after breakfast. The sky had been thick with cloud.

"Not quite," said Wootton. "Full moon's in three days time, but it was as near as dammit last night."

"Could you switch off the hall light for a minute, Bob," said Shand.

The room went black. Shand peered down at the road below. He could make out more detail now. The bedroom window was directly above the pavement, the other side of the road couldn't have been more than twenty-five feet away.

"Was she alone?" asked Shand.

“All alone,” said Wootton. “I thought it were strange at the time. Didn’t I just say that, Ruthie?”

“Yes, dad,” agreed a voice from below. Shand marvelled at the old cottage’s acoustics and looked down at the bare floorboards by the window – probably nailed directly onto the ceiling joists, just the one inch of wood between bedroom and lounge.

“Did you see where she went?” Shand asked as Taylor switched the hall light back on.

“No,” said Wootton. “I was starting to get cold. We got no heating upstairs and it was a bitter night so I just draws the curtain and jumps back into bed. Do you think she was on her way up to the circle?”

“I don’t know, Mr. Wootton. What do you think?”

“Well,” he said conspiratorially, “seeing as you asked and all. I can’t see her walking all the way up to the circle. Not at night. Not any time, really. Not a great walker, that one. I’ve seen her drive to the Oak. So that’ll tell you how far that one liked to walk.”

“So where do you think she was going, Mr. Wootton?”

“To meet someone on the green.” He tapped the side of his nose. “That’s what I reckon. The green’s always been a place to meet people. ‘Meet you on the green,’ that’s what we always used to say.”

“Who do you think she was going to meet?”

“Ah,” said Wootton, “now, wouldn’t we all like to know the answer to that.”

“How about a guess, Mr. Wootton?”

Mr. Wootton shook his head. “Not me, inspector. I gets in enough trouble as it is without pointing fingers at others.”

CHAPTER THIRTEEN

Shand and Taylor stood outside the Wootton's cottage. Annabel Marchant's house was about one hundred and fifty yards to the left. The green was fifty yards to the right. If she'd kept going she'd have reached the circle in another three-quarters of a mile, passing the Benson's cottage in the process.

What was she doing? Who was she going to meet? And why so late?

12:06. Annabel Marchant was alive at 12:06 and killed sometime between then and 1:45. But Helena Benson had been abducted around 10:30. Why the gap?

Then the thought struck him, he hadn't corroborated Helena's time of abduction. She'd said herself she'd been confused. Could it have been later? She'd been on the phone when the knock had come at the door. On the phone to ... he checked his notes, pulling out a torch, and flicking back through pages of almost illegible scrawl.

There it was - Ursula Montacute, chair Parish Council.

"Has anyone interviewed Ursula Montacute?" he asked Taylor.

Taylor borrowed the torch. "Doesn't ring a bell," he said, and then, "no, she's not on our list."

Shand flicked on his phone and rang Directory Enquiries. How many Ursula Montacutes could there be in Wessex?

Just the one. He jotted down her number and rang.

"Mrs. Montacute?"

"Speaking."

"Sorry to disturb you, but I'm Detective Chief Inspector Shand. Could I ask you a few questions?"

"By all means, chief inspector."

"Did you telephone Helena Benson last night?"

"She telephoned me. She wanted to discuss the upcoming parish council meeting."

"Do you remember what time that was?"

"About half past ten, I think. I believe the film had just finished. The one on BBC."

"Was it a long call?"

"No, quite short actually. Two minutes, I'd say. Then there was a knock at the door and she had to ring off." She paused, her voice hardening. "I actually heard them knock on the door, chief inspector. If only she hadn't put the phone down, I would have heard what happened next, and could have phoned for help."

~

"Shall we get something to eat?" suggested Taylor.

"What?" said Shand, busy juggling time frames in his head. Helena Benson abducted around 10:30, Annabel Marchant on the green at 12:06. How could he bring the two together?

"Food," said Taylor. "I only had a sandwich at dinner time."

Shand persuaded him to wait until they'd checked the last name on their list – Mark Acomb.

"And if he's not at home," said Shand, "we'll check the pub next."

He wasn't at home.

Bill Acomb thought his son might have gone drinking in Sturton. Or, at least, that was what he said as he stood in the doorway. A television set blared out from inside the house. Shand peered past him into the ill-lit hallway and wondered who he'd find if he pushed his way in. Was Mark Acomb hiding inside? Or was he usually this difficult to find?

Shand dwelt on the step for another second, then left.

He had a pie and a pint with Taylor at the Royal Oak, but couldn't settle. He wanted to write everything down, to spread notes all over the largest table he could find, and try and make everything fit together. He didn't want to eat or engage in small talk or even discuss the case. He wanted time by himself. Time to pull everything together. He'd been flying off at tangents all day, and it was time to step back and examine what had been discovered.

Taylor dropped him by his car in Sturton. Shand said goodnight and drove back to the station.

Alone in his office, he filed and collated, reading through all the reports and making notes as he went – creating lists of information he needed, questions to be asked, people to see. And then setting priorities. Tasks for the next day. Allocation of staff. He was not going to be unprepared again.

Hours passed. The station quiet except for the distant rumble of a cleaner's trolley. Shand leaned back in his chair and closed his eyes. If only he could make sense of the time line. Helena abducted around 10:32, Annabel killed at 12:45. Two and a quarter hours unaccounted for in between. Even if they moved Annabel's murder up to just after 12:06 there was still a 95-minute gap. How long did it take to bury Helena?

He went through the course of events in his mind. They arrive at 10:32, a few minutes to subdue Helena then tie her up. A few more minutes to look around the house, then into the car. That would make it about 10:40, 10:45 at the latest. A two-minute drive to the circle, they get out, dig the hole. Another twenty minutes. Eleven o'clock, maybe ten past. Then they tell her to lie down in the grave. She resists, they hold her down. Another minute. They explain about the breathing tube, they fill in the grave. Another few minutes. That would make it about 11:05 to 11:15. An hour before Annabel's last sighting.

So what did they do in the meantime? Did they stay at the circle? Were they waiting for someone?

He ripped out another sheet of paper from the pad and started to write. Facts in black, suppositions in red, switching between pens. Was it George they were waiting for? Had they rung him? Or did they go looking for him? Was that the cause of the delay? Had they driven to Sherminster and back?

He dived into a stack of papers he'd filed on the floor. How long did it take to drive to Sherminster? He tore through the pages, ran his finger down the text. There it was. Forty minutes. Forty minutes at night if you put your foot down.

He made the calculation. One hour twenty there and back, longer if they had trouble finding him. They leave at 11:05, back around 12:30 in time to kill Annabel at 12:45.

He collapsed back into his chair. *Why* would Annabel go to the circle? That was the problem. He rubbed his eyes and tried to massage the sleep out of them. He felt so tired – his body, his brain – he knew he needed to sleep, but couldn't bring himself to leave. He had to keep going.

He switched to a new sheet of paper. This time Annabel had seen the events at the circle. She'd driven past at eleven, but waited until she got home to phone a friend. A friend who just happened to be in on the abduction. A local man who'd planned the bank robbery and brought the men down from London.

The friend panics, suddenly he doesn't have all weekend to rob the bank. Annabel's going to tell everyone about what she saw at the circle. Someone's bound to get curious and take a look. So she has to be silenced. He arranges to meet her, takes her to the circle to investigate what she'd seen ... and kills her.

It fit the time frame. It even made sense – up to the point where they placed Annabel's body on Helena's grave. If you kill someone to hide a crime, you don't then place that corpse on top of the very body you were trying to hide.

Shand rolled the paper into a ball and tossed it into the bin. Was it at all possible that the crimes weren't linked? It sounded ridiculous but...

Another piece of paper. What if it wasn't Annabel, but Annabel's murderer who had witnessed Helena's burial?

Could they have used Helena's burial as a smokescreen?

Shand wasn't sure if it was desperation or lack of sleep but, suddenly, he could see the possibility. He could even envisage it. Someone driving by, sees the lights at the circle, goes to investigate, creeps up silently using the darkness as cover.

Shand stopped and shook his head. There'd been a full moon. And no cover if they came in from the road. They'd be seen.

Could they have come from another direction? The chalk track led into a wood. Someone could have come from there and watched from the cover of the trees.

He liked that. He put himself in their position, mentally crouching down on the edge of the wood, silently observing.

They'd watch, curious at first, maybe they'd think of intervening or calling the police. But they didn't. Why? Because they were alone and outnumbered, or because they'd already formulated another plan? A chance to get rid of a bigger problem - Annabel.

He started to write. Fast. They'd wait until the two men left, then they'd persuade Annabel to walk to her death.

How? He scratched it in large letters and underlined it twice. They'd have to be a friend, someone Annabel would trust - a husband, a lover, someone close - someone who could convince her to leave her house in the middle of the night.

But would she walk all the way to the circle? Mr. Wootton didn't think so. Neither did Shand. She had a car. Why hadn't she used it?

Another note. *Check car*. Had someone sabotaged it?

Or had she been offered a lift? From a car that couldn't risk being seen pulling up outside her house? A lover?

Shand could definitely see it. They'd meet at the Green. He'd drive her to the circle, feed her some story she couldn't resist - a moonlight tryst, a mystery - something to persuade her to walk over to the circle as he drifts behind her, spade in hand - maybe picked up from the car, maybe planted by the stones earlier. She stops, he grips the spade in both hands and then, by the light of the moon, he swings and - whack - she falls.

He'd then drag her body onto Helena's grave and leave, knowing the police would link the two crimes and waste days trying to figure out a connection that didn't exist. And, even better, if they caught Helena's abductors why bother to look any further?

He wrote it down while it was still fresh in his mind, writing so fast that passages became illegible and he had to go over them again, hoping that, unlike a dream, everything would still make sense in the morning.

CHAPTER FOURTEEN

Shand slept fitfully, haunted by a recurring dream that he'd blurted out a false lead in the middle of a press conference.

Then he'd wake up and the truth would overwhelm him.

By four o'clock he was a wreck. A 'wide-awake, staring at a hotel ceiling' wreck who couldn't stop going over and over what he'd done and what he should have done.

Why invent such a ridiculous story about an asylum seeker? It was so unlike him. He was the safe pair of hands.

Then came the realisation.

Perhaps it wasn't so out of character. Hadn't most of his adult life been spent trying to please others? Sacrificing everything for his job, never turning down a request to work late, cancelling holidays.

What was his asylum seeker remark but an extension of that? A ridiculous, senseless attempt to please others by giving them something they wanted to hear.

~

Shand was up early. The room, the bed, the inactivity was driving him crazy. He had to *do* something.

He drove to the stone circle, arriving just after first light. It was drizzling. He turned his coat collar up and strode along the chalk track, his mind already in the woods, going through his theory from the night before.

He stopped at the point the track entered the woods and looked back. The circle was visible, grey shapes against a grey sky. He imagined standing there the night before. What would he do next? Crouch down by the track's edge, use that branch for cover?

He studied the ground. It didn't look disturbed though the

earth was soft. He wondered if he should call SOCO back. A thought soon scotched. He needed Forensics to concentrate on what they already had. Everything else could wait.

And where did this chalk track go? It looked well maintained. The edges were distinct – no brambles or low branches encroached from the wood. Could it wind back to the village?

Shand followed the track deeper into the woods. After about a mile the trees gave way to fields and the track descended into what looked like a huge grassy bowl carved into the hillside. There were buildings in the distance, a large farm complex by the look of it, and the track curved down towards it.

Shand tried to take his bearings. Where was the village? He walked a bit farther. There was a spur of hillside to his left that blocked his view. He was sure the village was on the other side. In which case, where was this farm? Had it been overlooked in the house-to-house?

He swung around, scanning the sweep of the hills and woods. How many other houses had been missed? He needed a map. Yesterday, he'd assumed this track was a dead-end. He hadn't expected to find people living at the other end.

Shand looked at his watch. He'd arranged to meet Marcus at the circle in fifteen minutes. Interviewing the people at the farm would have to wait.

~

He found DC Ashenden waiting by his car, almost bouncing to attention as soon as Shand appeared out of the drizzle.

"I want you to go to Sherminster, Marcus," said Shand. "I've prepared a list of names and addresses. I want you to talk to all of them. Find out what George Benson's demeanour was that evening. I want to know if anyone phoned him or talked to him or gave him a message. Anything at all. If these people buried his wife, they had to get in touch with him. So I'm looking for a point of contact. A call, a stranger coming up to him, any unexplained absences. And trace the taxi driver who took him to his friend's house. Get a confirmation of the time. I've written everything down."

Shand fished the two pages of notes from his car and handed them over.

"About the Moleman, sir. Did you want my report now or later?"

"What did you find?"

"I think it's local kids, sir, targeting newcomer's gardens. At least that's what it looks like. Though the kids deny all knowledge."

"As they would," said Shand

"Exactly, sir. But..." Ashenden hesitated.

"But what?"

"It's a strange sort of vandalism, sir. It's not mindless, it's ... it's weird. Like they dig up shrubs and swap them around, rearrange flower beds, or they dig holes in someone's lawn and then arrange the piles of soil in a pattern – like a crop circle made of mole hills."

It still sounded like kids to Shand. Older kids, students probably.

"Has anyone been hurt?" asked Shand. "Any hint of violence towards animals?"

"No. As I said, it's just weird."

Shand was just about to dismiss the Moleman when something struck him.

"I take it this Moleman only comes out at night?"

"That's what it looks like."

"Any gardens hit Friday night?"

"Ah," said the constable, smiling as the significance hit him. "I don't think so, sir, but I haven't talked to everyone."

"Add that to your 'to do' list when you come back from Sherminster."

And with luck, thought Shand, our Moleman will have been both active and highly observant on Friday night. It was about time they had a breakthrough.

~

The breakthrough was closer than Shand realised. It was waiting for him when he returned to Sturton. Six pieces of paper lay on his desk. He grabbed the top copy. It was the phone log. They'd found four accounts – two fixed lines and two mobiles. The Marchant house, the Benson house and

Gabriel and Annabel's mobiles.

No mobiles though for George or Helena. A disappointment. He'd been hoping to see a late-night call to George from the kidnappers, a number he could trace.

He flipped through the pages. He found Helena's call to Ursula Montacute - 10:30, duration two minutes and twenty seconds. Then nothing. No call in or out until three the next afternoon. He scanned back. The previous call had been at six thirty, a local number.

Next page. Gabriel's mobile. A mass of numbers covering two pages, front and back. Every call in or out for the last week. Shand skimmed through the calls for Friday night. There was a gap. 7:34 p.m. to 6:47 a.m. Shand swore. If only there'd been a call around the time of the murder - they could have traced where Gabriel was. But now... The man could have been anywhere - London or Athelcott - it was only a three and a half-hour drive between the two.

Next came Annabel's mobile. A page of calls. Shand skipped to the end. 8:47 p.m., an incoming call, duration seventeen minutes.

Last came the Marchant's fixed line. A half page of calls. He skimmed back, looking for calls on Friday night, and there it was. An incoming call logged at 11:59 p.m., duration three minutes and sixteen seconds.

CHAPTER FIFTEEN

There was a phone number attached to the log entry. A local number according to the area code. Shand dived towards his computer. He tapped at the keyboard, scrolling through the screens, waiting for the right one to come up. There it was. He tapped in the phone number and waited, the cursor blinking like a metronome - yes, I have an address; no, I don't.

Seconds passed. Had the machine died? Should he reboot?

Then up it came. Name and address: public phone box, The Green, Athelcott.

Shand grabbed the phone. He wanted Forensics at the phone box now. Then he was out into the corridor, searching for the first face he recognised.

"I need all these numbers traced," he said, handing over the phone logs. "Names and addresses. And then go through and make a list of anyone who appears on Annabel's log more than once. I want to know who her close friends were."

He walked farther along the corridor until he found Taylor.

"Bob," he said. "We've found a phone call to Annabel Marchant at midnight the night she was killed. It was made from the call box on the green at Athelcott. Get a log of all calls made to or from that box since Friday. Go to the phone company if necessary and sit on them. We need that log now. I'll see you at the green."

~

Shand arrived at the green three minutes before the forensic team. Three minutes in which he secured the scene and inspected the ground outside the box. Asphalt and concrete. No chance of a print.

"Well," said SOCO, smiling as he stepped out of his van.

"Look at this, boys. A phone box, and it's still intact. I was expecting to find it all dug up by now. You're slipping, Mr. Shand."

Shand forced a smile and wondered how much more of this he had to endure.

"Phone call was made from this box at midnight Friday night," he said. "To the victim's house. Six minutes later she was seen walking to the green and forty minutes after that - maybe less, maybe more - she was dead."

Shand wondered how many people had used the box since. The phone logs should help. But it wouldn't be exhaustive. Anyone could have gone inside. And not just to make a phone call.

He hovered on the periphery, watching and waiting as white-suited men brushed and dusted.

"Good news and bad," said SOCO a short time later. "We've found prints, but there's a lot of them. Many are probably too smudged to generate a good match, but we'll process as many as we can."

"What about the coins?"

"We're opening the box now."

"You've told them not to shake the coins?" asked Shand. The killer's coin has to be near the top. Maybe at the top if the phone log confirmed no one had used the phone since.

"We know our job," said SOCO.

Shand waited. He wanted the coins dusted now. The prints on the door and the hand set could have been left by anyone at anytime, but those on the coins had a closer connection to the killer. And they were so easy to overlook. A killer might remember to wear gloves in the box, but would he remember to wipe his old prints off a coin?

This one had.

Shand closed his eyes and let out a deep breath. He'd had such hopes. But the second of the three coins found resting on the top layer of the cash box had been wiped clean. It had to be the killer's. Who else would clean a coin? Which meant they probably wore gloves as well. Which meant...

Dead-end.

Another one.

He waited for Taylor to arrive, clinging to a dwindling but

optimistic hope that maybe, just maybe, there'd be a second phone call from the box around midnight. A witness, or the killer deciding to ring home to check his answerphone.

No such luck. Taylor showed him the logs. One call at 9:47 Saturday night, another at 7:12 the previous evening.

"I've brought the Marchant's phone records," said Taylor. "They've been sorted by caller."

Shand took them and glanced through. He was hoping to find a male name at the top - the lover, the killer who had lured Annabel from her home - but was disappointed. A Ms. Jacintha Maybury headed the list - for both the fixed line and Annabel's mobile.

"Ms. Maybury, it is," said Shand. "If Annabel confided in anyone, this one's got to be favourite."

~

Larkspur House was on Upper Street, overlooking the green. An old thatched property with an undulating roof and what looked, at first, to be a traditional cottage garden - stepping stones curving through a small front lawn bordered by overcrowded perennials and shrubs. But, looking closer, Shand could see a strange mix of statues and earthenware pots - some of a very unusual design and colour - peeking out from amongst the border plants.

Jacintha Maybury opened the door. She was wearing a long, flowing dress with a heavy woollen shawl draped around her shoulders. Her hair was strangely unkempt - or maybe fashionably unkempt - part of it exploded over her shoulders and part was gathered up at the top, fixed by something that looked, to Shand, like an office bulldog clip.

She showed them inside. "Though I don't know what help I can be, chief inspector. I told your man yesterday. I didn't see a thing."

Inside, the house was disorganised and cluttered, filled by an eclectic collection of what looked to Shand like ethnic craft of unknown ethnicity. It was everywhere. It adorned the walls, hung from beams and covered the furniture. He'd never seen a sofa with so many throw cushions. Or so much macramé.

Artist, thought Shand, or maybe ex-model - Jacintha Maybury didn't so much walk across a room as flow between poses.

"Dreadful news, chief inspector," she said, scooping up a longhaired white cat from an armchair. "And poor Helena as well. You think you're safe in the country, don't you? But these days..."

"Quite," said Shand, taking the cat's chair. "We'd like to ask you some questions regarding Mrs. Marchant's personal life."

"Oh," she looked surprised. "I'll help in any way I can, of course, but..."

"Did Mrs. Marchant have a lover?"

She looked startled. "Why? I don't see ... why on earth would you ask me that?"

"I'm sorry to be blunt, Ms. Maybury, but it's important."

"I don't see how. I thought you had a suspect. The asylum seeker. It was in all the papers."

"You shouldn't believe everything you read in papers, miss," said Taylor.

Shand glanced over at his sergeant, wondering for a second who the remark was aimed at.

"Did Mrs. Marchant know anyone at the camp?" he asked, determined to bury the subject as quickly as possible.

"Of course not, she had no reason."

Thank God for that, thought Shand, subject buried now move on.

"You see," he said, leaning forward in his armchair and trying a softer, more conversational approach. "We know now that someone rang Mrs. Marchant at midnight. We think they persuaded her to come out and meet them. Who do you think that person could be?"

She shrugged. "I haven't a clue, chief inspector."

"Would she leave her house in the middle of the night to meet a stranger?"

"No, of course not."

"Then who?"

She thought for a while, stroking the purring cat on her lap.

"Well, me, I think. Not that I did. And Gabriel, of course, and Pippa."

"Pippa?" asked Taylor.

"Her daughter. She's away at Uni. Was away. I think she

drove back last night. Poor girl."

"Who else?" asked Shand.

"Her parents, though I hardly think they'd drive down from Norfolk. Andrew's not been well. And this can't have helped."

"What about people on this list?" asked Shand, reaching out to hand her the list of Annabel's callers. "Take your time. Anyone there that she was particularly friendly with?"

She squinted at the list, then held it out at arm's length.

"Oh, there's Gabe, I suppose. Gabe Marsh."

"Gabe?" said Shand. "As in ... Gabriel?"

"Yes, though everyone calls him Gabe. Something you'd never try with Gabriel Marchant. He's very correct."

Shand just sat there. How many more Gabriels were there? Were they like London buses? You wait forty years, then three come along at once?

"He doesn't work in London, does he?"

"Yes. He runs a property development company."

Shand was stunned. A part of him wanted to shelve the murder investigation and ask whereabouts in London Marsh worked. Could he know Anne? Were they sleeping together?

Jacintha was still talking. "He's Gabriel's friend really. Not Annabel's. The two of them are as thick as thieves. Not that they are thieves ... Chief Inspector?"

"What?" Shand was miles away. Ninety-three to be exact. Prowling his London flat trying to remember if Anne had ever had a property developer for a client. She'd had a six-month contract with an estate agent in Mayfair a few years back. Could she have met Marsh there?

Reluctantly, he dragged himself back to Athelcott. "Sorry. Anyone else on the list?"

Jacintha peered at the list for another ten seconds. "I don't recognise all these names. I've only known Annabel for two years, since she moved to Athelcott. Though," she paused and looked at the list again. "There's an address here in Harrow. That's where Gabriel and Annabel moved from. Might be an old friend."

Shand took the list. The Harrow address belonged to a Ms. Frances Pauli. A mobile account. He ran his eye down the list again, concentrating on the male names. Gabe Marsh had rung Annabel several times, at the house and on her mobile. And she'd phoned him back.

"You say that Marsh is primarily Gabriel's friend?" asked Shand.

"That's right."

"There seem to be a lot of calls while Gabriel was away."

"Was there?" She looked genuinely surprised. Shand watched her brow furrow and then suddenly unwrinkle. "Oh, that'll be the elections! They're both standing for the parish council. So am I actually - a sort of joint ticket."

"Joint ticket?"

"To clean up Athelcott." She grimaced. "Gabe's slogan, I'm afraid. I didn't want to join, but Annabel persuaded me. The village does need a face-lift. It could be such a pretty little village, if people would only try a bit harder. Some people treat the place like a tip."

"Like Bill Acomb?" asked Taylor.

"Especially Bill Acomb. Annabel thinks..." She stopped and corrected herself. "Annabel *thought* that the parish council should take the lead in improving the village. Have more flowers about the place, hanging baskets and communal planting. And, you know, get tougher with fly tippers, and farmers who leave mud on the roads and create those awful ruts on the grass verges. It's not much to ask. And it seems so sensible."

Shand could see the logic. He could also imagine Bill Acomb's reaction - interfering townies imposing their standards where they weren't wanted.

"And, of course, limit the use of those infernal pesticides. Do you know there are days when I can't leave my house? What with the smell of chemicals in the air and my allergies, I fear for the health of the entire village. Spraying chemicals should have been banned years ago, don't you agree?"

"Quite," said Shand. "This Mr. Marsh. Could there have been a relationship between him and Annabel?"

"Chief inspector, Gabe Marsh is genetically incapable of having a relationship. He's a terrible flirt and probably has a harem stashed away in London. I've never seen him bring the same girl twice to the village."

Harem? In London? Shand's attention wandered as his inner cuckold conjured scenes of red velvet curtains, wall-to-wall beds, swarthy Gabriels, Anne ... and Shand the eunuch standing in the corner waving a palm frond.

"He's a ladies' man?" asked Taylor.

"With the emphasis on the plural, sergeant. Not that he can help it. He's a congenital flirt. And it's part of his charm, though nobody in their right mind would ever take him seriously. Certainly not Annabel."

"What about ... Gabriel?" Shand almost said Anne, but stopped himself in time. "Is Gabriel the jealous type?"

"No. He liked to show Annabel off. I think he would have been offended if Gabe hadn't tried to chat her up. But he and Gabe go back a long way. Neither would hurt the other."

"What was the Marchant's marriage like?"

She looked uncomfortable. "Happy, I'd say."

"You don't sound that confident."

"It's not something I'm comfortable discussing. I'm sure they had their problems. Who doesn't? But I know that most of the time Annabel was happy. If she hadn't been, I'd have noticed."

"Is there anyone else Annabel might have confided in?"

"Annabel was not the confiding type, chief inspector."

"What kind of woman was she?"

She thought for a while before answering. "A born organiser, I'd say. Bags of confidence and immense energy. There was a lot of good in her, chief inspector. I know that some people found her bossy and abrasive, but she really did mean well."

~

Outside, Shand read through the phone logs again. The wind was picking up and the papers flapped in his hand.

"Shouldn't we have a look at this Gabe Marsh?" asked Taylor.

"Not yet," said Shand, suddenly noticing something. "There's someone we need to see first."

CHAPTER SIXTEEN

Gabriel Marchant reluctantly led them into his sitting room. "It's the police, darling," he said to his daughter.

"My condolences, Miss Marchant," said Shand. The girl barely looked at him, mumbling an acknowledgement before looking away, her long brown hair covering most of her face.

She'd been crying. That much Shand could see. Not that anyone could miss the red eyes, even under all that fringe.

Shand turned to Gabriel Marchant. "Perhaps the sergeant and Miss Marchant could make everyone some tea?" he said pointedly.

The girl looked up. "Da-ad," she said, looking daggers at her father.

Marchant hesitated. "Yes, darling. I think that might be best."

Taylor led the girl away, attempting to put a friendly hand on her shoulder, only to have her duck underneath and practically dive into the corridor.

Shand waited for Taylor to close the door. "Mr. Marchant, your wife took a phone call at midnight on Friday night. Within minutes of receiving that call she left the house on foot, and was last seen walking towards the green. Have you any idea who that caller might have been?"

"No idea."

Shand waited, letting the silence grow and watching every line, every contour of Gabriel's face. The man showed no curiosity, no surprise, no desire to ask or speculate where the call had come from.

"I'm going to be blunt, Mr. Marchant. Your wife left the house at midnight to meet someone who didn't drive round to your front door and didn't call on his own phone. Why?"

"Because he was the murderer. Obviously."

"Who your wife must have known very well."

"So? I thought you had the killer. It was on the news. The asylum seeker."

"That lead has been superseded," said Shand. "Unless you think your wife was friendly with one of the asylum seekers?"

"God, no."

Shand still couldn't understand Marchant's attitude. Unhelpful, antagonistic, incurious. Could he be in shock? Was this his own peculiar way of handling grief? Or was it guilt? A fear of saying too much.

Time to shake things up a bit.

"How many times did you talk to your wife last week?"

"What on earth has that got to do with anything!"

"According to the phone logs you didn't talk once."

"What phone logs?"

"Whereas you phoned a Miss Delacroix eleven times. She was having dinner with you on Friday night, I believe?"

"She's a colleague. I told you. Of course we talk frequently." Then he exploded. "You've been tracing my calls?"

"It's standard practice in a murder enquiry."

He shook his head. "No, inspector. You have no right. This wasn't the house phone you traced. It was *my* mobile." He clawed the air. "Don't you *realise* what position that puts me in? Mergers have been called off because a journalist just happened to learn of a clandestine meeting between interested parties. Imagine what a journalist would do to get hold of a list of my phone calls. Who I talk to is big news."

So's your wife's murder, thought Shand.

"There are a lot of calls to your wife from Gabe Marsh. Were he and Annabel particularly friendly?"

Gabriel exploded again.

"Good God, man, this is what you do with rape victims, isn't it? Slur the victim. My wife did not have a lover. And neither did I. But that doesn't matter to you, does it? All you want to do is persecute us."

Shand watched Marchant pace the room, still unable to work out if the man was exhibiting grief, outrage, guilt or paranoia.

"I have to ask these questions, Mr. Marchant. Do you want to answer them now, or shall we wait until your daughter comes back? I'm sure she'd like to know why you're more concerned about your own privacy than her mother's murder?"

For a second Shand wasn't sure if Marchant would acquiesce or spontaneously combust.

He chose the former.

"Get this over with."

"Do you know the password to your wife's computer?"

"No."

He stood there, glaring, arms folded, barking out quickfire replies. But at least he was answering the questions.

"We'll need a list of family birthdays and names of pets et cetera."

"I'll provide one through my solicitor. Next."

"I have to ask you questions about your wife's will."

"I inherit everything. We made our wills at the same time, leaving our money to each other. And before you ask, no, my wife was not independently wealthy. Quite the reverse in fact. All our money came from me."

Gabriel Marchant smiled. For the first time since Shand's arrival he actually looked happy. Although 'pleased with himself' might have been a more apt description.

"What about life insurance policies? Was your wife's life insured."

"No. I was the only breadwinner. My life was insured, not Annabel's."

Taylor knocked on the door and poked his head round. "Okay to bring in the tea?"

Shand nodded, he'd run out of questions. For the moment. He looked over at the daughter - head down and standing silently by the door, as far away from everyone else in the room as she could - and wondered how much she knew about her parent's marriage.

Not that he could ask her, not with her father present. Maybe he'd come back later, when Marchant was out. She was eighteen, after all. He wouldn't need parental consent.

"And I wouldn't abandon that asylum seeker lead if I were you, chief inspector," said Marchant. "Go and talk to that so-called farmer next door and ask *him* about asylum seekers."

"Why?" asked Shand.

"Because it might explain one question that no one in this village has ever been able to answer."

"Which is?" said Shand.

"How a man like William Acomb stays in business on his crappy little farm doing hardly any work when every other farmer in the county is on the verge of bankruptcy?"

"And the answer is..." prompted Shand.

"Asylum seekers, chief inspector. Now I think about it I've seen them hanging around his yard late at night. I bet he even smuggles them in and out of the country. Hides them in his outbuildings and then ships them out. It might even explain all those godforsaken vans he keeps beached in his fields. God knows, something has to."

~

Shand shook his head as he left the Marchant house. Asylum seekers and chickens, was there no end to Bill Acomb's infamy?

"You don't believe any of that rubbish?" asked Taylor as they left.

"I'm not sure I believe anything Gabriel Marchant says."

"I grew up around farmers like Bill Acomb," said Taylor, seething. "And there's a very simple reason why they survive and it has nothing to do with asylum seekers."

Shand stopped by the car and glanced back towards Lower Ash Farm and its ramshackle buildings. "Okay, I'm hooked. How does Bill Acomb survive?"

"By not spending any money. Look at the place. It's a tip. When's the last time anything new passed through that yard? If something breaks, he'll fix it. If he can't fix it, he'll tie it together with baler twine. And when that eventually goes, he'll borrow from a neighbour or make do without. That's how he gets by. No loans, no debts, no holidays, and no one on the payroll except family. Okay, so he might bend the odd rule here and there, but he'll cheat the tax man out of far less than Gabriel Marchant and his high price accountants."

It was the first time Shand had seen his sergeant so animated.

"You don't see Bill Acomb as Annabel's lover then?" said

Shand, keeping his face deadpan straight.

Taylor looked stunned - for a fraction of a second - until Shand raised an eyebrow and then the sergeant burst out laughing.

"I thought you were being serious."

"A mistake many people make," said Shand, feeling strangely liberated. His first joke since ... since a time so long ago he couldn't even remember.

"Anything from the daughter while you were in the kitchen?"

"Not a word. I tried to be chatty, but she wasn't having any of it. A few nods and a lot of mumbled yesses and noes. I didn't want to press."

No, thought Shand. Pippa Marchant seemed to be the only real mourner in that family.

Shand's phone rang. It was the Met.

"Got the information you requested on Gulliver's, sir. It's an upmarket drinking club with a bit of gambling thrown in - mainly cards. No criminal associations flagged, but some of the members are a bit interesting."

"In what way?" asked Shand.

"A few old lags from the sixties and seventies. You know, the celeb crims - the ones who've written books about the old East End gangs. From what I could gather the management pay them to mix with their real clientele - City types who like the idea of mixing with gangsters."

"Have you run the member and employee lists through criminal records yet?"

"Just about to, sir. But I thought I'd call first. It's one of the members. He lives in Athelcott."

CHAPTER SEVENTEEN

Yes! Gabe Marsh. Were the two crimes connected after all? Annabel's lover *and* the owner of the book of matches Helena found in the car?

Shand couldn't wait to find out.

"Big place," said Taylor as Marsh's house came into view. A large Victorian rectory, complete with gothic towers and at least a couple of acres of mature gardens. The whole set back from the village green and hidden behind an eight-foot high grey stone wall.

Two cars were already parked on the gravel drive outside the house. A small sports car and a large Jaguar. Shand lingered by the latter and peered inside. A four-door saloon with leather seats

"Looks like it's been cleaned," said Taylor walking around the other side. "You can't drive round these country lanes this time of year without getting mud splash."

Shand leaned closer to the passenger side window and shaded the glass with his hand. The inside of the car looked clean too. No books of matches left lying on any of the seats. He stood back and glanced at the tyres. There were a few white specks wedged in the tread. Would forensics get lucky and match any to the chalk from the track?

Not that that would prove much. A public track to a local landmark less than a mile away from the man's home. Why shouldn't he drive there?

"Can I help?" said a man's voice from the front door of the house.

Shand turned, startled.

"Mr. Marsh?"

"Gabe," said the man, advancing from the top step with

his right hand outstretched.

He was shorter than Shand had imagined - and less swarthy. But he did have the dark hair, the suntan and the gleaming smile. Shand took an instant dislike to him.

"Nice car, isn't she?" said the vertically-challenged gigolo. "And fully taxed. If you're interested I could make a few phone calls. I have contacts in the trade."

"That's not why we're here, Mr. Marsh," said Shand.

"Gabe, please. I haven't been Marsh since I left school."

They shook hands - briefly - then Shand produced his warrant card. "I'm Detective Chief Inspector Shand and this is Sergeant Taylor."

"And there was I thinking you'd come to read the meter."

Out came the gleaming teeth again. A ready smile, an easy confidence, not a trace of guilt or nerves.

"Where do you get your car cleaned, Gabe?" said Taylor. "I've been meaning to get mine done for months."

"A little garage on the Sturton road. Mason's, I think it's called."

"I thought they closed weekends?"

"Not yesterday, they didn't. I can get the receipt if you want." He turned and winked at Shand. "You can check out the CCTV cameras then, can't you? Dig up the drains and see what I was trying to wash off."

"You don't seem very upset by Mrs. Marchant's death," said Shand.

"Life goes on, chief inspector. Don't get me wrong, I liked Annabel and, of course, I'm saddened by her death, but..." He shook his head. "I've never believed in all that mourning stuff. Life's too short."

Like you, midget! Shand could feel his inner nine-year old untethering and spoiling for a fight. There was something about Marsh - his attitude, his smug self-confidence, his ... Gabriel-ness - that set Shand's teeth on edge.

Marsh shivered slightly. "Suddenly turned cold out here. You coming inside, or do you want to search the car first? I'll fetch the keys, if you want. I don't mind."

Shand declined the offer. Anyone that eager to have his property searched had to be either very stupid or very confident. And Gabe Marsh didn't look stupid.

Shand and Taylor followed Marsh inside. The rectory was

spacious, high-ceilinged and sparsely furnished to the point of being Spartan. The three men's footsteps echoed on the polished wooden floors. Marsh showed them through to a huge sitting room at the back of the house. A contrast to the studied precision of Annabel's rooms, it looked to Shand as though more money had been spent on electrical equipment than on furnishings. The hi-fi in the corner was enormous and speakers circled the room like acoustic standing stones.

"Drinks?" said Marsh, standing by a corner bar that stretched a good ten feet along one wall. Shand counted fifteen different bottles of scotch. "Don't worry about being on duty. I promise I won't tell."

"Thank you, but no," said Shand before Taylor could weaken. "You're a member of Gulliver's in London, I believe?"

For the first time since their arrival Gabe Marsh's smile slipped.

"However did you know that?"

"Did you ever take anyone from Athelcott to Gulliver's?"

He sat down. "I'd have to think. Gabriel, I suppose. Once or twice. I think he was living here then."

"Anyone else? We're checking the club records. If you signed someone in we'll find out."

"Check away, chief inspector. I have nothing to hide."

Back came the confidence. Shand couldn't fathom him out. He must know he was being questioned in connection with a murder.

"What was your relationship with Annabel Marchant?"

"My relationship with Annabel," repeated Marsh, pausing to sip from his glass. "Sorry to disappoint, chief inspector, but we hardly had one. I knew her, of course. Spent some time with her, but I'd hardly call it a relationship."

"You phoned her on six occasions last week."

"Did I? That'll be about the elections. Which I assume was not the kind of relationship you were asking about."

He smiled. The kind of smug smile a pop star makes in the company of adoring fans. Look at me. I'm clever, I'm pretty, and I'm shagging your wife!

"I thought you were standing on a joint ticket?" said Shand between hastily clenched teeth. "You, Annabel and Jacintha Maybury. Did you phone Ms. Maybury six times last week?"

Gabe smiled – to himself rather than Shand – and rolled the ice around his glass. "Have you met Jacintha?" he asked.

"I have."

"Then you'll know she isn't exactly organised. If you want something done, you go to Annabel. If you want something painted, you go to Jacintha. And by the way there are – there *were* – four of us on the ticket. Gabriel's standing as well."

"You have a reputation in the village, Mr. Marsh," said Shand.

"It's Gabe, and I'm sure whatever reputation I have is well deserved. The locals shock very easily."

Shand fought the desire to lean over and surgically extract the smugness from Marsh's smile with a chair leg.

"Would it surprise you to learn that Annabel was having an affair?" he said instead.

"Surprise – no. Offend – yes. I thought I would have had at least first refusal."

"You think this a joke, Gabe?" said Taylor, leaning forward in his chair. "You want us to take that Jag of yours apart so many times no one remembers where all the parts go?"

Gabe held his hands up in mock surrender. "Sorry, officers. I apologise. But really ... you're asking the most ridiculous questions. I wouldn't hurt anyone."

Shand couldn't believe it. The man was answering questions as though he was on a TV chat show. Slumped back in his chair, drink in hand, cute answers, playing to an invisible audience of sycophants.

"Answer the question," said Shand. "Do you think Annabel Marchant had a lover?"

"No, chief inspector. I do not."

"Why not?"

"I don't know really. I just couldn't imagine it. It would get in the way of all her other pursuits."

"What pursuits?"

"Her one-woman plan to overhaul the village. I think she would have had the green carpeted by next year."

"Gabe," warned Taylor.

"Sorry, but surely the others have told you about Annabel by now. She was a machine with a vision. An organisational whirlwind. Have you seen her house? She did all that. Bullied the builders for about eighteen months until they got everything just right. Kept them coming back for months. And there's all the committees she's on. And all the committees she's trying to get on. And the elections. The woman didn't have time for anything else."

"She had time to be murdered," said Shand. "Someone lured her to the green midnight Friday night. Who do you think that was?"

"No idea," shrugged Marsh.

"Think about it," said Shand. "Make a list. Annabel receives a phone call at midnight, two minutes later she's seen walking towards the green. Who would she leave her house for? You?"

"Maybe. If I was in trouble. Or if I told her someone close to her was."

Shand closed his eyes. He hadn't considered that. He felt like kicking himself. He'd been so invested in the lover theory he'd overlooked the simple threat. *I've got your daughter, Mrs. Marchant. Do what I say and she won't get hurt*.

Taylor filled the silence. "What do you do for a living, Gabe?"

"Property Development mainly. Here and abroad. I was over in Spain last month. Got a lovely new development down there in the foothills of the Sierras, up the coast from Malaga. There's a few spare units if anyone's interested?"

"I think I'll pass," said Taylor.

"Your business is based in London, I believe," said Shand.

"Yes, it is."

Part of him wanted to ask where in London. And if he had a flat there. An address Shand could file away to check later.

Or casually drop into a conversation with Anne.

"Where were you Friday night?" asked Shand.

"Let me see. Friday night..." He leaned back and looked up at the ceiling. Shand's inner nine-year old was ready to kill him. "My social life is so full, chief inspector."

"Gabe!" said Taylor.

"I was here," said Marsh. "Definitely. I was here all night. And a *very* long night it was too."

Another wink at Shand. What was this man's game? Did he want to be arrested? Wasting police time, possession of a stupid Christian name?

"Can anyone corroborate that?"

"They certainly can, chief inspector. I have the most impeccable witness. One with, shall we say, *police* connections." He winked again at Shand. "Someone I think you know *very* well."

CHAPTER EIGHTEEN

Shand's world cracked and fell apart. He'd been dreading this moment, beating himself up over it, expecting it every time someone mentioned a Gabriel, or a Gabriel opened his mouth, but ... never truly believing it would arrive. Not Anne.

"Do you want to meet her?" said Marsh.

"She's *here?*"

Shand couldn't believe it. Had Anne lost her mind? She had to know that he was investigating a murder in Athelcott. Why come down now of all times?

Didn't she care any more? Or was this deliberate? A ploy to rub Shand's nose in it. *Hello, Peter, meet the new man in my life. A* real *man.*

Or had Marsh tricked her? Turned her head, made her complicit in his plan to discredit Shand and the case against him. My client's sleeping with the investigating officer's wife – this case is nothing but a crude vendetta!

"*Darling!*" called Marsh. "You can stop hiding and come out now."

Footsteps padded along the hall floor, taking an eternity to arrive. Shand was on the edge of his seat, his body turned towards the door.

Then he saw her.

It wasn't Anne.

The woman was in her early twenties, long blonde hair, barefoot, and dressed – just – in a man's shirt and very little else. She stood in the doorway, one hand on the doorjamb the other on her hip.

"I'm the alibi," she said. "Julia Draycott. You might know my father. He's the Chief Constable."

Shand couldn't leave quickly enough. He needed fresh air, and he needed his heart to stop racing. He was sure his face was a deathly white - every drop of blood having drained from it while he awaited the barefoot arrival of his wife from the chief suspect's bed.

"You okay?" said Taylor when they returned to the car.

"Yes, it's uh ... stomach ache. I knew I shouldn't have had those eggs for breakfast." He rubbed his stomach to reinforce the lie. "And Marsh really pisses me off. It was probably listening to him that curdled them."

Taylor agreed. Marsh was too cool and too cocky.

"But it does put him in the clear," he said. "If she's telling the truth."

Shand strapped himself into the passenger seat. "Is she really the Chief Constable's daughter?" Marsh hadn't taken the interview seriously so why should his girlfriend?

Taylor shrugged. "I've never met him or his family. You going to ask him?"

Shand grunted and settled deeper into his seat. He supposed he had to, but it wasn't a conversation he was looking forward to. Hello, sir, about your daughter. Does she have this little tattoo...

And it still didn't put Marsh in the clear. He could have hired someone else to do his dirty work. He had the right car. He was a member of Gulliver's.

But he couldn't have been the midnight caller. Not if the girl was telling the truth about arriving at nine and never leaving Marsh's side until morning.

"Where did you say this farm was?" asked Taylor as they passed the pub.

"I'm not sure," said Shand. "Take the Sturton road and look for a right turn. It can't be far outside the village."

~

It took two wrong turns and a long winding lane before they found it - the farm Shand had glimpsed earlier when he'd been walking the chalk track. Shand recognised the curve of the fields, and there was the track - a white line striking down the green hillside from the woods at the top.

The road ended at the farm, fading into a courtyard partially surrounded by old stone buildings topped with terracotta red tiles. They drove in. The house was on the left, a long two-storey building with mullioned windows and covered in climbing plants – mainly roses and honeysuckle from what Shand could see. And it looked old. Jacobean, perhaps. An old manor house or a prosperous farmstead. The outbuildings looked of a similar age. Long, low and undulating at the roof line. The more modern buildings were in a yard beyond, over to the right, he could see their grey metal roofs peeking out above the long line of red tile.

He looked back towards the road. No gate. Two brick pillars and a low wall announced where the road ended and the yard began, but there was no sign of a gate having been hung in years. Anyone could walk in. And if the chalk track fed into the other end of the yard, there was a through route to the circle.

A dog barked. Then another. Two dogs burst out from behind the house and charged towards the two policemen. Shand braced himself. He'd never felt comfortable around dogs. The dogs skidded to a halt a few feet away and stayed there, alternating between barking and growling.

"All right, boys," said Taylor, squatting on his haunches and holding his right hand out for the dogs to sniff. Neither dog took the opportunity.

An elderly man appeared on the patio in front of the house. An elderly man in tweeds and carrying a shotgun broken over one arm.

"Who is it, dear?" came a woman's voice from the doorway.

"Jehovah's witnesses by the look of 'em," said the man, peering in a disturbingly shortsighted fashion towards Shand. "Fetch me another box of shells, dear. I've only got two left."

He snapped the gun closed and advanced towards the two policemen. Shand was stunned. Was the man going to shoot? For the second time in less than fifteen minutes Shand's heart contemplated stopping. He swallowed hard and fumbled for his warrant card.

"Police!" he said, his voice far higher than he'd expected. "Detective Chief Inspector Shand and..." For a second he forgot Taylor's name. All he could see were two snarling dogs staring at him and a deranged old man waving a gun at his face.

"Sergeant Taylor," the two policeman said in unison.

The man immediately broke his gun. "Sorry," he apologised. "We've been overrun with bloody journalists all weekend."

"You'll have to forgive my husband, chief inspector," said the woman now visible in the doorway. She was drying her hands on a towel. "He likes to play the fool."

"He does it very well," said Taylor.

"Years of practice and in-breeding," said the man. "Name's Sandy Montacute. Suppose you've come about the Marchant woman?"

He called the dogs back. They immediately circled around behind him and slumped by his feet.

"And I'm Ursula Montacute, chief inspector. I believe we spoke yesterday."

"Yes," said Shand, his pulse dropping below the one forty mark. "About uh ... Helena Benson's phone call."

"Terrible business," said Ursula. "I talked to her this morning. She hardly slept last night. Couldn't put the lights out apparently. Kept bringing back memories of being trapped in the dark."

Shand could imagine. He dreaded the kind of dreams his tortured subconscious was going to conjure up tonight.

"Come on, dear," said Sandy to his wife, "I expect the chief inspector would prefer to interrogate us out of this wind. What do you say, chief inspector? A spot of tea or are you allowed something stronger these days?"

"About your shotgun, sir," said Taylor as they made their way inside. "I wouldn't point it at any more journalists, if I were you."

"Ah, out of season, are they?"

Taylor smiled. "Unfortunately."

~

Inside, the house was a larger and less cluttered version of the Benson's house. Dark rooms, low ceilings, small windows and old furniture. Shand was tempted by the offer of a medicinal brandy, but declined both that and the tea. He didn't want to have anything breakable in his hand when the Montacutes told him about their wayward younger son,

Gabriel, who was wenching his way through London's IT departments.

He took a biscuit instead and accompanied it to a comfortable armchair in the Montacute's sitting room.

"Are the dogs kept loose at night?" he asked.

"There haven't been any complaints, have there?" asked Ursula.

"No, I was thinking about Friday night. Could someone have taken the chalk track to the circle without the dogs hearing them?"

"Not through our yard," said Sandy. "Our boys would have raised the roof. Though it's easy enough to cut across the fields and join the track farther up the hill. We're not Fort Knox."

"Did either of you hear or see anything unusual on Friday night?"

"Not a thing, chief inspector," said Ursula. "I checked the horses at seven-thirty. Everything perfectly normal. Then we watched the film, I took the telephone call from Helena, and shortly afterwards we went to bed. Slept like the proverbial logs, then up at dawn to see to the horses. Sorry, we can't be of more help."

"Does anyone else live in the house?" Shand scanned the room, gauging its size. The house must have at least five bedrooms.

"No, Sandy and I rattle around here by ourselves. Our children fled the nest years ago."

"No farmhands living in?"

Ursula laughed. "This isn't the Ponderosa, chief inspector. We don't have ranch hands sleeping in the barn."

"All the farm workers live in the village," said Sandy. "No one was here after evening milking. Ursula was the last to lock up."

"Do people use the chalk track at night?" asked Shand.

"Lisa might," said Ursula. "It's a short cut home for her."

"Lisa Budd?" asked Shand. "The girl who found the body?"

"Did she? Poor girl. Yes, she helps with the horses now and then."

"Was she helping Friday night?"

"I believe so. She left early if I remember. Long before

seven."

"Does she walk her dog along the track?"

"I wouldn't know."

It was slight, but Shand was sure he'd seen it. A change in Ursula's demeanour. As soon as he started asking about Lisa and Friday night her eyes lost that twinkling confidence and her answers became more clipped.

"I expect you want to ask us about the Marchant woman, sergeant?" said Sandy. "God knows we had the motive."

"You didn't like Mrs. Marchant?" asked Taylor.

"One doesn't like to speak ill of the dead, sergeant," said Ursula.

"But if one did?"

"Then one would say she was petty, vindictive, and should never have moved to the country. Did you know she sued her neighbour over a cockerel?"

"We did hear that," said Taylor.

"Then you know what kind of a woman she was. It simply beggars belief, where did the woman think she was moving to? This is a farming community, not suburbia."

Shand sat back and observed. Ursula was holding court again, the easy confidence flowing and her eyes twinkling.

"I hear she was standing for the parish council?" said Taylor.

"Ah, my motive, sergeant. Yes, she and I were political rivals. Fighting over the parish council. But rest assured, if I had planned to kill Annabel I wouldn't have left her body at the circle. No, sergeant, I would have left her head on a spike outside the village pub. *Pour encourager les autres.*"

"Pardon," said Taylor.

"It's French, dear," said Ursula. "To encourage the others. A sign to all the other incomers that trespass shall not be taken lightly."

Shand leaned forward to try and drag the interview back on track. "Was it turning into a bad-tempered election?"

"The potential was there," said Ursula. "I've certainly never experienced anything like it."

"It was all the Marchant woman's doing," said Sandy. "She was determined to win and didn't care how she achieved it. Gutter politics. In a parish council election, I ask you!"

"It was very disturbing, chief inspector," said Ursula. "Candidates rarely campaign – most years there's not even a vote – and if they do campaign, they do so by extolling their own virtues, not attacking the other candidates."

"Who did Annabel attack?"

"Who didn't she attack?" said Sandy. "The woman laid into the entire village. Everything we did was wrong. The way we farmed, the way we drove, the way we kept our gardens. Our entire way of life was anathema to that woman."

"It created a good deal of bad feeling," said Ursula. "And it affected the other parish councillors. Helena especially. She could never abide any form of unpleasantness. She became quite ill. I think she would have stood down if I hadn't persuaded her to stay. George certainly didn't help."

"In what way didn't George help?" asked Shand.

"He wanted Helena to stand down," said Ursula, "said it wasn't worth it."

"Nice enough man, but no stomach for a fight," said Sandy.

"And that's what the election had become? A fight?"

"That's where it was heading," said Sandy. "It was the only way the Marchant woman could win. She knew she didn't have the votes, so she set out to badger the older candidates into standing down."

Shand found it hard to believe. Was Annabel so driven that she'd do anything to win a tiny village election? Was she that competitive?

"Wouldn't other villagers have put their names forward to thwart Annabel?" asked Shand. He couldn't imagine Bill Acomb passing up the opportunity to get back at the Marchants.

"Some might have," said Sandy. "I didn't say it was a good plan. Just the only one she had. Demographics, chief inspector. There are more of us than there are of them. In a fair election, she'd lose."

"Not that one didn't suspect a more sinister motive behind the Gang of Four's candidature," said Ursula.

"The Gang of Four?" asked Taylor.

"The Marchants, Marsh and Jacintha," said Ursula. "Though perhaps Gang of Two would be a more appropriate appellation. Annabel needed four votes to control the council so she drafted Jacintha and Gabriel in to make up the numbers. They were to be her proxies."

"But not Marsh?" asked Shand.

"No," said Ursula. "I wouldn't be at all surprised to learn that Gabe Marsh put the idea into Annabel's head, so that she could do all the hard work while he sat back and waited."

"For what?" asked Shand.

"The man's a property developer," said Sandy with contempt. "What's he doing standing for election to a body that determines planning permission?"

"Does the parish council grant planning permission?" asked Shand. "I thought they made recommendations but the local authority had the final say."

"The local authority can be overruled, chief inspector," said Ursula. "This government likes property developers. It encourages them to appeal decisions that go against them, and if Marsh could say the parish supported him..."

Shand still couldn't see how any of the Gang of Four could hope to be elected by alienating the majority of their electorate. It didn't make sense.

Neither did it stand out as a compelling motive for murder. Annabel seemed capable of annoying her neighbours any time of the year. She didn't have to wait for an election campaign.

"Who do you think killed Annabel?" he asked.

"No one in the village, chief inspector. I'm certain of that."

"Why? The use of the stone circle suggests a degree of local knowledge."

"Ramblers," said Sandy looking as though he'd just bitten into a slice of lemon. "They memorise every right of way and place of archaeological interest. That's where I'd suggest you look."

"Ramblers?" repeated Shand.

"We've had terrible trouble with them, chief inspector," said Ursula. "Some of them become quite abusive."

"And don't forget the crop circles," said her husband. "If you're looking for people who use the track at night, they're the ones you should be talking to. Yobs from Sturton with nothing better to do than trample a man's crops. They do it every year."

"Bit late in the year for that," said Taylor. "Haven't you cut most of your fields?"

"True, sergeant, but these people know the area. Who's to say what they'd do next."

Shand listened. He could understand the unwillingness to believe that the murderer was a neighbour. But ramblers and yobs?

"We seriously considered having the track blocked," said Ursula. "But it's handy for the horses. It gives us access to the bridle paths on the other side of the circle."

"Ramblers!" said Sandy, once more biting into his virtual lemon.

"You'll have to forgive my husband, chief inspector. He hates ramblers."

"Oh, I wouldn't say that, dear. It depends how you cook 'em." He smiled and winked at Shand. "You should stop by for dinner one night. I have a brace of 'em hanging in the tack room."

He laughed. Ursula trilled. And Shand decided it was time to leave. He wasn't going to learn much more from the Montacutes.

CHAPTER NINETEEN

"Do you think we should check the tack room?" joked Taylor as they left the Montacutes.

"Drive," said Shand, pointing at Taylor's car. He felt dispirited. He could feel the momentum of the early morning falling away. The phone logs, the matchbook, Gulliver's. All that early promise. Now he was up against alibis and trying to uncover a motive for a pair of crimes that made no sense.

Which reminded him. The Chief Constable's daughter.

He rang his chief superintendent and, omitting the tattoo, described the girl.

"What do you think, sir? Is it her?"

Chief Superintendent Wiggins exhaled deeply.

"Sounds like Julia. Don't worry, Shand. I'll deal with this. If she's involved in any way, I'll find out. You keep her name out of the files. No need giving the press something to chew on. Oh, and talking about the press, I've pencilled in a press conference for four this afternoon."

Shand swallowed hard. "Is that..." He was about to say 'necessary,' but changed it quickly to 'in Sturton again?' Adding a bright and optimistic note to his voice as though he was really looking forward to it.

The rest of the conversation washed over him. He was wondering what hell awaited him at four o'clock.

"Which way?" asked Taylor as they reached the junction at the top of the lane.

"To the village," said Shand. "We need to have a word with Lisa Budd."

~

There was something about Lisa and the chalk track that had rattled Ursula Montacute. Shand mulled over the possibilities. Time was an obvious one. Maybe Lisa hadn't left at seven? Maybe she forgot something and came back?

He liked that. And he liked the timing. Ursula would be watching the film until 10:30 p.m. The phone rings, she gets up to answer. Then a short time after she looks out the window, or maybe the dogs bark and she sees Lisa in the yard. Lisa then goes home, back along the track, arriving at the stone circle sometime around eleven. Just in time to see Helena being dragged from the car.

Supposition. Every word.

But the girl did find the body. And she did use the track. The only person they'd found so far who was a regular user.

And there was the dog. Lisa had been walking her dog that morning when she found the body. Did she walk the dog in the evening as well?

He liked that even better. What would be more natural than taking your dog for a walk before bedtime? It was a full moon. No problem about lack of street lights. He could see her setting off for the woods, a brisk walk on a crisp night. Then she turns back, nears the stone circle, hears a noise and stops where the track leaves the wood. She crouches down, holds onto the muzzle of her dog and watches.

Then...

Then he hit the problem. Motive. Motive and the phone call. Would Annabel leave her house in the middle of the night for Lisa? Unlikely. And he couldn't see her luring or threatening Annabel either.

Or could he?

Mrs. Marchant, it's Lisa, Pippa's with me. She's hurt. I don't know what to do.

Would that be enough to rattle a mother? Daughter in danger, tearful girl on the phone, no time to think?

He bounced his theory off Bob Taylor.

"No," said Taylor after long consideration. "The witness says she was walking to the green. If she'd been worried about her daughter, she'd have been running."

~

The Budd household was in the midst of food preparation. Sunday dinner less than an hour away, and the kitchen full of steam and the smell of roasting meat. No one was happy to see the police.

"Can't this wait?" said her mother.

"No," said Shand. "I promise it won't take long."

The two policemen were shown into a small dining room, the table already laid for three. Shand and Taylor sat at the table. Lisa sat on the other side, arms folded and mouth set.

"I told your lot everything yesterday," she said. "You included," she added, nodding at Shand.

"I know," said Shand, "and we thank you for your co-operation. But I have some different questions. What time did you leave the Montacute's on Friday?"

The girl looked as though she'd been slapped. "What's that got to do with anything?"

"Ten-thirty, wasn't it?" said Shand casually.

"No! Much earlier. About seven. Why?"

Shand looked puzzled. Or, at least, he hoped he did. "That's odd. Are you sure it wasn't nearer eleven? We have a witness who saw you on the chalk track."

"You can't have I..." She stopped and then her anger turned into a sneer. "You ain't got no one, have you? You lot are all the same. You think we're thick."

Shand tried to retrieve the situation. "The witness says you were walking a dog. Did you walk your dog last night?"

He ended his question with a smile. The girl glared back.

"No," she said.

"Who did exercise the dog?"

"No one. I walk Joe in the morning."

More glares.

"Doesn't it have to relieve itself before going to bed?"

"*He* does that all by himself. The back garden's dog proof."

Shand glanced around the room. This was not going at all well. He tried a different tack.

"Pippa Marchant would be about your age, wouldn't she?" he said

"What about it?"

"Were you friends? Did you talk much?"

"No."

"Was there a problem between the two of you?"

"Am I gonna need a solicitor?"

Shand parted his teeth in a fixed but, by then, desperate smile, and tagged Taylor with a pleading look. Help!

"You like working at the stables, Lisa," said Taylor.

"It's all right."

"You haven't seen any dead ramblers hanging in the tack room?"

Lisa smiled. "He told you that one, did he? He's mad. One of these days he's really gonna shoot someone." Her smile faded as soon as she realised what she'd said. "Not that he would."

"Of course not," said Taylor warmly. "We know that. The person we're looking for doesn't use a shotgun. He – if it is a he – uses trickery. Do you know he rang Mrs. Marchant from the phone box on the green and tricked her into meeting him? In the middle of the night, can you believe that? Now, you know all the people in the village. Who do you think would be capable of something like that?"

Shand waited. Lisa was actually thinking. She even unfolded her arms.

"None of the locals," she said. "Annabel would slam the phone down if any of us called."

"So you think it'd be one of the incomers?" said Taylor.

"Have to be," she said. "Gabe Marsh is the creepiest. He's tried it on with me a few times. Wanted me to go to Newbury with him to help choose a stallion."

She raised both eyebrows. "Fat lot of horse flesh I'd've seen that weekend."

Taylor agreed. "So you reckon he's used to telling stories?"

"Definitely."

~

Shand thanked Taylor for bailing him out. And then sank into a pit of self-examination. Why did he need bailing out? Had he spent so much time analysing data that he'd forgotten how to relate to people?

Taylor suggested a pint and a meal at the pub. Maybe there'd be a carvery? Shand agreed, the smell of Sunday roast wafting in from Mrs. Budd's kitchen had given him an appetite.

But first he wanted to check in with Forensics. They had to have made some progress on yesterday's crime scenes.

They had. They'd found two good prints on the book of

matches Helena had found.

"We checked them against all the indexes," said SOCO. "Nothing. Including prints we took from the phone box this morning and the Benson's house yesterday. We're still processing the prints we took from the Marchants."

They had a wealth of other information. Crime scene analysis, clothes analysis, fibres. Too much to cover in detail over the phone. Shand said he'd come straight over, as soon as he'd had something to eat.

"And you know we didn't find any personal items on the victim," said SOCO. "No keys, no purse, no handbag. Not even a tissue. All her pockets were empty."

Probably kept everything in a handbag, thought Shand. Keys certainly. She'd stopped to lock up so she'd have needed keys to get back in. But she hadn't taken her purse. Gabriel Marchant had found that in the kitchen, complete with credit cards. Wherever she was going, she hadn't expected to need any money.

"Have you got a description of the handbag from the husband yet?" came the voice down the line.

Shand kicked himself. He hadn't. But then he wondered how many handbags Annabel had, and would Gabriel be able to tell which one was missing? Or even describe them? He thought of Anne's collection. Did she have three or four? And how would he describe them? *Well, one's kind of medium sized and black with a handle*. Was Gabriel Marchant any more attentive?

Anne. Her presence hung over the remainder of the phone call and pursued him to the pub. She still hadn't rung. He thought she might have last night. Someone must have told her about the press conference. It was on all the news. And the papers this morning.

But she hadn't. And he hadn't rung her. Part of him wanting to make a point – it's your turn to call. Part of him wanting to find out how long she could go before ringing. Days, weeks? Would she wait until the day she was supposed to drive down? Or would she just not turn up? Sorry, I couldn't get away. Are you sure it was this weekend? Must dash, there's a meeting I should have been in five minutes ago.

Conversations played inside his head. Replayed and rewritten, but always a tragedy.

CHAPTER TWENTY

There wasn't a carvery at the Royal Oak, just sandwiches or a basket meal – chicken or scampi.

Shand chose the chicken while Taylor had the scampi. Both had pints. Taylor out of habit, and Shand because he needed it. He collected the pints from the bar and gazed through into the packed lounge. Journalists and sightseers. The atmosphere heavy with raucous laughter and cigarette smoke. Everyone having a great time.

He thought about Annabel. Only one person seemed genuinely upset about her death. He wondered briefly if that was a consequence of her character or a condemnation of society. And then he decided to think about something else before he started contemplating his own demise and how many Gabriels would turn up for the funeral.

They ate fast and said little. Even the public bar was beginning to fill and people were noticeably straining to overhear any snatch of conversation from the policemen's table. Weather-beaten old men stared, and pointed, and nudged their neighbours. Others, reporters maybe, stood in a group, their coats almost brushing against Shand's table. Coats with deep pockets that probably hid running tape recorders.

Shand drained his glass and rose to leave. Out came the questions. *Any progress on the case, chief inspector? Anyone in custody? Have you interviewed any more asylum seekers?*

He pushed through the crowd. "Excuse me," he said and, "no comment." People reluctantly parted to let him through, though some seemed determined to stand in his way and bark questions at him.

He pushed, and side-stepped, and squeezed, determined to keep polite and non-committal. At least they'd let him finish his meal. Or had that been tactical – the hope of overhearing an unguarded statement?

The throng pursued him outside, their numbers growing as others spilled out from the lounge next door. It was becoming ridiculous. Shand turned and raised both hands.

"Please," he shouted. "I have a statement to make."

Instant quiet, except for the few latecomers who were still emerging from the pub doors. A collective call of 'shush' quietened them down.

"There has been a significant discovery in the case."

Shand anticipated the embryonic rush of questions and raised his hands again. "Please," he said. "I will be giving full details at the four o'clock press conference. Unless you keep me here talking, in which case it'll become a five o'clock press conference. So, enjoy your lunch, and I'll see you all at four."

He tried a smile, hoping he'd both made his point and exuded an air of approachable confidence.

It seemed to work. The crowd started to flow back inside. Shand turned away before they changed their minds, only looking back when he reached Taylor's car.

One journalist had remained outside. Kevin Tresco. He stood by the lounge door, staring directly at Shand. It was probably imagination, but Shand was sure the reporter's lips were curled in a sneer.

The car door lock clicked and Shand climbed inside.

"Er, this significant discovery, sir," said Taylor apprehensively. "What is it?"

Shand looked at him. "The midnight phone call."

"Ah, of course," said Taylor, smiling. He looked relieved.

Shand clicked his seat belt home. And wondered what Taylor was really thinking. Had he thought Shand had invented another lead? Was he wondering what kind of a man had been sent down from London?

Because just for a second, Shand hadn't been sure what he was going to tell them either. He'd wanted the press out of the way, and a part of him didn't care how he did it.

~

Taylor drove around the green and dropped Shand off at his car.

"Remember what I said," said Shand as he unbuckled his seat belt. "If Gabriel's no help, try Pippa or Jacintha Maybury. One of them's got to know what the missing handbag looks like. See if you can get some kind of a composite description ready for the press at four."

"Will do, sir. And I'll phone through the make and model of Annabel's mobile so the Press Office can release a picture."

"Good idea. And find out how Marcus is getting on in Sherminster. I want to see both of you the moment he returns."

~

The Forensics Department was in Langton Stacey. A new building on the outskirts of the town. Shand was collected from reception and shown to the first floor. As soon as he pushed through the swing doors at the top of the stairs, applause broke out.

Shand froze. Five white-coated police scientists stood in a grinning arc by the door of their large open plan office. There was a joke coming. Shand knew it. They knew it. All he could do was force a smile and wait.

"Chief Inspector," said SOCO. "Pardon the spontaneous outburst of admiration, but it's not every day our little office is graced by a presence such as yours."

Shand hung onto his grin and wondered what rank the Scene of Crimes Officer held. And what reciprocal hell he could dream up, for a reciprocal hell there would be. This ordeal was not going to go unavenged.

"I give you Mr. Shand," continued SOCO, "the new holder of the fastest fingertip search of a crime scene ever recorded. One cubic metre of soil sifted in ten seconds. You Met boys. Always showing us poor rustics how it's done."

"Very amusing," said Shand.

"We try to please," said SOCO. "Now, fun over, where do you want to start?"

SOCO spent the next ten minutes taking Shand through the minutia of evidence gathered and progress made. No prints had been found on the cardboard box, siphon or duct tape used at Helena's burial, but SOCO was confident they'd be able to trace the supermarket the box came from.

None of the hair or fibre samples gathered from the two victims looked likely to lead anywhere. The hairs on Annabel's clothes belonged to her and those on Helena's were grey and most likely belonged to her and George. The fibres could all be matched to sources at their homes and the policeman's coat that had covered Helena's shoulders.

"Though there is one thing we didn't find that might need explaining," said SOCO.

"What?" asked Shand.

"Annabel's hands and fingers. They're too clean. Think about. You're hit hard on the back of the head, you're going to pitch forward. Don't you throw your hands out to break your fall?"

"Depends if I'm still conscious," said Shand. "Or I might have my hands in my pockets."

"Possibly. It's just that I can't see any obvious impact marks on the clothes. I'd have expected to have seen staining around the knees, face or elbows when she fell. If her hands didn't break her fall, I can't see what did."

"Is that a problem?"

"Not really. But it's something to take into account. Maybe someone else was there to catch her. Anyway, the problem's yours now."

"As for the murder site," he continued. "You know all about that. The site was too disturbed for any meaningful analysis of footprints or tyre tracks."

Which brought them to the Benson's house. SOCO produced a file and handed it to Shand. They'd lifted eight different sets of fingerprints. Two belonged to George and Helena. None of the others had been identified.

"No hits at all from Criminal Records."

Shand kept reading. No threatening letters had been found or anything that could be construed as coded or odd. No roll of duct tape, no evidence of wine making, and no scissors that matched the pattern found on the cut tape.

"And we found a garden spade hanging on a hook in one of the outbuildings. No trace of blood or soil from the circle. Looks like our abductors came prepared with their own scissors, shovel, tape and tube."

“Can I keep this?” asked Shand, holding up the report.

“It’s your copy,” said SOCO. “The report from the Marchant house will take longer. We’re still running fingerprints. Not to mention the analysis of Annabel’s computer.”

”You’ve cracked the password?”

“It wasn’t difficult. She used her daughter’s Christian name. Prolific writer was our Annabel. And very efficient, she kept copies of all her correspondence going back three years.”

“Anything interesting? asked Shand. “Any emails?”

“Still ploughing through. Nothing noteworthy yet.”

“Yes!” A cry came from the other end of the room.

“What is it?” shouted SOCO.

“A match, sir. On the prints.”

Shand was already running. This was more than he’d hoped. A match! All they needed was a name and he was sure the case would crack open.

“Whose is it?” he shouted.

“It’s the prints on the book of matches, sir. They match one of the prints we took from the Marchant house.”

CHAPTER TWENTY-ONE

That was not what Shand had been expecting. Or hoping for. He'd wanted a name. A name with a record and a list of known associates.

But this? This complicated matters further. It linked two crimes that he'd almost convinced himself were unconnected. Why would anyone arrange a dead body on top of woman they'd buried alive? It didn't make sense.

And yet it had to. Fingerprint evidence had just linked the abductors' car with the Marchant's house. How else could that be explained?

And who owned the fingerprint?

He called Taylor.

"Get Gabriel Marchant's fingerprints. We've found a match between the print on the book of matches and prints lifted from his house."

Of course it didn't have to be Marchant. It could have been any of their friends. Marsh for one, he had the car that matched Helena's description, and he was a member of the London club.

"And get Marsh's too," he added.

~

Shand drove back to Sturton, his mind alternating between the case and what he was going to say at the press conference. Was there time to match Gabriel's fingerprints and file an arrest warrant? Could he announce Gabriel's arrest in front of Kevin bloody Tresco and the rest of world's media?

His car almost careered off the road. He was driving too fast. He always did when excited. He slowed down. Took deep breaths. But then, before he realised, he was away again, racing through case and country roads together.

Taylor's call came through just as he was entering Sturton.

"He's refused, sir," said Taylor. "Says we have no right, and his solicitor's on his way round."

"What about Marsh?"

"Can't find him. His car's gone and he's not answering his phone."

Shand almost hit the car in front. He hadn't noticed the lights change. Then he hit the steering wheel with both fists. Frustration! Why was nothing in this case straightforward?

Down came the rain. A heavy shower that burst out of a blackening sky. Shand crawled the remaining mile through a veil of brake light tinged rain and stop start traffic.

To make matters worse the station car park was full and he'd left his raincoat at the hotel. Shand hunched over the wheel and peered out at the mass of television company vans. Or what he assumed to be television company vans – he could barely see out – even with the windscreen wipers at full speed. And the car roof sounded like it was being beaten to death, and lightning had just tinged the sky electric pink.

He edged the car forward. He was *not* going to turn up at a press conference looking like a drowned rat. He drove as close to the station doors as he could and then ran for the entrance, hoping that Kevin Tresco was the owner of at least one of the cars he'd just blocked in.

He was still dripping by the time he reached his office. He shook his jacket and hung it on a hook behind the door. There was a file on his desk. The Post Mortem. He picked it up and flicked through the pages. Most of it was a confirmation of what he'd been told yesterday, but there were a few additions. She hadn't been drugged, poisoned or pregnant, and her health had been excellent. According to her stomach contents, her last meal had been about three hours before her death – most likely a pesto pasta with a single glass of red wine and probably two cups of coffee.

Nothing new that he could use. He tossed the report onto his in-tray and leaned back against his chair. He had a press conference in twenty minutes. Should he use it to put pressure on Marchant? Tell the media about the fingerprints and his lack of co-operation? It would be unprofessional, but if it got results...

But would it get results? Marchant's behaviour had verged on the paranoid from the beginning. Any extra pressure and he might stop co-operating completely.

And worse ... what if his fingerprints didn't match? Shand could see Kevin Tresco revelling in that. *Rogue cop hounds grieving husband*. And it wouldn't only be the press that would turn against him. He'd have jeopardised the case. Opened up the police to claims of defamation and prejudicing an enquiry. It wasn't worth the risk.

"Ah, there you are, Shand," said Chief Superintendent Wiggins. He stood in the doorway looking almost furtive. "About that matter this morning, I've..." He stopped, glancing up and down the corridor before stepping inside, and closing the door behind him.

He looked embarrassed. "I've spoken to the Chief Constable about his daughter and ... well, Julia's always been a bit of a handful, but she wouldn't lie over anything as serious as this. He's had a word with her, and she's adamant that Marsh was with her between 10:30 and 1:45. Those *are* the hours you're interested in, aren't they?"

"Yes, sir," said Shand. "Did she say what time she went to sleep?"

"Not exactly," said Wiggins, looking even more uncomfortable. "But according to the Chief she made it very clear that sleep did not feature very highly on the er ... night's activities."

"Ah," said Shand.

"Ah, indeed," said Wiggins. "Anyway, must dash. I've got to get back to Sherminster. This corruption enquiry's getting worse every day. Good luck with the press conference."

~

Luck was not on Shand's agenda for the press conference. He'd tell them what he wanted them to know, ask them for the help he wanted to receive, thank them, and get out. No questions, no heckling, and *no* cock-ups. First, he'd bury the asylum seeker story, then he'd hit them with the phone call lead. Something solid yet mysterious. A headline grabber. *Midnight caller lures wealthy woman to her death.* He liked the sound of that. Midnight Caller – menacing yet apposite.

And he would not be late. The lift doors opened and he strode out. Two minutes to go. A fact reiterated by Jimmy Scott, the press officer, who pounced the moment he saw Shand.

"Cutting it fine again, chief inspector," he said, his lips pursed together in what Shand took to be a sign of irritation.

"Sorry," said Shand, pushing through the swing doors into the long corridor.

"Hmm," said Jimmy, looking him up and down. "At least you're not wet. I've assembled and distributed the press packs. Pretty pictures of the mobile phone, and a sketch of the handbag."

"Good," said Shand, realising he'd forgotten to ask Taylor how the handbag enquiry had gone.

"Meanwhile," said Jimmy. "They're all champing at the bit wondering what your big announcement is going to be. As are we all, I might add. I don't want to complain, but it would help if you kept the Press Office informed. I know you're busy, but we're fielding questions all day. No one can do their job blind."

Shand apologised again. Jimmy was right. He'd been so focussed on conducting the investigation that he'd ignored the administrative side of his duties. He'd barely spoken to the Chief Super. He'd barely spoken to anyone besides Taylor and witnesses.

But what else could he do? He was running a major enquiry with a skeleton staff. The first two days were the most vital of any enquiry. He couldn't afford not to take an active role in the investigation.

"Oh, and who's this Moleman they've dragged up?" asked Jimmy.

Shand was surprised. "They've talked to you about the Moleman?"

"Yes, in between the Transylvanian asylum seekers and the serial killing druids."

Shand smiled. "Local kids," he said, "playing jokes on incomers and calling themselves the Moleman."

"Really? I think the Fleet Street boys have him down as a green-fingered Freddie Kruger."

"Not quite," said Shand, pulling the conference door open and standing back to allow Jimmy through.

Jimmy paused in the doorway and spoke almost in a whisper. "Watch out for Kevin Tresco," he warned. "He's *really* got it in for you. I think he sees you as the worst embodiment of the Antichrist - a copper *and* a Londoner."

~

The Antichrist took his place on the podium and made a point of smiling at Kevin Tresco. If the reporter wanted a fight, Shand was ready. He was not going to be intimidated by a self-important local hack.

The self-important local hack smiled back, and winked. Shand's inner nine year-old wanted to wink back, and raise him a smirk.

Shand swiftly poured a glass of water from the decanter and took a large swig. This was ridiculous. He was in the middle of a murder enquiry and, suddenly, all he could think of was getting the better of a lank-haired reporter who no one had ever heard of.

He glanced around the packed hall, wondering how many of the assembled media were called Gabriel. The way this case was going there had to be at least three. Gabriel O'Gabriel, Gabriel McGabriel, and probably a FitzGabriel or two thrown in for good measure. All reporting on the serial-killing druid asylum seeker murder for the Gabriels back home. *No Gabriels killed yet, but it's only a matter of time*.

Shand suppressed a smile. Perhaps he should start the conference with a request for a show of hands? How many Gabriels in the audience? Come on, don't be shy. There's enough wives to go round.

He took another drink, desperately trying to ignore the self-destruct gene that he could feel pulsing inside him.

But Shand's inner nine year-old could be very persuasive. *Why give a dry, factual press conference when you have the ability to put on a show. You can do this. You know you can. You're funny, quick-witted. Or, at least, you used to be. When you were at school, and didn't care what people thought. Now, here's your chance to shine in front of the world's media. Show Anne and all those senior ranks that you're the man. Don't rush through the facts and run off the stage like a frightened animal. Milk the situation, orate, be witty.*

And grind Kevin bloody Tresco into the ground. I double dare you!

Why not, thought Shand. He'd felt like a caged bear all day.

"We now know," he said, relaxing and projecting his voice to the back of the room, "that at midnight, a call was made to the murdered woman's house from the phone box on the village green. We need to know the identity of this ... midnight caller."

He emphasised the last two words and paused, waiting for the journalists to scribble down the epithet he'd become so proud of. *The Midnight Caller*. He could see it gracing tomorrow's headlines.

"So," he paused again. "We need to know who he," another pause, "or she-"

Or it, suggested Shand's inner schoolboy.

Shand suppressed a giggle. "Is," he finished. "Whoever they were, the murdered woman felt impelled to leave her house immediately and walk to the village green." He paused and addressed the press on the left-hand side of the room. "She didn't run." He turned to the right-hand side. "She didn't take her car..."

Or her ferret.

Shand had to look down. He could feel a monster giggle welling up inside him. Ferret. That one word, that one incongruous image – Annabel Marchant and her inseparable, furry companion – struck his funny bone an irrecoverable blow. It wasn't particularly funny. Another day, another hour it would have left him cold. But at that one, off-the-wall moment in Shand's life, it was funniest thing he'd ever heard.

He teetered on the edge of losing it.

I bet the ferret was called Gabriel.

He lost it.

"Eah!" It came out as a strangled shriek. Half suppressed giggle, half squeak. He raised a fist to his mouth and tried to pass it off as a cough. What was the matter with him? There wasn't anything to laugh at!

He forced himself to continue. He couldn't laugh. Not at

this. Not here.

He swallowed hard and tried to pull himself together.

"We call on anyone," he said, still looking down, trying to summon as much gravitas as he could muster, lowering his voice half an octave in the process. "Anyone who ... was in Athelcott Friday night."

His voice was cracking along with his face. He could feel the corners of his mouth reaching for his ears, his shoulders starting to shake. He had to laugh. He needed to laugh. The urge was irrepressible. Dissolve, thump the table, slump on top of it, roll on the floor. Let go!

But he couldn't.

He pinched himself – hard – using the table for cover, digging the nails of his left index finger and thumb into his inner right thigh, and squeezing as though his career depended upon it. Which it probably did. Pain shot through him. His eyes began to water. And the urge to giggle stopped.

For two whole seconds.

But he managed to get another sentence out. Holding Annabel's picture up, he looked straight at the cameras. "Did anyone see this woman? Eah!"

He had to look down again. He had to cover his squeak with a fist and a cough. And he had to keep pinching his leg. If he could just get to the end of his statement he could feign a pressing appointment and rush for the exit.

He soldiered on, unable to string more than a handful of words together before having to pause. Not trusting his voice, not trusting himself.

"We're still looking for ... the dead woman's ... handbag and phone."

A tear ran down his cheek. The pain from his thigh was excruciating, but he still needed to laugh. He'd explode if he didn't. His eyes felt like they were bulging out on stalks. He was having to contort his face to prevent the world's biggest grin from escaping. And a giggling fit that would last minutes, that would end his career.

"They may have been ... dumped on the roadside ... as the killers escaped. Please look."

Another deep breath, another squeak, another gouge at his leg. And then he was lifting up the pictures of Annabel's handbag and mobile phone. "Phone," he said, another tear. "Handbag ... That's all ... Pressing appointment." It was all he could manage. And then he was pushing his chair back, and hurrying off the stage.

He hit the wings and started to run - down the steps, through the door, into the corridor, and up the stairwell past the foyer - only stopping when he found the cloakroom, and threw himself into the first cubicle he found. Whereupon he collapsed, giggling uncontrollably, his laughter interspersed with high-pitched snorts.

CHAPTER TWENTY-TWO

Shand was red-eyed but firmly under control by the time he returned to his office and found Jimmy Scott waiting outside. He took a deep breath and wondered how much trouble he was in.

Jimmy turned and regarded Shand in what looked like wide-eyed shock. "I didn't realise you were so emotionally involved in the case," he said almost breathlessly. "I've seen emotional appeals from parents and spouses before but ... never from the detective in charge."

Shand blinked. Had people mistaken his tears and facial contortions for grief?

A plan articulated itself before he'd had time to think. "It's a little trick I developed at the Met," he lied. "Emotional appeals are three times more likely to achieve results than a straight forward request for information. Gabriel Marchant wouldn't do it so..."

"You faked that?" said Jimmy, his eyes widening farther.

Shand rubbed his leg. "The trick is to think of something sad and pinch the hell out of your leg. Works every time."

"I'm astonished," said Jimmy. "I'm ... speechless." And then he dived forward and grabbed Shand's hand. "Let me shake your hand, Mr. Shand. It's a pleasure working with a professional."

~

The professional dived inside his office and closed the door. What was the matter with him? Every time he opened his mouth a new lie popped out. And as for the press conference - what had he been thinking!

He slumped into a chair and dropped his head into his

hands. What had possessed him? People had been making jokes all day - mostly at his expense - and he'd taken it all in silence. But as soon as the situation was inappropriate, suddenly he's a music hall comedian! Did he want to fail? Was this what it was all about? Some self-destruct button that he couldn't leave alone? Some ridiculous plan to make Anne feel sorry for him?

Or was he in crisis? A mid-life 'what's it all about?' job-changing, life-analysing, full-blown Tourettes, male menopause crisis?

Or was he just tired and under stress? He'd barely slept for days, his marriage was God knows where, the case was baffling, he was beset by Gabriels, and he was in a new job in a new town.

And then there was Kevin Tresco. There was something about him. All that sneering and criticism. It was so personal. Something he'd never had to deal with. He was the safe pair of hands. A man who cruised through his career accepting plaudits. Never an object of ridicule or criticism.

One thing was certain. He would never face another press conference. He'd hand over to Jimmy Scott and bury himself in the investigation. No press, no interviews, and no more run-ins with Kevin bloody Tresco.

~

A knock on the door heralded Marcus Ashenden's return from Sherminster.

"I thought I'd bring him straight up," said Taylor, ushering the breathless DC into Shand's office.

"You look like you've run all the way from Sherminster, constable," said Shand.

"I had to park in town," said Marcus, "the car park was blocked."

Shand closed his eyes. He'd forgotten about his car. He dug out his car keys and handed them to Taylor. "Sorry," he said, "I was late for the press conference. See if you can find someone to move it."

"No need," said Taylor. "It's all sorted now. They didn't know whose car it was so they broke in."

"Broke in?" Shand could see his day spiralling ever deeper down the plughole of misfortune.

"It's not damaged," said his sergeant. "They released the door lock, disengaged the hand brake and pushed it clear."

"Where is it now?" asked Shand, half-expecting to be told it had been towed away.

It hadn't. By some miracle of good fortune it had been shunted into a space by the front gate. Shand pocketed his keys and asked for Marc's report.

"Everything appears to check out, sir," he began. "I talked to the friends George stayed with - Duncan and Elaine Shepherd. They said George arrived about 8:15, they had a coffee and rang for a taxi that arrived about 8:45."

"Did they notice anything about George's demeanour?" asked Shand.

Marcus ran a finger back over his notes. "He was excited about the evening ahead."

"Excited?" said Shand, wondering if excitement could be confused with nerves. "Did you ask them if he was nervous at all?"

"I did," said Marcus, flicking onto the next page. "They didn't think so. Duncan said he looked at his watch a few times during the evening, but he put that down to George not being used to staying out late. A 'real home bird' is how he described him."

Shand gestured for Marcus to continue while he leaned back in his chair and listened.

"I confirmed with the taxi company that two men were picked up from Duncan Shepherd's address at 8:51 and taken to the Crown and Anchor in Sherminster. A ten-minute ride. The taxi driver doesn't remember any conversation. 'Just two men on the way to the pub,' he said."

"Did anyone notice anything odd in George's demeanour that evening?" asked Shand.

"No, sir. One of his friends - a Clive Farleigh - said he was quiet for about twenty minutes around midnight, but no one else noticed. And Farleigh put it down to the drink. He thought George was feeling queasy."

"Did anyone see George talking to someone outside their party?"

"No. Nor any phone calls, sir. Not that anyone saw. He went to the gents a number of times and would have passed a phone box, but no one saw him use it."

Nor would they, thought Shand. Helena's abductors were hardly likely to ring the Crown and Anchor's public phone on the off chance that George was passing at the time.

"When did they leave?" he asked.

"The party broke up just after midnight. Some walked home, the others waited outside for taxis."

"Was George ever alone?"

"No, sir. The taxi for George and Duncan arrived at 12:30, dropped them off at 12:40, then the two of them stayed up talking for at least another hour. Elaine came down and made them coffee. And she made them both drink a pint of water."

"Wives," said Taylor. "What would we do without them?"

"So George went to bed about a quarter to two?" asked Shand.

"That's right," said Marcus. "He stayed the night and left after breakfast. About eight o'clock, they think."

Shand leaned back farther in his chair. Why hadn't Helena's abductors made any attempt to contact George? Didn't they know where he was? Helena hadn't mentioned anything about being quizzed over her husband's whereabouts. But then she was only just coming out of shock. It was a wonder she was as lucid as she was.

He juggled times in his head. From 8:15 to 1:45, George was barely alone. Take away the handful of trips to the gents and he was never alone. Could anyone have made contact and not been seen? Slipped a note in his pocket, maybe? Something that he might not have read until the next day?

No. It was too hit and miss. If someone slipped a note in Shand's pocket it might be days before he noticed. They'd leave the note in the house. Somewhere prominent that George couldn't miss.

Which they hadn't or Shand would have seen it. He'd been the first in the house that morning.

"Come on," he said, pushing his chair back. "It's time we talked to George and Helena again."

~

Marcus stayed behind to write his report while Taylor drove Shand to Athelcott.

"How did the press conference go?" asked Taylor as he

buckled himself in.

"Don't ask," said Shand.

"That bad?"

"Worse. But it's the last one I'll ever do."

He swiftly changed the subject, recounting his trip to Forensics and then unveiling his plans for the next day.

"How would you like a trip to London, Bob? I need you to check out Marchant's alibi and his relationship with Miss Delacroix. Check the restaurant, the hotel and Gulliver's if you have the time. And make sure you visit his office. I want Marchant's colleagues to know we're investigating him. Let him know there's a price for non-co-operation."

"It'll be a pleasure, sir."

~

George and Helena were watching television when Shand knocked on the door.

"Why, chief inspector," said a startled Helena, "We were just watching you on television. Such a ... such a powerful presentation."

Shand grimaced. If he ever survived this case he could see a battered video tape coming out at every Christmas party for the next ten years. Look boys, this is how a professional conducts a television appeal. Cue raucous laughter and break out the beers.

"I have some follow up questions from yesterday," said Shand once he'd declined the offer of tea, biscuits, cakes and a choice of assorted chocolates. "The men who abducted you, did they use any items from here? I'm thinking about the breathing tube and the duct tape and the cardboard box."

Helena looked at George. "Have we any duct tape, dear?"

"No," said her husband. "There are some boxes in the old stables. We use to store fruit in."

"Would you know if any were missing?" asked Shand.

He shrugged. "They're boxes, chief inspector. I couldn't tell you anything more about them."

"What about a siphon? Do you do any wine making?"

"Not for years, chief inspector," said Helena. "To let you into a secret, I don't think George liked my elderflower wine."

"Nonsense, dear. I loved it."

Helena smiled conspiratorially at Shand. "Which is no doubt why my bottles collected so much dust every year."

"Do you still have a siphon?"

"I really couldn't say," shrugged Helena.

Shand looked around the room at the clutter of furniture and countless drawers. Helena's kidnappers didn't have the time to stumble upon the materials they needed here. They had to have arrived prepared.

"When the man tied you up," said Shand. "Where did he produce the duct tape from?"

Helena considered the question for several seconds. George edged closer to her on the sofa and took her hand.

"I think he took it from a pocket, chief inspector."

"How did he cut the tape, Mrs. Benson? Did he rip it or did he use something else?"

"I can't remember. It may have been a knife. I don't know."

She rubbed her right temple and smiled apologetically. "I'm a terrible witness, chief inspector, but it all happened so fast."

Shand moved down his list. Hair samples.

"This may sound a strange request," said Shand, "but we found two types of hairs on your clothes, Mrs. Benson. We think they're from you and your husband, but we need to be certain."

"You want hair samples, chief inspector," said Helena. "I don't think that's a problem. Though it might be for George." She smiled and rubbed her husband's balding head. "Don't take too many."

"I'll do my best," said Taylor, taking out a pair of sample bags. "I'll hunt out one that looks like he's about to jump."

Shand watched. Helena seemed to have recovered remarkably. A different generation, thought Shand. More robust. More used to adversity. Then he realised he was talking about a woman who wasn't much more than ten years older than he was.

"Are you going to extract our DNA, chief inspector?" asked Helena.

"I don't think so," said Shand. "They should be able to match the hair under a microscope."

"Ah," said Helena. "It is extraordinary what science can do these days, isn't it? Must make your job easier."

Shand wondered if it did. It opened up new avenues, certainly, and increased the amount of information. But did it make the job easier?

"It all depends on the type of case," he said. "Sometimes you can have too much information."

Like this case? He wondered how an old-time detective would have approached the murder/burial. Freed from the necessity to don white coats and search for minutiae would they have made faster progress? Would they have rounded up Marsh and Marchant and beaten a confession out of them? Or gambled everything on a hunch that led them straight to the murderer?

He really didn't know.

But he did know that forensics alone couldn't solve every case. The assessment of character, the analysis of motive and relationships - some procedures hadn't changed in a hundred years.

"How would you describe your relationship with the Marchants?" he asked, suddenly remembering that he was supposed to be conducting an interview.

"We lived in the same village, chief inspector," said Helena. "We spoke occasionally. That was all."

"I heard there was some ill-feeling over the election."

She rubbed her temple again. "There was some nonsense, yes. Annabel was not an easy person to get along with. She has ... had ... very strident views on most things and little appreciation for the feelings of others."

"Not that anyone would kill her for it," added George.

"Of course not," said Helena.

"Why do you think she was killed?"

"Do you know, chief inspector, I really have no idea. If only I could remember better. It must have happened right on top of me. But," she shrugged. "I'm sorry. I don't know if I heard people up there, or rats, or if everything was a dream. I have tried."

She suddenly looked frail, her eyes full, her lower lip quivering.

"What about Gabriel Marchant? Did you see much of him?"

"Very little. I think he only lives in the village at weekends. We know him to speak to, but that's all."

"What about you, Mr. Benson? Did he ever call on you professionally?"

George swallowed. Shand watched his Adam's apple rise and fall. "At the bank you mean?" he said. "No, no, not at all."

"That match book that you found, Mrs. Benson. It came from a drinking club in London called Gulliver's."

"Really. Has it been any help?"

"Mr. Marsh is a member of that club."

"No!" She seemed surprised. "You can't ... No. I'm sure the men were taller and thicker set. Mr. Marsh is such a slight man."

"Maybe they were associates of his? What do you think, Mr. Benson?"

George almost jumped. "I ... I really can't say."

Shand pressed. George had to be holding something back. The nerves, the look of near panic whenever Shand asked him a question.

"Is Mr. Marsh a customer at your bank?"

"No, not at all."

"When's the last time he spoke to you?"

"I ... I don't know. Maybe at that party he threw. When was it, dear?"

George looked pleadingly at his wife.

"August," said Helena. "He invited the whole village to a garden party at the rectory."

Shand looked at Helena. Hadn't she noticed the way her husband almost jumped every time Shand asked him a question? Or was this normal behaviour for George – a shy man who felt guilty under questioning?

"Yes," said George, recovering some of his lost bonhomie. "A regular open house. Very lavish. The Brigadess thought he was trying to bribe his way into village society."

"The Brigadess?" asked Taylor.

"Ursula Montacute," said Helena. "Her husband's a brigadier. I don't recall who labelled her the Brigadess, but it stuck."

"And very apt too," said George, "she runs the parish council like a military machine."

"I wouldn't say that, dear. She's organised, but she doesn't boss anyone about."

"Unlike Annabel Marchant," said Shand, watching for a response.

"Very unlike Annabel Marchant, chief inspector," said Helena. "Ursula thinks about others and acts accordingly. She can be stern, and she can dig her heels in, but she's always fair and prepared to listen."

"Whereas Annabel Marchant wasn't?" prompted Shand.

"She had a very narrow view of life, chief inspector. It was her way or no way. Maybe some of her ideas had merit, but … she didn't appear interested in compromise or accommodation. It was 'this is what I want, now give me your support.'"

"I bet she made a lot of enemies with an attitude like that," said Shand.

Helena's face immediately set. "You won't find the murderer in the village, chief inspector."

And Shand wasn't going to get much more from Helena Benson. He glanced down at his notes. Had he covered everything?

Not quite.

"I've one more question, Mrs. Benson. Did either of the intruders ever ask if you were alone in the house?"

"No. I don't believe they did."

"Or search upstairs?"

"No. They went into George's study, but certainly not upstairs."

"Did they ask where George was?"

"No, they didn't. Do you think that's significant?"

He did. They knew she was alone. Intruders would have checked every room. Especially if George was their target. Which meant he wasn't.

"Who else knew that George would be away that night?"

"Most of the village, and most of the customers at the bank, I should think. It wasn't a secret, and George had been making jokes about his wild night out in Sherminster for weeks. He's very outgoing."

Except when answering questions from me, thought Shand.

CHAPTER TWENTY-THREE

Shand didn't say much on the drive back to Sturton. Not at first. He was too busy throwing ideas around inside his head. Facts, and theories, and wild guesses bouncing back and forth.

Helena had been the target all along. Not George. They'd known he was elsewhere, but hadn't cared. Why? Had they already contacted him? He was nervous enough. But Shand couldn't understand why he was still nervous – Helena was safe, and he'd declined all offers of police protection.

It didn't make sense.

Unless the threat was current. We've taken your wife once, we can do it again.

But to what end?

If the plan had been to rob George's bank over the weekend, why waste a day? Logic dictated you kidnap the manager and his family on the Friday night, rob the bank, then have Saturday and Sunday to make good your escape. You don't let the bank manager go gallivanting off to Sherminster, and you certainly don't continue with the plan once the police have been alerted.

So why was the threat still current? Were they stubborn, stupid, fixated?

Or wasn't it robbery they had in mind?

Extortion! Shand started to fidget in his seat. It didn't have to be a robbery at all. *You work in a bank. Give me money, or your wife gets it.*

Once started along that avenue of thought, he could see other possibilities. Money laundering, fraud. Approve this loan, open this account. They could have approached George at any time and threatened him. Maybe he didn't take them seriously, so they snatched his wife.

It would explain everything.

Except Annabel Marchant and the annoying fingerprint that tied the two cases together.

"What do you make of George Benson, Bob?" asked Shand, seeking a second opinion.

"I'd swap my bank manager for him any day."

Yes, thought Shand. There was an avuncular quality to George Benson. He didn't look like a person who turned down too many loan applications. But then, presumably, he must. He was, after all, a bank manager who had to turn a profit. There had to be a harder side, however well he hid it.

"Did he seem nervous to you at all? Uncomfortable about certain questions?"

"A bit," said Taylor. "He didn't like the questions about Marsh and Marchant."

"No, he didn't," said Shand, glad of the confirmation.

Gabe Marsh and Gabriel Marchant. Could it be that neat? The two of them extorting money from George Benson, abducting his wife when he threatened to tell the police, then killing Annabel because ... because what? Because Marchant couldn't afford a divorce, or because she knew something?

Shand bounced his latest theory off Taylor, who could see the logic – with one annoying exception – if both the Gabriels had alibis, who made the phone call? The men who abducted Helena? The men with rough London accents? Would Annabel have strolled to the green in the middle of the night to meet one of them?

"Go on home, Bob," said Shand when they reached the station car park. "We're not going to make much more progress tonight, and I want you in London first thing. Break Marchant's alibi and we've got a case."

~

Shand raced back to his office. The case was approaching the forty-eight hour mark and the steep decline into failure and the unsolved crime file. He picked up the phone. He wanted background checks on Marchant and Marsh. Bank statements, tax records – anything that could be found.

"Look for any links to dubious companies, unexplained income, or cash flow problems," he told them.

And he added George Benson to the list. The extortion

might have started months ago. The abduction of Helena triggered by George's reluctance to continue.

The bank would have to be audited too. A search for suspicious accounts – money laundering, false loans, missing money. Maybe it would convince George to cooperate? He'd soon find out when the auditors arrived at his branch.

A knock came at Shand's door. Chief Superintendent Wiggins stood in the doorway.

"Ah, Shand," he said, swiftly closing the door behind him. "How are ... er things?"

Shand noted the hesitancy in his voice, and a look that most people reserved for visiting the terminally ill in hospital.

He braced himself. "Fine," he said.

"The case not too much? Must be a strain catching a big murder in your first week?"

Oh, God, he's seen the press conference, thought Shand, fixing his face in an optimistic smile.

"No strain at all, sir," said Shand. "I'm thriving on the challenge."

Shand's brain left the conversation at that point and hurried three sentences into the future. He was going to have the case taken away from him. Stress, inexperience, the need for a fresh mind. Everything was leading towards the inevitable.

"I er ... saw the press conference earlier. You looked a tad strained, I thought."

Shand found himself smiling. "A bit of a risk, but I thought it justified."

"Risk?"

Shand's brain snapped back in panic. It couldn't work twice. Not the 'emotional appeal has three times the success rate' speech.

Too late. The words were already greased and hurdling teeth.

"It's a technique they use in the States, sir. If the family won't cooperate."

Wiggins looked blank.

"Emotional appeals have three times the success rate of ordinary appeals."

There it was – a statistic he'd dragged out of the ether. A

statistic that someone was certain to check if he didn't stop talking about it.

"So if the family won't cooperate," he continued, "you try to find someone else. I was the closest."

"Oh, so it was..." The Chief Super struggled to find the word.

"Planned," suggested Shand. "Yes, sir, entirely. As I said it was a bit of a risk, but it had to be done. Anything to break the case."

Shand pushed a confident smile to the fore and hid behind it. Wiggins had to go soon. The corruption enquiry, an overstretched department – something had to drag him back to HQ.

"Ah, yes, er ... good work."

He didn't look entirely convinced. So Shand hit him with a quick-fire progress summary. The matched fingerprints, the new motives of extortion and money laundering, the husband's refusal to be fingerprinted, Taylor's trip to check out his alibi, the audits.

The Chief Super's face brightened. Solid police work, good ideas, and a plan to move the case forward.

"Keep up the good work, Shand," he said. "But er ... I'd go easy on those American practices, don't you think?"

~

The police station emptied as the evening progressed. Shand toiled at his desk, writing up the day's progress, planning for the next. The case was moving into the middle game. The long slog through statements and facts, looking for the inconsistency, the mistake. Just like chess. The novelty of the opening, the long grind for position, and then the rush to the end game.

Top of his list for tomorrow was one word – fingerprints. Whose were they? Marchant's, Marsh's or someone else's entirely?

Shand stopped by the front desk on his way out to see if his somewhat manic appeal to the public had yielded any results. The desk sergeant smiled and handed him a sheaf of messages. The one at the top was unfortunately representative of the others.

'Is that nice policeman all right?' it said.

Shand went back to his hotel room and tried to sleep, tried to watch television, tried to read, and failed at all three. He was over-tired, scratchy-eyed, yawning, and on the verge of passing out. But held on that verge by a mind that refused to still – always finding some niggling thought to dwell upon.

Like Anne. Even with the lights off, even with his eyes closed, he could still see the phone, resting on the bedside table, silently goading him. Daring him to pick it up. Would she be at home? Would she still be at work? Or was she sleeping elsewhere?

It was stupid. It was self-destructive. It served no purpose. But he couldn't let it go. A part of him wanted to call home, to make himself listen as it rang and rang without answer, each ring cutting deeper, each ring adding substance to a picture he didn't want to see, but couldn't shake off.

~

Sleep eventually claimed him, and for the first time in several days he slept through to his alarm. Maybe his obsession had been cathartic?

He dressed and went down for breakfast. A selection of newspapers lay on a table by the fruit juices. He flicked through the headlines. Midnight Caller was everywhere. Which was good to see. Both the broad sheets and the tabloids. Then he found the local paper, the *Echo*. 'Out Of His Depth,' ran the headlines. Below came an unflattering picture of Shand taken from the press conference, and then three pages of advice from Kevin Tresco entitled. 'So here's the real Athelcott story – crop circles, witchcraft and the Moleman.'

Shand read on. Tabloid sensationalism of the worst kind. It read like a cheap horror film written by a fifteen year-old, painting Athelcott as a village gripped by satanic cults. Shand threw the paper down. He couldn't finish it. The story was ridiculous. How could Tresco call himself an investigative journalist and write that rubbish?

A question he didn't have time to answer.

His phone rang. It was the station, a breathless constable on the line.

"Sir, you better get out to Athelcott immediately. There's been another burial at the stone circle."

CHAPTER TWENTY-FOUR

Shand blocked the entrance to the chalk track with his car. He wasn't going to make the same mistake as Saturday. This crime scene was going to be protected. One police car was already parked along the track by the circle, but there wouldn't be any others.

Shand hurried along the track. Two uniformed policeman were standing by their car talking to a third man, a youth in a dirty green coat.

"Haven't touched a thing, sir," said one of the constables. "We called it in straight away."

Shand walked slowly towards the circle, watching every step, determined not to contaminate the scene any more than he had to. But he had to get closer. He could see something in the circle, but not enough to make a judgement. Was it another burial? Or a trick of the light?

And was that a line of police tape inside the circle?

He reached the outer edge of the stones. There was a new mound, covered in turfs, identical in size and shape to the one that had covered Helena Benson. But this time it was on the side nearer the road.

And someone had moved the police tape. Yesterday, it ran in a circle around the outside of the stones. Now, it ran in a circle around short metal poles, the circle of tape transecting the circle of stones like a pair of Olympic rings.

"Why did you move the tape?" he shouted to the two policemen.

"We didn't," came the reply. "It was like that when we arrived."

Shand swung back to look closer at the tape circle. Why would anyone do that? Had someone from the County

Archaeologist's department moved the tape?

Or was it linked to the crime? An added layer of ritual.

A car screeched to a halt behind Shand's and a car door slammed. Shand turned to the two uniformed coppers. "Get some tape across the track entrance and make sure people stay back."

His eyes were drawn back to the mound. He couldn't see a breathing tube, but should he check? He could walk carefully up to the mound. He lurched forward, then stopped. Indecision. What if he couldn't see a breathing tube? What next? A fingertip search, feeling for a tube breaking the surface? And if that didn't work?

He looked to the road. Where was Scene of Crimes? He checked his watch. He'd called them out as soon as he'd received the call. They should have been here by now.

Another glance at the mound. Maybe he could shout a message to whoever was inside? Give them hope. We're on our way.

"Hello!" he shouted, cupping his hands around his mouth, trying to focus the call. "We're here!"

Then he felt foolish. He was shouting at a mound of earth. He glanced back to the road. More cars arriving. People looking his way. What if Kevin Tresco was there? Wouldn't he love to twist Shand's words? *Novice cop talks to mound of earth.*

And then he felt guilty. Thinking about himself while someone lay buried, helpless and frantic, unable to move, too frightened to cry out in case they lost the tube in their mouth, not knowing if help was on its way or even possible.

He called again. "Stay calm! We know where you are!"

Another glance at his watch. Come on! Frustration rising. How much longer should he give them? A minute, five?

More cars, more people. He strained to see a white coat and shook his head in frustration. Three uniformed coppers were jogging down the track towards him. And Marcus Ashenden, his DC.

Shand shifted his weight from foot to foot. Come on! Another minute and he'd dig up the entire crime scene if he had to.

"SOCO's behind me," said Marcus, breathing hard. "They're just getting changed."

Thank God, thought Shand. How long would it take before they dug this person out? Would they walk along the track or run? Would they wait for photographs to be taken? Would they take the mound apart piece by tiny piece to preserve evidence?

He couldn't take his eyes off the mound. He thought he saw it pulsing with the breath of the person trapped inside. He thought he heard them gasping, crying for help, shouting accusatory words – what is taking you so long!

He had to look away. Four white suits ambled along the track. He couldn't believe it. "Come on," he pleaded, then again louder. "Come on!"

He willed them to hurry. He waved. He beckoned. He didn't care what people thought. A life was at stake.

They began to jog, then they were at the circle, through the gap between the stones. A camera clicked, several times, lights flashing around the stones. And then people were crawling and probing and brushing. White shapes slithering like maggots all over the mound. Shand waited, unable to recall the last time he'd breathed, praying, and hoping, and wondering who it would be. Helena? George? Someone else?

A white-rimmed face turned to Shand. A reluctant shake of the head.

No! Not dead! Shand almost burst into the circle. They couldn't be dead!

"No tube," said SOCO.

Shand couldn't accept it. They hadn't looked hard enough. There had to be a tube!

"Let's start removing the turfs," said SOCO.

Shand watched, edging forward as each turf was lifted. Couldn't they go any faster?

The top layer removed, they started probing the earth. Still no tube. And no body. How deep was it buried?

They kept digging. They kept probing. The pile of soil growing higher and wider.

Until...

SOCO stopped and looked at Shand. "There's nothing here," he said.

"Go deeper," said Shand.

"We've hit bedrock."

Shand turned away. A hoax? He'd been put through the ringer for a hoax?

He stormed away from the circle, looking for the youth he'd seen earlier. The one in the dirty green coat. He had to be the Moleman. Right age, right place. Call in the cops and have a front row seat. *Look what I found. I think it's another body.*

"Name?" snapped Shand, grabbing hold of the youth's shoulder and swinging him around to face him.

"Lee," said the boy. He was in his late teens, unkempt and wiry. "Lee Molland. Did you find anything?"

"What do you think?" said Shand.

"I wasn't sure. I thought I'd better ring, just in case."

"Just in case of what?" snapped Shand.

"In case there was a body. I didn't think there was but..."

"Why didn't you think there was a body?"

Shand kept pressing. He didn't want to give the boy time to think.

"Because of the legend. You know? About the stones."

Shand looked at the boy closely. Was this another wind up? You've fallen for my body in the circle hoax, now here's another?

"What legend?"

"They say the stones dance at full moon. And when they stop they don't always go back to the same place they come from. You can see how they've moved away from your police tape." He pointed at the circle. "I expect you'll find that new mound's really the old one popped back out again."

Shand waited for him to finish, then added another five seconds to control his temper.

"Here's another legend, Lee," said Shand between clenched teeth. "If I hear of one more molehill where a molehill shouldn't be, or flowers switching beds, or police tape dancing by the light of the moon, then you, my boy, will materialise magically in Sturton cells. Understand?"

"You think I'm the Moleman?" He spoke like a choirboy, eyes widening in innocent surprise.

"Doesn't matter what I think. See those men over there? The ones with the white coats and short tempers. They're going to take that circle apart until they find the proof. DNA, fibres, hair. I bet you shed cells like a regular leper."

For the first time doubt spread across Lee Molland's face. "You wouldn't do that for a hoax?"

"*I* wouldn't," said Shand. "But *they* would. Don't get enough work, see? Not many murders in this part of Wessex so any chance they get to use their shiny new machines and they're unstoppable."

Lee bit his lip and glanced at the circle.

"Of course, I could call them off if I wanted," said Shand. "If someone was to be helpful. Like telling me where they were Friday night."

"I already told your lot. I didn't see anything. I stayed in."

"Stayed in," said Shand, looking for every facial twitch and deviation of eye contact. "Let's take a leap of imagination and pretend you're the Moleman."

Lee started to complain, but Shand raised a finger. "No, Lee, stay with me, we're only pretending. Now, if you were the Moleman, what might you have seen on Friday night, early Saturday morning."

"Nothing."

"Lee," warned Shand.

"I'm helping, really, but think about it. Would the Moleman really go out on a moonlit night when anyone could see him?"

~

Shand took a deep breath, then shook his head. Kids. This case was trying enough without hoaxers nearly giving him a heart attack.

"Do you think they really dance at full moon, sir?" said Marcus staring at the circle of stones in what could only be described as a look of awe.

"No, Marcus and when you've got time, check the dates the Moleman struck against the moon and weather conditions."

Shand left his constable and told SOCO he could stand his team down. It was a hoax. The burial mound, the police tape – all an elaborate hoax to make it look like the stones had moved.

"Are you sure they haven't?" said SOCO. "Those trees look a lot closer to me."

Shand fell for it and looked, staring at the trees until the laughter registered.

"Gotcha, Mr. Shand," said SOCO, smiling. "I must say your crime scenes are nothing if not entertaining."

Shand hovered on the brink of a caustic reply but, failing to come up with anything better than 'big nose,' decided to walk away.

Only to find Kevin Tresco sitting on his car bonnet.

"Did you read my story this morning, chief inspector?" said the reporter getting up, his lips already curling into his trademark sneer.

"Your story?" said Shand, feigning surprise. "I can't remember. Was that the one with 'Now wash your hands' stamped on each page?"

Shand pushed past and dived into his car, leaving the reporter trout-like in his wake. A couple of uniformed officers cleared bystanders out of the way and Shand made his getaway, accelerating hard until the circle was out of sight.

A mile out of Athelcott Shand's inner adult addressed him. 'Well done, Shand,' it said, using its sarcastic schoolteacher voice. 'Less than a day after vowing never to speak to the press again, you pick on the worst jackal in the pack and insult him. One second of triumph that will undoubtedly come back in a re-arranged and out of context quote in tomorrow's Echo.'

'So what?' said his inner nine-year old. 'Kevin Tresco hates you anyway. Nothing you could say to him would ever make a difference.'

Which was true. Even his inner adult had to agree with that.

And it felt good. Liberating even. The way he'd handled the Moleman too. After the ordeal of the buried body, he'd cut loose, thrown off the old repressed Shand and started speaking what he felt instead of what he thought people expected to hear.

And he'd been intuitive. Acted on a hunch without stopping to analyse the minutiae. He'd jumped straight from hoax to Moleman to the boy who'd called in the burial.

And he'd been right.

Probably.

~

Shand, and his thankfully now quiet inner family, had barely settled in his office when the phone call came. It was from one of the few members of the Forensics team who hadn't been called to the stone circle.

"We've traced the store where the cardboard box came from," she said. "You know the one from Mrs. Benson's burial?"

"Yes, I know," said Shand, expecting to be told it was another dead end.

"It's from a supermarket in Harrow. Pricerite on Edgware Lane. It was part of a consignment sent there three years ago. Do you want the exact date?"

Shand sat bolt upright. "Yes, please."

He found a pen, jotted the date down. Three years ago. Harrow. Didn't someone say that Gabriel and Annabel had used to live in Harrow?

CHAPTER TWENTY-FIVE

He scrabbled through papers and reports on his desk. Where were they? The witness statements. Jacintha Maybury's. He was sure she said something about the Marchants living in Harrow.

She had. He found the entry cross-referenced to the phone logs. He remembered now. There was an entry for a woman living in Harrow. Someone who Annabel had called last week.

He fished out the phone logs and started dialling. If she could tie Gabriel Marchant to the supermarket, they'd have the box and the book of matches connecting Gabriel to the abduction!

And when was it that the Marchants had moved to Athelcott - two, three years ago? It all fitted.

The phone rang. Shand tapped on the desk with a finger. Waiting. The dial tone taking forever. Click. A woman's voice. "Hello."

Shand introduced himself briefly, his mind racing towards the first question.

"Do you know the Pricerite supermarket in Harrow? The one on Edgware Lane?"

"Yes," came the slightly puzzled answer.

"Did Annabel and Gabriel Marchant shop there?"

"I ... I believe so. Why do you want to know?"

"Were they living in Harrow three years ago? Specifically the months of June and July?"

He was thinking fast. How long did a box stay at a supermarket? Would it be months before it was discarded for shoppers to use?

"Yes, they moved to Athelcott that autumn. September, I

think."

Shand punched the air. He had the information he wanted, enough to bring Gabriel in surely. Could he find more?

"Did you know the Marchants well?" he asked.

"Not so much Gabriel, but Annabel certainly."

"What kind of a woman was she?"

"Annabel?" she let out a deep sigh. "Now that's a question. She was a complex person. A lot of fun, boundless energy, very outgoing but ... at the same time she was a very private person. There was a social Annabel and a private Annabel. Very few people knew the private Annabel."

"Did you?"

"I think so, though it's been such a long time since we had a real talk. We chat, but it's different over the phone."

"What about Gabriel Marchant? How would you describe their relationship."

"Loving, I'd say. As much as Gabriel can love anything that's not to do with work or himself."

"You don't like Gabriel?"

"I don't like men who are obsessed with their work, and with Gabriel there are times when you can barely get a sentence out of him that's not work-related."

"Would you say she had a happy marriage?"

"She once joked she had the ideal marriage. A rich husband who was never at home."

"What did you think she meant by that?"

"Nothing risqué, chief inspector. Annabel was a woman who had expensive hobbies and loved to see them indulged. Have you seen what she did to her home? She designed the lot – interior and exterior. All Gabriel did was pay the bills."

A not insubstantial contribution in Shand's eyes. But then, he was a man.

"Did she ever mention any special friends she had in Athelcott?" said Shand, skirting around the use of the word 'lover.'

"Someone called Jacintha, I think. I've met her several times. An artist, I believe."

"Any men friends?"

A long pause before the clipped denial. "Definitely not."

"I have to ask these questions," said Shand. "Any

particular friends from her time in Harrow, school friends she kept in touch with, old flames?"

"Not that I recall. You'd have to ask Gabriel."

Shand could see himself doing that. One request for a list of old boyfriends and Gabriel would run screaming to his solicitor complaining of harassment and character assassination.

"How about enemies? Did she ever mention any problems she was having with anyone?"

"You mean besides that awful neighbour? The one who lives in a tip."

"Bill Acomb," said Shand. "Yes, we know about him. Anyone else?"

"There was a woman with a strange name. Brigadoon or something like that."

"The Brigadess?"

"Yes, that's it. The local squire's wife, she used to think she ran the village until Annabel arrived."

"Was there much friction between them?"

"I don't really know. When I last spoke to Annabel she gave me the impression that the woman was not going to be a problem for much longer."

"What did she mean by that?"

"She wouldn't say. Annabel can ... could ... be very secretive when she wanted to."

Shand replaced the phone and leant back in his chair. What *had* Annabel meant by that? The election? Surely not? From the feedback he'd received from the village he couldn't see either of the Marchants winning a popularity poll.

He filed the question aside for later. He had a more pressing matter to organise. And this one he was going to enjoy.

~

Shand knocked on Gabriel Marchant's front door and waited. A reporter had noticed his arrival and stood by the gate. Thankfully it wasn't Kevin Tresco.

Gabriel Marchant's face appeared in a nearby window, then quickly disappeared. Shand waited, then knocked again.

The door opened.

"My client has nothing to say to you, chief inspector."

The lawyer, a very expensive lawyer by the look of him, stood in the doorway, his hand on the door, blocking access to the house and his client who stood behind him in the hallway.

"And you would be?" asked Shand.

"Charles Rathmell," he said as though the name should be familiar – which it wasn't – and delivered with the aristocratic disdain of a Regency buck. "My card," he added, handing Shand an embossed work of art.

"Very nice," said Shand, fighting the sudden urge to rip it up and cast the tiny pieces over the lawyer's crocodile skin shoes.

"Well, Mr. Rathmell, perhaps you'd be so kind as to inform your client that he has two choices. One, he comes to the station voluntarily or, two, I arrest him here and all his colleagues and clients can read about it in tomorrow's papers."

"You have no grounds for an arrest."

"Do I not? You want me to read them all out in front of the press? That's a reporter standing by the gate." Shand turned to stab a finger in the direction of the lone bystander. "I've got a loud voice and I bet he's got big ears."

Gabriel lurched forward. "No," he said, grabbing his lawyer by the arm. "It's all right. I'll go voluntarily."

~

Shand placed the supermarket box in the middle of the table in Interview Room One. He'd leave it there, not say a word about it, and let Gabriel's imagination do the rest.

"Take a seat," he said as Gabriel and his lawyer came through the door.

"My client has nothing to say, Mr. Shand. This is a totally nugatory exercise."

"Indeed, sir," said Shand, dismissively. "They were always my favourite. Now, Gabriel, have you heard of a club called Gulliver's? A drinking club off Hanover Lane."

Gabriel looked at his lawyer who answered for him. "My client refuses to answer any questions."

"Perhaps he's confused as to the whereabouts of Hanover Lane," said Shand, placing his hands on the table and leaning forward. "It's not in Swindon, Gabriel. It's in London. And your name appears in the guest book."

Both solicitor and client sat silent and implacable.

Shand produced the evidence bag with the matchbook and dangled it in front of Gabriel's face.

"Ring any bells yet, Gabriel?"

"This is a pointless exercise, chief inspector," said the lawyer.

Shand ignored him. "This was found in the car used for the abduction of Helena Benson."

Gabriel started. "I thought this was about Annabel," he blurted.

"Now that's interesting," said Shand. "What makes you think the crimes are unconnected?"

Gabriel looked pleadingly at his lawyer.

"He doesn't have an opinion one way or the other," said Rathmell. "He was merely expressing surprise."

"Surprise," echoed Shand. "Well, let's give him another one. We found fingerprints on this book of matches and guess what – we found a match to ones found in your house."

This time it was the lawyer who looked towards his client. Gabriel shook his head. "You're lying," he said.

"I wouldn't know how to, Gabriel. But you see, it's not just the fingerprints, and the club in London with your name on the guest book. It's this as well." He tapped on the large cardboard box on the table. "I expect you thought this was where you put your clothes when we perform the strip search."

Rathmell leapt to his feet. "Chief Inspector!"

Shand held himself in check. The words were there, waiting. *It's all right, Mr. Rathmell, we'll bring in a box for you too.*

Instead he raised his hands and apologised. "Do you know where this box was found?" he said, introducing a more sombre tone to his voice.

Neither man spoke. Rathmell flounced back into his chair.

"This is the box that Helena Benson's head was put into when she was buried alive. Look," he said, turning the box to make sure both men could see the punctured hole. "This is where the breathing tube went. Can you imagine what it was like? Buried alive for nine hours with nothing to see but the inside of this box. The darkness, the weight of the soil on your body, the only air coming through a tube held between your teeth. Imagine if you had to sneeze. What would you do? Grit your teeth and hope you didn't lose the tube?"

Rathmell spoke. "I fail to see what this has to do with my client."

"Do you recognise this box, Mr. Marchant?" asked Shand, pushing it towards him. Gabriel backed off, not wanting the box to touch him.

"Take a good look," said Shand. "It came from your house too."

Gabriel stood up violently, so violently his chair overturned. "What is this! I had nothing to do with any burial, or murder, or anything. I'm innocent!"

"I think this interview has just concluded, chief inspector," said Rathmell reaching for his briefcase.

"I wouldn't advise it," said Shand. "Unless you want to walk through the media circus by the front door."

"What media circus?" asked Gabriel, his eyes widening.

"A press conference. In about...." Shand checked his watch. "Five minutes. They're like a pack of wolves in the corridors. If they see you here with a lawyer... Well, you can guess what they're going to think."

"Did you arrange this?" snapped Rathmell.

"Not me. I can't stand the press. All I want is to conduct this interview then smuggle you out the back door. Another ten minutes, that's all."

Both men sat down.

"So, you have no idea how this box of yours got into Helena's grave?"

"My client refuses to answer. As he will on every other question for the next ten minutes."

"Then I'll just talk," said Shand. "Perhaps your client would like to know how the investigation is going into the murder of his wife? He hasn't asked yet. Perhaps he's just shy?"

Gabriel was very close to exploding - eyes narrowed, arms folded so tightly they almost dug into his chest.

"And he might like to know about George Benson."

Shand turned to observe Gabriel's reaction. "We're

auditing his bank, you know?"

No reaction. The same rigid mask staring at a point on the wall behind Shand's shoulder.

"Any financial irregularities and we'll find them. We'll be checking all accounts *and* account holders. Every loan, every security."

Still no reaction. Shand placed himself in Gabriel's eye line.

"And we'll be talking to George as well. Very talkative man, George Benson, don't you think?"

Gabriel blinked and turned away, finding another patch of wall.

Shand checked his watch and sighed. "Well this is a waste of time, isn't it?"

"At last we agree, chief inspector," said Rathmell. "Shouldn't you check to see if the corridors are clear?"

Shand nodded to the constable by the door. "Take a look, constable." And then turned and took a kick at the skirting board.

"It's clear, sir," said the constable coming back into the room.

"Then show our two guests out the back way. Make sure they don't meet any reporters."

"Thank you, chief inspector," smiled the Rathmell, his oily confidence returning. "Good day."

Shand turned his back, counted to ten, then rang next door.

"We've got it!" he shouted. "Bring your stuff and let's get started.

CHAPTER TWENTY-SIX

"It's that chair over there," he said as the technician came in. "His finger prints are all over it."

Simple, but effective, thought Shand. Carefully clean all four chairs in the room, push them tight against the table and wait for Gabriel to pull one out. The rest of the interview was a bonus - spurred on by the mythical press conference - though he had expected more of a reaction when he mentioned George and the bank.

He watched as the chair was sprayed and dusted. A clean set of prints. No smudges or distortions. He watched as each print was lifted and attached to its own card. And then joined the procession along the corridor towards the waiting computer.

Minutes passed in growing anticipation. Shand paced at the back of the room. Would the fingerprints be enough to charge him?

The prints were scanned and uploaded. Shand alternated between pacing and darting forward to peer over the technician's shoulders. What was taking so long? There was only the one print to match.

The cursor blinked, the screen changed. And...

The prints didn't match. Shand stared at the screen, unable to speak. He'd been so sure. And yet...

"Marcus," he said. "Find Gabe Marsh. Tell him we want to see him. Now. If he can't come to us, we'll go to him."

The print *had* to belong to Marsh.

~

Shand was simmering in his office, checking through the Marsh file when Marcus found him.

"Can't get through, sir. He's still not answering his home phone, and he's switched off his mobile. I've sent a unit round to check."

Shand could have kicked something. Had he let Marsh escape? Had he been so invested in Gabriel Marchant's guilt that he hadn't followed up on the obvious? Marsh had the car, the membership of the London club, access to the Marchant's house. He should have gone for Marsh first!

But Marsh couldn't have made the phone call. He had the alibi. The Chief Constable's daughter.

"Thank you, Marcus," said Shand. "Get back to me the moment they report in."

Shand closed the file and leaned back in his chair. Was he placing too much emphasis on the book of matches? It could be a red herring. Something dropped in the back seat by an innocent passenger, an acquaintance of the kidnappers not in any way involved with the gang.

Or it could belong to a kidnapper hired by Marchant – a kidnapper who'd been to Marchant's home, a kidnapper he'd met at Gulliver's.

He so wanted Gabriel Marchant to be guilty. He looked guilty. He acted guilty. His wife was dead, and yet not once had he asked how the case was progressing.

"Sir?" a knock on the open door heralded Marcus's return. Shand looked up. Bad news by the look of it.

"No sign of Marsh at the rectory, sir. The car's gone and the place is locked up."

Shand waved Marsh's file at the detective constable. "Find him, Marcus. Check all his business numbers. Someone's got to know where he is. Pretend you're looking for a holiday home in Spain. That should get his attention. Oh, and find out if either of the Gabriels have a gardener. I want to know if someone would notice a garden spade going missing."

Shand threw himself back in his chair. He felt like he was getting nowhere. That everything was taking too long and failing to work out as planned.

He checked his watch. Taylor had been gone for hours. He must have found something by now. He picked up the phone and tapped in the numbers, desperate for some good news.

"How's it going," he asked the moment Taylor answered.

"Not good, sir," said Taylor. "I've talked to the staff at the restaurant and they say Gabriel was definitely there Friday night. He's a regular apparently. Had a table booked for nine and didn't leave until eleven thirty."

"They're sure about that? Eleven thirty?"

"I've seen the credit card receipt. It's timed at 11:24."

"And they're sure it was Gabriel?"

"Positive. They showed me his picture from one of the Sunday papers. There's no way Gabriel could have made it back to Athelcott before two."

Shand had to agree. Reluctantly. His imagination clutched at the passing straws of a late night helicopter dash from London, or the hiring of a double, or an identical twin...

But he let them float on by.

"I'm on my way to his hotel now," said Taylor. "To see if they remember what time he got in."

Shand told his sergeant to keep digging and put the phone down. Another lead going nowhere. And an even bigger question left unanswered. Who was the Midnight Caller? If it wasn't either of the two Gabriels, who was left? Jacintha Maybury? The mystery lover?

That's when he remembered Annabel's computer. There had to be emails, letters – something to identify this mystery person. Had Forensics released their report yet?

He rummaged through his in-tray and there it was – nestling under a pile of memos and office circulars. A one-page summary and a memory stick containing the files. According to the summary there were over a thousand emails and a couple of hundred letters, mostly business related: uninteresting correspondence with clubs, societies, mail order companies, builders and estate agents. And a hundred or so emails and letters to friends and family.

They hadn't read everything, but they had found several letters from Annabel to her solicitor concerning Bill Acomb. The lawsuit over the chicken was just the beginning. She wanted him out.

Shand loaded the stick and read the letters. They went back eighteen months, starting with a request for legal advice and ending with a dossier cataloguing his crimes. She was gathering evidence for a series of prosecutions. Health and Safety violations, under-declaration of income, false accounting, noise pollution, anti-social behaviour. Anything she could find. She wanted him put out of business and gone.

Was Bill Acomb aware of this?

He sampled her other letters, scrolling through Annabel's life in a series of literary snapshots – terse communications with tradesmen, loving letters to her daughter, amusing letters to friends. The latter perhaps the most revealing as it mentioned people in the village – mostly to their disadvantage. Annabel's wit was biting, and often cruel.

The Acombs and the Montacutes fared the worst. The Acombs were depicted as ignorant louts, 'no better than travellers' and the Montacutes as doddery dinosaurs, clinging to a lifestyle that no longer existed.

But no sign of a lover. The only man who merited a warm mention was Gabe Marsh. But there was nothing in her letters that hinted at a deeper relationship.

Had Annabel kept this lover a secret – even from her computer? Did he – or she – really exist?

He looked again at Jacintha Maybury. She was unmarried. She was a close friend of Annabel's. And there was no correspondence between them. Not even an email.

Shand leaned forward and scrolled back through the folders. Nothing. Was that significant? Could Jacintha Maybury be both mystery lover and Midnight Caller?

Or was it nothing at all – they lived close by and preferred the phone?

A question interrupted by the shrill ring of Shand's phone. It was the desk sergeant. He'd just received a call from Helena Benson. One of her garden spades was missing.

CHAPTER TWENTY-SEVEN

"You have two spades?" asked Shand, gazing into the half-light of the old stables. Tools of all kinds hung from hooks on the far wall - forks, rakes, shears, a strimmer. And one spade.

"We're both keen gardeners, chief inspector," said Helena. "A garden this size needs two people to work it."

It *was* a large garden. Enormous by London standards. Lawns, borders, trees and a huge vegetable plot in the far corner. Most of it already dug for the winter. Only a few lines of cabbages and leeks stood out against the deep black of the bare soil.

"You don't have a gardener?"

"Of course not," said Helena. "Why pay someone else to do what you love?"

Indeed, thought Shand, wondering if he'd ever love gardening. Not that he'd had the opportunity - he'd lived in gardenless flats all his adult life. But maybe...

There was something about the Benson house. Every time he visited, he left with the idea that this was the kind of the house he could be happy in - *they* could be happy in, he and Anne.

"I didn't think to look until today," said Helena. "Then I saw it was missing. It should have been hanging on the same hook as the other."

Shand stepped inside the old stables. All signs of horses had long gone. Now it was an old stone shed, crammed with tools and boxes of garden produce. Cobwebs and strings of onions hung from nails in the low cross beams. It wasn't a surprise SOCO hadn't registered the missing spade. There was nothing obvious to suggest its removal.

Shand examined the flooring. Dirt, by the look of it. Too dry and too hard to take a footprint. There'd be nothing here.

And the men had worn gloves.

"The man you thought went out the kitchen door," said Shand. "Was he gone long?"

"I don't think so. Is this where you think he went?"

It had to be, thought Shand. Did that mean he already knew where to look?

He pointed at the stable door. "You don't keep this locked?"

"No," said Helena. "We've never had to. The missing spade's identical to the one there. If that helps. We bought them at the same time."

Shand hadn't thought to ask. Somehow he'd assumed all spades were alike. He took a closer look. Wooden shaft, wooden handle. Was there a maker's name?

There was - of a kind - on the metal part of the shaft. Two words badly worn - one said 'England,' the other was mostly lost but ended in 'ton.'

Strange, thought Shand, they take the box from the Marchants, but the spade from the Bensons. Why? Didn't the Marchants have a spade?

"Why are you auditing George's bank?" asked Helena.

"Pardon," said Shand, his mind still on the spade.

"George rang. He's very upset. He says you ordered an audit at his branch."

Helena looked accusingly at Shand.

"I had to," explained Shand. "The only motive I can find for your..." Words eluded him. She was standing in front of him. The victim. Her eyes accusing. Why are you hurting my husband? Haven't we suffered enough? And now he had to take her back to Friday night with stark words like burial, and attack, and abduction. Wasn't there a better word?

He started to say 'misfortune,' then stopped. It sounded ridiculously Victorian. He took a deep breath and started again. "The only motive we can find for your abduction is that someone wanted to put pressure on your husband. You yourself thought it was a bank robbery."

Helena nodded, listening intently.

"But according to your husband no one contacted him. Which doesn't make sense. Unless..." He had to say it. "Unless your husband's still being threatened. Is he Mrs. Benson?"

Helena looked surprised. And shocked. Her mouth opened a good half-second before she found anything to say.

"You think someone's still trying to rob George's bank?"

"What do you think Mrs. Benson? Has your husband been more nervous than usual this last week?"

He could see Helena thinking. She looked worried. Which made Shand feel even guiltier.

Helena lowered her eyes. "I had noticed. But that's because of what happened to me. I'm certain of it. He would have told me if there was anything else."

"Even if it put you in danger? We're looking at the possibility that someone wants George to do something for them. Something at the bank. And they're using you as leverage. Now we can only help if George cooperates."

"Do you want me to speak to him, chief inspector?"

"Someone has to, Mrs. Benson. Impress upon him that we're going to catch these people. We already have some excellent leads. But we can catch them quicker with his help. If it's a matter of protection, we can give him anything he wants – twenty-four hour armed guards, a safe house, the lot. Or if it's some other hold they have over him – if they've already coerced him into breaking the law – we can talk about that too. We want the gang prosecuted, not George."

'Thank you, chief inspector," said Helena, clasping his right hand in both of hers. "I'll talk to George this evening."

~

It was midday and Shand was starving. He'd missed breakfast in his rush to get to the stone circle. And he wasn't going to share his meal with a pack of inquisitive journalists. So he drove past the Royal Oak and onto the next village, assuaging his rumbling stomach with promises of something special. He'd hunt out a proper village pub with a roaring fire, draught cider, and a real restaurant.

Eventually he found a place, following a sign off the main road that promised good pub grub in three miles. He ordered a steak and kidney pie, and braved a half pint of something that called itself rough farmhouse cider – a brew so cloudy that he couldn't see his fingers on the far side of the glass.

And tasted on the dry side of vinegar.

But the food was excellent, and there wasn't a journalist

in sight. He sat and ate, and sipped, and tried to forget about Athelcott and the case that consumed him. Failing, of course, the case having all the survival instincts of an infant cuckoo, stretching, and pushing, and heaving every other thought from his head.

Did he have enough to press charges? Should he order the arrest of Gabe Marsh, alert the ports?

He was torn, and beset by the probability that whatever he did, it would be wrong. If he acted hastily, the man would be innocent. If he waited for more evidence, Gabe would disappear, and hindsight and Kevin Tresco would maul him unmercifully.

This was his first case. He couldn't afford any mistakes. He had to impress. He had to present the perfect case to the Crown Prosecution Service, something they couldn't throw back at him later for lack of evidence.

But neither could he wait too long. Witness's memories would start to fail, and suspects would have more time to rehearse their alibis. Perhaps he should be more aggressive? Arrest anyone he suspected of not telling the whole truth, and lean on them until they did?

Something that didn't appeal to Peter Shand. The people who needed leaning on always had lawyers, which left who? People like George Benson who would make Shand feel like an unconscionable bully.

Maybe he wasn't cut out to be a detective? Self-doubt, there it was, perching on his shoulder waiting for an ingress. Give up, go home, go back to what you were good at.

He drained his glass and went in search of the gents. Self-doubt followed, pointing out the phone on the wall. *It's a long time since she called.*

He lingered by the phone again on the way back. Vowing alternately to call and then not to call. As usual he made the wrong choice.

Laughter – in the background of her office, and in the timbre of her voice as she answered her name. "Anne Cromwell," she said, her voice bubbling.

"It's me," he said, two quiet words, and suddenly the laughter stopped.

She tried to cover it up, tried to sound upbeat and positive, but he'd heard the pause, the implicit groan, and in that brief second he was thrown – if not into despair, into somewhere very close.

"Oh. I've been meaning to ring," she said. "It's chaos here, as usual."

Words deserted him – all the good words, leaving him with nothing words that filled the silences between his pain.

"Did you go live as planned?"

"Yes, we did."

"Good."

Good. He breathed heavily into the phone – nerves – and quickly covered the mouthpiece with his hand.

"I ... I heard you were on the TV," she said.

"Did you see me?" Panic. Had she seen his debacle of a press conference? Followed by hope. Was she concerned for him?

"No, I read about it in the papers."

"Ah."

"You must be very busy."

"Yes. Very busy." His voice clicked with the dryness of his throat.

A long silence and then, "Well, I've got to go now. Another meeting. I'll ring you er ... tomorrow. Bye."

"Bye," he said to the dial tone.

~

Shand slouched into his office and slumped into a chair. There was a message on his desk from Marcus.

Can't find Marsh. He might be in Birmingham, or Bristol, or possibly London. No one's sure. They say he travels around a lot and rarely calls in.

Shand rang Marcus.

"Doesn't he keep an office diary?"

"Apparently not, sir. I received the impression he doesn't like to commit much to paper."

Shand gave him Julia Draycott's number.

"See if she knows where he is. But be polite, she's the Chief Constable's daughter."

He stared at the files on his desk, trying to summon the energy to open one of them, or do something constructive, but all he could think about was Anne and that stupid phone call. Why couldn't he say what he felt? Why did he morph into that inarticulate wimp? Why? Why? Why?

And several more whys. All unanswered. He'd script the next conversation. Practice his delivery, add some jokes, show her what a good time he was having, and what a great person he was to be around.

And every word would be punctuated by nervous clicks. He'd come across as manic and strange. Worse than the press conference, he'd be a wild-eyed, drug-crazed, heavy-breathing, husband-from-hell, cackling jokes down the phone line.

He slumped even farther back in his chair, closed his eyes and let his head loll over the back.

Not the most flattering position to be seen in by your boss but, given the day it had been, the inevitable one.

"Shand?" said Wiggins. "Are you all right?"

Shand opened one eye. The ceiling blinked back.

"Postprandial breathing exercise, sir," said Shand, not moving an inch. "Helps clear the mind after a meal."

"More American practices, eh, Shand?"

"Samoan," said Shand, slowly straightening his head and wondering why his imagination could reach such heights only to desert him whenever Anne was on the other end of the line.

The purpose of the Chief Superintendent's flying visit from Sherminster HQ soon became clear. He'd decided to take charge of the afternoon press conference – thank God – and wanted Shand to brief him.

"Can I say an arrest is imminent?" he asked.

Shand wanted to say, yes. In his eyes, an arrest had been imminent since the first second he'd viewed the body. That vital clue always just an hour away, waiting to be discovered.

But, instead, he took the Chief Super through the case and its progress. It wasn't what Wiggins wanted to hear. Nothing juicy to tell the press. No asylum seekers or Midnight Callers.

"You can say we have an important lead concerning the murder weapon," suggested Shand. "And that we've matched a set of fingerprints, but can't reveal any more for obvious reasons."

Wiggins liked that. Mysterious yet professional. He jotted down the lines on a notepad and left.

Shand shook off what was left of his earlier despondency, and threw himself back into his work. He'd keep busy, and not give himself time to think of anything else.

Out came Annabel's memory stick. There were still several folders he hadn't looked at. One of them was entitled 'Parish Council' and contained dozens of files. Shand went through them all – the manifestos, the plans, the letters. Annabel meant to win, that was obvious, and by the tone and content of the letters, she didn't care how. Shand was amazed, and wondered if the letters were libellous. She accused her fellow candidates of being incompetent and self-seeking, detailing instances where they'd ruled in favour of their friends, and generally casting dirt liberally around the community.

Most of the criticism was aimed at Ursula Montacute. There was even a file on her, listing her failings which, according to Annabel, were legion. Mrs. Montacute ignored complaints against her friends, consistently blocked planning permission for houses, plotted to keep outsiders off the council, and ran an illegal fox hunt.

It looked like Annabel had analysed every parish council decision for the past fifteen years looking for dirt. And failed to find it, decided Shand nearly thirty minutes later. Everything was anecdotal or circumstantial – a catalogue of innuendo and conjecture. Mud to be thrown with the hope that enough would stick, or deter Ursula from standing.

Then he found something he wasn't expecting. A folder entitled '6P,' and inside it a scanned image of a bank statement.

Ursula's bank statement.

CHAPTER TWENTY-EIGHT

It was dated a year ago. The Montacute's current account. All their payments and receipts for June last year. How had Annabel got hold of that?

Then Shand noticed the heading - Provincial Bank, Sturton - and made the link. George. His bank, his branch. Had Annabel somehow persuaded him to give her details of the Montacute's finances?

His mind joined up other dots. Was this the hold that the Marchants had over George? He'd been providing them with personal information about his customers? Something he wanted to stop, so they arranged for Helena to be abducted?

No, too much of a leap, there'd have to be more to it than just providing bank details. Maybe that was how it started? A few bank statements, a few favours in return - money maybe - then came the real requests, dragging George deeper and deeper into their schemes until he threatened to pull out.

Shand had just convinced himself when he clicked on the next file. And found a scanned image of the Montacute's Building Society account.

He stared at the screen. How could George have obtained that?

And what was Annabel's interest? Both statements were from June last year, was there some payment that Annabel was trying to track down to incriminate the Brigadess?

Several seconds passed. Dots dissolved and joined up again. Could George have been handling the Montacute's investments? He was their bank manager after all.

He checked other scanned images. Copies of unit trust holdings, farm accounts, estate valuations. Annabel had all the Montacute's financial details.

Another line of dots flared in Shand's head. What was Gabriel's job in the City? Market analyst? He scrolled through other files, skipping through letters until he found it. A copy of a letter from Gabriel to Ursula and Sandy. It was dated July last year and entitled, 'Investment Portfolio.' Shand raced through it. Gabriel thanked them for the information they had provided and suggested a re-balancing of their finances. A list of proposed acquisitions and disposals followed.

Gabriel Marchant had been the Montacute's financial adviser.

Shand tried to square that with the antipathy between the two families. Had something happened since last July?

Shand checked the remaining files, stopping at a letter dated barely a month ago. It was from Annabel to an estate agent, asking if they'd approach the Montacutes on her behalf, and make an offer for Sixpenny Barton, the Montacute's estate. 'The buyer's name must remain a secret,' it said. 'She mustn't know it's me.'

He delved deeper. More files. A valuation of Sixpenny Barton, a Land Registry map of the estate, and plans for its development. Annabel was looking to finance the purchase of the estate by selling off a parcel of land for development. Marsh's name wasn't mentioned, but Shand could see it pencilled in between the lines. Was that the motivating force behind the election campaign and the Gang of Four? A drive to remove dissenters from the Parish Council and force through planning permission?

~

He found Ursula Montacute by the stables, carrying a saddle into the tack room.

"To what do we owe this pleasure, chief inspector?" said the Brigadess, pausing by the door.

"I've been looking through Annabel Marchant's computer files."

"Ah," said the Brigadess, "and you've found her file on me."

Shand was surprised. "You knew about it?"

"I think everyone did. Annabel dropped enough hints.

Sorry to be rude, but this saddle weighs a ton, and I've got to put it away." She turned and heaved the saddle up onto a support protruding from the far wall.

Shand stayed in the doorway. "Did you know what the file contained?"

"All manner of nonsense I should imagine." She turned and smiled. "Really, chief inspector, you don't have to stand in the doorway. Sandy's moved the bodies."

"Bodies?" said Shand.

"The brace of ramblers? Sandy's little joke? You should pay more attention, chief inspector. A man in your profession."

Shand was not in the mood for jokes. "Did you know that Annabel had your financial details on her computer?"

Ursula stepped into the patch of sunlight by the tack room door. Her face set. "Gabriel gave them to her, I suppose? Or she took them." She shook her head. "I wouldn't put anything past that woman."

"Gabriel Marchant was your financial adviser then?"

"'Was' being the operative word, chief inspector. And another motive for you to add to my list. Except that it would have been Gabriel I'd've staked out in the circle, not Annabel. Sandy wanted to horsewhip the horrid, little man. I'm sorry I stopped him."

"He lost you money?" asked Shand.

"Oh, no, chief inspector," said Ursula sarcastically. "Men like Gabriel never *lose* other people's money. It's always unforeseen market forces."

"Did you lose a lot?"

"Oh, yes," said the Brigadess. "It was our own fault really. We bought into Gabriel's pretty charts and projections. More fool us, but he seemed to know what he was doing. And we, rather stupidly, expected him to warn us if there was ever a problem."

"Which he didn't."

"No, he did not. The markets tumbled and we thought, 'Well, it can't be that bad, or Gabriel would have said something. Maybe it's better to hold on and wait for the markets to rally.' But they didn't rally, and suddenly Gabriel was unavailable. Always in meetings, or out of the country. And when we did contact him, he just shrugged and said, 'we were lucky it hadn't been worse.'"

"I take it he's not your financial adviser any more?"

"You take it correctly, chief inspector. And believe me, If we were going to take our revenge upon that little oik we would have done so then. We don't believe in putting off revenge in this family."

"Did you take revenge?" asked Shand.

The Brigadess smiled. "Chief inspector, how could I possibly answer that?"

Shand persisted. "Off the record, Mrs. Montacute."

The Brigadess considered the request, twirling a strand of hair that had escaped from under her riding hat.

"Off the record," she repeated. "You could always ask Bill Acomb who gave him the idea for the cockerel."

For the first time that afternoon Shand smiled. A smile broadening into a grin. And then a laugh.

"The Athelcott One was your idea?"

The Brigadess laughed. "We prefer to call him 'The Marchant's Bane.'"

Shand had one more question to ask.

"Did you know that Annabel wanted to buy Sixpenny Barton?"

Her smile dissolved. "That was her was it? The couple from Devon looking for a small estate?" Anger flared. She looked away. "I should have known."

"Were you thinking of selling?" asked Shand.

"Of course not," snapped the Brigadess. "Sixpenny Barton has been in the family for generations. I'd go to the workhouse before I ever considered selling."

"What if someone made a very high offer?"

Ursula shook her head. "It wouldn't matter what anyone offered. The estate's not for sale."

~

Shand returned to his office, wondering if Gabriel would deliberately impoverish a client to force them to sell up – if his wife told him to, or if Gabe Marsh showed him how much money they could both make from developing the land?

It had to run into millions. An estate that size in a location like that – an unspoilt valley only three hours from London.

And how far would the Montacute's go to protect it?

Another line of thought. The Brigadess as Midnight Caller. *I'll sell, but on one condition – meet me on the green in five minutes.*

Would that be enough to tempt Annabel from her home?

He thought it might. And then proceeded to join up the remaining dots. He had to place the Brigadess in sight of the circle at eleven o'clock. How? A late night walk with the dogs? It was possible.

But would she have let her friend be buried alive without calling the police? Could she have watched from the cover of the trees, deciding instead to seize the opportunity and murder Annabel? Even if she hadn't seen who was being buried, was she that calculating, willing to do anything to stop Annabel destroying her beloved Sixpenny Barton?

Marcus Ashenden appeared in the doorway clutching a file.

"The girlfriend thinks Gabe's in London, sir. But reckons he'll be back later in the week. He's supposed to be taking her to Newbury on Thursday."

"Is that Marsh's file?" asked Shand.

"No, sir, this came for you earlier. It's that asylum seeker."

For a second, Shand thought his career was about to flash before his eyes. "What about the asylum seeker?" he said, dreading the answer.

Marcus darted forward and thrust the file towards Shand. "The missing asylum seeker, sir. He's still missing. This is the official notification."

Shand took the file. There was a yellow sticker on the front with a handwritten note – *thought you'd be interested*. He wasn't. He glanced at the single page inside, and the photo, and then passed the file back to Marcus.

"You'd better deal with this," he said. "Very low priority."

The rest of the afternoon dragged, waiting for calls that kept his concentration returning to the phone. Taylor in London, Marsh God knows where, auditors at the bank, financial background checks promised any second. He couldn't settle.

When the phone did ring his mood worsened. The audit at the bank was progressing slowly. Nothing suspicious had been found so far, and it would take another two or three days to be sure.

A similar report from HQ. Nothing flagged against any of the names or Gabe Marsh's companies. No bankruptcies, prosecutions, reprimands, or passing mentions in any criminal enquiry. Gabe's companies all filed their returns on time, and appeared to be in profit.

"It'll be another day before I have everything you wanted," said the constable. "Some of the banks take their time, but I should have all the bank account information by tomorrow afternoon."

More waiting. Another day, another drop in the statistical probability of success.

He tried Marsh's phone again. Nothing. Rang round his various offices. Sorry, try again tomorrow.

Shand slumped back in his chair. The afternoon had gone downhill since that stupid tongue-tied phone call to Anne. And all these Gabriels! He was surrounded by them. A constant reminder of the rocky state of his marriage. Maybe he should call her? Have it our with her? End the doubt. Are you having an affair?

But what if she said, yes?

Was it better to live in life-sapping doubt or gut-wrenching certainty?

He stared at the phone. To call or not to call? Shand's inner procrastinator counselled delay. *Call her from the hotel tonight when you're alone and you can both talk.*

Except she never picked up when he called in the evenings.

He had to do it now or he'd never do it all.

His hand was hovering over the phone when it rang. He snatched his hand away. Then slowly leaned forward, his heart thumping, and picked up.

"I've got some interesting news about Gabriel," said Taylor.

"What?"

"I've just checked the hotel's CCTV camera and it shows him arriving at the hotel five minutes before midnight. He's not the midnight caller."

"Oh," said Shand, thinking he'd have classified that as depressing news rather than interesting.

"There's more," said Taylor. "There was a woman with

him. Late thirties, short dark hair, called herself Mrs. Marchant."

Shand froze. Anne was in her late thirties. And she had short, dark hair.

CHAPTER TWENTY-NINE

For the second time in two days Shand entered the marital twilight zone. All colour, and hope, and sound drained from his world leaving a silent, black and white wasteland. Despair. Shock. And an inevitability that had been building since the moment he left London. His marriage was over. Anne had moved on...

"Sir?" Taylor was still talking. "Are you still there?"

"Just," said Shand, staring bleakly into the distance.

"Anyway, according to the receptionist, this Mrs. Marchant has been a regular visitor to the hotel over the past three months. Always with Gabriel Marchant. I've got a picture of her from the CCTV and I'm off to interview Sabine Delacroix."

"Sabine Delacroix?"

"The woman who was at the restaurant with Gabriel. The one he made all the phone calls to."

Shand closed his eyes. What was the matter with him? Of course the woman couldn't be Anne. He'd have recognised her number in Marchant's phone logs.

"Right," said Shand. "Good work, Bob. Uh, did they make any calls from their room?"

"No. I checked."

"Right." Shand paused while he racked his still traumatised brain for something else to say. "Ask her if Annabel knew about her and Gabriel. Oh, and see if she knows anything about Marsh, George Benson or Gulliver's."

He could see the semblance of a motive for Annabel's murder forming out of the fog. A mistress pressing Gabriel for something more than a fling, and a wife who would have taken half of everything he had.

And from what Shand had seen of Gabriel, he didn't come across as the sharing type.

"I'm on my way,' said Taylor.

Another thought.

"Oh, and see if Gabriel mentioned anything about buying Sixpenny Barton from the Montacutes."

A re-energised Shand phoned Annabel's estate agent next.

"You're lucky," a female voice answered. "I was just leaving."

He introduced himself and swiftly moved on to the subject of Sixpenny Barton.

"How did the Montacutes react to the enquiry?"

"Not very well. They didn't reply to my letter, so I rang and was told in no uncertain terms that the estate was not for sale."

"How did Annabel react to the news?"

"She was disappointed but ... I think she saw it as the opening salvo in a long campaign. She was a very determined woman. She asked me to conduct an informal valuation of the estate for her without the Montacutes knowing."

"Did you?"

"I was going to do so this week, but then..."

She let the sentence hang. Annabel had died and Sixpenny Barton had been saved.

"Did she mention any plans to develop Sixpenny Barton?" asked Shand.

"Yes, she asked about the possibility of planning permission and how she should go about it.'

"Would she have got planning permission?"

There was a long pause. "I think it would depend upon how she went about it. If she kept the development small – a dozen or so executive homes – and had local support, I think it would have sailed through."

"What if the Parish Council opposed it."

"It would have made things difficult, but not impossible. There's a shortage of building land in the county and Sixpenny Barton's part of the village envelope."

~

Shand sat with his chin in his hands, staring into space. He couldn't see how Annabel could ever hope to buy Sixpenny Barton. The Montacutes would never sell. Even if they were desperate for money, all they had to do was sell off a portion of the estate to a developer.

Or did Annabel think the idea of developing Sixpenny Barton would never occur to the Montacutes?

He supposed it possible. From what he'd read of her correspondence she had a low opinion of the villagers' intellect.

Or maybe she had another plan?

An hour later he'd had enough. He'd gone over and over every aspect of the case until all the facts had begun to coalesce into one incomprehensible mass. And Anne was starting to intrude on his thoughts again. He'd run out of Gabriels for her to run off with, now he was lining her up as Annabel's mystery lover.

He needed to get out. The room, the station. He needed somewhere to unwind and forget. Somewhere noisy and brash.

He found what he was looking for in Sturton High Street. Maybe not as loud and brash as he'd been planning, but the smell of food drew him in. The *Taj Mahal:* red flock wallpaper and piped Indian music. Strangely, it reminded him of home, a little piece of essential urban living transported into the wilds of the countryside.

And it sold cider, a brand he'd never heard of - Wessex Imperial Number Seven - he'd have to try it.

He ordered a half-pint while he read through the menu. Sipped it carefully - an interesting taste - slightly sparkling, dry, very clean, almost an apple wine taste without the alcoholic burn at the back of the throat.

He ordered another half with the meal. A Chicken Jalfreezi with a spicy Keema Nan, Onion Bhaji and Bombay Aloo. And another when he realised how hot the Jalfreezi was and needed something chilled to cool his throat. And then another because, after all, they were only halves and he was used to drinking three pints of lager with his curries. And then another...

The first intimation that three pints of Wessex Imperial Number Seven might be slightly stronger than three pints of watered down London lager came when the night air hit him outside the restaurant. Suddenly he felt light-headed and his legs turned to rubber. Either that or Sturton High Street had developed an unusual camber.

He carved an extravagant path to the hotel, concentrating hard on the art of walking and avoiding obstacles. He collected his keys from a swaying receptionist and mounted the stairs, clutching at the rail with both hands. The door was more of a problem. For some inexplicable reason someone had magnetised both key and lock, giving them an identical polarity that repelled on contact, forcing his hand to slip left or right, but never into the hole he was aiming for.

Sleep came unexpectedly swiftly that night, a deep sleep rich in dreams and a strange feeling that sometime during the night he'd got up to use the phone.

And in the morning he awoke to an unexpected call.

CHAPTER THIRTY

"He's escaped, sir."

Taylor's voice broke into Shand's befuddled consciousness.

"Who?" he asked. "Marsh?"

"No, the Athelcott One. Someone broke him out of the pound last night."

Shand was halfway to Athelcott before he considered the reason for jumping out of bed and missing breakfast for the second day running. Was he really rushing to Athelcott to arrest a chicken?

Taylor's words came back to him.

"Gabriel Marchant's been on the phone three times. The cock's been crowing since six thirty."

Was Bill Acomb crazy? If he wanted his chicken back that badly, why advertise his whereabouts to the entire village? Gabriel was bound to complain. The chicken would be impounded, and Bill Acomb would be fined. All for what – a few hours fun at Gabriel's expense.

Still, it was an ill wind...

And as Shand's head began to clear, he could think of a much better reason to visit Athelcott.

~

Bob Taylor was waiting in Bill Acomb's yard. Shand called him over. There were a few questions he had to ask first.

"Was the woman at the hotel Sabine Delacroix?"

"Oh, yes. She's been seeing Gabriel for about three months, nothing serious. Annabel didn't know, but according to Gabriel she never loved him anyway."

"Gabriel told her that, did he?"

"Probably just after telling her his wife didn't understand him."

A cockerel crowed loudly – very loudly – the sound appearing to emanate from an outbuilding close to the Marchant fence line.

"Now that," said Taylor, "is a cock with a fine pair of lungs."

An unnatural pair of lungs, thought Shand. The sound was piercing.

"What about Marsh?" he asked. "Did Gabriel ever talk about him?"

"Never talked about anyone from the village, apparently. Annabel included."

Too close to home, thought Shand, his mind already turning to the coming interview.

"Come on," he said. "I want a word with Gabriel first."

"What about the cock?"

"The cock hasn't got a lawyer on his way over."

~

Gabriel Marchant threw the door open at the first knock. "I can still hear that damned creature. Why haven't you stopped it?"

"It's being attended to," said Shand angrily. "I've had enough lip from Bill Acomb this week. Making us look like fools by breaking out his chicken is the final straw. I want you to make a formal complaint, Mr. Marchant. It'll strengthen our case. I want him done for contempt this time."

Gabriel Marchant relaxed and actually smiled.

"Can we come in, Mr. Marchant? It won't take long."

"Yes, of course."

Shand followed Gabriel through to the living room. Still no sign of the lawyer. He wondered how much time he had. And how long he could keep up the pretence.

"I take it Miss Delacroix phoned you about last night?" he asked, the moment everyone was seated.

Gabriel jumped up, his earlier amiability shattered. Shand put his hand out.

"It's okay, Mr. Marchant, we're not here about that. We know you were in London now. Miss Delacroix's given you a cast iron alibi."

Gabriel sat down slowly, suspicion still etched in his face.

"Oh, no!" said Shand, annoyed and going through the motions of searching his pockets. "I've left the complaint form in the car. Nip out and get it, Bob."

Taylor's eyes flickered in surprise before he replied. "The white form?"

"Of course the white form," said Shand impatiently. "Now, come on, get off your backside and fetch it."

Shand waited for Taylor to leave before turning to Gabriel and raising his eyebrows.

"I don't know how you put up with these bolshy yokels. I really don't. I've only been here a week and already I can't wait to get back to London. I suppose you'll be selling up now and looking for a place closer to civilisation?"

"I hadn't really thought about it."

"I would," said Shand. "There are people in this village trying to fit you up. Did you know that?"

Marchant looked puzzled.

"And not just the locals. Some of your so-called friends as well."

"What are you talking about?"

Shand glanced left and right, beginning to enjoy his new conspiratorial role.

"I shouldn't be telling you this but..." He leaned closer and lowered his voice. "A person who you know very well fed us this story about you and the Provincial Bank in Sturton."

"What? Who?"

Shand tapped the side of his nose. If he'd had a moustache he'd probably have twirled it.

"I'd lose my job if I told you. But they can't stop me warning you, and I expect you know already know who I'm referring to anyway, don't you?

"Gabe?"

Shand smiled. "Ironic isn't it? Gabe Marsh goes missing, no one can find him, and yet my superiors say 'shake up the husband.'" He shook his head. "No imagination. The wife's dead, therefore the husband must have done it."

"Gabe's gone missing?"

"Like a shadow in the night. Gone. No sign of him or his passport. I don't suppose he contacted you at all?"

"No."

Gabriel was definitely thinking. Hard. His eyes had lost their focus and there was a distraction in his voice.

"Not since he came round to see how you were, I suppose?" said Shand.

"What?" said Gabriel, miles away.

"I was just saying the last time you saw Marsh was probably when he came round to see how you were. He did come round, didn't he?"

"No, he phoned."

"Oh." Shand feigned surprise. "I thought he would have called in person. Living over the road and being an old friend."

Shand wondered how much longer he had to push. Someone as paranoid as Gabriel should have been retaliating by now – listing all Marsh's possible whereabouts and countering with accusations of his own.

"No, he didn't," said Gabriel, suddenly snapping back. "What did he tell you about me and the bank?"

"Sorry," said Shand. "I really would lose my job if I told you."

Shand watched him, willing him to snap, pick up the phone and have it out with Marsh now.

"He's probably in Spain," said Gabriel quietly.

"That new development of his? The one in the Sierras?"

"That's the one. He was there last month. He intimated to me then it would make the perfect hideaway."

"He did, did he?" Shand tried another tack. "Some friend that Gabe Marsh. Did you know he gave us the name of that solicitor, you know the one that Annabel consulted?"

Gabriel looked blank. Shand waited a little longer.

"What solicitor?" asked Gabriel.

"You know, the one she consulted recently?"

Still blank, but Shand pressed on. "About the development at Sixpenny Barton?"

"Annabel consulted a solicitor about that?"

"I think she was worried about planning permission and the appeals process. So, Gabe said. They were working very closely together on the project. Whose idea was that by the way? To buy Sixpenny Barton and develop the land?"

"Annabel's. She always loved that house. And the location."

"Bit of a long shot though. How on earth were you going to get the Brigadess to sell?"

"Money," said Gabriel. "We were going to make them an offer they couldn't refuse."

Shand resisted the sudden image of a horse's head under the blanket and continued. "The Brigadess told me she'd never sell at any price."

"Everyone has a price, chief inspector."

Shand wasn't so sure. He checked his watch. Any second a lawyer or Taylor could burst in. Time to play his last card.

"You know, there's still something that I can't see," he said.

"What's that?"

"How you and Annabel could be planning such a huge venture in the middle of a divorce?"

Gabriel exploded. Shand immediately raised both hands and apologised.

"I'm sorry, Mr. Marchant, but I'm only repeating what I was told. Annabel had found out about Sabine and was–"

"Annabel never knew about Sabine!" Gabriel had risen, red-faced, to his feet.

Shand fired his final volley. "Gabe did though. And he and Annabel had become very close."

Shand watched. Surely he'd done enough to poison Gabriel's mind against Marsh? If the two men were working together, now was the time for Gabriel to crack and start incriminating his partner.

He didn't. He turned on Shand. "Get out!" he shouted, stabbing a finger at the door. "Get out of my house!"

Shand left.

~

"Sorry about that, Bob. I had to do it to get Gabriel to open up."

"Did it work?"

"Up to a point." There was something about Gabriel Marchant that defied analysis. From the outset he'd behaved counter to Shand's expectations. He'd never grieved. He'd been angry, defensive, paranoid. And yet given the opportunity to rail against Gabe Marsh, he'd spurned it. Why?

He discussed it briefly with Taylor before giving up. "Come

on, Bob. Time to arrest the chicken."

The chicken house was a ramshackle construction of corrugated iron and wood that looked like it had been built from driftwood on a dark night. Bizarrely, the building did not look out of place. A similar motif ran through the entire yard.

A white cockerel perched in the doorway at the top of a rickety ramp. It stood up and flapped its wings as the two men approached.

"Is that it?" asked Shand.

Taylor shrugged his shoulders. "It's the right sex."

The animal craned its neck and crowed. A reedy, pale imitation of the crow they'd heard earlier.

"'Ere, what you doin' with my chickens?"

Bill Acomb hurried across the yard towards them, wiping what looked like the remains of his breakfast from his face.

"Pretty expensive joke don't you think?" shouted Shand, pointing at the cockerel. "What on earth did you think you'd achieve?"

Bill Acomb's weather-beaten face cracked into a sly smile. "I've done nothin' illegal."

"What do you call breaking into a police pound?" asked Shand.

The farmer scratched his chin. He appeared to be enjoying himself. "I reckon I'd call that ... breakin' and enterin'. Next question."

Shand shook his head in disbelief, then stabbed a finger in the direction of the white cockerel. "Is that the Athelcott One?"

Bill Acomb peered around Shand's shoulder and then smiled. "No, that ain't 'im."

"Is he in the shed?" asked Taylor.

"I 'as no idea where 'e is. I ain't seen 'im since your lot took 'im away."

A cockerel crowed – unnaturally loud – the call emanating from inside the chicken shed.

"You mind explaining what that was?" said Shand becoming impatient.

"Now that *was* the Athelcott One. You can tell by the purity of the–"

"Open the shed," snapped Shand.

"You won't find 'im in there, inspector."

Acomb was still smiling – which Shand thought strange for a man on the verge of losing both his prize chicken and several hundred pounds in fines.

"Why not?" asked Shand, feeling like a straight man feeding lines to a bucolic comic.

The farmer's smile expanded to show a set of imperfect and slightly blackened teeth. "It's a recording, that's all. I told you we'd get our revenge on Mr. Fancy Marchant, didn't I?"

His smile matured into a throaty laugh, eventually ending in a series of hacking coughs.

"Turn it off," said Shand. "Now!"

Acomb unlatched a door at the back of the shed and retrieved a large portable radio cassette player. Both Shand and Taylor leaned in to check the rest of the shed was empty.

"The cassette, please," said Shand, holding his hand out.

"It's the only one I got. I needs it to train up the other cock. Show 'im 'ow it's done."

"Don't push it," said Taylor, pulling the cassette recorder from the farmer's grasp and removing the cassette. "You can have this back when you tell us what you've done with the Athelcott One."

"I don't know nothin'. I was as surprised as you lot when I 'eard about it on the radio."

Shand looked closer at the white cockerel. Did they have a description of the Athelcott One? And was this really what he should he be doing in the middle of a murder enquiry?

"Mr. Acomb," he said. "Prove to me that that's not the Athelcott One or we're taking him with us."

"You can't do that!"

"He can," said Taylor, hooking a thumb at Shand. "Look at him. He's a townie like Gabriel Marchant. Do you think he cares if he gets the wrong chicken?"

Shand blinked, somewhat taken aback by the vehemence of Taylor's outburst.

Acomb wrestled with a pocket somewhere deep beneath his overalls. "Look!" he said, his hand suddenly flying out and thrusting a creased photograph in Shand's face. "That's the Athelcott One. See!"

Shand did. The chicken in the picture was black with

flecks of red and gold around the neck. And huge muscular legs.

Bill Acomb's smile returned. "Different breeds. That white one's a Sussex, whereas old Athelcott, 'e's an Italian Singing Chicken."

"Italian Singing Chicken," repeated Taylor sceptically.

"It's a rare breed. Specially bred for its purity of note, length and loudness."

"Not to mention it pisses off the neighbours."

"Only the townies," winked Bill.

Shand felt that somewhere between the car and the yard he'd entered an alternate ruralverse. A feeling confirmed when the white cockerel crowed.

"See," said Bill. "You can tell 'e's English by 'is accent."

~

"Sorry about that back there," said Taylor as they walked across the yard. "I thought I'd get more out of him if I labelled you a townie."

Touché, thought Shand, noticing a movement out of the corner of his eye. He turned. Someone had just opened the Acomb's front door.

"It's Mark Acomb," said Taylor. "Hey, Mark! I've been looking for you."

The figure slipped back inside and slammed the door.

"I'll go round the back," shouted Taylor, already running. Shand sprinted for the front door. Why was the boy running?

Shand flung the front door open and followed inside. Everything was dark and cluttered. Music blared from a radio, the smell of fried food everywhere. He followed the sound of running footsteps, snaking past the obstacle course of a hallway into the kitchen. The back door banged against its hinges. And Mark Acomb ran straight into the waiting arms of Bob Taylor.

"Don't be stupid, Mark!" shouted Taylor to the struggling youth who quickly gave up.

"'ere what you doin' to my boy?" shouted his father.

"Your boy was trying to run away."

"Wasn't!" said Mark, dusting himself off. "Just thought you were someone else, that's all."

"A likely story," said Taylor. "You've been avoiding me all

week. Why? Where were you Friday night?”

“Can’t remember.” The boy was looking everywhere but at Taylor.

“Perhaps a trip to the station will refresh your memory,” said the sergeant.

“You can’t arrest ’im for nothin’,” said his father.

“He can,” said Taylor, hooking a thumb towards Shand who was beginning to dislike his unasked for role as urban bad cop. “Give him an excuse and he’ll have you locked up like that,” continued Taylor, snapping his fingers.

Shand tried to look intimidating and felt the desire to pretend to chew gum. A bizarre image culled from childhood of what a really tough kid should look like.

“I was in Sturton,” said Mark. “Drinking.”

“Until when?”

“Closing time, a bit after.”

“And then what?”

“I come home.”

Shand made the calculations. Closing time on a Friday night would be eleven. Add on fifteen minutes drinking up time and another fifteen to say goodbye to his mates and find his car, couple that with a twenty-five minute drive home and you get Mark Acomb passing the village green very close to midnight on Friday night.

“How’d you get home?” asked Taylor.

“In the van.”

“By yourself?”

“Yeah.”

“What time did you get home?”

Mark Acomb shrugged. “Dunno.”

“Did you see Annabel Marchant?”

“I didn’t see anyone. The place was dead as it always is.”

“You saw no one walking on the green? Or by the phone box?”

“I told you. I didn’t see them.”

“Them?” asked Shand. “Why did you say ‘them’?”

The boy shrugged. “No reason. Anyway what you hassling me for? You should be up at the circle looking for the missing boy.”

“What missing boy?”

“The one in the paper. Davy Perkins. He’s been missing a

year now. And that's where he was last seen. Right on the spot Annabel was found."

CHAPTER THIRTY-ONE

It was plastered over the first three pages of the Echo. *Stone Circle Claims Second Victim*. An exclusive by Kevin Tresco. Intrepid Echo reporter uncovers secret history of killer stones.

Shand could barely continue reading. There was even a picture of a sneering Kevin Tresco above his by-line. And such prose. *Murder village rocked by new revelation. Terrified villagers flee death stones. Satanic serial killer murders by moonlight.*

Beneath the rhetoric, it was worse. Shand could see the germ of a real story. If any of it was true.

"Did you know this Davy Perkins?" he asked Mark Acomb.

"Yeah, it's like it says there. He went missing about a year back. No one ever knew why."

This was worse than worse. A potential lead he'd overlooked. A potential lead found by Kevin bloody Tresco.

He read on, avoiding as many adjectives as he could. A seventeen year-old boy, Davy Perkins, had gone missing on September 16th the previous year. He'd been last seen having an argument at the stone circle with two men. After that - nothing. His parents had filed a missing person report, but the police had found nothing. The boy had vanished. Gone. 'Totally out of character,' said his mother. 'He was always such a nice boy, and he'd never forget my birthday.'

Shand handed the newspaper back to Mark Acomb and strode towards his car.

"Well?" said Taylor, hurrying after him.

"Find another copy of the Echo. Discreetly. And get Marcus to check it out."

He paused by the door to his car and glanced back. It seemed stupid to take two cars everywhere. "Wait up, Bob," he said, jogging back to his sergeant. "I'll come with you."

"What about your car?"

"It's better where it is. I want Gabriel Marchant to see it every time he looks out the window."

The call to Marcus brought more bad news. The financial checks on the two Gabriels had just been faxed through. Both were clean, and both were solvent. Gabriel Marchant especially so. He had a substantial portfolio of investments.

Shand could see another motive sliding the way of the others. The two Gabriels didn't need money – so why extort it?

Shand answered his own question – greed and stupidity – but with a diminishing conviction. Maybe they were both innocent? Maybe there was no plan to extort money from George's bank, and Annabel had been killed by someone else?

He refused to believe it. Something was going on at George's bank. It was the only theory that made sense. And there was always money laundering. Maybe that was the source of the two Gabriels' wealth? They'd pressured George into helping them, he'd got cold feet and needed to be taught a lesson.

But...

There was still the question of Annabel and the Midnight Caller. And where was the evidence against Marsh and Marchant? Something he could go to court with, something other than supposition and gut feeling.

Which brought him back to the missing boy and the horrendous possibility that Kevin Tresco had found an important lead that Shand hadn't even bothered to look for.

~

They found a newsagents in the next village. Shand stayed in the car, praying that Kevin Tresco wouldn't suddenly appear with a camera team in tow, while Taylor went inside to buy the paper.

For once, Fortune left the brave to their own devices and favoured the man sliding down the front seat of his car.

It would be but a brief accommodation.

Shand read the paper again and culled the facts from the purple chaff. The parents. He had to interview the parents.

Reporters were already gathered outside the Perkins

family home, a brick-built Victorian mid-terrace. He ignored the bevy of questions thrown at him and led Taylor through the gate and up the short garden path.

There was no answer to his first knock, so he tried again. Louder.

"Go away!" shouted a woman from inside. "I've already told you. I've got nothing to say."

"It's the police," said Shand. "We'd like a word."

The door opened a crack, through which Mrs. Perkins squinted suspiciously at the two warrant cards.

"About bloody time," she said, unlatching the chain. "You should've been here a year ago."

They were shown through to the kitchen and a table covered in flour and mixing bowls. "Sit yourselves down and keep your hands off the table. I'm in the middle of baking."

The two policemen sat down, Shand drawing his chair as far away from the table as he could.

"I'd like to go through the circumstances surrounding your son's disappearance, if that's okay, Mrs. Perkins," said Shand.

"Where were you a year ago? That's what I'd like to know," said the woman.

"I was in London," said Shand. "Now, it says here that your son left home on the evening of September 16th and you never saw him again. Is that correct?"

"Yes," she said, her voice softening. "He got up from that table there – we'd just had tea – grabbed his coat and left."

She turned away, her voice breaking, and rubbed her eyes.

Shand gave her a few seconds. "Did he say where he was going?"

She sniffed back the tears. "'Out,' that's all he said. You know what kids are like."

Shand didn't. But he could imagine.

"Did he have much money with him?"

"I don't think so. He didn't have a bank account or anything like that. Just a few pounds he got from his gardening jobs."

"It says here that he worked for Annabel Marchant."

"Yes, three days a week." Her voice hardened. "Until she sacked him."

"Did he say why she sacked him?"

"No, he left before he could tell me. I only found out through Ruthie. She works for the Marchants – cleaning and such."

"Did Ruthie say why he'd been sacked?"

"She thought it was something to do with the girl – Pippa. From stuff she overheard. Reckoned the Marchants thought he was getting too friendly, so they sacked him and shipped the girl off to some expensive boarding school."

"Would Davy have tried to follow her?"

She shook her head. "I thought he might have. I even wrote to Pippa. I got Ruthie to get me her address. But she hadn't seen or heard from him. Nice letter."

She stared vacantly into space.

"It says here that Davy was sacked the day before he left. Is that right?"

She shrugged. "You'd have to ask Gabriel Marchant, but it sounds about right."

"Did he have other gardening jobs?" asked Taylor.

"Oh, yes. He mowed most of the incomer's lawns. And some of the holiday cottages. He wasn't short of work. Not over the summer."

"Not much gardening work over the winter though," said Taylor.

"No. That's why we didn't contact the police straight away. He'd been talking about going to London to look for work. We thought he might have just upped on the spur of the moment and gone to stay with his brother."

"His brother?" asked Shand.

"Jason. He's got a bed-sit up there. Davy was talking about staying with him for a few days until he got himself sorted out. He's the first person I rang. But you know those bed-sits – one pay phone at the bottom of the stairs and twenty flats sharing. And most of them don't understand English. It wasn't easy getting hold of him."

"I can imagine," said Shand. "So Jason hadn't heard from Davy?"

"No, and then my birthday came around – November 4th – Davy never misses my birthday. Always a card. But not last year. Or a Christmas card. Which is not like him." Her voice started to crack again. "Something must have happened."

Shand looked down at his notes and waited for her to compose herself.

"Did Davy have any friends that he confided in?"

"Not many. He was a quiet boy. I asked around. No one knew anything."

"What about Lee Molland? It says here that he saw Davy arguing with two men on the evening of the 16th – *after* Davy left here. Did he tell you that?"

Her face hardened. "No, he didn't. I wish he had. It might have made your lot take a bit more notice."

"Can we have a look at his room?" asked Shand.

"Yes, I've kept it exactly the same as it was."

The room may have not been a shrine, but it was close – a space, frozen in time, awaiting the prodigal's return. Though probably a good deal tidier than it had been in real life. Shand couldn't imagine a seventeen year-old boy with such neatly stacked possessions.

"Do you think this missing boy has anything to do with the case?" asked Taylor as soon as Mrs. Perkins had left the room.

"It's an avenue we can't be seen to ignore."

A sentiment reinforced by two phone calls in three minutes. The first from the Press Office, the second from Chief Superintendent Wiggins. Both began, 'About this missing boy...'

Apparently, the other papers had picked up the story and were catching up fast. Shand oozed a practised confidence – everything was in hand, he was at the boy's house now. If there was a link, he'd find it. A politician couldn't have projected a rosier picture.

Back in the real world, Shand and Taylor picked through the missing boy's life. The CDs, the books, the clothes, the magazines and posters. And found nothing. No hidden notes, no job application forms, no informative letters. Whatever caused the boy's disappearance, its answer was not there.

They thanked Mrs. Perkins and left.

~

Lee Molland was not at home. "He's out somewhere," said his mother with as much interest as if Shand had enquired about a stranger. His follow-up question of, "When will he be back?" was met with a shrug and a swiftly closing door.

"Drive," said Shand to his sergeant. "Circle the village. He won't be far."

They found him by the stone circle, talking to a group of journalists. He seemed to be enjoying himself. Something that Shand was determined to stop.

"Do you want to join us, chief inspector?" said Lee as Shand strode towards him. "I'm giving a guided re-enactment of what happened here a year ago."

Shand smiled for the journalists before turning, grasping Lee by the upper arm and pulling him close. "Do you want me to tell them about the time you were arrested wearing women's clothing?" whispered Shand into the boy's ear.

"I was never!" said Lee, trying to pull away.

"You think they care?" hissed Shand, nodding towards the journalists. "All they want is a story."

Lee stopped struggling. "What do you want?" he said sullenly.

"A private tour, Mr. Molland. You're going to walk me through this story of yours. No embellishments ... and no audience."

He turned to Taylor. "Tell our friends over there there's been an unexpected intermission. Young Lee here needs a ten-minute break. Don't you, Lee?"

Lee mumbled a grudging acceptance and led the two policemen back to the mouth of the chalk track.

"I was here," said Lee. "Walking down the lane towards the village."

"Where had you come from?" asked Shand, looking up the lane towards open fields and woods.

"There's a pub at Nethercombe."

"That's a fair walk," said Taylor. "Must be close on three miles."

"I like walking. Besides you're not supposed to drink and drive, are you?" he added with a smirk.

"How old are you, Lee? Seventeen?" asked Taylor.

"Nineteen. You can check. Which means I was eighteen last year and legal."

"How much had you had to drink that night?" asked Shand.

"A couple of pints. I was perfectly sober. You can't walk three miles drunk, can you?"

"So what time did you reach here?"

Lee shrugged. "Late. I'd say about eleven, eleven thirty."

"And you say the moon was full?"

"A proper hunter's moon. You can check that too."

There was something of Kevin Tresco in the way the boy smirked. The same twisted smile, the same lank hair, the same smug confidence. Shand wondered if they were related. Or worse, that there was some recessive gene at large populating Wessex with hundreds of Kevin Tresco smirk-alikes.

"So what did you see?" asked Shand.

"Two men, like I told the papers. They were arguing with Davy inside the stone circle."

"You sure it was Davy?" asked Taylor.

"Positive."

Shand looked back towards the stone circle. What was it? About a hundred and fifty yards away?

"How could you be sure?" he asked.

"I recognised his voice. It was a still night. Sound travelled."

"What about the two men? Did their voices travel?"

"Of course. They were shouting. That's how I recognised their accents. They were both Londoners."

Shand glanced down at his notes. "That's not in the paper, Lee. There's nothing about the men coming from London."

"Isn't there?" He looked surprised. "There should be. I'm sure I told him."

Shand looked at the boy closely, trying to gauge whether he was lying. Without the smirk, the boy looked quite plausible.

"So what were they arguing about, Lee?" asked Shand. "With the air so still you must have heard everything they said."

"I wish I had. But they stopped almost as soon as I got here. Maybe they saw me. The hedge would have blocked their view until I reached the track here."

Convenient, thought Shand, though – he had to admit – not implausible.

"So what *did* you hear them say?"

"Something about a sacrifice. One of them was shouting that a sacrifice had to be made. The other was going on about how Davy had no choice and it was all for his own good anyway."

"What do you think they meant?"

Lee shrugged. "Don't really know. At the time most of us thought he'd got Pippa pregnant and legged it."

Shand was torn – again – this time between a natural suspicion of everything Lee Molland said, and the dot-joining portion of his brain that saw Gabriel Marchant and two men from London. Were they the ones he turned to whenever he needed a problem removed – an unsuitable boyfriend or a troublesome wife?

Or was he being spoon-fed connections by a meddlesome teenager?

"Why didn't you mention any of this before?"

Lee shrugged again. "Like I said. I thought he'd legged it. And if he didn't want to talk about it, I didn't see why I should. Course, now I see it all differently. I don't think he ever left the village."

Shand could see what was coming next. "I suppose you think he's buried up there in the stone circle, don't you?"

Lee glanced back towards the stones. "Yes, I really do."

Yes, thought Shand, and you'd have us digging the whole lot up again just like yesterday. The boy was obsessed.

"How long did it take to think up this story of yours, Lee?" snapped Shand.

"It's not a story. It's true. As the Goddess is my witness."

He held his right hand over his heart, his face moulded into an expression of angelic probity

Shand shook his head. "What Goddess is that, Lee? Are you telling me you're one of those pagans that Kevin Tresco writes about?"

"I'm not a Satanist. I'm Wiccan. It's a recognised religion."

"And that stone circle's your church, is it?"

"The whole world's our church."

CHAPTER THIRTY-TWO

"Did you believe any of that?" Shand asked his sergeant on the way back to the car.

"I don't know," said Taylor. "Sometimes I think teenagers belong to a different species."

Sometimes Shand thought the whole human race was an alien species.

"Come on, Bob," he said. "I want to have another word with Helena."

They found Helena in the front garden, pruning. She carried a pair of secateurs in one hand and a wicker basket in the other. She looked up when the car stopped.

"Good morning, Mrs. Benson," said Shand, racing through the pleasantries. "You were going to talk to your husband yesterday evening."

Helena put down her basket. "Yes, chief inspector, I did."

Shand waited, fighting back the urge to say, 'and?' He could tell Helena was uncomfortable.

"I ... I think something *is* wrong," she said slowly. "No, I'm *sure* something is wrong." She looked away, her eyes following her left hand as it brushed distractedly through the flowering tops of a bed of phlox. "He said there wasn't, but I know there must. He can't fool me after all these years."

"Did he say–"

She cut Shand off as though she hadn't been listening, suddenly lifting her head and almost pleading. "You have to understand my husband, chief inspector. He's ... he can be very stubborn. Especially when he thinks he's being boxed in. If he digs his feet in, no one can shift him. And ... and this audit has made things worse. He's clammed up entirely. If you could stop the audit, I'm certain I could get him to talk."

Her eyes had filled, making Shand feel even worse. He needed that audit. It was his best hope of finding a motive for Helena's abduction. He'd given George chance after chance to tell what he knew. He'd offered protection, amnesty. What more could he do?

Helena must have read Shand's answer in his eyes. She looked away, appearing to age ten years in the process.

"There might be a way of making the audit unnecessary," said Shand. "If we could have a look through your husband's things?"

Helena brightened. "Yes, of course. I'll show you where everything is."

Shand and Taylor spent the rest of the morning taking George's study apart. No one had checked the contents of the room during the forensic search. Then they'd been more concerned with fingerprints and fibres.

Now everything counted.

Luckily George was an inveterate record-keeper. He kept everything. All of it neatly organised and filed. Every bill and bank statement for eight years. Shand hadn't needed to run a financial check – he could have just asked. It was all there. Building Society passbooks, premium bonds, share certificates, bank statements.

But no unusual payments or withdrawals. George's salary went in every month, interest and dividends were paid annually. They saved regularly and lived frugally. No debts, no expensive habits, and no unexplained windfalls.

They extended the search. Every cabinet and drawer. Piles of correspondence, guarantees, catalogues and brochures. Every page was read, scrutinised and discarded. Every book was held up by its spine and unfurled. No cryptic notes, no letters to or from the two Gabriels. Nothing.

"I'm sorry," he told Helena after they'd finished. "There's nothing here. Is there anywhere else where your husband might keep things?"

"No," said Helena, her voice barely audible. "He's very particular. He keeps everything in the one place."

Shand could barely look at her. She looked so frail, so despondent, standing there rubbing her forehead. Three days ago two men had buried her alive and now he – Shand – was torturing her again by pressurising her husband. And yet what else could he do?

"You'll continue with the audit?" she said, her voice

devoid of hope.

"I'm afraid so," said Shand, feeling like an ogre.

~

He almost threw himself into Taylor's car. "Drive," he snapped, reaching for his mobile.

After what seemed to Shand like an age, George Benson answered the phone. There was a small but noticeable intake of breath from the other end of the line the moment Shand introduced himself.

"I've just come from your wife, Mr. Benson, and this has got to stop. Whatever it is you've done or were being strong-armed into doing, it doesn't matter any more. We're not interested in you, we're only interested in the men who were threatening you. Understand? Everything else can be made to go away. But for Christ's sake talk to us!"

There was a long silence.

"Mr. Benson?"

"I have nothing to say." He spoke almost breathlessly. Nerves. Stress. Shand could hear it in every syllable. "I keep on telling you. No one is threatening me. No one at all."

Shand sighed heavily and closed his eyes. He felt like smashing the phone against the dashboard. Why wouldn't the man speak to him! It was obviously tearing him apart.

"Look, Mr. Benson, whatever it is, we're going to find it. So why not make it easier on everyone concerned and tell us now?"

Shand waited for an answer, but all he could hear was George's ragged breathing.

Then a quiet voice said, "there's nothing to tell."

Shand hung up, frustrated and angry.

~

Shand's mood wasn't improved after a visit to the Rectory. The house was still locked up – no sign of life inside, no cars outside. He was tempted to claim he heard a suspicious noise from inside and break in, but knew that Gabe Marsh would have a lawyer that would not only see through the subterfuge, but use it to taint every piece of evidence they subsequently produced.

So he phoned Marcus instead. "Any news on Gabe

Marsh?"

"Not yet, sir. I've tried all his numbers again this morning, but no one knows where he is."

"What about the missing boy? Any luck?"

"If he's still alive he's not working or claiming benefit. And I've pulled the missing person report. Shall I leave it on your desk with the financial reports? The other two just arrived."

Shand checked his watch. Lunch time. And he still hadn't eaten since last night.

"Anything interesting in the reports?"

"Nothing in the Benson file, but the Montacutes have a large overdraft. £50,000."

"Bring everything with you. We'll meet up for lunch at..." The name of the pub he'd eaten at the day before deserted him. He put his hand over the phone and turned to Taylor. "What's the name of the pub in Tarrant Marshall?"

"The Plough."

"The Plough, Tarrant Marshall. As soon as you can."

~

They found a quiet corner in the lounge bar of the Plough and waited for Marcus. After the excesses of the night before, Shand kept away from alcohol and sipped at a glass of orange juice instead.

When Marcus arrived they ordered food and sifted through the files. The Montacutes had had an overdraft for a year during which time their balance had fluctuated wildly. The nature of farming, explained Taylor.

"Only the milk provides a regular income, everything else comes in lumps. Crop harvest, subsidy payments. The outgoings can be the same. A big farm like that could easily spend fifty grand on one piece of kit."

But even given that, it wasn't hard to see that Sixpenny Barton was not doing as well. Two years ago the Montacutes had been comfortably off. Now they had a farm that was losing money and a personal wealth cut in half.

Which might give them a motive for killing Annabel, but why bury Helena?

"Could the Montacutes be behind the bank robbery as well?" suggested Marcus. "They need the money."

"Who would the Brigadess know from the East End of

London?" asked Taylor. "For George Benson to keep quiet this long, someone has got to have one hell of a hold over him. Something that would continue even if they were arrested. Like other gang members ready to exact revenge. I don't see the Brigadess running a gang."

Neither did Shand.

"What about this missing boy?" he asked, picking up the missing person report. "Does anyone really believe it has any bearing on this case?"

Marcus looked hesitant. He opened his mouth to speak, then swiftly looked down and started tapping his feet.

"What do you think, Marcus?" asked Shand. "This is a brainstorming session so all contributions welcome."

The food arrived and Marcus paused while the plates were handed around.

"I think it has possibilities, sir," said Marcus. "There's a strong ritualistic element to all these crimes. The use of the stone circle, the placing of a dead body on top of a live one. We've all tried to find a connection between Annabel and Helena, but what if there isn't one?"

He spoke more freely, growing in confidence. "What if the only connection is one of opportunity? That Annabel and Helena were two women alone in their homes that night. It could have been anyone."

"But what about the phone call from the green?"

"One of Annabel's friends. Or someone who could impersonate them."

Shand wasn't convinced. "What about the missing boy? If you have him down as the first murder, where's his body? It's a different MO. Serial killers don't change MOs."

"This one might. Or it's a sect, or ... or maybe he *was* buried alive, but never found. So this time the killer puts another body on top as a marker."

"To make sure his handiwork was discovered," said Shand, staring into the distance. He could see the twisted logic. A killer fixated on live burials and publicity. "But where would he bury the missing boy?"

A woman's voice answered.

"I think I can help you there, chief inspector. I saw them bury the body."

CHAPTER THIRTY-THREE

Shand's eyes focussed on a woman in her late twenties, curly blonde hair and enormous earrings that resembled a pair of wind chimes. In one movement she'd pulled up a chair from an adjoining table and sat down.

"Got to eat first," she said breathlessly. "I'm starving. D'you mind if I join you?"

"Who..."

Shand's voice trailed off as the woman swivelled in her chair and waved at a passing waitress. "Could you take my order? No, don't bother about a menu. I'll have the chicken and chips. Thank you."

She turned back to the table and smiled. "I expect you're wondering who the hell I am."

"The thought had crossed–"

She cut Shand short. "Saffron," she said, thrusting a hand across the table, the palm facing down making Shand unsure as to whether he was supposed to kiss it, or shake it.

"I'm the answer to your prayers," she continued, barely taking a breath. "The witness you've been waiting for."

"What–"

"...can I tell you?" said Saffron, not only finishing Shand's sentence but wresting it from his mouth. "Well, for one thing, he wasn't killed at the stone circle. That was where it started, but it wasn't where it finished."

"Wh–"

"Where? In the woods. I saw it all. They were struggling in the circle, he broke free, ran towards the woods. He thought he could lose them, but they were too fast. They caught up with him by a twisted beech tree, and buried him within the sound of running water."

She paused for breath, and beamed another smile. Shand wanted to ask her why she hadn't come forward a year ago, but doubted he could complete the sentence.

Taylor obliged. "How–"

"...do I know all this? Simple, I was there. Not physically, of course, but as good as."

Shand experienced a frightening premonition of exactly where this conversation was heading.

"The stones helped, of course. Wonderful channellers of psychic energy. I just stood in the circle this morning, and let them show me what happened. I'm surprised you didn't think to do that, chief inspector."

"So am I," said Shand.

"You're a psychic?" said Marcus, his eyes even wider than usual.

"Didn't I say? I'm the one who found that missing girl in Devon last year. It was in all the papers. That's why the Echo brought me in to help with the case."

"Kevin–"

"...Tresco. Yes, him. He could do with a good dandruff shampoo, but his heart's in the right place."

"Is..." Shand paused, waiting for Saffron to interrupt. But this time she didn't. She smiled instead, eyes twinkling and daring Shand to finish.

Shand looked away and surveyed the bar. Was this a set up? Had they been followed? Was Kevin bloody Tresco watching all this?

He turned back to Saffron. "Is Kevin Tresco here?"

She looked surprised. "Of course not."

"Then how did you know we were here?"

"Really, chief inspector! I'm a psychic. Duh!" She reached over and punched him playfully on the arm.

Shand closed his eyes. If it wasn't for the fact that he was halfway through his meal and starving, he would have walked out. He looked at the others. Taylor seemed to be enjoying himself, and Marcus looked like he was about to ask for an autograph. And as for her ... she looked like a person several crowbars couldn't shift.

He forced a smile, and picked at his pie.

"Did you see the two men's faces?" asked Marcus.

"Sorry, they had masks on. Black ski masks. But if I could touch something of theirs – you know like something they left at the crime scene."

"No," said Shand.

"But, sir," said Marcus.

Taylor rested a hand on his shoulder. "Maybe later, Marc. I'm sure Mr. Shand'll change his mind if we find a body under a twisted beech within the sound of running water."

Taylor winked at Shand who thankfully had his mouth full and couldn't reply.

Saffron shivered. "Did you feel that? That's another one."

"Another what?" asked Marcus.

"Restless spirit. He's been following me all morning, but for some reason he can't - or won't - speak to me."

"Perhaps he's headless," said Shand.

Saffron dissolved into laughter, looking for a second as though she was about to fall off her chair, and then punched Shand on the arm.

"No! You can't decapitate a soul. Whatever happens to the body, the soul remains whole. It's inviolate. Otherwise reincarnation wouldn't work, would it? Everyone would be born with clogged arteries, and bad eyesight."

"She's got a point," said Taylor, joining in.

"Talking of which," continued Saffron. "Reincarnation, that is - has anyone thought to ascertain the chicken's date of birth."

Shand flinched. The conversation - if that indeed was what he was experiencing - was diving towards uncharted depths.

"The Athelcott One?" said Marcus.

"That's the one," said Saffron. "I wouldn't be at all surprised if we find that the Athelcott One was hatched on the exact day that Davy Perkins disappeared."

She nodded knowingly at Marcus who responded with a hushed, "the Athelcott One is Davy Perkins reincarnate?"

Saffron nodded extravagantly. "Returning to avenge his death."

Taylor laughed. "You'd have thought he'd have come back as something bigger?"

"You don't always get a choice," said Saffron. "It's pot luck from what I've heard."

"The Marchants!" said Marcus. "The Athelcott One was always shouting at the Marchants."

"Crowing," said Taylor. "And he only crowed at the

Marchants because Bill Acomb housed him there."

"Or was told to," said Saffron. "A murdered spirit has the power to influence others."

Shand couldn't take any more. "Has it ever occurred to you that the boy might have been turned into a chicken by an evil wizard?"

Saffron and Marcus stared open-mouthed at Shand. Unfortunately, not in disbelief. Shand recognised the glow of admiration for a kindred intellect.

"That was a joke," he said.

"Ah," said Saffron, "but many a true thing is spoken in jest, chief inspector."

She wagged her little finger in his direction and then pouted. "I can't keep on calling you chief inspector – such a mouthful – what do people call you? Guv, is it?"

She deepened her voice and said, "'ello, guv," then punched his arm. This sent her rocking back and forth on her chair, giggling. Until she screamed, "No!" and gushed, "I bet they call you Shandy? Right? I bet I am. What do you say, Shandy?"

Shand considered the very real possibility that he'd died some time on Friday night and had been floating around the nine drug-crazed levels of Hell ever since. This one being by far the worst. Maybe if he banged his head on the table he'd wake up? He shifted his plate to one side and looked longingly at the hard, nut brown wood.

"I can tell exactly what you're thinking, Shandy."

Shand's eyes remained fixed on the table. "No, Saffy, I don't think you can."

CHAPTER THIRTY-FOUR

The telephone call was as welcome as it was unexpected.

"I think we've found it, sir," came the excited cry down the line. "The murder weapon. Out on a lay-by on the London road just north of Athelcott. A driver was stopping for a pee when he saw it on the other side of the hedge."

Shand was on his feet before the station sergeant finished. "Sorry, Saffron, we have to go. Come on you two."

~

The lay-by was already sealed off. Police tape across one exit, and a car on the other. Taylor pulled alongside the police car, and wound his widow down.

"Where is it?" he asked.

"In the far corner, behind the hedge. The bloke who found it's in the black car."

It was a small lay-by. Barely more than a hard shoulder with room for five cars. A waist high hedge ran along a low bank that separated the lay-by from the wide expanse of fields at the back. A wind whipped in across the flat open fields.

Shand knocked on the door of the black car. "DCI Shand. Can you take us through exactly what happened?"

"Without unzipping your trousers," added Taylor.

Shand pivoted slowly and gave his sergeant a look. Happy hour had ended ten minutes ago.

The driver introduced himself as Jason Oldfield, a sales rep based in Taunton. He'd stopped off to relieve himself when he noticed the spade on the other side of the hedge.

"I thought it was a strange thing to throw out, then I remembered the press conference."

Shand tried to remember which one that had been - the one where he'd invented a false lead, or the one where he'd burst into tears.

At least some good had come from them.

And more good news came five minutes later when SOCO lifted the spade and found traces of blood and hair on the back.

"We were lucky," said SOCO. "The spade was lying with the front of the blade uppermost. Otherwise the rain would have washed most of it off."

Shand recognised the spade too. Wooden shaft, wooden handle, and even through the plastic he could read 'England' and something that ended in 'ington.' Helena Benson's missing spade. It had to be.

Shand hovered in the background as the site was processed, jumping up whenever anyone shouted out, or held up a hand. This was the breakthrough he'd been waiting for, he was sure of it.

Next came the handbag. A few yards from the spade amongst a pile of rags and food wrappers. It was Annabel's. A quick glance inside confirmed that. Her mobile phone and library card. But no letters, or notes, or anything to suggest a name for the Midnight Caller.

Then came the surprise. A half-used roll of duct tape was wedged deep into the hedge, a few feet from the spade.

Shand ran over to look. Was it *the* duct tape? The tape used to bind Helena? It had to be, surely? Discovered so close to the spade and handbag. And who stops at a lay-by to throw out a half-used roll of duct tape?

Which meant...

Shand joined up the dots. The murder and the abduction had to be done by the same person. Or the same gang. The duct tape came from the abduction, the spade and handbag from the murder. They *were* connected. The same person disposed of the evidence.

Another dot clanged into place. Helena's spade, Annabel's blood. If Forensics confirmed the blood and hair belonged to Annabel, and Helena identified the spade, then the link was solid. They were dealing with one crime. One mind.

"Can we get these analysed now?" asked Shand.

"We need another hour here to finish," said SOCO.

"Split the team," said Shand. "Send half back with the

evidence now. I really need a break in this case."

"I suppose if I don't agree you're going to get your boss to ring my boss, right?"

"The number's pre-programmed and ready to press."

SOCO split his team.

"Marcus," shouted Shand. "Stay here and liase until they've finished. We're going to Langton Stacey with Forensics."

~

Shand barely said a word in the car. His mind was racing ahead to what they might find. Fingerprints, DNA, fibres, something! All murderers made one mistake.

And then he was tumbling back into doubt. Had he been correct in his assumption that the two crimes were linked? Could the murderer have seen where the spade and duct tape had been dumped, and then woven them into a complex plan of murder and deception?

He bounced his concerns off Taylor.

"I think you're in danger of overcomplicating things, sir. My old sergeant always used to say that the simplest answers were invariably the right ones. Unless, of course, Professor Moriarty has moved into the district."

It was meant as a joke, but a certain section of Shand's brain felt an overpowering urge to get hold of a telephone directory and search through the M's.

~

They started with the spade. More photographs, more preliminaries. Shand fidgeted in the background, wanting them to get on with it. The blood, the hair, a scan for prints.

Someone offered him coffee. He drained it in four gulps.

Then came the scans. Wands of light, sprays, white-coated technicians hunched over the spade blocking Shand's view.

"There are prints on the handle," said one of the technicians – Julie, if Shand remembered her name correctly.

He fidgeted some more, getting up, sitting down. Wondering if he should ask to borrow a white suit, wondering if he'd get in their way.

"The shaft's clean. Looks like it's been wiped. Several

prints on the handle."

Shand mimed picking up a spade and delivering a lethal blow to the back of someone's head. How would he grasp the spade? Not by the handle. He'd hold it like a bat. His left hand at the top of the shaft, the right about eight inches lower.

But why would someone wipe the shaft if they were wearing gloves?

The prints were lifted. Six good and three partials. More time, more coffee as the prints were scanned into the system and compared. Two matches came back. George and Helena Benson. For all nine prints.

Shand swore silently. He'd hoped ... but then it had always been an unrealistic hope. They'd worn gloves. Helena had said so.

But at least it proved one thing. The spade was Helena's.

Next came the blood and the hair. And soil – there were traces stuck to the blade.

"It'll take a while for a full DNA match, but we can do hair and blood type," explained Julie.

"And we can run a soil analysis and compare it to the sample we took from the circle," said her colleague.

"Whichever's quicker," said Shand.

Time dragged. Taylor looked bored, and Shand had started pacing. He knew the procedures, he knew they took time for a reason, he knew about cross contamination and accuracy but...

Did it have to take so long?

The hair sample matched. Not a conclusive test, but good enough for Shand. He had the murder weapon!

The blood type matched too.

"Don't bother with the DNA," said Shand. "That can wait. Print the bag and tape."

Shand checked his watch. SOCO should be on his way back now. He phoned Marcus.

"Any news?"

"They've just finished, sir. They've taken casts of several footprints and bagged anything they found that looked recent. Most of it's rubbish from the bin."

And most of it would turn out to be rubbish too, thought Shand. This gang was careful. He didn't see them leaving a

DNA-laden tissue in a bin.

"Prints on the handbag," said Sandy.

Shand's spirits soared once more only to plummet a second later. It would be the same as the spade. Old prints. Annabel's no doubt.

"And there's one on the duct tape. On the inside of the roll."

"The inside?" said Shand, rushing over.

"Yeah, easy one to miss."

"Process that one first," said Shand, his excitement mounting. This could be the mistake. So easy to overlook. You wear gloves, wipe the outside of the roll, your mind fixed on the tape. And you forget about the inside.

The print was lifted, scanned, input. Shand followed its progress. The cursor blinked and...

Match.

The print on the duct tape, the print from the Marchant's house, and the print from the book of matches – all came from the same person.

CHAPTER THIRTY-FIVE

Gabe Marsh, thought Shand. It's got to be him. He had access to the Marchant's house, he was a member of Gulliver's, and he'd run off. What else did anyone need?

And it was time to be creative. He tried Marsh's mobile first – no answer – then the London property company.

"May I speak to Gabe Marsh?"

"Sorry, he's not in the office at the moment, can I take a message?"

"That's a shame," said Shand. "I'm only in the country for two days. I was hoping to put a business proposition his way. I've got a hundred acres of beach property, and I was told Gabe would be a good man to help develop it."

Shand heard a distant pair of eyeballs spark dollar signs as they spun in their sockets.

"I'm ... I'm sure he'd be very interested. If I can take your name and number, I'm certain he'll get back to you."

"I'm not sure I can wait. I really need to get things moving fast." He paused to build up the tension. "Tell you what – I'll give Gabe first crack. If he can get back to me within the hour, I won't go to the next name on my list."

Shand left his name – opting for the affluent sound of Mr. Grosvenor – then his phone number, then hung up.

"If that doesn't drag Marsh out of his hole nothing will."

"Are you sure the print's his?" asked Taylor.

"Ninety-five per cent," said Shand, who then immediately started thinking about the other five per cent. Doubt being the unfortunate by-product of a vivid imagination.

Had he become fixated on the two Gabriels? Everything appeared to point their way – the way they behaved, their connection to Gulliver's, the two prints in Gabriel's house. But what about the Midnight Caller? Both men had alibis. Was there a third conspirator? Someone else in the village?

Like Jacintha Maybury. She was Annabel's friend, she lived on the green and she had no alibi. And she *was* part of the Gang of Four, so why not part of the Gang of Five – the two Gabriels, Jacintha and their two hired muscle from London?

"Bob, get back to Athelcott. I want Jacintha Maybury, the cleaner, and anyone else who might have visited the Marchant's house last week printed. I'm sure there's a kit around here somewhere you can borrow. Tell them it's routine – elimination purposes only – you know the drill. And if anyone declines, be resourceful. Hand them a piece of paper to read. Whatever it takes. No one gets out of this."

Taylor left. Shand paced. How long should he give Gabe Marsh? The full hour or a bit longer?

The analysis of the prints on the handbag came back. All of them belonged to the dead woman. No surprise. Then SOCO arrived with the rest of his team and several bags bulging with garbage.

Shand pulled away from the noise and the crowd and took his mobile to a corner desk where he could listen and think.

And jump when his phone rang.

"Hello," he said tentatively.

"Shand," said the Chief Super. "What's this about the murder weapon being found?"

"Can you can call me back on..." he leaned forward and read the desk phone number back to Wiggins. "I've got to keep this line clear."

Wiggins obliged. "Why the cloak and dagger?"

"I'm trying to lure Gabe Marsh out of hiding, sir."

"Ah." The Chief Super's voice brightened. "Does that mean an arrest is imminent?"

Shand hesitated. He had every intention of arresting Marsh, but he didn't want it turned into a media event.

"It depends if he takes the bait, sir. And there are other leads. He's not the only suspect."

"A shame," said Wiggins. "Still, finding the murder weapon should go down well with the press. When can you get to Sturton? I'll get the Press Office to set up a conference for as soon as you arrive."

"No! It's too soon. There's–"

"Nonsense, Shand. It's never too soon for good news. And

we can't keep the press waiting too long. You of all people should know that. They start becoming imaginative, and God knows what they'll print. I'd do it myself, if it wasn't for this damned corruption enquiry. I'm booked solid all afternoon."

"What about Jimmy Scott?"

"Too lightweight. The press like to hear it from the man in the charge. Gives it more credibility. More gravitas."

Shand couldn't imagine two press conferences with less credibility or gravitas than the two he'd given.

"But, sir, I'm waiting for a phone call, and the moment I receive it I have to pretend to be someone else. It's an undercover sting. I can't leave here for at least an hour."

"Nonsense, Shand. Get someone to drive you. You can do your cloak and dagger from the back seat. I'll tell them to expect you in an hour."

For the second time that day Shand stared at an expanse of wooden table and contemplated meeting it head-on.

Then his mobile rang and he almost juggled the phone past his ear and over his shoulder onto the floor.

It was Anne. "It's me," she said. "I said I'd call."

She made it sound like a chore.

"Yes," he said, tongue-tied, knowing he had to ask her to ring back on another line, but unsure if she would. She might think he was doing it deliberately to make a point.

He closed his eyes. Indecision. Fear.

"I'm sorry about this," he started. "But ... can you call back on another line?" He gave her the new number. "I've got to keep this line clear. An important call..."

An important call. His choice of words as ham-fisted as ever. Your call's not important, so get off the line.

"Oh," she said. "Of course."

Click. He put down his phone and tried to compose himself. As though ten seconds would make any difference. He tried to think of something bright and chatty to say. Something that didn't revolve around dead bodies, fingerprints, and are you sleeping with Gabriel!

The office phone rang. He took a deep breath and picked it up.

"Sorry," he said. "Work."

"Work," she echoed. "It's all we ever do, isn't it?"

There was a resigned sadness in her voice. He'd known

her too long not to recognise the signs. She had something bad to tell him. Something she wasn't sure how to phrase. It was going to turn into one of those conversations, wasn't it? He hated the superficiality of their usual conversations, but superficiality was preferable to truth. He didn't want to know it was all over, or which Gabriel she was seeing, or the wisdom of a trial separation, or anything like that. He wanted ignorance. False jollity. Someone calling her away to a meeting.

"I don't know," he said, defensively, then ran out of things to say.

"Do you ever think about giving it all up?"

"No!" he said, not allowing a breath before he answered. "We shouldn't give up. It can still work. It..."

He sounded frenetic, and he could feel people across the room staring, their conversation dropping away. He stopped, self-conscious.

"What are you talking about?" she asked.

"Nothing," he said. "Nothing at all. Sorry, I think that call's coming through now. I'll talk to you later, bye."

He slammed the phone down. Stupid, stupid, stupid! Would he never learn?

~

Shand sat silent and reflective as Marcus drove him to Sturton. Gabe Marsh hadn't called. Maybe he really was incommunicado. Yet another failure of judgement in an afternoon that had begun so brightly.

He slumped even lower in the passenger seat. Maybe he wasn't cut out for CID? He certainly wasn't cut out for marriage.

The car radio pumped out something that sounded exactly like the last song and the song before that. And Shand replayed that phone call, over and over, until he was sick of the thought of it.

~

The station car park wasn't as full as last time – the press interest waning at last. Shand bounced out of Marcus's car, trying to motivate himself, mentally slapping his thighs as he strode across the car park, trying to flood his mind with positive thoughts. The hour wasn't quite up, Marsh might still ring. And the press conference – now he thought about it – was a good idea. He could appeal for witnesses. Someone might have a seen a car parked at the lay-by early Saturday morning.

He made his way straight to the conference room. No preparation this time. No time to think himself into doubt. He'd walk on, give the facts, ask for help, take three questions maximum, then leave. Important leads to follow up, sorry, can't stop.

He slapped his thighs for real this time. Walking down the long corridor towards the conference room, his eyes fixed on the door ahead. Again, he felt like a boxer, but a champion this time. Someone who was going to attack from the first bell and go for a knockout with every punch.

He shoved the door open – hard – slamming it flat against the wall. The sound echoed through the room like a pistol shot. Heads turned. He trotted up the stairs to the stage. Jimmy came rushing over.

"You're early, have you–"

Shand pushed past him, a swagger in his step, his eyes cold. This was going to be an emotionless, professional display.

He didn't even bother to sit down. He planted both palms on the table, leaned forward towards the nest of microphones, and spoke, not caring that half the audience were still milling around and chatting.

"We've found the murder weapon," he began.

Instant quiet.

Shand was alone on stage. The other chairs empty. Jimmy hovering in the wings looking confused.

Shand pressed on, all cameras swivelling his way, people sitting down.

"The garden spade was found in a lay-by on the London road, north of Athelcott. Anyone, I repeat anyone, who was driving along that section of road in the early hours of Saturday morning is asked to contact the police. If you saw a car parked at a lay-by, or anyone behaving suspiciously your evidence is vital."

"Which lay-by?"

Shand glowered at the reporter. "Do I look like I've

finished?"

The reporter apologised. Shand glared for another half-second.

"Maps will be provided showing the exact location. I'd suggest you take camera crews out there and film the stretch of road to jog the memory of any potential witnesses."

Kevin Tresco stood up. "Is it true you were led to the murder weapon by a psychic?"

Heads swivelled in Tresco's direction. Except Shand's, which tracked slowly – contemptuously – towards the smirking reporter.

"Who are you? The reporter from the Beano?"

Laughter. Tresco shrugged it off, ratcheting his smirk wider. "Do you deny you talked to a psychic today?"

"A psychic? Listen, lad, why don't you sit quiet and let the grown-ups ask some real questions?"

"I have pictures," said Tresco.

"I expect you've got a colouring book and crayons too."

Shand was just getting warmed up when his phone rang. He dug it out of his pocket. "What?" he barked.

"Mr. Grosvenor?"

CHAPTER THIRTY-SIX

Shand's boxer persona staggered under the unexpected blow. Gabe Marsh was on the other end of the line. He recognised his voice. And, unless Shand put on an accent in the next two seconds, Marsh would probably recognise his.

A matter complicated by the proximity of about five microphones and a room full of journalists.

He muted the phone. "I have to take this call. Thank you." He turned and hurried towards the wings, grabbed the startled press officer, and told him to coordinate with Marcus about the location of the lay-by and the distribution of maps.

"Sorry," he said, heading towards the steps. "Got to go."

Kevin Tresco stood at the bottom of the steps, blocking his path. "Another call from your psychic?"

Shand couldn't help himself, the telephone call momentarily forgotten as a red mist descended. His sneering nemesis was within strangling distance. He feigned a trip from the third step, pitched forward, and launched himself at the reporter, catching him hard on the chest with both hands, shoving him off his feet.

"Sorry," said Shand, shrugging in the direction of the sprawling reporter. "I tripped."

He ducked through the door, closed it behind him, and ran, not slowing down until he'd cleared the corridor. A deep breath, then he deactivated the mute button.

"Sorry," he said, putting on an Irish accent and praying Marsh was still there. "I had a call on another line."

He waited, pressing the phone tighter against his ear as he hurried along another corridor.

Gabe Marsh spoke. Relief. "That's all right. I'm sorry I missed you earlier. Sounds a fascinating project. Whereabouts did you say the beach was situated?"

"On the Med. Forgive me, but I make it a policy of not talking business over an open phone line. I'm sure you understand. Where are you now? If you're not too far we could meet for dinner?"

"I'm at my house in Wessex. A little village called Athelcott. You might have heard of it. It's been all over the news. The murder village?"

Shand tried to remain calm. "No, I've been out of the country, but I'm sure my driver can find it. We're quite close, I think."

Shand pretended to take down the address and directions, trying to stay in character while desperately wanting to get off the phone and sprint to the nearest car.

They arranged to meet in two hours. Any less and it would look suspicious. He rang Taylor and passed on the news.

"Don't tackle him yet. Watch his house and stop him if he tries to leave. I'm on my way."

~

Shand hitched a lift in a police car. Taylor was waiting by the Rectory gates.

"His car's still there, sir. Can't tell if he's alone or not."

Taylor opened the gates and the police car sped through, skidding to a halt in the gravel a few yards behind Marsh's Jaguar.

Shand jumped out. This was it, he could feel it. The case was nearing its end. He hammered on the door, waited, then hammered again.

The door opened.

"Chief inspector?" said Marsh. "What an unexpected–"

"Believe me, Mr. Marsh, the pleasure's all mine. Now grab your coat; we're going for a drive."

Gabe smiled. A smile of confused amusement. "What on earth are you talking about?"

"I call it 'helping police with their enquiries.' We're taking the fingerprints of everyone who had access to the Marchant's house, and you're next."

Gabe's smile widened. "What a shame. I'd love to help, but I've an important business meeting in an hour. Tell you what, I'll come in tomorrow. How's that?"

"Unacceptable," said Shand. "Get your coat now, and we'll have you back within the hour."

Marsh looked uncertain. He glanced back inside his house.

"Alternatively," said Shand. "We can arrest you now, and keep you in overnight. Your choice."

~

They took Marsh to Sturton in the back of Taylor's car. Taylor drove while Shand began the interrogation.

"Where've you been the last two days?"

"Around," said Marsh casually, looking out the window, showing no nerves or interest in what was happening to him. Had to be guilty, thought Shand. No innocent man could be that relaxed in the back of a police car.

"Why did you turn your mobile off?" asked Shand.

"I didn't want to be disturbed. I was with a friend. If you know what I mean."

"Does the friend have a name?"

"Several."

"Look, Gabe, you might think you're funny, but we don't. This is a murder enquiry. Now who were you with?"

Gabe didn't even acknowledge the question. "Don't the trees look spectacular this time of year."

~

They rushed Marsh into Interview Room Two where one of the Forensic team was waiting.

Shand held his breath, expecting Marsh to have second thoughts and call his lawyer. But he didn't. He treated the entire process as a joke. Which made Shand even more nervous. Was there something Marsh knew that he didn't?

He followed the technician next door to where the computer had been set up. Marsh's prints were added to those Taylor had collected earlier - Jacintha's and Annabel's cleaner's. All were scanned and input into the computer.

Shand waited. Everything quiet except for the hum of the computer. Could he be wrong? Did the print belong to someone else? Would another day end with the case no nearer to being solved?

Back came the answer. A match. The print on the roll of

duct tape and book of matches belonged to Gabe Marsh.

"Yes!" said Shand, punching the air. They had him!

~

A smiling DCI threw open the door to Interview Room Two.

"Guess what, Gabe. We've matched your fingerprints to two found at the scene of the crime."

Gabe Marsh stopped smiling. He looked shocked. "That's impossible," he said, shaking his head.

"Afraid not," said Shand. "You see, when you were wiping your prints off that roll of duct tape, you forgot about the inside of the roll. Silly mistake. And you left a book of matches in the car your blokes used to drive Helena Benson to the circle. Not very clever, Gabe."

Shand shook his head and tutted. He was going to enjoy this. He'd suffered for days, now it was someone else's turn.

Gabe Marsh swallowed hard. "I'm innocent," he said. "I don't know anything about this. I swear."

Shand paused, considering his next move.

"Now, Gabe, there are two ways we can play this. One, we bring in the lawyers and sit around the station all night glaring at each other across the table. Or, two, we sort this out now. You surrender your passport and go home on bail to your important meeting. What do you think?"

Shand watched him, wondering if the temptation of Mr. Grosvenor's millions would be strong enough.

Apparently it was.

"Look, I'm innocent. I don't know how my fingerprints got anywhere."

"Then you won't mind us searching your house and car?"

"No ... Yes! I'm expecting a client. I can't have him arrive with the house full of Old Bill."

"We'll get you a hire car. You can meet him at the gate. Take him for a meal."

Marsh didn't answer. He leaned forward and held his head in his hands. Seconds passed. He ran his hands through his hair, then looked up, resigned. He dug his hands into his pockets, and threw his keys across the table.

Shand took Taylor outside and handed him the keys. "Take as many men as you need. Concentrate on papers and correspondence. And get Forensics to look at the car. I'll join you shortly. Oh, and get Marcus down here."

Shand returned to the interview room.

"Where did you say my fingerprints were?" said Marsh.

"On the roll of duct tape and the book of matches."

Marsh shook his head. "That's rubbish." He looked more confident. The initial shock appeared to be wearing off. "How could my prints get on any tape? I was in bed with the Chief Constable's daughter at the time."

"Easy. You handled the tape earlier."

"That's ridiculous! If I hired someone to kill Annabel, do you really think I'd supply the duct tape? I'm not stupid."

"Everyone makes mistakes."

"Not me. Someone's trying to fit me up. Even you must see that. What possible motive could I have for any of this?"

"Well, let's see. What about George Benson and his bank?"

Shand waited for a reaction. Marsh stared back blankly. Shrugged.

"What about his bank?"

"We've nearly finished the audit," said Shand, pressing on. "We'll know everything by tomorrow."

Still no reaction.

"And then there's Annabel's plan to develop Sixpenny Barton. Maybe you thought you didn't need a partner?"

"That? That was Annabel's little pipe dream, not mine. The Brigadess would never sell that house of hers."

"You might be right. About someone fitting you up, that is. Gabriel, for example. He could get rid of you and Annabel at the same time. Why share the proceeds when he can have it all himself?"

For a while Gabe Marsh looked pensive. Shand pointedly checked his watch.

"What time is that meeting of yours?"

~

Fifteen minutes later Shand left the interview room. Marsh wasn't talking no matter how hard Shand pressed. The lure of Mr. Grosvenor's millions had been replaced by a desire for legal representation.

Still, Mr. Grosvenor might be useful later on.

"Put on your best accent and call this number," Shand

told Marcus. "Tell our friend in there that you're Mr. Grosvenor's personal assistant. There's been a family emergency, Mr. Grosvenor apologises, and asks if he can reschedule the meeting for later this week."

"What if he asks any questions?"

"Apologise and tell him there's a call on another line."

Shand left soon after that. There was nothing more to be gained talking to Marsh and he wanted to oversee the search of the Rectory.

On the way out he stopped to have a word with the desk sergeant.

"Mr. Marsh's solicitor should be here in three hours. But if anyone else asks, Gabe Marsh isn't here, okay? And that includes senior management. I don't want the press nosing around."

Marcus drove while Shand rehearsed his next interview with Marsh. He had enough to charge him – he was certain of that – but doubted it would be sufficient for a conviction. Unless they found something in the next three hours, he'd have to let him go.

The Rectory was a mass of lights against the black background of a star-less night. Every window shone – all three floors – and, inside, voices and footsteps echoed through the sparsely furnished house.

"Nothing so far, sir," said Taylor. "We've just started on his computer. And Forensics say the car's been detailed. Inside and out."

Shand moved from room to room – watching, listening, suggesting. The house looked barely lived in. Some rooms were totally empty, others looked like hotel bedrooms – sterile.

Hours passed. The computer contained nothing but games. The little correspondence they found was mostly circulars or bills. And the only files they found contained nothing but house details – thousands of them from properties all over the UK and Europe.

Then, at 10:38, Shand's phone rang.

It was the station sergeant from Sturton.

"Just had a call from an Ursula Montacute. Says something's happened to George Benson, and thinks you should get over there quick. She's at Ivy Cottage with his missus."

CHAPTER THIRTY-SEVEN

Shand left Taylor in charge and grabbed Marcus. "The Benson house. Now!"

They ran for the car, the gravel crunching underfoot. Each footfall grating on Shand's conscience. Not another death, not George. He couldn't bear the responsibility. Had he driven the man to suicide? Had he let him be murdered?

The passenger side door was locked. He tugged harder. Come on, Marcus! The constable climbed inside, reached over, the door clicked open, Shand scrambled inside, the engine already roaring, the car shooting backwards. Shand flapped at his open door as it swung out of reach. The car swerved onto the grass, then lurched forward. Shand grabbed the door and pulled it shut.

Then they were flying, the car accelerating, sluing around corners. Shand hung on, his mind pulled back into the past, wondering how he could have handled the situation better. He knew George was under pressure. Should he have stopped the audit, taken him into protective custody? What?

Marcus revved the engine, hedges flew past in a rapidly moving cone of light. But all Shand could see was Helena Benson's accusing eyes and the Brigadess, her hand outstretched, finger pointing. It's all your fault, chief inspector. Everything!

The car rocked to a stop. Shand was out and running. The house lights were on, the door wide open. He ran inside, almost colliding with the Brigadess in the hallway.

"It's George," she said. "He's missing. His car's in the garage, but no one knows where he is. We've rung everyone he could possibly be with."

"Where's Helena?"

"In the kitchen. She's beside herself. I've sent for a doctor."

They exchanged looks. The Brigadess was expecting the worst as well, ensuring a doctor was on hand to treat the grieving widow.

He had to ask. "You've checked every room?"

"We've checked everywhere. Do you think..." She glanced back towards the kitchen, then lowered her voice. "Do you think he might have been taken to the circle?"

Shand hadn't considered that. Another burial?

"Do you want me to drive up there?" asked Marcus from the doorway.

"Not yet." He turned to the Brigadess. "Have you checked inside the car?"

"We looked through the windows. We didn't..." She lowered her voice again. "We didn't look in the boot."

"Have you got the keys?"

"I'll fetch them."

The Brigadess disappeared into the kitchen and returned with an ashen-faced Helena Benson.

"Sit down," Ursula remonstrated with her. "I'll fetch them."

"No," insisted Helena, her voice frail and tearful. "I'll do it."

She picked the keys off of the sideboard and immediately dropped them, her hands shaking so much. The Brigadess scooped them up before Helena had a chance to react and brought them over to Shand who passed them to Marcus.

"You know what to do," he said. Marcus nodded and left.

Shand glanced at Helena and quickly looked away. Guilt. Her eyes were already sinking into the back of her head. Black and lifeless. She'd looked old enough at lunchtime, now she'd aged another ten years.

The Brigadess took her to the sofa by the fire and sat her down.

Shand stood as close to the door as he could, wanting to be anywhere else but in that room.

But there were questions he had to ask.

He caught the Brigadess's eye. "May..." He didn't know how to put it. "Could ... could you take me through what happened this evening?"

"We had a parish council meeting, chief inspector," said the Brigadess, sitting on the arm of the sofa with one hand resting on Helena's shoulder. "I picked Helena up from here at six, and took her back to the Barton. We like to have a talk before the meeting. A bit of a ritual I suppose. George," she stopped and looked at Helena.

"Go on," said Helena, her voice thin and ghost-like. "It has to be done."

"George wasn't here. He usually comes home about six thirty, doesn't he, dear?"

Helena nodded. "I leave his dinner in the oven." She started to sob softly.

"Has anyone checked the oven?" asked Shand, trying not to look at Helena.

"It's not there," said Helena.

Shand excused himself and walked through into the kitchen. There was a plate in a rack on the draining board. Along with a teacup, a wineglass, a fork and a tea spoon. George's meal? He took a tea towel from a hook by the sink and used it to cover his hands while he opened the oven door and looked inside. It was empty.

He returned to the lounge. "There's a plate on the draining board," he said. "Is that George's?"

"Yes," said Helena. "He always washes up." Her face dissolved. The Brigadess pulled her towards her and held her tight. Shand slipped back into the kitchen.

There was a bottle of red wine on the table. He squatted next to it and peered through the tinted glass. It was practically empty – just a few dregs remaining.

He stood up and slowly surveyed the rest of the room. Everything looked as it should. George had come home, eaten his meal, drank a glass or two of red wine, made himself a cup of something, and washed up.

"You came home at what time?" he asked the Brigadess from the kitchen door.

"About half past ten."

Three hours or so unaccounted for. Three hours which he could have spent watching TV. Or being driven to London at gunpoint. Or...

He didn't want to think about the other possibilities.

The scrape of shoes on a coconut fibre mat heralded

Marcus's return.

"Nothing in the garage, sir."

Shand turned back to the Brigadess. "Have you checked the back garden?"

"Not thoroughly. I called out and shone a torch from the kitchen door."

Shand turned and looked for the torch. It was on the kitchen windowsill. He picked it up and beckoned Marcus over.

"Watch where you step and follow me," he said, opening the kitchen door. Once outside, he made sure the door was firmly closed before speaking again. He didn't want Helena to hear. "Keep your eyes peeled for anything that looks like a pile of clothes or a patch of disturbed earth."

He swung the torch in a slow arc over the lawns and borders. Nothing in the foreground and the light barely touched the far end of the garden. They moved forward slowly, fanning the light ahead of them, carving a corridor towards the old stable block.

The door was closed. Shand reached forward to unlatch it, then pulled the top half open.

He shone the torch inside and froze. He couldn't believe what he was looking at. Beside him, Marcus inhaled so fast he sounded asthmatic.

They'd found George Benson. He was lying stretched out on the floor, his lifeless face caught in the torchlight staring towards the door. But that wasn't what grabbed the two policeman's attention. It was what was standing on his back. An enormous black chicken with flecks of red and gold around his neck.

"The Athelcott One," said Marcus, awe-struck.

CHAPTER THIRTY-EIGHT

Shand stared, his brain trying to catch up with events. This was too surreal. Even for Athelcott. The chicken started to move, strutting up and down the dead man's back. His well-feathered legs impossibly far apart, giving him a rolling gait that reminded Shand of a disreputable pirate after a particularly hard night ashore.

"You don't think..." said Marcus struggling to complete the sentence. "That, you know, what Saffron said ... about Davy Perkins and reincarnation."

The thought had crossed Shand's mind – fleetingly – not that he was going to say anything, least of all to Marcus.

"Can you see anything to put him in?" he said, changing the subject. The chicken had jumped onto the ground and was now scratching up the dirt floor and pecking. Shand could see vital evidence being destroyed if they didn't act soon.

"There's a box over there," said Marcus pointing to a stack of cardboard boxes in the corner.

Shand opened the bottom half of the door for Marcus. The chicken eyed the DC suspiciously, even more so when he came at him with a box. Pandemonium. Marcus mistimed his lunge and the Athelcott One flapped out of range. A scene replayed from every angle and almost every inch of the outhouse. Dust rose in the torchlight as man and chicken circled each other.

Shand held the torch and speculated which god held sway over crime scenes. And what he'd ever done to offend them. A week ago he would have been angry. Now he was more sanguine, knowing that the crime scene was destined to be destroyed whatever decision he made. If he waited for SOCO, the chicken would defecate on the little evidence he didn't scratch up or eat.

Marcus lunged again and this time succeeded in scooping up the squawking chicken, its wings flapping wildly as he brought it back to the box in the doorway. Shand held the flaps open while Marcus manhandled the bird inside.

Shand glanced back towards the house, thankful that Helena didn't have to witness such a scene. Then he prepared himself. Someone had to break the news.

"Get SOCO over here," he told Marcus. "I'll be inside."

~

He stood in the doorway between the kitchen and the lounge, two faces turned his way. Expectation, fear. He knew whatever he said would bring pain. And whatever words he used would be inadequate.

"I'm sorry," he said. The two women held each other tighter. "We've found your husband, Mrs. Benson."

Helena dissolved, turning her face into the Brigadess's body.

Shand looked away, feeling like an intruder. He looked around the room, anywhere but at the sofa, trying to close his mind to the grief and force himself to step back, to look at the scene clinically. How had George died? Had he left a note?

He stepped noiselessly around the room, checking the surfaces – the table, shelves – anywhere a note could be left. Then he slipped back into the kitchen. Again no note. He returned to the stable, took the torch from Marcus and played the light on George's face. Was that a bluish tinge to his lips? Heart attack? Poison?

"Go to the front gate," he told Marcus. "Keep everyone away from the house for now. Show them through the garden."

He'd let Helena grieve for as long as he could.

~

SOCO was the first to arrive, his white suit glowing in the torchlight.

"Has anything been moved?"

Shand searched for the words to best present what had happened, but felt like a Scrabble player dealt a hand of Qs and Xs.

"The body hasn't been moved," he said. "But … we might have left some scuff marks on the scene when we removed the chicken."

"The chicken?"

"It was contaminating the crime scene. In hindsight, if I'd known how difficult it was going to be to catch I–"

SOCO raised his hand. "No need to explain, Mr. Shand. The moment we heard it was one of your crime scenes, we knew we were in for something different."

Shand took it all, his reputation cursed and fast becoming a byword for mirth.

"And rest assured," SOCO continued, "the words 'fowl play' will not pass my lips."

Shand forced a smile and prayed for a minor fault-line to open up beneath his feet. Nothing too large, just wide enough to hide one man. And the bloody chicken.

SOCO found a light switch at the side of the door and carefully switched it on. A single forty-watt bulb flickered into life, spreading a grey light over the crime scene. Curious, thought Shand. The light had been off, but the door had been closed. Why would George shut himself inside a dark outhouse? Had he been killed elsewhere, and carried inside?

He looked closer at the body. It looked as though he'd fallen forward. There was none of the theatricality of Annabel's murder. The arms and legs hadn't been arranged. Everything looked natural. Except for the chicken, and the door being closed and the light switched off.

Did that make it murder? Proof that a second party had been involved?

"Mr. Shand?"

The doctor had arrived. The local GP, a rake-like man so tall he had to bend low to pass under the stable door. Shand wondered how he managed home visits in an area plagued by so many low ceilings.

Minutes passed. The doctor knelt by the body, Shand waiting for a pronouncement.

"Heart attack?" he asked, unable to contain himself any longer. "I noticed the bluish tinge to the lips."

"I'd be surprised," said the doctor. "George has no history of heart problems."

"An overdose?"

"Possibly. Or poison. There's no obvious sign of trauma or asphyxiation. You'll need a post mortem, but I'd take samples of everything he ate or drank. Is anyone else ill in the house?"

"No, though you'll need to see Helena before you go."

"I'll see her now," he said, getting up.

"What about time of death?" asked Shand.

"Very recently. Within the hour, I'd say."

Shand accompanied the doctor into the house and waited, hovering in the background while the doctor treated Helena. He felt like a ghoul, waiting to pounce with his questions while her husband was still warm. But he had to do it. The tranquillisers would kick in soon. He couldn't afford to wait.

The doctor left, ducking between the beams. Shand took a deep breath. And began.

"I have to ask some more questions," he said.

The Brigadess stiffened, but Helena squeezed her wrist. "It's all right, dear," she said. "It has to be done."

"Did you and your husband eat the same meal?"

Helena rubbed her eyes with her sleeve and sniffed. "Yes, a beef curry. I ate at five thirty. I put George's in the oven."

She talked with her head lowered, her left hand resting on her right, her right thumb gently caressing her wedding ring.

"Did you drink the same wine?"

"No, I didn't drink. I ... I had the meeting."

"Did you lock up when you left at six?"

"I think so–"

"I'm sure so," said the Brigadess, interrupting. "I remember waiting while you locked the front door."

"What about the back door?"

"I ..." She dropped her head lower and slowly shook it, her voice breaking. "It's all my fault. We never had to lock doors before. George was going to be back in half an hour. I ... I forgot."

"It's not your fault," said the Brigadess. "Don't *ever* think that."

Shand looked away. If blame was being apportioned...

He waited, time hanging heavy in the grief-laden atmosphere. Eventually the tears subsided.

"Can you ... can you think of any reason why your husband

would go out to the stables?"

Helena looked up, surprised. "He was in the stables?"

"Yes."

"Why would he go there?" She rubbed her eyes with a sleeve and looked from Shand to the Brigadess.

"Were you…" Shand felt stupid even asking, but … If only he could find the words that didn't make the question sound absurd. "Did you keep chickens in the old stables?"

"Chickens?" Helena and the Brigadess spoke as one.

"We found a chicken with your husband. Bill Acomb's chicken. The Athelcott One."

Both women looked stunned.

"How…" The Brigadess broke off and looked apologetically at Helena. "I'm sorry," she said. "It's none of my business."

"No," said Helena, squeezing her friend's hand. "Don't worry about me."

The Brigadess turned to Shand. "How did George die?"

"We don't know yet," said Shand. "But we know he didn't suffer."

Both women looked relieved.

"There was nothing … ritualistic then," asked the Brigadess. "About the…"

"Oh, no, nothing like that," said Shand, suddenly realising the picture he must have placed in both women's heads at the mention of a chicken being found with the body.

"Sir?" said Marcus, appearing at the kitchen door. "Can you come outside a minute."

Shand excused himself and followed Marcus outside. "What is it?"

"Footprints on the lawn."

Shand increased his pace. The stables and the ground nearby were now illuminated by arc lights. A frosty dew glistened over the exposed areas of lawn, leaving islands of dark grass around the trees and the buildings. And there, about five yards beyond the stable, ran a ragged line of footprints – dark patches in the dew – running from the outbuilding to the back wall of the garden.

It had to be recent. The dew could only have formed in the last few hours.

Shand looked closer, shoulder to shoulder with SOCO, both men peering at the tracks in the dew. There seemed too many for one person. And it was impossible to tell which direction they were moving. They were shapes rather than imprints.

"One was walking, one was running," said SOCO.

Shand stared harder, trying to see what SOCO saw. He couldn't.

"I'd say it's one man," said SOCO. "He climbs over the back wall, walks to the house, then leaves running."

They followed the trail to the back wall, walking a parallel track several yards to the right. SOCO shone his torch on the shrub border, then pushed through to the shoulder-height brick wall and eased himself up, balancing precariously on the fulcrum of his stomach.

Shand waited.

"There's a good print on the other side," said SOCO, his voice contorted by the pressure of the wall on his stomach. "We can get a cast. He must have jumped down with some force."

He jumped back down and Shand took his place. And his torch. There was a small patch of exposed soil at the base of the wall. He could see the zigzag marks of a tread from a shoe. Just the one. He panned the torch from left to right. It looked like a track, running parallel to the back wall, bounded on the far side by a wood and grassed over.

Which way had the intruder gone? Where had they come from? Shand shone the torch to its limits. The track might have opened up into a field on the right, but it was too dark to tell. To the left, the track faded into the night.

"We'll take that cast tonight," said SOCO. "The rest can wait until tomorrow."

"There's a bottle of wine in the kitchen too," said Shand, clambering down. "It's the one thing George had, that Helena didn't."

Shand returned to the house, trying to make sense of what he'd seen. What was the point of the chicken? A way of luring George out of the house? Put a cockerel in the outhouse, then wait for it to crow?

Or was it another elaboration? Like arranging Annabel's body on top of a live burial. A red herring to confuse the investigation?

And where did Gabe Marsh fit in? Was this the reason for his sudden reappearance? He'd arranged for George's murder so he wanted an alibi? Had he planned his own arrest?

Too many questions. He needed to focus. The wine bottle. How long had it been open? Had Helena drunk from it at all?

He pulled a plastic evidence bag from his pocket and carefully bagged the bottle before taking it through to Helena.

Neither woman had moved. They were wrapped together on the sofa gently rocking back and forth. Shand hesitated. "Excuse me," he said. "One more question if I may."

The Brigadess glared in his direction. "Can't it wait?"

"He's only doing his job, dear," said Helena mumbling into the other woman's shoulder.

Shand walked around to the other side of the sofa so he could talk to Helena without her having to turn her head.

He showed her the wine bottle, holding the evidence bag between finger and thumb. "Did you drink any wine from this bottle?"

She peered at it, her eyes barely open, blinked several times, then peered again.

"Where did you get that?" she said, surprised.

"From the kitchen table."

She looked confused. "*Our* kitchen table?"

Shand wondered if she was too drugged to understand. "Yes, this is the bottle that George finished for dinner. Did you have any yesterday?"

Helena shook her head, her eyes closing. "No," she said. "It's the wrong bottle."

"What do you mean – wrong bottle?"

"Not ours," she said, her voice drifting away sleepily. "Always buy the same wine. There's a box by the door. For the bottle bank."

Shand ran back into the kitchen. There was a cardboard box full of empty wine bottles in the corner behind the door. He knelt down to check. Every one was the same. Bordeaux Superior 2004. The one in the evidence bag was a Chateauneuf-du-Pape.

CHAPTER THIRTY-NINE

"I'm putting Helena to bed," said the Brigadess.

"Yes, of course," said Shand, his mind elsewhere. Someone had planted a bottle in the house. When? Between six and six thirty was the logical answer. In the half-hour the house was empty and the back door unlocked.

He went to the lounge door. Helena was leaning heavily on the Brigadess en route for the stairs.

"Do you need any help?" he asked.

"We'll manage," said the Brigadess.

Indecision. He wanted to ask Helena if George could have brought the bottle home with him. A present from a customer maybe? If he could only help her up the stairs it would make him feel better for the intrusion.

But...

Shand's phone rang. It was the station sergeant.

"I've got an irate lawyer here wanting to know where everyone is, and why his client's still locked up."

~

Shand arranged for Marcus to give him a lift to his car. "And get that bloody chicken to the pound."

"It'll be closed for the night," said Marcus. "I'll have to take him to the station."

Shand contemplated the tactical benefits of housing the Athelcott One in the cell next to Gabe Marsh. But decided the less he had to do with installing a chicken into the cells at Sturton the better.

And he still hadn't decided what he was going to do with Marsh. He could keep him in custody for forty-eight hours if he wanted to - he had the fingerprints. But little else. The search of his house and car had yielded nothing. The forensics on the second murder wouldn't come back until tomorrow. And the same for the bank audit.

Shand drove, weaving along the winding country lanes, hardly ever having to dip his headlights until he reached the outskirts of Sturton. The case pursued him. Every aspect of it. From planning to execution. Could Marsh have planted the wine bottle himself? It must have been about 6:15 when Taylor first stationed himself outside the Rectory – he'd have had the time.

Shand pulled into the almost empty police car park and climbed out. It was nearly midnight and the last thing he wanted was a verbal duel with an irate lawyer. He stretched his arms and yawned. Another long day in a week of long days.

The lawyer buzzed around Shand the moment he identified himself. The lobby echoed to the sound of the lawyer venting – *it's an outrage ... deliberately kept waiting ... no one here knew what was going on, or where the investigating officer was...*

And finally: "I demand to see my client!"

Shand waited to see if he'd finished. For a small man he had a powerful pair of lungs, he'd barely taken a breath during the one minute long tirade. And he reminded Shand of someone. Someone he couldn't quite place.

"Sorry," said Shand. "But there's been a second murder."

"So my client can go free? He's been in custody all evening. We'll be filing a wrongful arrest charge..."

The lawyer was off again and Shand suddenly realised who it was he reminded him of. The Athelcott One – minus the rolling gait and feathers admittedly, but he had the lungs.

"...when are you going to let me see my client!"

"Follow me," said Shand, deciding he might as well have one more go at Gabe Marsh before calling it a night.

"I want to see my client alone first," the lawyer insisted as they reached the door.

"No," said Shand. "I ask my questions first. You have him afterwards."

Gabe Marsh jumped up the moment the door opened and shouted at Shand. "At last! Where the hell have you been?"

"I'll cut straight to the point, Gabe," said Shand. "This time you've really screwed up. And I'll tell you why."

He had Marsh's attention. The initial anger disappeared, replaced by a mixture of curiosity and apprehension. Even his lawyer shut up.

Shand took his time, slowly drawing out a chair before sitting down. And then waited for Marsh to sit down too.

"Believe me," the detective said. "I know that George was a liability. He was ready to crack. I can see why you had to do something about him."

"I keep telling you, I hardly know the bloke!"

Shand ignored the outburst. "And now he's dead. Murdered."

The lawyer interrupted. "As I said in the lobby–"

Shand slapped the table, hard. "I already have enough to hold your client for forty-eight hours, and I'm prepared to take every minute of it. Unless..." He paused to make sure he had their full attention. "Unless he cooperates, and answers every question to my satisfaction. Does everyone understand that?"

Shand took the silence as an implicit acceptance and moved on.

"Now," said Shand. "This second murder–"

Gabe couldn't wait. "It couldn't have been me! I've been here all evening."

"So you know when the murder occurred?"

"No! I just..." He looked at his lawyer.

"My client was simply making the obvious inference."

"Maybe," said Shand, glaring at Gabe. "And maybe he thought we were too stupid to realise the murder was set up earlier. Now, think on this, Gabe. We found the bottle, and we found footprints we can match to the shoes that made them. Very sloppy."

It was Marsh's turn to slam both hands down on the table. "I am innocent!" he shouted.

The interview hit a wall. The lawyer began interrupting again, and Marsh refused to be baited.

Shand gave up. He was tired, it was late, and he couldn't see anything more being achieved that night.

"What about my client? Can he go now?"

"Not until after tomorrow's post mortem."

Shand left, the lawyer's complaints pursued him down the corridor. Halfway along, Shand bent both arms into an approximation of chicken wings and flapped them. Adding several squawks for good measure.

It had been a very long day.

He pushed the station door open, and took a deep lungful of crisp night air. He was ready for his bed.

"Is it true you've arrested someone?" said a voice.

Shand turned. Kevin Tresco stepped out of the shadow.

Shand kept walking. "No comment," he said.

"Look, Shand, I could have you up for assault. Who've you got in there?"

Shand turned and feigned confusion. "Sorry, do I know you?"

It was the worst insult that Shand could think of for an egotist like Tresco.

The journalist appeared to agree. He was speechless, unable to decide which insult to hurl first, his lips ran the gamut of form and shape.

Shand increased his pace, his car thankfully close by.

"You won't be laughing tomorrow," shouted Tresco as he pulled away.

~

Shand was too tired to dream - or analyse the mistakes of the day, or even remonstrate with the iniquities of Fate. He slept. Right through to his alarm the next morning.

Outside, the sun was shining and Shand felt refreshed. He had a PM to look forward to, and forensic analysis of the bottle and shoe print. This was the day the case broke wide open. He could feel it.

Then, going into breakfast, he saw the newspaper headline. A folded copy of the Echo sat atop a pile of morning papers on a side table by the door.

Second Murder rocks Athelcott : Police Arrest Chicken.

CHAPTER FORTY

Shand picked up a copy of the paper and took it to his table. It was another hatchet job; the facts pushed aside in favour of ridicule – all at Shand's expense. They even had a cartoon on the front page showing the Athelcott One holding up a card with his prisoner identification number on.

Shand read the rest of the article while he picked at his breakfast, unable to believe that a responsible newspaper could publish such drivel. It made him out to be incompetent, a loose cannon who had to be replaced. It even implied that his lack of experience had led directly to George Benson's death.

Shand had just reached the point where he was wondering if the day could get any worse when a familiar voice cut through the quiet calm of the breakfast lounge.

"Shandy!"

Heads turned. All except Shand's, which kept perfectly still, his eyes fixed on the table. Maybe she'd go away?

"There you are!" said Saffron, ending the sentence with a playful punch to Shand's shoulder. "Don't pretend you didn't see me. I saw you looking."

Another punch. Shand rolled with it, wondering how he could extricate himself from the woman's clutches without making a scene. And tarnishing his reputation further. A man who arrests chickens cannot afford to brawl in public with a psychic.

"Saffy," he said, gathering the courage to look up and force a smile.

She pulled out a chair and plonked herself down, exhaling heavily. "Good to get the weight off. What are you reading?"

She tugged the newspaper towards her and swivelled it around before he could answer.

One glance at the headlines and she waved her hand

dismissively. “Don’t mind him. What does he know?” She reached out and grabbed Shand’s right hand, giving it a friendly squeeze. “You definitely did the right thing. And very brave too. Not many coppers would have thought to arrest the chicken.”

It was probably the first thing she’d ever said that Shand could agree with.

“Why–” he began.

“...am I here?” She let go of his hand. “I thought that was obvious now you’ve got the chicken in custody.”

Not to Shand it wasn’t.

“Duh!” said Saffron. “I’m offering my services as interpreter – for the chicken. You know, Davy Perkins’ spirit? You’ll want to question him, won’t you?”

Shand blinked. This had to be a dream. The newspaper headline, Saffron, the chicken. If it hadn’t been for his bruised leg from Sunday’s eye-watering press conference he would have pinched himself.

“So, Shandy, where did you find the chicken? No, don’t tell me!” She placed the back of her right hand theatrically over her eyes. “Hmm, I see a man. Does the name Gerry mean anything to you?”

Shand declined to answer, in the hope that psychics, like wasps, eventually go away if ignored.

“It’s something like Gerry though. Gary, Gordon. George! That’s it! Isn’t it? You found him at the crime scene.”

“How–”

“... did I know? Really, Shandy.” Another playful punch. “Does the Pope shit in the woods? I’m a psychic. I know these things.”

Shand looked down at his plate and felt the siren call of the table reaching out to his forehead. How long would it take before he lost consciousness?

“So, when do we start?” said Saffron. “I was thinking we should take him back to the circle. You know – scene of crime, powerful source of psychic energy. I’ll have the chicken regressed in no time.”

Shand took a deep breath and looked up. The psychic beamed across the table at him, exuding boundless enthusiasm.

“Saffy,” he said, searching for words that might make her

go away. "I'm tied up this morning – post mortem, forensics. But the moment I'm free, I'll give you a ring."

Saffron looked suspicious. She held his gaze for two full seconds, then dived down to rummage in a voluminous handbag by her feet.

"My card," she said, handing it to Shand, but keeping the card firmly between finger and thumb as he tried to pull it away. "Remember," she continued. "You can't hide from a psychic."

"Rest assured, Saffy, the moment I'm ready to interrogate a chicken, you'll be the first to know."

~

George Benson's naked body lay on the slab. Shand couldn't bring himself to look. The nakedness of a man he knew. Guilt over his death. The knowledge of what the pathologist was about to do.

He switched himself off. Glazed his eyes and filtered the proceedings through a gauze of detachment.

There were no marks on the body – according to the pathologist. No signs of struggle or restraint. And he hadn't been smothered. A thorough examination of the airways yielded no fibres. Shand was offered the opportunity to see for himself, but declined.

"Does that mean he was poisoned?" asked Shand, looking for a quick answer and a reason to leave.

"Far too early to tell," said the pathologist who then launched into a list of other possible explanations for George's cyanotic lips and fingernails – a list which included seizures, pulmonary hypertension and drowning.

Hypertension? Shand fastened on the word. Did that mean what he thought it meant? Stress. Stress exacerbated by a bank audit and a DCI who wouldn't leave him alone?

He daren't ask. He withdrew farther towards the back of the room. He didn't think he could cope with a stress-related verdict. He'd have to resign.

The post mortem continued. Blood samples were taken and then the cutting began. Shand waited, listening to the pathologist's dictated commentary, his ears tuned to the one word – hypertension.

It never came.

George had been in good health.

"An overdose, most likely," said the pathologist. "Narcotic, sedative, benzodiazepine. The blood analysis will tell."

"How long will that take?" asked Shand.

The pathologist shrugged. "Hours, days. Depends how much work the lab's got on."

Shand phoned Wiggins. "I need a blood sample fast-tracked."

"And I need to see you, Shand. Now!"

~

Shand left as soon as he'd organised a messenger to rush the samples to the lab. Then he made his own angst-filled run to the Wessex Constabulary HQ at Sherminster. It had to be about the headlines in the Echo. Or yesterday's press conference. Or the second murder. Or the fact that Shand had arrested Gabe Marsh without informing the Chief Super or calling a press conference. Or...

The more he thought about it, the worse his situation appeared. The case would be taken off him. It might already have been.

He paused outside Detective Chief Superintendent Wiggins' office and straightened his tie. A quick brush of his suit, a tug at his sleeves and then a confident knock.

"Enter!"

Shand strode in. "You wanted to see me, sir?" he said, injecting a breezy optimism into his demeanour.

"Shut the door," said Wiggins tersely.

Shand closed the door and swiftly sat down. Wiggins looked uncomfortable. He had a copy of the Echo on his desk.

"Have you seen today's Echo, Shand? What is it with you and Tresco? First the press conference, now this!" He picked up the folded copy of the Echo, and slapped it back down on the desk.

Shand crossed his legs, grasped his top knee with both hands and leaned back, trying to exude a confidence he'd last seen running down the corridor towards the fire exit.

"Yes," he said, desperately plucking an idea out of the ether. "It does seem to be working, doesn't it?"

"Working?"

"My plan. I was told at the outset that Kevin Tresco had it in for the Wessex Constabulary. You know, the corruption allegations..."

"You don't have to tell me about the corruption allegations–"

"Exactly. It's detrimental to everyone. So I refocused his antipathy towards me, and you'll notice there hasn't been one word about the corruption enquiry since. The only copper he's attacked is me."

"You did this deliberately?"

"For the good of the force, yes. I'm drawing him out. Letting him make a fool of himself attacking me, so that when I produce the murderer his credibility is blown for good. No more irritating Kevin Tresco."

Shand sat back and smiled. Lee Molland couldn't have generated more angelic probity.

~

Shand left, inventing a pressing appointment with Forensics while his thin veneer of plausibility still held. The more stories he invented the shorter their shelf life became. This one had started to smell the moment he left the room.

He ran, ignoring the lift and fleeing down the back stairs, turning his mobile off in the process. If Wiggins changed his mind and took him off the case, he'd have to find him first.

Shand drove to Langton Stacey, bulldozing all negative thoughts aside. Forensics would have analysed last night's finds by now. There'd be a breakthrough. He'd solve the case and everything would go away.

He was almost right.

"Where've you been?" said SOCO as soon as Shand arrived. "I've been trying to ring you all morning."

"What have you found?" said Shand, still out of breath from running up the stairs.

"Plenty," said SOCO. "We identified that shoe print at the base of the wall. Astrella, size eight. Trainers. A cheap Italian import sold from discount warehouses and some of the lower end supermarkets. A list of outlets is being compiled, but don't hold your breath. Unless your man bought them with a store card, I doubt you'll trace him that way."

Size eight. Shand wondered what size Gabe Marsh took. And what he'd been wearing the evening they arrested him. Not trainers. At least, he didn't think so.

He phoned Marcus.

"Find out Gabe Marsh's shoe size and see if you can find any trainers at his house. We're looking for a pair of size eight Astrella trainers, okay?"

"Now it gets better," said SOCO. "We've analysed the dregs in that bottle of wine."

SOCO waited, infuriating Shand by drawing out the moment.

"Well?" said Shand.

"You don't want to guess? I thought an enquiring mind like yours–"

"Just tell me," snapped Shand.

"Diazepam. Valium to you and me. And in lethal concentrations."

"Was there Valium in the house?"

"See," said SOCO, turning to his colleagues. "The value of a forensic mind. Straight to the point. Could it have been suicide, he asks?"

"Well?" said Shand.

"Unlikely. No note and no bottle of Valium – either in the house, or on the deceased's person. If he did commit suicide, he cleaned up after himself. There's nothing in the bins either."

Murder. Shand had been ninety-five percent certain from the outset, but it was an immense relief to remove that five percent of doubt. And guilt. The fear that Shand had pushed George into suicide or a stress-related accident.

He phoned Taylor.

"I need you to ring round all the local GPs and chemists. Someone put Valium in George's wine. Enough to kill him. Find out who uses it. And make sure it didn't come from the house. Check with the Benson's GP first."

He flicked the phone shut. Things were moving. Maybe this *was* going to be the day the case broke?

"And now the really good news," said SOCO. "We found prints on the wine bottle."

Again he prolonged the moment, smiling smugly like a stage magician about to produce something unexpected from his hat.

"Whose?" said Shand unable to resist the bait.

"Two sets. George Benson and Gabe Marsh."

CHAPTER FORTY-ONE

"Can I borrow this?" said Shand pointing at the wine bottle.

"Be my guest," said SOCO.

Shand gripped the evidence bag between finger and thumb and held it up to his face.

It couldn't have been better. George's prints when he poured wine from the bottle and Marsh's when he delivered it.

Shand took the bottle and sped back to Sturton. He had enough to charge Marsh now. Maybe enough to convict. All he needed was a link between Marsh and some kind of fraud at George's bank and he'd have the lot.

And then he thought of something else and rang Marcus.

"Check the Rectory for any sign of Valium. Bottles, prescriptions, anything. That's what killed George."

He was still buzzing when he reached the station. Even the sight of an Athelcott One wanted poster on his office door didn't faze him. What did it matter? He had the murderer.

He paced his office floor, trying to decide how to handle the next phase. The end game. Should he wait for Marcus and Taylor to report back or face Marsh now? He was undecided. Marsh had shown little proclivity to crack. He'd probably dismiss the prints as yet another fit-up. And yet?

Surely the weight of evidence would begin to hit home. His fingerprints in the car, on the duct tape, on the wine bottle. The discovery of the duct tape next to Annabel's handbag and the murder weapon. The man was linked to both murders and the abduction.

More pacing. And then a quick trip to the canteen for a sandwich. No lunch break today. He was going to work through until he closed the case.

Preparation. That's what he needed. Map out the interview with Marsh, work out the order of questions, go over the points Marsh might raise in his defence. Make sure every eventuality was covered.

He sat, he planned, he typed. He edited, rewrote and polished.

And then Marcus called.

He hadn't found any trainers or Valium at the Rectory, and Marsh's shoe size was nine.

"Nine?"

"Yes, sir."

"You're sure?"

"Positive. I checked every shoe he's got. They're all nines."

Doubt. Niggling, annoying doubt. Could Marsh squeeze into an eight? Was he that devious to try? Would he deliberately leave a false shoe print to signal his innocence?

But then leave his fingerprints all over the wine bottle?

It didn't add up.

Shand sat in silence, moving evidence around his head like pieces on a chessboard. Did he need the shoe print? Now that he thought about it how could Gabe have made it in the first place? The prints were in the dew. Still reasonably fresh at 10:45, but Gabe had been taken into custody at 6:45. The dew wouldn't have formed until later. Much later.

Which meant?

He didn't like to think what it meant. A second person? The murderer returning? Both possibilities begged the same question. Why? To see if George was dead? To remove evidence?

Or to plant the chicken?

Yes, thought Shand. To plant the chicken and arrange the crime scene. To make the death look like another ritual murder when it was all about greed and profit. It made sense. Gabe could hardly sneak about the village in daylight carrying a chicken. But someone could at night, using the grass track.

Then the phone rang. The bank audit had just been completed. It was negative.

~

Shand couldn't believe it. Everything pointed to the bank. Helena's abduction, George's anxiety, his murder.

"Are you sure?" he pressed.

"Positive. We've checked everything. No discrepancies, no hint of money laundering or dodgy loans. It's a typical small country bank. And very well run."

Shand sat in shock, staring at the phone long after the conversation had ended. He'd been so sure! It was the only part of the case that made any sense. Why else involve George and Helena?

He wouldn't let it go. George had been cleverer than the auditors. He'd covered his tracks. Or it was something planned for the future – you do this or next time we'll kill your wife. And don't think you can tell the police or hide – we've friends on the outside who'll make good our promise. That would work. Wouldn't it?

He started pacing again, unable to sit still. He had to be moving, doing something. He was so close to solving the case. If only, if only, if only...

One more push, one more shoe to drop, and the case had to break open.

He couldn't wait any longer. He grabbed the wine bottle and left. Time for one more crack at Gabe Marsh.

~

Marsh's solicitor was already downstairs. He stood up the moment he saw Shand.

"The post mortem's been completed. Now are you going to release my client?"

"Follow me," said Shand.

Gabe Marsh was brought up from the cells. He was unshaven, slightly dishevelled, but far from cowed.

"Is that a peace offering, chief inspector?" he said, nodding at the wine bottle.

"Sit down," said Shand. He placed the wine bottle centrally on the table and switched the tape recorders on.

"Do you recognise this bottle?" he asked.

"No, why should I?" Marsh leaned back in his chair, his feet spread out under the table.

"Take a closer look. It has your fingerprints on it."

Gabe leaned forward and took a closer look. "Okay, I recognise the label. I bought six cases of the stuff last month. Is that a crime?"

"If you fill it with Valium and poison someone with it, yes."

Gabe snapped bolt upright. "I don't believe this!" He looked at his lawyer. "They're fitting me up. Can't you do something about this?"

The lawyer turned to Shand. "We will challenge every piece of forensic evidence you have–"

Shand cut him off, never taking his eye off Marsh. "Do you think that's going to work with a jury, Gabe? We uploaded the fingerprints from the book of matches into our system long before we ever heard of you. It's all on file – a complete audit trail. We couldn't have fitted you up."

"Look," said Marsh. "I'm not stupid. Do you really think I'd leave my fingerprints all over the place? Only an idiot would forget to wipe a bottle."

"Or someone very daring. Who thinks they can double bluff their way out of jail by saying – look at me, I'm too clever to make a mistake, therefore someone's trying to fit me up."

"Yeah, right," said Marsh sarcastically. "So I get myself arrested and become the prime suspect? That's a real plan, isn't it?"

"Where did you get the Valium? One of your girlfriends, or do you have a prescription?"

"I've never taken Valium in my life. I wouldn't even know what it looked like!"

"We're checking the records now. We'll find out."

"Good for you."

Still no headway. Gabe picked at his fingernails. Shand tried a different tack.

"What I don't understand though is why your accomplice didn't remove the bottle from the table when he went back last night."

Gabe looked up. "What accomplice?"

"The one you sent to make sure George was dead. And arrange the body, of course. You'd have thought he would have at least wiped your prints from the bottle, wouldn't you?"

"I've got no idea what you're talking about."

"Or maybe that was his plan? Did he tell you he'd already wiped the bottle before you planted it? Is that the way it happened? The two of you working together, planning the murders, and all the time he's setting you up?"

Marsh clenched his fists. "I am innocent!" he said, spitting the words through gritted teeth. "There's no plan, no conspiracy. When are you going to get that through your thick head!"

"When you tell me how your prints came to be on that bottle."

Gabe exhaled deeply. His frustration building. He looked as though he was fighting hard not to hit something.

He took another deep breath. "It's *my* bottle!" he said, barely controlling his frustration. "Of course my fingerprints are on it. Someone must have taken it."

"Without leaving their own prints?"

"They probably wore gloves."

"How do you dispose of your wine bottles, Mr. Marsh? Do you leave them in the dustbin for serial killers to pick through?"

"Look!" said Marsh. "Half the village were in my house last month. Anyone could have taken a bottle. I put out four cases of the stuff."

"What were half the village doing in your house last month?"

"The garden party. Part of Annabel's charm offensive. You know, for the elections? She couldn't bear the idea of Wellington boots on her carpets, so she volunteered the Rectory instead."

"Half the village turned up?" said Shand, not liking the direction the interview was taking.

"Probably more. You know how nosy neighbours can be. It was supposed to be a garden party, but everyone wanted to sneak a look around the house."

"The house was open?"

"It had to be. For the toilets. And somewhere to keep the food cool, and store the drink."

Shand had a very bad feeling.

And a crisis of conscience. If he asked the questions he now wanted to ask, he'd be handing Marsh a defence strategy. But if he didn't ... and Marsh really had been framed...

"Did you employ staff to hand out the drinks?" he asked.

"I hired a couple of waitresses to keep the food and drink circulating. They opened the bottles and took them out to the tables. Buffet tables on the lawn. It wasn't a sit down affair."

"So how would your prints get on any of the bottles?"

Marsh considered the question. He was calmer now.

"I unpacked half the crates before the waitresses arrived. And I'm sure I poured drinks for several people. Playing the host, you know?"

The smile was back, the easy confidence.

Shand felt manipulated. He had to ask the next questions. About the duct tape and the book of matches. But he already knew the answer. True or not, Marsh would swear both were in the house that day.

Shand delayed the moment.

"Did anyone take a bottle home with them that day? Or behave suspiciously?"

Marsh shrugged. "Not that I can remember."

His confidence bordered on smugness. He slouched back in his chair, his eyes fixed on Shand's, daring him to ask about duct tape and matchbooks.

Shand didn't want to give him the satisfaction. But he had to ask.

"Is there anything else you'd like to add? About duct tape and matchbooks?"

"There is actually," said Marsh, straightening himself up. "I remember now, there would have been a roll of duct tape in the drawing room that day. I'd been repackaging some books I had to send back that morning. They'd sent me the wrong size."

"Size?"

"For my library. You know, old leather books you buy by the yard to fill up the shelves. They sent the wrong ones. Too tall. You can check, if you like."

"And the book of matches?"

"Now *they* definitely would have been there. I'd dropped into Gulliver's the week before. You can check that too."

"Well," said the lawyer, shuffling his papers. "I think that provides a reasonable explanation for the fingerprints. I suggest you release my client now and concentrate on finding the real murderer."

Shand was torn. He had the evidence to charge Marsh, and yet he didn't. A competent lawyer would convince the jury there was reasonable doubt. But if he let him go, he'd be opening himself up to a storm of criticism. Especially if Marsh absconded.

"Okay," said Shand. "But he surrenders his passport and promises not to leave the area. Do you hear that, Gabe? I want to know where you are at all times."

~

Shand returned to his office, demoralised. There was a report waiting on his desk. He picked it up and flicked through it. It was the blood analysis from the post mortem. Positive for diazepam. A lethal dose which would have brought about death in a few hours for a man of George Benson's weight.

He dropped the report back on his desk. Nothing that he hadn't already surmised.

Doubt. It surrounded and suffocated him. The deeper he delved into the case the less he understood. All his theories were unravelling. The bank, the money laundering, the plot between the two Gabriels. The only evidence he had – the fingerprints – was now questionable. The two main suspects had cast-iron alibis, and as for motive the only credible one left was Gabriel wanting to get rid of Annabel without losing half his money in a messy divorce.

He slumped in his chair and stared up at the ceiling. Where had he gone wrong? Had he missed something? Had he become so invested in Marsh, Marchant and George's bank that he'd overlooked everything else?

The image of a serial killing druid fluttered into his mind.

He refused to acknowledge it. There was a logical answer to this puzzle. The two murders, the abduction, the burial – all were connected if only he could see the link.

He leaned back in his chair and let it swing round full circle. Perhaps he *should* start again. Forget about connecting the murders and concentrate on the fingerprints. They were the only firm piece of evidence he had linking anyone to the crime. So how had they got there?

He pushed off with his feet and took another spin. There were three possibilities that he could see. One, Gabe Marsh was careless. Two, he was trying to be clever in case he accidentally left a print at the scene or, three, someone had deliberately set out to frame him.

He went through each in turn. Was Gabe Marsh careless? He was intelligent, a self-made man, wealthy. But did that preclude carelessness? He was a womaniser, he was irreverent, he ran off in the middle of a murder case. Might not that be associated with a more slapdash approach to life?

No. Shand couldn't see it. The book of matches, the duct tape – yes, an easy mistake to make. But the wine bottle? That took carelessness to a new extreme.

And would Gabe have known that the Benson house was empty between six and six thirty? Or that the back door was unlocked?

Which brought him to option two – Gabe left the prints deliberately.

Another swing of the chair, clockwise this time. How devious was Gabe Marsh? Did he have the foresight to plan an open day a month before the murders and make sure all those objects – the matchbook, the duct tape, the wine bottle – were all on display? And why do it? He said himself it was stupid. It immediately made him a suspect.

Unless he already knew that that was inevitable. He was certain to be a suspect therefore he decided to fabricate evidence that he knew he could discredit later and taint the rest of the case against him?

Was Gabe Marsh that calculating?

And then there was option three – the fit up. Which immediately begged the question – why? A partner-in-crime looking for a fall guy? Shand had put that to Marsh and he'd dismissed it. Would he really risk jail rather than give up a partner who was framing him?

Which left whom? Someone with a grudge against both Annabel and Marsh? Gabriel, the cuckolded husband? Jacintha, the spurned lover? The Brigadess?

Which brought him back to George and the rock that all his theories foundered on. Where did George fit in? He could find plenty of motives for murdering Annabel, he could see a reason for framing Marsh. But as soon as George entered the equation everything collapsed.

Or did it?

What if the crimes had nothing to do with George or his bank? What if Helena had been the target all along? She was the one who'd been buried. What if the poisoned wine had been meant for her too?

He pushed his chair around even faster, trying to spin the doubt away. So many possibilities, so many red herrings. The chicken, the stone circle, the way the bodies had been arranged. It was all so theatrical.

That's when it hit him. It *was* theatrical. All of it. Burying someone alive in a stone circle, placing a dead body on top, placing a chicken on top of the second victim. It was pure theatre.

He jabbed his foot down and stopped the chair.

Why hadn't he considered that earlier? The murders did have a pattern - theatricality! That was the link, not the victims. And it was a theatricality he'd seen elsewhere in the village. The rearranged flower beds, the fake molehills, the fake burial, the stones that danced by moonlight.

The Moleman.

CHAPTER FORTY-TWO

Shand rang Marcus.

"Run a background check on Lee Molland. I want everything, including his shoe size. And then run a house-to-house in Athelcott. I want to know who went to last month's garden party at the Rectory and if anyone took anything home with them. There's a possibility the wine bottle, the duct tape and the book of matches were all taken from the Rectory that day. See if anyone video'd the affair."

He put the phone down. Things were moving again. He had a new suspect and a credible motive. Lee Molland, the attention-seeking fantasist. The murders a natural progression from his Moleman activities – the need for a wider audience, bigger thrills, the victims nothing more than props on a macabre tableau vivant.

Or was that tableau mordant?

He bounced out of his office in search of Taylor. Could Lee's mother be on Valium? It was about time they had a break.

"Bob?" said Shand, throwing open the door to the CID office.

Taylor was in conversation on the phone. He held up his hand to ask for quiet. "You're sure?" he asked the other person on the line.

Shand waited.

"Thank you," said Bob, his excitement growing. "Thank you very much. And don't forget to fax over the other names."

"We've got her!" said Bob, clutching a piece of paper.

"Her?" said Shand.

"Jacintha Maybury. She collected a bottle of Valium on

Monday."

Shand's new theory wobbled for a good second before reasserting itself. If Lee Molland could steal items from Gabe Marsh he could steal from Jacintha too.

"Who else is on your list?" he asked, hoping to hear the name Molland somewhere near the top.

"Jacintha Maybury's the only one from Athelcott. Apparently there's not much call for Valium these days. Most of the local GPs have stopped prescribing it."

Shand was silent for a moment. How easy would it be for Lee Molland to steal Valium from Jacintha? Would he have to break in? Or did they know each other? Did he mow her lawns, perhaps?

Or would he buy it over the internet? And risk having his purchase traced? Shand didn't think so. There was a pattern to this case and that pattern was theatre and planted evidence. He'd steal the Valium and use it to add another layer of confusion and disinformation.

"And I rang the Benson's GP," said Taylor. "He wouldn't go into details, but he confirmed he'd never prescribed Valium for either George or Helena."

~

The press were everywhere. Outside the police station and camped on the village green by the Royal Oak.

Shand asked Taylor to pull over by the pub.

"What's the name of a village about fifteen miles farther on?" he asked.

"There's Buckland Abbas, I suppose. Why?"

"You'll see."

Shand climbed out. Heads immediately turned, then came the rush and the barrage of questions. *Is it true you've made an arrest? Have you found another body. Are you here to arrest any more chickens?*

Shand raised his arms and quietened them down. "I have a quick statement to make," he said. "This afternoon we're conducting a series of important interviews and searches. Something we can do a lot quicker without an audience, so I'd appreciate it if you could all steer clear of Buckland Abbas for the next three hours. Thank you."

"Why Buckland Abbas?" said several journalists at once.

Shand ignored the question and dived back into the car.

"Drive," he said. "The Buckland road."

Taylor accelerated away. "I take it we're going to turn off before Buckland Abbas and double back?" he asked.

"Got it in one. I'm not interviewing Jacintha with a circus watching."

A circus that would have undoubtedly followed them to the Molland house as well, cameras snapping, faces pressed against living room windows, microphones thrust through letterboxes. Anything for a story.

And Sturton didn't have the manpower to stop them. The only unit Division could spare was stationed outside Helena's house.

Taylor took a quick left after a bend and gradually circled back through a series of winding single-track lanes.

"I'm still not convinced about Molland," he said out of the blue. "How would he persuade Annabel to come out and meet him?"

Something that Shand had difficulty with too. Lee Molland was not the obvious candidate for Midnight Caller.

"He's resourceful," said Shand. "He'd think of something."

"And the two Londoners, where'd he find them?"

"College, the pubs in Sturton, holidaymakers, the Internet. London's not that far away."

"But why work with a gang? Everything else he's done, he's done alone. The farce up at the stone circle, digging up people's gardens. He's a loner."

"Not necessarily," said Shand. "What about the crop circles? I can't see Lee not being involved in something like that. And he had to have someone else abduct Helena or she might have recognised him."

"Well, I still like Jacintha for it. She had the Valium, she lives on the Green, she has no alibi, and she's still the best bet for the Midnight Caller."

~

When they arrived at Larkspur Cottage the Green was clear. Curiosity and a good story having routed any thoughts of press cooperation with the police.

"You can have first crack," said Shand as he opened the

garden gate. "I want to have a look around first."

He knocked on the door.

Jacintha seemed surprised to see them.

"Oh," she said. "Chief Inspector, whatever brings you here?"

"Can we come in?" said Shand.

"Oh, sorry, of course." She opened the door wider and stood back for the two policemen to enter. Shand made for the room they'd been shown into before, the same eclectic jumble of arts and crafts.

But no photographs. Not that Shand could see. No family snaps, no holiday pictures, no men friends.

Taylor settled in a chair and produced his notebook.

"I believe you use Valium, Miss Maybury?" he asked.

"How..." she paused, narrowing her eyes. "Occasionally, yes. Why do you ask?"

"Do you have any in the house at the moment?"

"I ... yes, I collected some on Monday."

"Can you show me?" said Taylor, getting up. "It's very important."

Jacintha looked to Shand. "What's this about, chief inspector? Am I a suspect?"

"We're talking to everyone in the village who has recently purchased Valium, Ms. Maybury. Quite routine."

Jacintha led them through the house, ducking under a low door to a steep staircase boxed in against a side wall and finally into an upstairs bathroom. Shand followed at the rear, taking his time, peering into each room as they passed, all of them in their own way mirror images of the first - cluttered, low-beamed and devoid of photographs.

The upstairs bathroom was small and built into the roof with a single eyebrow window sunk into the thatch. A bathroom cabinet teemed with bottles.

"There," said Jacintha pointing to one of the larger bottles. "Is ... is that how George Benson died? An overdose?"

"Why would you say that?" asked Taylor.

"No reason," said Jacintha defensively. "It's just. If you're looking for Valium..."

"Do you mind if we borrow this," said Taylor, nodding at the bottle while he slipped on his gloves.

"No ... I will get them back, won't I?"

"As soon as they've been eliminated from our enquiries," said Taylor. He picked up the bottle and showed it to Shand. It was full. And the seal was unbroken.

"Have you got any more?" said Shand. "An older bottle, perhaps?"

Jacintha shrugged. "I thought I had." She rummaged through the cabinet, lifting and tilting bottles. "But I couldn't find them. That's why I had to go for a new prescription."

"If you'd allow me," said Shand, sliding past the narrow gap between Taylor and the wall. Jacintha stepped aside to make room. The three people almost filled the entire bathroom.

"Is this the only place you keep your tablets?" asked Shand as he started to rummage.

"Yes, it's a small cottage."

And a large number of tablets, thought Shand. It was like an amateur pharmacy. Medication for this, supplements for that. And so many of the bottles were nearly empty or past their sell-by date. The woman was a hoarder. And, by the look of it, a budding hypochondriac.

"I've never been well," said Jacintha, reading his mind. "One of the reasons I moved out to the country. Of course if I'd known about the pesticides..."

She laughed nervously.

"Does anyone else have access to this bathroom?" asked Shand.

"How do you mean? I live alone."

"Quite," said Shand. "But do you ever have any guests stay over, or do any of your friends use this bathroom?"

"It's the only bathroom in the house. Anyone who comes to see me uses it."

"Which would include Gabe Marsh, I suppose."

"Yes, and half the village. Look, chief inspector, are you saying that someone stole my old bottle of Valium?"

"We're looking into the possibility," said Shand. "Do you remember how full the bottle was?"

Jacintha shrugged. "Half full? Maybe three quarters. I only take the tablets now and then so... My memory's not that good, I'm afraid."

"Do you know Mrs. Molland at all. She lives in the village,

has a teenage son called Lee?"

Jacintha shrugged again. "I may do. I host some of the WI gatherings here. You know, the Women's Institute? I help out with the knitting circle, and one year we had a go at pottery. But I'm terrible at names."

"Did any of them have a son come to fetch them? In the last month perhaps? A teenage boy who might have used your bathroom?"

"Possibly," said Jacintha. "Sometimes the place is like a madhouse. People going up and down the stairs, in and out the kitchen making tea. If the weather's nice, we like to have our sessions outside, in the back garden. Anyone could have come and gone without my noticing them."

Convenient, thought Shand, no one locks their doors, and no one can be ruled in or out. He thought fondly of London and the double locks, and the thousands of CCTV cameras. What he wouldn't give for a CCTV camera set up on the Green.

"Would you like some tea?" asked Jacintha. "Unless you're finished?"

There was a tinge of hope attached to Jacintha's last question. Which Shand immediately dashed.

"We'd love a cup," he said.

Shand followed Jacintha into her kitchen, pausing in the doorway to signal to Taylor that it would be an opportune moment to take a quick unaccompanied look around the house.

Jacintha didn't notice. She was busy filling a kettle. An Aga range in the corner pumped a steady stream of heat into the room. Jacintha flipped back the range lid and placed the full kettle on the hotplate.

"Have you ever been married, Ms. Maybury?" Shand asked, trying to make the question sound conversational.

"No," she said. "Never found the right person."

Shand considered her choice of word. Person, not man.

His next question stuck in his throat. What was he going to say? *Are you a lesbian, Ms. Maybury? Were you Annabel's lover? Did she spurn your advances? Did she dump you in favour of Gabe?* It all sounded so sordid.

And what would it achieve? If it was her motive for murder, she'd lie. And if it wasn't, then what? Embarrassed silence and a hostile witness.

And possibly poison in the tea.

He smiled nervously and changed the subject.

"Nice flowers," he said, nodding at a vase in the window over the sink.

"Yes, they're from the garden."

Shand plotted a circuitous, and hopefully well-concealed, route to his next set of questions.

"You do the gardening yourself?" he asked.

"Yes, I love gardening. It's so rewarding."

"You wouldn't employ a gardener then?"

"Never, my garden is my own little fiefdom. I couldn't bear to share it with anyone else."

He walked to the window and looked out over the back garden; a large lawn dotted with small specimen trees, their leaves turning various autumn colours from yellow to scarlet, the whole surrounded by an irregular border of perennials and shrubs.

"Annabel was a keen gardener too, wasn't she?" he asked.

"Yes, she loved her garden almost as much as her house."

"Did she employ a gardener?"

"Several," said Jacintha, smiling. "She was always firing them. They had trouble working to her exacting standards."

"Local lads, were they?"

"Some were. She was using a landscaping firm in Sturton the last time I heard."

"You wouldn't happen to know the names of the local lads she used?"

"Davy someone – the boy in the papers. I remember him. There was some trouble with..." She stopped and eyed him suspiciously. "Why do you want to know?"

"Sorry," said Shand, smiling easily. "I'm a policeman. We can't help it. We like to know everything. You were saying about the trouble..."

She hesitated. "Something to do with Pippa," she said coldly. "Annabel didn't go into details."

Shand smiled and took another turn by the window while he worked out how to continue. He should have brought a picture of Lee Molland. He could have shown it to her. Has this boy ever been in your house? Did he work for Annabel?

He decided on the direct approach.

"I have a problem, Ms. Maybury. And I think you can help. A brown cardboard box about twenty inches square," he used his hands to indicate the size, "was used in the abduct-ion of Helena Benson. That box came from a super-market in Harrow. A supermarket that the Marchant's frequented. Now, you knew Annabel better than most, and you know their house well. Can you remember seeing such a box?"

She shrugged. "Have you asked Gabriel?"

"I have, but I got the impression he doesn't notice that much about the house."

"No," she smiled, "He doesn't."

Shand tried prompting. "Perhaps she kept Christmas decorations in it, or old toys, or something she hadn't unpacked from her move? Just an ordinary box that she kept in a cupboard, or the garage, or a garden shed."

Jacintha started to shake her head, then stopped.

"There was a box. Full of bric-a-brac and ornaments she brought from her old house, but could no longer find a home for. I helped her carry it from the car."

"The car?"

"When we took our jumble to the village fete."

"When was this?"

The kettle whistled. She turned to make the tea. "Some time in early August."

"What happened to the box? Did it stay with the jumble or did you take it back?"

"I'm pretty sure it got thrown out. We all met up the next day..."

"We?"

"The jumble committee and volunteers. We went through all the boxes and piles of clothes, and sorted them into lots and worked out prices. Everything else was discarded. All the boxes and wrapping paper."

"Do you remember the names of the committee members and volunteers?"

"I'm terrible with names, chief inspector. The Brigadess would know. She organised everything."

~

Shand left after the tea.

"Did you find anything?" he asked Taylor as they approached the car.

"Not really. I couldn't find any letters from Annabel or Gabe. I looked through her bookshelves. A lot of books on arts and crafts and poetry, nothing on poisons or witchcraft."

"You thought she might be a witch?"

"I was looking for a reason for her using the stone circle."

Shand's door clicked open and he climbed inside.

"Don't you find her too disorganised to be the murderer?" Shand asked.

"No. I think she fits the bill perfectly. You said the murders were theatrical, and she's theatrical. From the way she dresses, to the way she decorates her home."

Shand disagreed. Jacintha was artistic. The murderer was an exhibitionist. And a planner.

"Hold on a second," he asked Taylor. "I need to phone the Brigadess first."

The Brigadess answered just as Shand was about to give up. Her tone changed the moment he gave his name.

"Tired of harassing Helena are you?" she snapped.

Shand apologised and tried to explain, his words sounding empty and rehearsed. As indeed they were. *I was only doing my job, those questions had to be asked.*

The Brigadess appeared to relent. "It can't be a pleasant occupation."

"No," said Shand, swiftly moving the conversation along. "The reason for my call concerns the village jumble sale. I was told you organised the sorting of the jumble."

"Yes, chief inspector, I did."

"Could you tell me who helped with the sorting?"

"I assume you have a good reason for asking?"

"The cardboard box that Annabel's jumble came in, could have been used in Helena's abduction."

The Brigadess was silent for a while.

"Mrs. Montacute?" he asked.

"I'm thinking," she said. "I believe the boxes were put aside with the other rubbish to be thrown out. But..."

"But what?"

"I can't recall what happened to them. Some of the stronger boxes would have been reused. There's usually someone looking for a decent box. Stall holders, exhibitors, helpers."

"Who was present during the sorting?"

"Myself, of course, Annabel, Jacintha, Lisa Budd, Helena, Tracey Molland..."

"Tracey Molland? Is that Lee's mother?"

"Yes, she likes to see what items are coming in before they go on sale. I suspect she has an arrangement with some of the stallholders to hold things back. But she needs the money so I look the other way."

Standing on the step outside the Molland house, Shand could feel the adrenaline flowing. He could be one knock away from closing the case.

Tracey Molland answered the door, holding it open a crack. A television studio audience screamed in the background.

"What do you want?" she said.

"Is Lee at home?"

"No."

She started to close the door. Shand pushed his foot into the gap.

"Can I see his room?"

"You won't find him there?"

"I can come back with a search warrant and a dozen heavy-footed coppers, If you want?"

She let go of the door and turned away. "Make yourself at home," she said over her retreating shoulder. "See if I care."

The two policemen entered. "Check the back," shouted Shand as he rushed upstairs.

There were four doors at the top of the landing. He tried them all. Two bedrooms, a bathroom and an airing cupboard. No sign of Lee. He peered out the back window, over the small back garden, the rickety wooden fence and the hillside beyond.

Nothing.

"He's not down here," shouted Taylor from below, fighting with the television to be heard. Jerry Springer or one of his clones judging from the shouts and invective.

Shand went back to Lee's bedroom. There were shoes on the floor. Trainers. Not Astrella. But every one was size eight.

CHAPTER FORTY-THREE

Shand charged into the lounge. Tracey Molland was sitting on the edge of a dilapidated sofa watching TV.

"Where is he?" he asked. "Where's Lee?"

"Out," she said, her eyes never leaving the screen where two under-dressed, overweight women, urged on by a wild studio audience, screamed abuse at each other.

"When will he be back?"

A shrug. And more screams from the TV as the two women began to fight.

Shand marched over and turned off the set.

"Hey, I was watching that!"

"Then answer my questions. The quicker I get answers, the quicker I leave."

She folded her arms and slumped back in the sofa, her face set like a spoilt child denied a treat.

"Did Lee go to the garden party at the Rectory last month?"

"Might have."

"Did he or did he not?"

"Ok, so he went. We all did. So what?"

"Did he bring anything back with him?"

"Like what?"

"Like a bottle of wine?"

"A bottle of wine!" She sprang upright. With the right studio audience, she'd have flown at Shand, fingers scratching. "Is that what this is all about? People being murdered all over the village, and all you care about is a bottle of bloody wine?"

"Would you rather I asked Lee's whereabouts at the time of the murders?"

That quietened her. For a second. "Might have known you lot would try to pin everything on the likes of us. Never were no murders until them incomers started buying up the village. That's where you should be looking. Not here."

Taylor came in. "He's not out back."

Shand looked at Mrs. Molland. She glared back, arms folded once more, eyes glistening with hostility. He wasn't going to get any more out of her. And there were other things he could be doing – like searching the house before she thought to withdraw permission.

"Your turn," he told Taylor and left.

He tried the bathroom first, a small damp room that looked like it hadn't been updated since the fifties – the enamel on the bath had worn away under the taps leaving two dirty brown stains. And black mould crept down from the ceiling, dotting the white tiles in the cleft between the two outside walls.

He pulled open the mirrored door of the cabinet over the sink, lifting and tilting every bottle. No Valium.

He moved onto the airing cupboard. An uninsulated hot water tank and three shelves of warm clothing. He lifted each in turn, then dropped to his knees and felt behind the tank with his hands. Nothing, except for dust and cobwebs.

Snippets of conversation percolated up from downstairs. Taylor was chatting to her now, putting her at ease, doing all the things that Shand should have done. All the things he'd forgotten in his head-down charge for answers.

Back to Lee's bedroom. Clothes and magazines strewn on the floor. Shand picked through them – and the battered wardrobe, and the chest of drawers – nothing. No Valium, no incriminating papers, no spare bottles of Chateauneuf-du-Pape.

He skimmed the solitary bookshelf. Text books mainly. Mostly on Mythology – Greek, Norse and Celtic. A student's union card rested on the last book. Lee was enrolled at Sturton College.

Was that where Lee was now?

He put the union card down and flicked through a pile of CDs – could one be a computer disc? Did Lee Molland own a computer?

A quick glance around the bedroom. No computer. No sign of a hi-fi either. There was a cheap clock radio on the floor by the bed and a personal CD player on the chest of drawers.

The Molland's didn't look like a family that had money to spend on expensive items.

He returned to the lounge, trying to slip in quietly.

"Had a good look?" said Mrs. Molland, her mood changing the instant she saw Shand. "If any of my underwear's missing, I'm ringing the papers."

Shand smiled weakly – he could imagine the headlines – and pointed to the front door.

"I'll be in the car," he said.

~

Taylor emerged fifteen minutes later.

"Did you get anything?" Shand asked.

"Not much. She's been to Jacintha's house on a couple of occasions with the WI, but is sure that Lee never has. Though from talking to her, I don't think she has much idea what Lee does or where he goes."

"What about the jumble sale? Did she remember anything about the cardboard box?"

"Nothing at all. Says she was too busy pricing up the jumble to notice what happened to the boxes."

"Did she say if Lee was there?"

"He was there all afternoon helping set up the stalls."

It was enough for Shand, but not enough for a warrant. Not anywhere near enough.

He looked beyond the two rows of terraced houses towards the end of the short cul-de-sac. There was a stile. Did it lead to a footpath? *The* footpath, the one he'd seen the night before when leaning over the Benson's back wall? It was heading in the right direction – if his bearings were correct.

"Stay here," he said, starting to walk away backwards. "I want that house under twenty-four hour surveillance. And see how Marcus is getting on with the house-to-house. I won't be long."

He turned and jogged the short distance to the end of the road, climbed the stile and set off across the field, following a line of crushed grass towards the wood on the far side.

Was this Lee's back way into the village? A deserted track he could use without fear of being seen? Slip over people's back garden walls at the dead of night, then sneak away?

Maybe this was how he gained access to Jacintha's medicine cabinet? He broke in at night.

The track ended in another stile. A woodland path lay on the other side. Shand followed. The path bent and twisted between the trees. He could see a wall ahead, framed between the leaves. A long high wall – probably the back wall of the Rectory garden, it was built of the same dark grey stone and had to be at least eight feet high.

Shand followed the path along the base of the wall until he noticed a door. An old wooden door, its brown paint flaked and peeling. Was this a back way into the Rectory?

He tried the handle. It was stiff, but turned, the door juddering as he eased it open a crack. There were bushes on the other side. He opened it farther and slipped inside. A line of rhododendrons formed a high screen that ran along most of the northern wall. Shand found a gap between the branches and peered out. Across a wide expanse of lawn, lay the Rectory.

He stood there thinking for a while. Did the presence of the door make it easier for Lee Molland to slip out with a stolen bottle? Marginally, perhaps. But there was something else it most definitely did do – it provided Gabe Marsh with a way of leaving the Rectory yesterday evening without Bob Taylor seeing him.

He slipped back through the door and followed the path farther along the garden wall. It was almost a tunnel – trees on one side, a high wall on the other, a canopy of branches overhead and in the distance a circle of light.

Which turned out to be an entrance to a cow pasture. He ducked underneath the single strand of electric wire that marked the end of the path and stopped to get his bearings. He was standing in a small L-shaped field. One leg of the L stretched uphill, probably towards the Benson house and the stone circle, while the other ran straight ahead towards the road and a field gate. To his right the field continued downhill for another hundred and fifty yards, ending in the line of back gardens from the houses in Upper Street. The third house along caught his attention. Larkspur cottage, Jacintha Maybury's home.

He followed the field boundary down the eastern wall of the rectory and along to Jacintha's back garden, keeping one eye on the cows who reciprocated by staring back, their cudding jaws rotating slowly while their heads swivelled to track his progress.

He stopped at Jacintha's garden wall. It was no more than four feet high. Jacintha's back door was ... what? About fifty yards away? And with those small windows and the trellis blocking the view from the front garden, Lee Molland could have been over that wall, in the house, up the stairs and out again without anyone seeing him. He didn't even have to pass the lounge - the stairs came off the rear hall - if the back door was unlocked he could even slip in while Jacintha was preoccupied. He'd know there were tablets. A small village like Athelcott would know everything. Half the village had probably used her bathroom and Jacintha made no secret about her health concerns.

He retraced his steps, following the field boundary back along the rectory wall and then uphill along the woodland edge. There was another field beyond separated by a hedge. Shand clambered over the metal field gate. He could see the ridge of the Benson's thatched roof in the distance. He hurried, crossing the empty field, his eyes set on the gate in the distance where the field narrowed to a point. Beyond it was the Benson's back wall and the narrow grass track that ran alongside it - ending in a gate to the large field that ran up to the circle.

He stopped and leaned up against the gate, breathing hard. There was a direct route between Lee Molland's house and the Benson's. He'd proved it.

Two words came from a little voice inside his head.

So what?

~

He returned to the Molland house crestfallen. Like so many of his endeavours of the past week, what had seemed a good idea at the outset had quickly become tarnished. What had he proved? That Lee Molland could walk to the Benson house unobserved? Okay, but the same held true for Gabe Marsh, Jacintha Maybury and all the other residents of Upper Street, Hill Street and the two terraces on Jubilee Road.

The news from Marcus wasn't encouraging either. The

only villagers who hadn't attended the Rectory garden party were two families from the holiday cottages. And those that had attended hadn't seen anything unusual – other than the lack of furniture in the Rectory. 'Why buy a big house like that and leave it half empty?' was a recurring comment.

And no one had seen anyone leaving with a bottle of wine.

As for Lee Molland – he'd disappeared. He wasn't in college – which he should have been – and no one had seen him since yesterday.

The final piece of bad news concerned the surveillance of Lee's house. No one was available. Not from Uniform branch, not from the other CID Divisions. If Shand wanted a stake out, he'd have to use his own team.

Taylor volunteered to take the first shift, citing Mrs. Taylor's reluctance to let him stay out all night. Marcus had a dog to feed, but could relieve Taylor at ten. And Shand, with no encumbrances, agreed to take over at four. Six hours each. And if Lee still hadn't shown by tomorrow morning they'd review the situation.

If Shand was still on the case, that was. Not that anyone said that, but Shand could feel the confidence ebbing. Yesterday he'd been convinced of Gabe Marsh's guilt, today it was Lee Molland, who would it be tomorrow? Was he losing perspective? Becoming desperate? Jumping on hunches?

He hitched a lift with Marcus to the station car park in Sturton, indecision hitting him the moment he said goodbye. Should he return to his office and catch up on paperwork, or go to the hotel and try and grab some sleep? Neither appealed. He wanted to be sat across the table from Lee Molland. Everything else was marking time. All he'd need was half an hour and the boy would break.

He glanced up at his office window. Wiggins hadn't called since the morning. Maybe he was up there waiting? *Sorry, Shand, but it's for the best. I've reassigned the case. Why don't you take a few days leave?*

He looked at his car. Maybe he could search for Lee himself? Sturton wasn't that big, he could quarter the town in his car, check all the pubs.

He drove, he walked, he covered Sturton – the pubs, the shops, the car parks. Everywhere where people gathered.

Plenty of false alarms, but no Lee Molland.

He called Taylor.

"Anything?"

"Quiet as the grave."

Shand checked his watch. Nearly ten. He might as well join Marcus. If Lee was going to show it would be sometime in the next few hours. Better to be close by, sleeping in the back of a car than tossing and turning in a hotel room thirty minutes away.

He parked his car outside the Royal Oak and walked the short distance to Jubilee Road. The moon lit his way, streetlights unnecessary in the still, clear night. He spotted Marcus's car tucked in between a group of four cars parked opposite the Molland's terrace. He checked to see if anyone was watching, then stepped into the road, opened the front passenger-side door and slid inside.

A dog growled from the back seat. Shand swung round. A large black Alsatian snarled at him, its lips curling back to show teeth that, even in the half-light of the car, glistened menacingly.

"Satan!" hissed Marcus. "Be quiet."

The dog took no notice. Shand, never too confident around dogs, froze.

"Satan!" hissed Marcus again. "Bad dog! Lie down!"

The dog stretched out its front paws and gradually sank lengthways along the back seat, emitting a constant growl in the process.

"Sorry, sir, but I had to bring him. He doesn't like staying in the flat by himself at night. He's no trouble really."

Shand took another look at the dog. He practically filled the entire back seat. And was it his imagination or could he feel the car moving in time to the dog's breathing?

"Anything from the Molland house?" he asked.

"The parents are inside. Mr. Molland came home about six. He works for the Montacutes by the way. A farm labourer."

But no sign of Lee. Not even for dinner. Shand wondered how much money the boy had on him. Enough to feed himself and find a room? Or was he with friends?

A tap on his window made him jump. He swung round. The unexpected face of Saffron filled the passenger side window, her fingers waggling a friendly greeting.

The car bounced suddenly as Satan belatedly sprang at the window, barking ferociously in Shand's ear and nearly sending Shand crashing into the windscreen in fright.

"No, Satan!" shouted Marcus. "Down! Bad dog! Lie down!"

The dog obeyed, after a fashion, slumping heavily against the back seat.

Shand took a deep breath and wound his window down.

"What are you doing here?" he hissed.

"You said you'd ring," said Saffron, resting her forearms on the window and leaning into the car. "Hello, Marcus."

"Hello, Saffron."

"This is not a good time," said Shand.

"Of course it is," said Saffron, ignoring him. "Come on, Marcus, open the door. It's freezing out here."

Shand thanked God for the occupant of the back seat. "Sorry, Saffron," he said. "There's no room. Satan's in the back."

She peered past him at the nine stone of muscle panting on the back seat. "Not another reincarnation, I hope."

Shand braced himself for the playful punch on the shoulder. And there it came, accompanied by the usual trill of laughter.

"Come on, Satan," said Marcus, leaning behind Shand to unlock the back door. "There's a good boy. Move over."

Shand opened his mouth to object, but what could he do? She never took any notice of anything he said. If he tried to arrest her, there'd be a scene. If he ignored her, there'd be a scene. The stake out would be compromised whatever he did.

Saffron tapped him twice on the shoulder. "Be a love and take the back seat, would you? I only bought these tights yesterday, and I don't like the look of those claws."

"Perhaps–" started Shand.

"Unless you want me to sit on your lap?"

Shand took the back seat, squeezing in next to Satan who sat upright, his front paws pressed hard against Shand's right leg and his top lip curled back in warning.

"Who are we watching?" asked Saffron, turning to Shand. "Is it another chicken?"

Shand closed his eyes. "I thought you'd know," he said,

finding some small comfort in sarcasm.

"Hmm, let me see," said Saffron. "Is it ... is it that man creeping along the hedgerow?"

Shand shot forward. "Where?"

Saffron laughed and gave him a playful push. "You're far too easy, Shandy."

Shand felt a large mass squeeze between him and the back of the seat. Satan had seized the opportunity to stretch out along the back seat leaving Shand perched on the front lip of the seat.

"Anyway," said Saffron. "I can help your cover."

"How?" said Shand, shuffling his buttocks in the hope of finding a more comfortable niche.

"We can pretend we're a courting couple."

Shand shook his head in disbelief. "Saffron, there are three of us in the car."

"So? I'm a popular girl."

Not from where I'm sitting, thought Shand, as he slid along the lip of the back seat trying to find some room. Surely Satan had to have a waist or somewhere his body went in?

Which was when Shand's phone rang and the back seat erupted.

"He's frightened of phones," explained Marcus as Satan bounced backwards, barking furiously and snapping at the phone in Shand's hand.

Shand fell backwards, trying to fend off Satan who was lunging at the phone, snapping a few inches short with his teeth every time. Shand dropped the phone, pressing himself as far back into the angle of the seat and door as he could and bringing his hands up to protect his face and throat. Marcus tried to grab Satan from the front seat.

Saffron picked up the phone. "Mr. Shand's phone. Who shall I say is calling?"

Nine stone of dog barrelled forward and pinned Shand against the door.

"He's only playing," said Marcus with less conviction than Shand would have liked.

The dog fastened his teeth around Shand's tie and attempted to kill it by throwing his head back and forth at great speed. Shand grabbed for Satan's collar and held on.

Marcus grabbed the dog by the waist.

And in the midst of the tumult all Shand could hear was Saffron's voice, talking on his phone as though nothing was happening.

"I'm afraid he's wrestling with Satan at the moment, Mr. Wiggins. Can I take a message?"

Oh dear God, thought Shand. Could the day get any worse?

"Me?" said Saffron. "I'm Mr. Shand's personal psychic."

Shand closed his eyes. It could.

"Oh," said Saffron. "He rang off."

"Leave, Satan! Drop!" shouted Marcus, wresting the dog away from Shand. "Come on, boy. Bone. Bone for a good dog."

The mention of food transformed Satan. He bounced away from Shand and presented himself behind the driver's seat, sitting perfectly still, eyes alert, tongue lolling happily from the side of his mouth.

Shand looked away and slumped in the corner waiting for his career to once more flash before his eyes. But saw something else instead. Movement at the end of the lane. Two men. They must have come from the track.

"Down!" he said. "Someone's coming!"

He sank down in the back seat, trying to present the lowest profile. Saffron and Marcus did the same. Two men were on the far side of the road, walking fast, approaching the Molland house. One of the men looked like Lee. The other was of a similar age, but thicker set. He turned at the gate and looked almost directly at the car.

Shand couldn't believe it.

"It's the missing asylum seeker!" hissed Marcus. "It's Marius Lupescu."

CHAPTER FORTY-FOUR

Shand watched the two men disappear inside. What were they doing together? And what should Shand do now? He hadn't expected Lee to have company.

"Marcus, call for back up."

He watched the upstairs landing light come on in the house. Where were they going? Was the asylum seeker staying with Lee?

Marcus called the station. It would be thirty minutes, twenty-five if they were lucky, before anyone arrived. Should they move in before? Cover the back in case Lee left by the kitchen door?

Or make the arrest now? One cover the front, one go in the back?

Indecision. He couldn't afford anything to go wrong. If he went in early and was rushed by two men, could he hold them? He'd never had any form of combat training. Marcus would have, but could he guarantee that it would be Marcus's door they rushed?

Best to wait. Play it by the book. Two men on each door.

"Should I check round the back, sir? In case they slip across the fields."

"Okay, but make sure you're not seen. Find some cover and stay out of sight."

Marcus left, crouching low and scurrying towards the far end of the terrace. Satan watched intently from the back seat.

"He didn't need to go, you know?" said Saffron. "They'll come out the front."

Shand ignored her, shutting everything out except for the house, his eyes fixed on the windows, looking for shapes, changes in the mix of light and shadow. Minutes passed. The landing light flickered, then went out. The front door opened.

Lee came out, a hold-all in his right hand. Then came the other man. They turned left at the gate, towards the path at the end of the lane.

Shand checked his watch, holding his wrist in the patch of moonlight that filtered through the rear window. Back up was fifteen minutes away. Fifteen minutes if they'd responded immediately and the traffic was light.

The two men reached the end of the lane. Little time left to think. He'd have to follow.

"Stay here," he told Saffron. "When back up arrives tell them where we've gone."

"Shouldn't I go with you? I can help find them if you lose them."

Shand closed his eyes. The last thing he needed was Saffron tagging along.

"What about your new tights? The woods are full of brambles."

"I can take them off."

"No!" he said, louder than he'd meant. Panicked by the vision of back up arriving just as Saffron had her tights around her ankles.

"Why don't you stay here and..." He grabbed the first idea that came to him. "Scry. That's it. You stay here and scry for them. Find out where Lee's going and meet us there?"

It appeared to work. Saffron reached behind her neck and unhooked her necklace. "I'll use this as a pendulum," she said.

Shand's mind was already elsewhere. The two men would be halfway across the field by now. Far enough away not to notice a light coming on from inside a parked car. He eased the rear door open and slipped outside, crouching down to push the door to and quietly click the lock home.

The night was still, and silent except for the muffled sound of music from one of the houses and the distant cry of an owl. Shand slipped along the side of the parked cars then the fence line of the front gardens. He could see two shapes at the far side of the field, heading for the track through the woods. He crouched down and ran noiselessly to the first stile and waited. The men disappeared. Shand gave them another five seconds, then climbed the stile and skirted the field to his left to look for Marcus. Marcus was already on his way.

"They took a hold-all from a shed out back," he whispered.

Shand glanced across the field. Was it safe yet? How deep in the woods would they have to be not to notice two men running towards them across an open field?

The alternative was worse. Once in the woods they could disappear – the back door to the Rectory, countless trails into the woods. And what was in the hold-all? More poison? More duct tape? Were they heading for Helena's?

"Come on," he hissed and started running, crouching low and running as fast as he dared over the uneven pasture. Several times he almost fell, several times his feet found unexpected holes, but he kept going. He stopped at the second stile and listened between ragged breaths. A second owl hooted in the distance, the two birds calling to each other. And somewhere deep in the woods a twig cracked.

Shand studied the track ahead. How many dead twigs were scattered across the path? On a night like this the sound would carry for miles.

He peered into the gloom, the moonlight only penetrated the edge of the wood, beyond that it was pitch black.

But they had no choice. They had to follow.

Shand went first. Over the stile into the woodland edge. The path snaked between the trees, a line of dark grey between the black, his eyes slowly becoming accustomed, his ears pricked for the slightest sound.

There was earth beneath his feet, or grass – something yielding, and quiet. Then came the wall and the swish of leaf litter. Shand froze. It was brighter here on the woodland edge. He could see shapes up ahead, a hundred yards, maybe closer. One had his head illuminated by moonlight, the other was hidden in the shadow of the Rectory wall. Neither stopped or glanced back.

Shand waited, unable to move, listening to the blood pound in his ears and the faint, dry swish of shoes through dead leaves. He was visible. His face moonlit. If one of them turned he'd be seen.

An age passed. Wherever Lee and the asylum seeker were going they weren't in a hurry. The shapes ducked under the electric fence at the end of the track and turned left.

Towards Helena's.

Shand started to run, sticking to the higher, woodland side of the track where the leaf litter was less. A twig cracked. He pressed on. Fear. Apprehension. A terrible foreboding. How long would they need to kill Helena? A few seconds? A minute? What was in that hold-all? A knife? A baseball bat? Could he get to them in time?

He slowed a few yards short of the electric fence and peered through the underbrush between him and the two men. They were a hundred yards away, walking past a herd of sleeping cows. Should he ring Helena and warn her? Or would that make it worse? What if they were only planning to break in – to plant another bottle of wine? Timing the break in for after Helena had gone to bed, but then Shand's phone call brings her downstairs and they have to kill her?

He darted forward for a better look. He could call out. That would stop them. The moment they climbed Helena's back wall he'd shout and keep on shouting, at the top of his lungs if need be. There was not going to be a third murder!

Lee and Marius climbed the metal gate into the next field. Shand counted the seconds – five, six – waiting for Lee's head to drop below the top of the intervening hedge. Then he ran, keeping low, aiming for the hedge to the left of the gate. A cow started as he ran by. It leapt ungainly to its feet, bellowing in fright. Shand threw himself to the ground. Other cows got up. Two bellowed.

Shand neither moved nor looked up. He pressed himself flat on the grass. And prayed that the two men wouldn't come back to look.

And that the cows would settle down.

Silence, broken only by the bark of a dog in a nearby house. He waited. A few seconds, then a few seconds more ... then he was running, head down and couldn't care less about the cows. He had to save Helena!

He slid into the base of the hedge and looked for a gap to peer through. The two men were approaching the next gate. From there it would be forty yards to Helena's wall. He had to get closer. He started to rise. A hand grabbed his shoulder.

"Shouldn't we wait?" whispered Marcus.

"No," said Shand, shrugging off the hand and reaching for

the top bar of the gate.

He climbed the gate as silently as he could, then set off across the field, crouching low, willing his feet to silence, ready to throw himself to the ground the moment anyone looked round.

No one did. Lee and his friend climbed the far gate. They were approaching Helena's wall. Shand watched, and waited – ready to shout, ready to sprint, ready to raise the entire village if he had to.

They kept going. Past the place the intruder had climbed the wall the night before. Past the gate at the far end of the wall. Were they circling around to the front door?

They weren't. They walked straight on, heading uphill. Uphill towards the stone circle.

Marcus came alongside. "Where are they going?"

Shand was more concerned with what they were going to do when they got there. And what was in that hold-all?

He climbed the gate and crept along the grass track, passing the Benson's back wall. At the entrance to the large field he stopped. This was going to be difficult. The field was huge with no cover. To be safe, they'd have to wait until Lee cleared the brow of the hill some five hundred yards distant.

Shand couldn't wait that long. Someone might have been lured to the stone circle. He let a gap of two hundred yards develop, then set off along the field boundary towards the woodland edge.

The cold night air bit through Shand's clothes. He hadn't thought to bring a coat. He pulled his jacket tighter to his chest and pressed on. At the stone circle, Lee and his companion stopped. Shand slowed, peering on tip toe to see over the brow of the hill. He could only see their heads. He looked up at the moon, hoping to see a cloud nearby. Something to give him cover so he could take a closer look. But the clouds were on the other side of the sky and showing no inclination to move closer.

The two men entered the circle. There was a snatch of conversation, too muffled for Shand to decipher. He strained to hear more. Both men laughed. Then began to run. Lee towards the chalk track through the woods, Marius towards the road. Had they realised they were being followed?

Shand raced up the hill. There was something in the stone

circle. The hold-all. They'd left it behind. He signalled Marcus to follow Lee while he stopped to look. It was a canvas hold-all with a single zip fastening lengthways down the middle. He snapped on his gloves and pulled the zip back.

And immediately recoiled. The stench of rotting flesh hit him the moment he opened the bag. He stood up, walked away, and took several deep breaths. Then returned, knelt down and, bracing himself, slowly pulled the two sides of the bag apart.

It was empty.

Whatever – or whoever – had been inside they'd taken with them.

~

Shand rang the station. He wanted the hold-all secured and taken back to Sturton.

"Cancel the back-up request," he said. "And get them to pick up the hold-all. It's at the stone circle."

And then he was running, legs pumping towards the chalk track and Marcus, who had to be somewhere up ahead. He could hear the clatter and crunch of running feet in the distance. He set off in pursuit, running fast and blind, black walls of trees towered either side of him, a grey gloom in between.

After a quarter of a mile, Shand fell back. Age and lack of fitness slowing him to a rubber-legged walk, ragged breaths burning his lungs with cold night air. He stopped, hunched over, and clutched both knees with his hands. He wasn't cut out for this.

Minutes passed with barely a sound – no running feet, no raised voices, or sounds of distant struggle – just Shand's breathing and the plaintive calls of a pair of hunting owls.

He started to walk, trusting that Marcus hadn't turned off the track. More minutes passed and then, turning a bend, he saw a dark shape against the light grey of the chalk track up ahead. Someone was walking his way.

He waited, bracing himself in case it was Lee. Then he heard Marcus's voice.

"I lost him," he said, breathlessly. "He must have turned off somewhere."

~

They retraced their steps, stopping at anything that looked like a path into the woods.

"Did you hear him turn off?" asked Shand.

"I didn't hear anything. I just ran."

"But you saw him?"

"No. I just assumed he ran down the track and set off after him. I thought I'd see him when I got to a straight bit."

And Shand had run after Marcus. Leaving Lee to hide in the trees until they passed, or maybe he'd turned off before Marcus had even reached the chalk track.

A dog howled in the distance. Shand knew how he felt.

"Sorry, sir. I should have stopped and listened."

"It's not your fault," said Shand, seeing no point in apportioning blame. When it came to making mistakes, a certain DCI had already filled the Division's quota for the week single-handed.

Another dog howled. Then another. Several dogs all barking at once. It was coming from behind, along the chalk track over towards Sixpenny Barton. Was that where Lee had run to? Had he woken all the dogs in the neighbourhood?

Shand turned to look. It sounded so close. A trick of the night, perhaps. And how many dogs was that? It sounded like at least half a dozen - barking, howling and baying.

They saw the glow first. Like a dull, yellow ball on the horizon between the trees.

"What's that?" asked Marcus.

Shand had no idea. It appeared to be on the track or floating slightly above it. And it was changing shape, like a small cloud composed of dozens of dancing, fuzzy lights.

The baying grew louder. And closer. And there was another noise - a scraping, clattering sound.

A rush of cold air blew against the back of Shand's neck. Small branches rustled overhead. And then ... silence. Complete and utter silence. No dogs, no owls, no rustling leaves. Nothing. And how *black* everything had suddenly become. The moon had gone. The dancing lights had gone. All definition had gone. It was like the two walls of trees had closed over them, squeezing every last bit of light out of the world. He'd never experienced a darkness like it. In a town there was always light somewhere - the fuzzy glow of street lights on the horizon, a light from a window, a shop, a car.

But this ... this was taking black to a new level – a silent, timeless black as though a portal to the past had been opened and he was alone in a wood in some Dark Age past.

And then the baying started up again – louder and closer – making Shand jump in surprise. The dancing, spectral lights returned too.

"It's the Wild Hunt!" said Marcus, already turning. "We've got to get out of here!"

Another time Shand might have stayed and debated the point. But it was pitch black, they were alone in the woods, a pack of wild spectral dogs were heading their way, and Marcus had started to run.

Shand followed – fast – his mind trying to rationalise the situation while his imagination fought him all the way. Why were the dogs glowing? And what was that scraping, clattering sound? Was he really being pursued by a spectral hunt?

The track turned revealing a small patch of light up ahead. It had to be the mouth of the chalk track. Marcus ran faster, moving farther away. Shand flinched in sudden pain. Stitch. He ignored it, kept going. And then felt stupid. What was he doing? Running away from a bunch of glowing lights. He was a detective. He should be running towards the lights to see what they were.

Or, at least, looking for a place in the woods where he could hide and watch unobserved.

He slowed to a walk, hands on hips and taking deep breaths. The sounds from behind were more muffled now. And where was Marcus? There was neither sight nor sound of him.

"Over here!" hissed Marcus from the trees on the left. "We can hide down here."

Marcus had found a narrow path winding off into the woods. They followed it for thirty yards before Shand stopped and turned. He positioned himself behind a tree and waited. Was this going to be another of Lee Molland's stunts? A Wild Hunt put on for Shand's benefit? Or were those stories of Satanic cults in the village more than wild conjecture?

The sounds came closer. Dogs and the clatter of horse's hooves – many horses, trotting along the track. A glow flickered through the trees away to Shand's right. A glow that fragmented and stretched back along the chalk track as though a caravan of glow-worms was approaching.

The procession slowed, then stopped at the entrance to Shand's path. The lights at the front danced back and forth. Shand strained to make out the shapes. Some looked like spectral hounds - dog-like shapes that glowed dirty yellow - others were just blurs - formless clouds of fuzzy light.

Then they started baying - frantically - one shape bounded onto the path towards Shand and the others followed.

Shand fell back instinctively. Four short strides away from the path and then he dived for the ground, pressing himself flat against the soil and what felt like bramble. He braced himself, not daring to look or breathe. Sounds all around. Dogs, horses, shouts, the crack of a whip. He could feel soil hit the back of his legs. He waited for the first dog to find him, the jab of the nuzzling nose, the frenzied claws.

It never came. The baying passed by and moved off. It wasn't Shand's scent they had. He rolled slightly to his left and looked up. Spectral horses and riders, parts of them glowing like the dogs, were thundering past. At least a dozen of them, probably more. What the hell was going on?

He stayed on the floor several seconds after the last rider had passed. Then got up, disentangling his clothes from the barbed strands of bramble.

"Marcus," he hissed.

A groan came from deeper in the wood.

"Are you all right?"

"I will be, sir," said Marcus, clutching something white to his cheek. "I ran into a tree."

"Can you walk?"

"Just about."

"Then follow me. I think I know where they're going."

CHAPTER FORTY-FIVE

The moon had re-emerged by the time they reached the yard at Sixpenny Barton. A yard full of 4x4's and horseboxes.

"Take down the registration numbers," said Shand. "Run every one of them through DVLA. We're going to talk to the lot of them."

Shand checked the outbuildings, looking for fluorescent paint or dye. What was the Brigadess playing at? Was she running a coven, or in league with Lee Molland?

One thing was certain - he wasn't going to leave until he found out. Even if he had to arrest every single rider and drag them back to Sturton.

Hours passed. Then the procession of dancing lights appeared on the horizon where the chalk track left the wood at the top of the ridge.

"You take Lee, I'll deal with the rest," Shand whispered to Marcus. "Stay out of sight until they're all in the yard."

They waited, crouching in the shadows in the lee of the outbuildings. The procession getting closer, the clatter of hooves, a snatch of broken conversation on the wind.

The first rider pulled into the yard, then another, then the dogs, swarming over the yard, their noses pressed to the ground, their tails erect. Shand waited for the last rider to arrive, then stepped into the moonlight.

"Mrs. Montacute," he said, trying to keep his anger under control.

Her horse shied at Shand's sudden appearance and danced backwards.

"Easy, boy," said the Brigadess. "Easy now." She pulled the horse around and walked it back towards Shand. "Chief inspector, this *is* a surprise."

"What the hell is going on here?" snapped Shand.

"Isn't it obvious? We've been drag-hunting."

"At night?"

"It's the only time the bloody sabs aren't about," said Sandy Montacute, pulling his mount alongside.

"Hunt saboteurs don't target drag-hunts, Mr. Montacute. Even a townie like me knows that."

"If only the yobs from Sturton shared your powers of discrimination, chief inspector," said the Brigadess. "Unfortunately the lure of a good punch-up is their only motivation. None of them care about animals. They just like to cause trouble."

It almost sounded plausible. But how could it be? A clandestine meeting in the middle of the night, the proximity of Lee Molland...

But on the other hand ... Where was the guilt? He looked around the yard. People were dismounting, unlatching the rear gates of trailers, loading their horses. No sense of urgency, no one trying to make a run for it. If it wasn't for the fact that it was three o'clock in the morning, it couldn't have looked more natural.

"So why paint the animals?" he said, turning back to the Brigadess.

"It's a matter of visibility. Moonlight's fine in the open, but you need something to follow in the woods."

"And it helps keep the pack together," said Sandy. "Without the paint the whipper-in would never notice the strays."

Shand had to turn away. He felt like he was in the middle of a well-rehearsed practical joke. They had answers for everything, they sat on their horses, and smiled down at him while the yard teemed with glowing animals. It just wasn't right.

And then something hit him.

"What scent were the dogs following tonight?"

"Part of a fox carcass, I believe," said Sandy. "Killed humanely, of course. We'd like to use aniseed but..." He shrugged apologetically. "The hounds are bred to hunt foxes. Eventually we'll train them onto aniseed, but it takes time."

Shand looked from Sandy to his wife. Were they really telling the truth? It sounded so plausible – in a raw, countrified kind of way. The foul-smelling hold-all. Lee running off. The spectral-looking hunt.

"So Lee Molland was your hare?" he asked.

"Yes," said Sandy, "Bright lad. It was all his idea – both the hunting at night and the fluorescent dye."

Shand didn't doubt it, the whole episode had Lee Molland's imprint; drag-hunting by moonlight, the facsimile of the Wild Hunt. It would appeal to his sense of theatre.

"Where's Lee now?" he asked. "Is he coming here?"

"He shouldn't be far behind," said the Brigadess, her horse straining forward and nodding its head up and down. "Easy, boy," she said. "You're have to excuse us, chief inspector, we have a pair of bored and hungry horses here who were promised food."

They both dismounted and started to lead their horses away.

Shand followed alongside. "Did Lee run the course alone?"

"No, he shares the running with a friend," said Sandy. "One drags the sack while the other walks to the next rendezvous. Very clever really. They plan the route meticulously and if we're getting close, they lift the sack off the ground for a short spell and make the hounds work to find the scent again."

"Do you know the name of Lee's friend?" asked Shand.

"No," said the Brigadess, abruptly. "We liase through Lee. We don't know anything about his friends."

Shand knew she was lying. And why.

"You don't hunt asylum seekers then?" said Shand, watching the Brigadess for a reaction.

There was a flicker of surprise. Barely discernible. And then a smile. "Don't give my husband ideas, chief inspector."

"They'd probably enjoy it," joked Sandy. "A good chase through the woods. It'd remind 'em of home."

~

Shand watched them stable their horses, and then glanced towards Marcus who was still standing in the shadows watching for Lee. The rest of the yard was emptying – horses and dogs disappearing into their respective trailers and boxes. It looked innocent enough. And yet ... the involvement with Lee Molland, the secretive way it was organised, the asylum seeker who just happened to go missing the night of the murder.

Shand froze. The night of the murder had been cloudless too. A full moon. Had they…

He ran to the stable door. “Were you hunting Friday night?” he asked the Brigadess.

She didn’t answer at first. She continued stuffing hay into a rope net.

“We might as well tell him,” said her husband from the adjoining stall. “He already knows about the hunt.”

Shand waited, his anger bubbling up. Had they *all* been on the chalk track that night? Had they put their own secrecy above the search for the killer? He couldn’t believe it!

“None of us saw anything, chief inspector,” said the Brigadess. “If we had we’d have come forward.”

Shand could barely get the words out. He was stunned. All that time he’d been searching for witnesses, and here were a dozen riding up and down the chalk track at the time of the murder! None of whom could be bothered to come forward!

“Why?” he asked. “Why on earth couldn’t anyone come forward?”

“To keep the hunt secret,” said Sandy. “If the press got wind of us hunting at night, the sabs would have been alerted.”

“Not to mention the tabloids. There were enough rumours about Satanists and cults without dragging the hunt into it. We’d have been branded as witches.”

Shand didn’t doubt it. But this was a murder enquiry for Christ’s sake!

“What time did you start out?” he asked.

“Five past twelve,” said Sandy.

“That’s very precise.”

“We had to give the runners a twenty minute start. They left at eleven forty-five.”

“Lee and Marius,” said Shand, more to himself than a question. He was already constructing the time line – Lee and Marius would have reached the woods about eleven fifty. One takes the drag and runs off, the other…

The other is alone to do whatever he wants.

“Did you ride past the stone circle?”

“No, we turned off as soon as we entered the woods,” said the Brigadess. “We didn’t go within a mile of the circle all night. Otherwise we'd have come forward."

Shand let it pass – with difficulty – a part of him wanted to arrest the entire hunt for obstructing a murder investigation.

"Who set the course?" he asked. "Lee?"

"Yes."

Perfect. He plans the murder, arranges an alibi, and plots the course to keep the witnesses out of the way.

"Did you see Lee at all during the hunt?"

"Not until we caught him. Which would have been about two thirty."

"And then what happened?"

"We turned around and came home."

"And Lee?"

"He fetched the other boy, and came back too."

"We lay on an early breakfast for everyone," said Sandy. "And have a collection for the runners."

Shand glanced up towards the chalk track. The curving line caught the moonlight as it swung up the valley towards the trees on the crest of the hill. No sign of Lee or Marius yet. But it shouldn't be long. Not with food and cash waiting to be handed out.

"Is there anything else you haven't told me?"

The Brigadess looked at her husband and then at Shand. "You might want to have a word with Lisa," she said. "I'll come with you."

~

They found Lisa coming out of the tack room.

"Shall I start breakfast…"

Her words froze on her lips the moment she recognised Shand.

"It's all right, Lisa," said the Brigadess. "He knows. You can tell him when you really found the body."

Shand listened as yet another brick in his understanding of the case was pulled out, dusted off, and placed somewhere else. Lisa hadn't been walking her dog at seven. She'd been walking home from the drag hunt at six, noticed the glint of Annabel's coat and walked over to investigate.

"Then I panicked," she said. "I thought the killer might still be about, so I run home. Then I started thinking about calling the police, but I didn't want to get anyone in trouble – you know, with the hunt and that – so I thought I'd take the dog out, and see if she were still there."

Shand took it philosophically. It might have taken people five days to come forward, but at least they were tying off their own loose ends. He'd sensed a nervousness in both the Brigadess and Lisa's original accounts of what had happened Friday night. Now he could account for it. Lisa had gone home at seven – as they'd both said. But she'd returned at ten to help with the hunt.

"What time did you pass the stone circle on the way over?" he asked.

"About nine thirty."

"Did you see any cars parked nearby?"

"No."

"Anyone parked outside the Benson house?"

"No one at all. The road was clear."

~

He stayed with the Brigadess after Lisa had left. "You realise I'm going to have to interview everyone who rode on Friday's hunt?"

"Yes," she said. "I'll provide a list."

He took another glance around the yard. The horses and dogs had been stowed away, the ramps pulled up and secured. People were drifting towards the house in their twos and threes – a few looked over their shoulders towards Shand, most ignored him. Most probably played golf with the Chief Constable.

He turned back to the Brigadess. It was a long shot, but so many other loose ends had been tied that evening.

"Was George involved with the hunt?" he asked.

"George? No, George didn't ride. Whatever gave you that idea?"

"It's just that ... I've been trying to find an explanation for George's behaviour all week. And I can't."

"Really, chief inspector, the man had his wife abducted and buried alive. How would you feel?"

Relieved I knew where she was. The thought came out of nowhere – nowhere he wanted to admit to. He immediately hated himself for it. How could he wish that on anyone? Was he that insecure?

He changed the subject.

“Helena commented on it herself,” he said. “She was worried about him too.”

The Brigadess sighed and looked hard at Shand who braced himself for another admonition.

But what she had to say was far worse.

CHAPTER FORTY-SIX

"This absolutely must not go any further," she said, taking him aside. "Do I have your word?"

"Of course."

The Brigadess took a deep breath. "Helena had some bad news two months ago. She has a brain tumour. Inoperable ... and terminal."

Shand could barely take the news. He felt connected to Helena – responsible even – ever since her hand had shot out of the ground and grabbed his ankle. How much more did the poor woman have to suffer?

He clenched his fists. If Lee Molland entered the yard in the next five minutes, he'd kill him.

"I only found out last night," said the Brigadess. "She and George had been arguing about chemotherapy. He wanted her to try it. She wanted to die with dignity. They'd been arguing about it the night he'd left for Sherminster. He blamed himself for not being at home."

Shand felt numb. All those times he'd pushed George, asking him what was wrong, pressuring him to speak. If only he'd known, if only George had *said* something!

He had to leave, walk away. "Sorry," he said. "I'm so sorry," and then he was pushing past the Brigadess into the moonlit yard. How had he got things so wrong?

~

When Marcus found him he was still in a daze, re-evaluating everything he'd done, everything he'd said. Had he misread other witnesses? Should he apologise to Gabriel Marchant and Gabe Marsh?

Doubt. It found nourishment in the dark and the lateness of the hour. He hadn't slept well all week and...

"It's him, sir," said Marcus. "Marius. He's coming down

the chalk track."

It was like throwing a bucket of water over a drunk. All Shand's negative introspection fell away. If he could get Marius to talk, he'd get Lee Molland.

They hurried back into position, using the shadows and the sides of the stables as cover. And waited. Marius took his time, walking slowly down the gently shelving track. As soon as he entered the yard, Shand stepped into his path.

"Hello," he said, smiling and holding out his hand. "Marius, isn't it?"

Marius looked surprised, and slightly nervous. "Yes," he said, wiping his right hand down his trousers.

They shook hands, Shand keeping a firm hold while Marcus circled behind the asylum seeker.

"Police," said Shand, maintaining his grip. "We'd like to ask you a few questions."

Marius tried to pull away, but was enveloped by Marcus. There was the barest of struggles before the asylum seeker gave up, his hand going limp in Shand's grasp.

They took him into an empty stall, and switched on the light. Three straw bales were pushed up against the rear wall, the rest of the box was bare – grey concrete floor, wooden partition walls and an underlying smell of ammonia.

Marcus stood by the door while Shand questioned the asylum seeker.

"Where's Lee?" he demanded.

Marius cowered, backing against the partition wall and flinching as though expecting to be hit. Shand backed off, and softened his voice.

"We're police officers, Marius. We're not going to hurt you. All we need to know is where Lee is. We need to find him."

Marius shrugged his shoulders and looked down at his feet.

"Is he meeting you here?"

"Maybe."

"Look at me, Marius," said Shand, bending his knees and trying to establish eye contact. "Do you need an interpreter?"

Marius continued to speak into his chest. "No. I speak English very good."

"Okay, Marius," said Shand, enunciating slowly. "I'm going to ask you questions about Friday night's hunt. Do you understand?"

"Yes."

"Who ran the first leg? You or Lee?"

He hesitated before answering. "I … I run first. Lee, he meet me second checkpoint."

"Checkpoint?"

Marius pulled a folded piece of paper out of his back pocket and slowly unfolded it.

"Map," he said, handing the paper to Shand. "Checkpoint red."

Shand took the map. It was a black and white photocopy of an Ordnance Survey map. One on each side. One with Wednesday scribbled at the top, the other Friday. Both had coloured lines tracing the route of that night's drag hunt. Red crosses marked the places where the two men were scheduled to meet and two lines ran between each cross – a long blue line that, according to Marius, marked the circuitous route of the drag run and a short dotted line the other had to walk.

Shand studied the map. Friday's drag run left the chalk track as soon as it entered the wood from Sixpenny Barton and then snaked northwards. The first checkpoint was north-east of the start – maybe a five or ten minute walk. He made the calculations. They left Sixpenny Barton at eleven forty-five. They would have reached the wood at eleven fifty. Lee would then be on his own. How long did he have before he met Marius at the first checkpoint?

He asked.

Marius shrugged. "Thirty minutes? Lee, he say we run thirty minutes, rest twenty, walk ten. But many times it feel longer."

Could Lee get to the Green and back in thirty minutes, phone Annabel and kill her?

He stared at the map. It would be one hell of a run. He'd be out of breath by the time he reached the phone box and then he'd have to run another half-hour leg after he ran back up the hill.

It was impossible.

Unless he had a car. Parked on the chalk track waiting.

Driven there by the two men who'd abducted Helena.

"Did you hear a car?" he asked.

Marius's demeanour changed instantly. Up came his head. "No," he said, shaking it violently. "I see no car. I see nothing!"

Shand saw the fear, the pleading in the man's eyes. He reached out and placed both hands gently on Marius's shoulders. Marius flinched, and Shand pulled back. He'd meant it as a supportive gesture.

He tried another approach. "Look at me, Marius. Please. We are not going to hurt you. Do you understand? You are *not* a suspect. You tell the truth and you go free. You have nothing to fear."

"I see nothing," he said quietly, his eyes looking everywhere but at Shand. "No want trouble."

"What did you see?" Shand continued. "Tell me. I can protect you. You don't have to worry."

Marius looked up. "You no deport me?"

"Of course not. We're not Immigration. We only want to know what you saw. That's all."

Marius's head moved from side to side as if assessing the pros and cons. Then he spoke, the words exhaled like a sigh. "I see car."

"Where did you see the car, Marius? Show me on the map."

Shand held out the map of Friday's hunt and pointed to the chalk track where it ran through the woods. "Was it here?"

Marius looked at the map, taking his time. Then pointed to the other end of the track, by the stone circle. "There," he said.

Shand stared at the map. Friday's course didn't go anywhere near the stone circle. How could he have seen anything that far away?

"When was this? What time did you see the car?"

"After I leave farm. Four a.m."

"You saw a car by the stone circle at 4:00 a.m.?"

Marius nodded gravely, then added. "I see them carry body from car."

CHAPTER FORTY-SEVEN

It took several seconds for Marius's statement to sink in.

"You saw someone carry a body from a car?"

"Yes."

Shand still couldn't believe it. "You're sure it was a body?"

"In my country I see many bodies. I know dead body when I see one."

"Did you see who was carrying it?"

"I no stay look. I see car. I see body. I turn fast."

"What did they look like? Were they tall, short?"

Marius shrugged. "They were people. Light not so good then. More clouds, not so many moons."

"What about the car? Was it large, small?"

He shrugged again. "It was car."

Shand paused. Was Marius telling the truth? All his instincts said he was. The body language, the way he spoke. Which meant that Annabel *had* been killed elsewhere. The pathologist had speculated as much - the cleanliness of her fingernails and clothes. This was the proof. There was another crime scene to be found - the place where Annabel had been killed, and her body stored between midnight and four.

"Why didn't you tell anyone what you'd seen?" Shand asked.

"If I speak, people say I kill woman. Send Marius home."

"But you came back tonight to go hunting?"

"I need money. Where else I go?"

Shand let Marcus conclude the questioning. Where Marius had been staying since Friday, his contacts with Lee, Lee's friends, whether any were from London. Shand sat on a straw bale at the back of the stall, sampling the answers, drifting in and out between the interview and a running analysis he'd constructed in his head.

Annabel had been killed elsewhere and moved later. Why? Because the killer – who until proven otherwise he'd call Lee – was pressed for time? It made sense. Up to a point. Up to the point he introduced the two Londoners and their car. Why hadn't *they* moved the body? They abducted Helena at 10:30, buried her between eleven and eleven thirty, drove down the chalk track to wait for Lee at eleven fifty, drove him to the phone box for midnight. Then what? Lee killed Annabel and they drove him back to the chalk track? So why didn't they dump the body at the same time? They had to drive past the circle.

Or did Lee insist on arranging the body himself? Which he couldn't do earlier because he was rushing to meet Marius at the next rendezvous?

Shand liked that. And Lee would want to take his time. It was his trademark. Attention to detail. He didn't vandalise gardens, he rearranged them. He'd wait until he'd finished with the drag hunt then meet up with the others and take Annabel's body to the circle. Then he'd choreograph the scene, taking his time, imagining the reaction he'd induce, the publicity, the cameras.

Just like George's murder – another tableau constructed post mortem, Lee returning to the scene to make sure George and the chicken were found together.

But if so...

Where was Lee during Helena's abduction and burial? He had nowhere else to be. He wasn't expected at the hunt until later. Wouldn't he want to be there? Wouldn't he need to be there – to watch, to oversee, to get whatever sick kick he got out of that sort of thing?

Or had Lee been one of the two men?

'Yes!' thought Shand, suddenly noticing the quizzical glances from both Marius and Marcus. And the fact that his right foot was tapping wildly on the concrete floor.

"Sorry," he said, shifting his weight to press down and contain the errant foot. Then he was away again. Lee as one of Helena's abductors. Lee putting on a London accent. All he needed was a driver. Someone to taxi him back and forth and help carry the bodies. Which was why Annabel had to be taken to the stone circle later. Two people were needed to carry the body, and Lee didn't have time at midnight. But he did at four. After he'd finished with the hunt.

Everything fitted. The motive, the MO, the timing.

All he lacked was a single shred of evidence.

~

Shand's mobile rang.

"Remember me?" said an annoyed Saffron. "The girl you're always running away from, promising to call."

He'd forgotten all about her.

"Sorry," he said, a lie forming and rising unbidden from his throat. "I would have rung, but you know how Satan reacts to phone calls."

Silence. Perhaps Shand had tried it on once too often?

"I have half a mind not to give you this message," she said.

"What message?"

"The one that starts – remember that boy you were following..."

"You've found him?"

"I'm looking at him disappearing through his front door as I speak."

"He's returned home?"

"That's what I just said. Shandy, are you paying attention? I thought my scrying powers had deserted me when I couldn't get the pendulum to move. But now it's obvious. I was in the right place all the time. Isn't that..."

Shand stopped listening.

"We've got to go," he told Marcus. "Lee's back home." He turned to Marius. "Go and get your money and something to eat. We'll send a car to pick you up later. We'll need you to sign a statement, then you can go."

Shand commandeered a car from the Montacutes. He wasn't going to wait twenty-five minutes for a car from Sturton.

~

Shand took the front door, while Marcus ran around the terrace to the back. The house was in darkness. He rang the doorbell. And waited. He rang the bell again. Then hammered on the door with his fists. The landing light came on.

"Who is it?" someone called from inside.

Shand hammered again.

"All right, I'm coming."

Shand leaned into the door the moment it opened, wedging his foot in the crack and flashing his warrant card at a startled Lee Molland.

"A word, Lee," he said, stepping inside and closing the door.

"What do you want?"

Lee was still fully dressed. Black tracksuit – top and bottom – ideal for sneaking around the village at night. And black trainers.

"What size are they?" he asked, nodding towards Lee's feet.

"What?"

"Your trainers. What size are they?"

"Eight, why?"

"And what's that logo I can see on the side? Astrella, is it?"

Lee cocked his foot on one side and looked down. "Something like that, yeah,"

"Congratulations, Lee," said Shand. "You're nicked."

~

Shand was elated. He had his suspect in custody and a real prospect of closing the case before breakfast.

If he could ditch the psychic.

"Do you need a lift to your car?" he asked, keeping his tone warm and friendly.

"Don't I get to sit in on the interview?" asked Saffron.

"We'll be waiting an hour or more for the duty solicitor. And you need to sleep. I've got a job for you later today. There's a number of things I need to pick your brain about."

Saffron eyed him suspiciously. "You're not just saying that?"

"Saffy," said Shand, placing his hand on his heart, and projecting an aura of integrity that most politicians would have sacrificed several small children for. "Could *I* fool a psychic?"

~

The duty solicitor arrived at five thirty and was rushed into Interview Room One. Shand had been like a caged bear for over an hour, only held back from starting the interview early by the fear of jeopardising the case. This was one interview that had to be played by the book. He'd made too many mistakes to risk a confession being thrown out for not following procedure.

He started the tapes, introduced those present. And began.

"What were you doing at the Benson's house on the evening of George's murder?"

Lee shrugged. "I don't know what you're talking about."

"Wrong answer," said Shand. "We can place you at the scene. Which makes me wonder why you'd lie. What do you think, constable?"

"I think it means he's guilty, sir," said Marcus. "Why else would he lie?"

"Why else indeed," said Shand. "Now, Lee, do you want to change your answer or do you wish the presumption of guilt to stand?"

"I was at home. I never went out."

Shand shook his head. "No, no, no, Lee. That won't do. We have the forensics. You left traces all over the Benson's garden. Traces that had to be made between six and ten thirty. Why do you think we took your trainers? We don't make a habit of interviewing suspects in their socks."

Lee was wavering. His posture hadn't changed. He was still slumped in his chair, arms folded and legs stretched out under the table, but his eyes had lost some of their sparkle. And they shifted occasionally.

"Juries love their forensics, don't they, Marcus? Makes their job that much easier. All that sitting around the courtroom trying to work out which witness is lying. Much easier to listen to the expert, and when he says it's a million to one shot that you're innocent they're going to know what to do. Million to one. Gotta be guilty."

Lee shuffled in his seat, crossed his legs, then uncrossed them again.

"And of course you're not a juvenile any more. Nineteen years old. That means life if you're convicted. Thirty years minimum, I'd say. Unless the judge takes a dislike to you.

Which seeing as you're a young male is highly likely. You know how many young males a judge sees in a year? Too many. All that insolence and testosterone. Gets right up their noses."

"Have you finished?" said Lee.

"Just getting warmed up, Lee. Looking forward to the big trial. Kinda spoils it if you plead guilty. All that free publicity wasted. Not that you could benefit. Not with the law preventing criminals from profiting from their crimes. But we could. A book, I think. How I trapped a monster. Of course, with me writing it, I'd have license to paint you however I liked. What do you think? Pathetic attention seeker? Posterity would know you through my words. And posterity has never cared for the truth. Look at Shakespeare. Ever done any cross-dressing, Lee?"

Lee yawned. For effect, thought Shand. Trying to show how bored he was. Unlike the duty solicitor who showed real signs of drowsiness – his head tilting forward and his eyes almost closed.

Which was a definite advantage, thought Shand, deciding to restrain from raising his voice or making any sudden movements.

"Nothing to say, Lee?" he asked. "Of course it's your prerogative. And it's not as though I need anything from you. I've got the forensics. I can go to trial now." He leaned back in his chair and smiled. "We're only here now for your benefit. The law says we've got to give you a chance to explain yourself. But if you can't, you can't. So one more time, Lee. What were you doing at the Benson's house?"

Lee looked up at the ceiling, refusing to even look at Shand.

"Prison it is then," said Shand, turning to Marcus. "Are the cells here still full?"

"Er ... yes," said Marcus, flustered by the unexpected question.

"Shame," said Shand, turning back to Lee. "Still, you've got to get used to life inside. There's no bail on murder charges. But look on the bright side – a pretty boy like you is going to be very popular inside. All those hardened criminals looking for a friend."

Lee looked worried. "I didn't kill anyone," he said.

"Good to hear it," said Shand, gathering up his papers, and feigning a practised indifference. "Where's the nearest prison?" he asked Marcus. "Can you give them a ring and arrange Lee's transfer?"

"Okay," said Lee, sitting upright. "I was there, but I didn't kill anyone. He was already dead."

"Who?" said Shand.

"George. He was lying on the floor of the outbuilding."

"Which you were visiting, why?"

Lee hesitated. "I was going back to check on the cock."

"The Athelcott One?"

"Yes, I'd shut him in there. I thought it was the last place anyone would look. But I needed to go back that evening to make sure he had enough food and water."

"The Athelcott One had been there all day?"

"Since midday. I hid him in my room first, but when you questioned me I knew I had to move him. So I thought of the last place you'd look. You'd searched the Benson's house so many times it had to be safe."

There was a frightening plausibility to Lee's story. And gone was the cocky self-assurance and the knowing smirks.

Was he actually telling the truth?

"When you found George was the door open or closed?"

"Open. And the light was on. I thought he'd found the Athelcott One and I'd have to explain. Then I saw his feet."

There appeared to be real shock in Lee's eyes.

"And the chicken?"

"He was roosting on a pile of boxes. I bent down and felt for George's pulse. But there wasn't one. Then I panicked. I thought the shock of seeing the Athelcott One had given him a heart attack. Then I heard the car pull up outside and I switched off the light, shut the door, and legged it."

"What time was this?"

"About ten thirty."

It fitted. But then it would if he'd been there arranging the crime scene.

"What about the night of Annabel's murder? Where were you at midnight?"

"I was in bed."

Shand noticed the hesitation and the downward glance before answering. Was he starting to read Lee Molland or was he being led a dance?

"That's not very clever, Lee. A dozen witnesses saw you leave Sixpenny Barton at eleven forty-five. Marius left you on the chalk track at eleven fifty."

Lee's mouth opened in shock.

Shand continued. "Marius, your asylum-seeking friend, then ran the first leg with the drag leaving you alone in the woods for forty minutes."

"Thirty minutes," said Lee. "We ran thirty minute shifts."

"You checked your watches in the moonlight, did you? Forty minutes gives you plenty of time to kill Annabel and get back."

"We had torches. And I didn't kill anyone!"

Lee's outburst brought the duty solicitor's head snapping back upright. He glanced at his client, then at Shand, with the puzzled look of someone who wasn't quite sure where he was.

Shand was not going to enlighten him.

"Where did you go after Friday's drag hunt?"

"Home."

"What time was that? About four?"

"About then."

"And that would have taken you past the stone circle?"

"I never went anywhere near the circle!"

"But that's your route home, Lee. We followed you tonight."

"Not when I'm on the other side of the woods. Friday, I was at the Barton so I went home along the roads. It's quicker." Then something hit him. "You took my bag, didn't you? I couldn't believe someone nicked it."

"Maybe the stones moved it while they were dancing?"

Lee turned to his solicitor. "I want it documented that they've got my bag."

"Forensics have your bag," said Shand. "Along with everything else they took from the stone circle. Not that Annabel was killed at the stone circle. She was dumped there at four. Funny how all these events happen during gaps in your alibi."

The interview stalled at that point. Lee folded his arms and became less and less co-operative, and the duty solicitor decided to earn his call-out fee. Shand kept the interview going for another fifteen minutes, then gave up. Lee wasn't going to confess, and he had nothing left to confront him with.

"Are you going to charge my client, or badger him to death?" asked the duty solicitor.

"He'll keep," said Shand, getting up to leave. "We'll check his statement and make a decision later today. In the meantime he stays here."

CHAPTER FORTY-EIGHT

Tiredness hit Shand the moment he left the interview room. He'd been kept alert by the buzz of adrenaline. Now he felt like a wreck.

"Go home," he told Marcus. "Get some sleep, then tomorrow, or today, or whatever day this is, hunt down all of Lee's friends. One of them's got to be his driver."

It was all he could do to finish the sentence. He yawned all the way to the stairwell and forced himself up the steps. A cup of coffee and he'd be fine. He needed to check through Helena's statement. See how she described her assailants.

He took two black coffees from the machine. The first one tasted foul. Bitter and lukewarm. The second was better. Then he felt a craving for sugar and pressed the hot chocolate button. Very nice.

He staggered to his office, slumped in his chair and fired up thc computer. He pulled down Helena's statement. She described the men as taller than George and stocky. Lee was smaller than George and slim.

Sleep claimed him soon after that. His car was stuck in Athelcott and he didn't feel like walking to the hotel.

~

Shand might have dreamed that Detective Chief Superintendent Wiggins was standing in the doorway. He might also have dreamed that he was snoring at the time, his head lolled to one side, and a substance which could only be described as drool, overflowing down his cheek onto the back of the chair.

Unfortunately he'd have been wrong. It wasn't a dream.

"Shand!" bellowed the DCS, slamming the door behind him.

Shand jumped. "Sir," he said, clamping both hands to the

chair's arm rests for support.

"Is everything all right?" said the DCS, leaning forward and peering down at Shand. "You look terrible. Is that ... is that bramble in your hair?"

Shand patted his head and found a four-inch strand of dead bramble. He held it gingerly between finger and thumb and stared at it. How long had that been there?

"I had a fall in the woods, sir," he said, feeling an explanation was necessary.

"When you were wrestling with Satan, I suppose?"

"No, that was in the car. This was later." He threw the bramble in the waste bin by his desk, and then noticed the state of his trousers - were those blackberry stains?

"How are you feeling?" asked the DCS, the concern on his face deepening.

"Fine," said Shand, his hands reaching towards the knot of his tie which, as expected, he found hanging loose and twisted over one shoulder. He pulled it back to the centre and tightened it.

"This business with Satan-" said the DCS.

"He's a dog," said Shand, interrupting swiftly.

"Is he?" said Wiggins, in a tone normally reserved for encounters with the mentally unbalanced. "I hadn't heard that one."

"No, sir. He really is a dog."

"You uh see him do you, Shand? Satan? Is he ... is he here now?"

Even half-asleep Shand could hear the alarm bells.

"No! Satan is Marcus's dog. We were all in the car together."

"With the psychic?"

"She's not part of the case, sir. She just turned up."

Shand could feel himself fighting a desperate rearguard action. But with no support. His brain was half-asleep and what had happened to his knack for finding the opportune lie?

"She said she was working for you, Shand. She had your phone."

"Only because Satan knocked it out of my hand!"

"You can't blame Satan for everything, Shand. There is such a thing as free will."

Shand's brain fled. The battlefield strewn with white flags and discarded excuses. He opened his mouth in ever-optimistic hope, but not one lie deigned to poke its head over his tonsils.

"Go home, Shand. Take the rest of the day off. I've arranged for a DI from Eastern Division to be released early. Tom Morrison, good copper and very experienced. He'll join us tomorrow morning and we'll go through the files together. No reflection on you, Shand. If anyone's to blame, it's me. Now go home. I'll see that Taylor brings all the files up to date."

~

Shand was not going anywhere. He collected his things together in case Wiggins returned, and hovered by the door, listening. He heard the door opposite click shut, and then footsteps retreating down the corridor. He slipped his head outside and saw Wiggins leaving – he'd probably left a note on Taylor's desk.

Shand waited for the corridor to clear, then retrieved the note. He had other plans for Taylor. Not that he knew what they were, but he was sure something would come to mind.

He returned to his office and stood by the window monitoring the car park. As soon as Wiggins drove off he relaxed. Now all he had to do was close the case before the new DI arrived.

Which was still feasible. He'd done all the hard work. All he needed now was to find the place where Annabel had been murdered...

And then what? Pin all his hopes on forensics again? The case was awash with forensics – most of it dubious. Fingerprints that had been planted, shoe prints that could be explained way. He didn't have one piece of evidence that conclusively proved guilt.

What he needed was to find Helena's abductors. That was where Lee, or whoever was guilty, had made their mistake. A secret shared is a secret jeopardised.

Which brought him back to his theory that Lee would need to be present at Helena's abduction. He dug out Helena's statement again in case he'd dreamed the answer he'd found last night. He hadn't. There it was on screen. Two stocky men, taller than George. Neither of which could be Lee.

Doubt, doubt and more doubt. Was he wrong about Lee? His entire case rested on Lee's predilection for publicity and the bizarre. And the shoe print. But what if he really had been hiding the Athelcott One in the outbuilding? That was in character too. Take the chicken out of the equation and you had a simple murder. And no reason to search for a murderer obsessed with spectacle.

Doubt again. He was plagued by it. It used to be an advantage - a safety mechanism that made him check and double-check everything before proceeding. It had made him the 'safe pair of hands.' Now it was a curse. Something that impeded progress. He didn't have the time that he used to have. When he was lecturing, he had months to examine old cases. He could sit down and mull over the decisions and evidence, show his students where the mistakes had been made, what should have been done and when. But now he was under constant pressure - Wiggins, the press, his own vanity, countless Gabriels. Everyone wanting something. An arrest, someone to blame, good publicity, his wife.

And now he wasn't sure if he was cut out for the job.

Even more doubt. He'd stepped out of a career he'd been good at, into one that consistently refused to be what he'd expected it to be. Okay, he'd needed the operational experience to be considered for promotion, but what if he'd burned his boats? Damaged his reputation so much he couldn't even get his old job back. Forever tarnished as the man who arrested chickens and wrestled with Satan in the back seat of cars!

No. He refused to be dragged any deeper into this self-created mire. If Wiggins wanted a fresh eye on the case, he'd have one. Shand's. He'd throw everything up in the air, rid himself of preconception and examine the case anew.

Starting from the beginning.

Shand gathered up his notes, pulled his chair in close to the computer, and started reading. He re-read every file, highlighting anything he deemed important, taking notes as he went, constructing timelines for events and people, checking alibis and their corroboration.

Then he read through the notes of what he'd extracted,

and suddenly noticed something that he should have seen before.

~

"You wanted to see me?" asked Taylor, poking his head around Shand's door.

Shand was still deep in thought. He'd barely moved since his epiphany. And would his plan work? It was probably the only way, short of an unexpected confession, to bring the murderer to justice.

He filled Taylor in. The sergeant had his doubts, but grudgingly accepted the logic of Shand's argument, if not the practicality of his plan.

"The Chief Super will go spare," he said.

"Only if he finds out," said Shand. "And if he does, I'll take full responsibility." He smiled. "I'll tell him Satan told me to do it."

~

Taylor executed the first part of the plan – the release of Lee Molland. Shand arranged a venue, and then rang Marcus to collect the equipment. Everything was running smoothly. Until Shand saw Chief Superintendent Wiggins drive into the station car park.

"Your car keys," said Shand, holding out his hand to Taylor. "Wiggins is downstairs. I've got to run. Tell him you're working in here bringing all the files up to date like he asked."

He grabbed the keys and ran. Along the corridor and down the back stairs. He waited for a full minute by the fire exit, trying to judge Wiggins' progress, giving him enough time to park his car and walk to the front desk.

Shand had barely taken three steps towards Taylor's car when his phone rang. It was Wiggins. Shand's first thought was to switch the mobile off, but then decided it might look suspicious.

"Hello," he answered, feigning a yawn.

"Where the devil are you, Shand? The station sergeant says you're still in the building."

Shand yawned again. "My car was parked out back so I left via the rear exit."

He added another yawn. "Do you want me to come in?"

"No, of course not. Sorry, Shand. I shouldn't have woken you."

Shand dashed across the car park, hunched low and praying the DCS wasn't close to a window.

The car key danced nervously in his hand, sliding off the lock three times before finding the hole. The door opened. Shand threw himself inside, glanced towards the station foyer, then gunned the engine, pulling away far faster than he'd intended and almost hitting a wall as he slued the car into a turn too tight for the speed.

He pulled into traffic, turned left, then right, not caring where he was going as long he was putting distance between himself and the station. He left Sturton, found the smallest turn off he could find, to a village he'd never heard of and, after two miles, pulled over, parking by a farm gate.

He leaned over the steering wheel and tried to catch his breath. If he still had a job by the end of the day it would be a miracle.

And what was Wiggins doing checking up on him? Had he heard about the surveillance equipment requisition?

Shand flopped back in the driver's seat, and took several deep breaths. Was his plan compromised? He needed another person to set the trap. Someone outside CID. He'd intended to ask one of the uniformed branch to volunteer, but now...

Could he trust anyone at Sturton? Wiggins had probably put the word out – DCI Shand's having a nervous breakdown, inform me if he contacts you.

Shand looked at the steering wheel. And visualised banging his head against it repeatedly. To be so close...

And then he had another thought.

It was a measure of Shand's desperation that that thought centred upon a card nestling in the top pocket of his jacket.

Saffron.

The 'con' column was immense, but the single entry under 'pro' was telling. She'd do it. Everything else can be overlooked when you're desperate.

He checked the 'con' column again. Yes, she thought she was psychic; yes, she was slightly batty and ,yes, she couldn't stop talking. But she *had* helped last night. She could have left the car outside Lee's house and gone home. But she'd stayed. For five hours in a cold car with a neurotic dog.

She *could* be trusted.

And if he got a result, what did any of it matter? Wiggins wouldn't care if he used a team of psychic monkeys.

He took out the card and phoned.

CHAPTER FORTY-NINE

Saffron volunteered with a squeal. A squeal that a less desperate Shand would have taken as a warning sign. But he pressed on and explained what she had to do.

"We'll run it through several times," said Shand. "First run through, I'll be you, and you be the murderer."

"Ok, Shandy, fire away."

"The phone is ringing, you pick up and I say, 'I saw you.'"

He paused to let the words sink in before continuing. "Four o'clock, Saturday morning, up at the circle, carrying that Annabel."

"Who is this?" said Saffron. "You sound very scary."

Shand closed his eyes. Doubt hovered ever watchful over his shoulder.

"A friend," he said. "A very good friend if you get my drift. Someone who deserves a birthday present. Ten grand will do for a start. Unless you want me to tell the police. You can write me a cheque, I'm not going anywhere."

"Why are we asking for a cheque?" said Saffron. "That's stupid. We should be asking for cash."

"Because we haven't got time. A cheque they can write now. Cash they can stall for. I want the meeting at lunchtime, in public, and in daylight."

"They're going to think me a pretty stupid blackmailer asking for a cheque."

"That's the plan."

~

They practised for twenty minutes. Shand coaching, trying to cover all possible variations. What if the murderer wanted more time, denied being at the circle, said they couldn't make it at lunchtime?

Saffron coped with each variation – eventually – and

began to sound more natural and less like a bad B movie actress.

It was time.

"Are you ready?" Shand asked.

"As ready as I'll ever be."

He rang off. And waited for Saffron to make the call. A tractor engine droned in the distance. Everything else was silent. Minutes passed. Hadn't Saffron got through? Had it all gone wrong?

He checked his watch, gave it a shake to make sure it was working. Surely more than four minutes had passed?

Still she hadn't rung back. He checked his phone. Had the battery gone dead?

It rang.

"All set," said Saffron. "I'll meet you at the pub."

~

At the pub, Shand went over everything again. Was there anything he'd overlooked? The surveillance camera blended into its surroundings so well it was practically invisible. The sound levels were perfect. And there was no car outside that could be recognised. He and Marcus had driven to the pub in the next village to meet Saffron and hitch a lift back with her in her car.

They'd even been given a storeroom in the back to watch the monitor from.

But did the restaurant look too empty?

Shand left the storeroom and took another look. He'd chosen the pub on Taylor's recommendation.

"There's a separate restaurant area that's practically empty at lunchtimes. All the food trade's in the evenings, but they keep the room open lunchtimes for coffee and young families."

It was exactly what Shand wanted. Somewhere quiet. But was it too quiet? Saffron was on her own in there. Would it look like a set up?

He stood by the entrance to the restaurant. There were over a dozen tables, seating for forty-eight. A buffet bar along one side and a carvery in the corner. Did it look closed? It certainly looked empty. Maybe he should seat Saffron more visibly? He'd agonised over that for twenty minutes, they'd changed the camera angle twice. Which is better? To tuck Saffron around the corner in the quietest part of the room, or have her visible from the foyer?

Both had their advantages. He should have brought more people into his plan, maybe rung Langton Stacey and populated the restaurant with a few more couples.

He checked his watch. Thirty minutes to go. He'd better leave. He was looking suspicious enough as it was.

Thirty minutes came and went. Shand stared at the monitor willing them to arrive. Had they taken one look at Saffron and left?

"Do you want me to check the bar?" asked Marcus, even more nervous than Shand.

"Not yet," said Shand.

Saffron looked bored. Which worried Shand more than when he thought she looked nervous. Would she...

Saffron smiled and sat up. A shape appeared on the monitor. They'd arrived.

~

Shand watched intently, his face less than a foot away from the screen. Saffron was still on script. And the waitress had played her part - he'd told her to check the restaurant every five minutes from one thirty. Now she was returning with the coffees.

"Do you have the cheque?" asked Saffron.

"I might. If you answer me one question."

"What's that?"

"What were you doing at the stone circle at four o'clock in the morning?"

This was one Shand had covered. He willed Saffron to remember.

"I was walking back from the drag hunt. You know, the one the Brigadess runs?"

"Ah, the full moon. I should have realised."

There was an acceptance in the voice, almost a dry amusement that on that night of all nights so many people had been abroad.

"Who shall I make the cheque payable to?"

They'd covered that one as well. Shand wanted her to say 'cash,' but Saffron insisted on a pseudonym. "It's more in character," she'd said.

"Sharon Sprott."

"Is that two t's?"

"Two t's to a tee," said Saffron, adding a trill-like laugh.

Shand buried his head. Then rebuked the monitor. "This is not the time to make bad jokes, Saffy." She'd done so well up to then. Was she about to lose it?

Saffron accepted the cheque and scrutinised it.

"Don't worry," she said. "Your secret's safe with me. Though I must admit to being the teeniest bit intrigued. Why did you do it?"

Shand couldn't believe it. They'd agreed. No questions about the murders. It couldn't look like a set up. Her job was to take the money, then get out.

"Nice weather today, don't you think?"

They weren't taking the bait. Shand wasn't sure if he was relieved or worried. Did they sense that something was wrong?

"You know," said Saffron. "I think I'll just go and powder my nose. Won't be long."

At last, thought Shand, staring even more intently at the screen. This was when it should happen. He waited. A hand reached out across the table and hovered over Saffron's cup. There was a bottle in the hand. It tipped. Then the other hand reached over, picked up the teaspoon and started stirring. The rattle of spoon on cup resonated through the speakers.

"That's all we need," said Shand, heading for the door. "Keep the tape running. Everything else is a bonus."

Shand strode along the back corridor, through the foyer and into the restaurant.

He slid into the vacant seat and grabbed Saffron's cup. "I'll take this, Mrs. Benson."

CHAPTER FIFTY

The look of surprise on Helena's face was fleeting.

"What a pleasant surprise, chief inspector. Have you been here long?"

"Long enough."

Helena looked down at her cup. "Oh," she said, and then she looked at Shand and smiled. Which surprised him, he wasn't sure what he'd been expecting – tears, an impassioned denial? But definitely not this.

"What gave me away?" she asked, her voice calm and without the slightest tremor of nerves.

"Little things," he said, watching her closely. "Little things I didn't even notice until today."

"Such as?" asked Helena, taking a long sip of coffee.

"Such as the two men who abducted you. It made sense at first. They drive down from London. They abduct you at 10:30, bury you at eleven, then disappear – probably back to London. But then it seems they stay in the village for Annabel's murder. And this morning I discover that Annabel wasn't moved to the circle until four. So what were these men doing all that time?"

"Did it ever occur to you that Annabel might have hired the two men to abduct me?"

It hadn't. The merest flutter of doubt grazed his confidence. "Why would she do that?"

"To frighten me into withdrawing from the council elections."

"Was she trying to frighten you?"

Helena took another sip of coffee. "Then the two men find out my husband's a bank manager and they get greedy. Why settle for the thousand pounds that Annabel promised when they could blackmail George into robbing his bank?"

Shand was confused. "What are you saying?"

"But they still have one loose end to contend with – Annabel. So they phone her from the village green and say they want their money now. When she comes out, they take her to the circle to prove they did the work. As soon as she pays them, they kill her. What do you think of that?"

She looked at him over the rim of her cup and raised both eyebrows, challenging him.

He didn't know what to say. Or what Helena was doing. He'd solved the case. Helena was guilty. None of what she'd said had happened.

Had it?

"George was never contacted," he said, barging away the doubt. "There never was a plan to rob his bank."

"No," said Helena, wistfully. "I considered planting more clues, but George was never any good at dissembling. I thought it better to hint at the possibility and keep George's role to a minimum."

"So you admit it?"

"Chief inspector, you're holding a cup of coffee laced with poison. I'm hardly in a position to deny anything."

"Then why..."

"Professional curiosity. I've read crime novels since I was a little girl. I wanted to know if you'd considered the same scenarios I had. Don't you think that Annabel would have made a splendid murderer? She was cunning, amoral, single-minded. I thought you would have at least considered her as a suspect in my abduction."

"I hadn't. I–"

Helena interrupted him with a wave of her hand. "No mind, chief inspector. You were saying about the two men..."

Shand paused for a second to observe Helena. She seemed so in control. This was supposed to be his big moment – the denouement. Not hers.

"So," he said, "this morning I reassessed all the information we had and where it came from, and realised that so much of it came from you. The existence of the two men, the time of the abduction, the abduction itself, that the match book came from the car, that there was a car, that the drugged wine bottle wasn't on your table when you left home at six.

"All of that came from you. Even the spade that killed

Annabel. And all of it was uncorroborated. Take away the abduction and suddenly two irreconcilable crimes become one – Annabel's murder – everything else is alibi. And brilliant."

Helena smiled broadly. "It was, wasn't it?"

"And once I understood that, then everything else fell into place. You had to move Annabel's body to the circle at four because that was the earliest George could return from Sherminster without waking his hosts. You staged the fake abduction for 10:30 to give yourself an alibi, and murdered Annabel at midnight to give George an alibi. Perfect.

"Then at four, the two of you moved the body to the circle, dug the hole. You climbed in, George covered you up and placed Annabel on top. The perfect alibi. How could the person buried beneath the body be the murderer?

"But what about the spade?" said Helena, draining the last of her coffee. "How could Annabel's blood be on the spade if it was used afterwards to dig the grave?"

"You took two spades to the circle," said Shand. "One to dig with and the murder weapon that you pressed soil onto to make it look like it had been used to dig with."

Helena nodded as he spoke and smiled like a tutor listening to her prize student.

"We spent hours agonising over that," she said. "George didn't think anyone would notice. He wanted to use the same spade, but I knew we couldn't risk Annabel's blood being smeared or removed by the digging. The murder had to be seen as occurring after the burial, not before. Of course it meant an extra journey for George. He had to clean the other spade and take it home. But I knew it was necessary."

"I'm still not sure how you got Annabel to come to meet you. I imagine it was something to do with the Brigadess. Some piece of tantalising information that you promised her if she'd come to you immediately. Though how you got her to walk is beyond me."

"I told her I couldn't risk anyone seeing her car outside my house. People would then know who'd given her the information."

"About the Brigadess?"

"I said I'd found something too shocking for words. That I knew the Brigadess was in financial straits, but I couldn't believe she'd stoop to fraud."

Shand smiled to himself. That would definitely make Annabel leave her house in the middle of night.

"Let me guess," said Shand. "You made sure she had the impression that if she didn't come over straight away you might change your mind?"

"Exactly," said Helena, reaching over and touching Shand on the back of his hand. She looked pleased, he thought, and animated. The relief, maybe, of finally being able to talk.

"I dithered," she continued. "And wondered aloud if I was making a mistake talking to her. And that, perhaps, if I took the papers to the Brigadess in the morning she'd be able to explain that it was all a silly mistake."

And Annabel came running – or, more accurately, walking – to her death.

"What did you use?" asked Shand. "Sheets on the floor to make sure Annabel left no trace?"

"Polythene sheets," said Helena. "I laid them out on the study floor and told her we were decorating. I said the papers were on George's desk, picked up the spade I'd placed behind the door and hit her. I'm a lot stronger than people think. You can't dig a quarter acre garden for thirty years without building up some muscles, chief inspector."

"So you laid Annabel on her stomach–"

"Lividity, chief inspector. So many people forget the importance of keeping the body in the same position that you intend it to be found."

"Then when George came back, you wrapped her in the polythene, put her in your car and drove her to the circle."

"I had to change my clothes," said Helena. "Twice. I had to be found in the same clothes I'd been wearing that evening, but I couldn't risk any fibres or hairs from Annabel. So I changed in between and George got rid of them along with the polythene sheet and the scissors I cut the duct tape with. He put them in a skip outside a house in Sherminster. They should be gone by now."

Shand sat back and listened. He hadn't thought to ask anyone what clothes Helena had been wearing that day. Or to search for material the body might have been wrapped in. As soon as they'd found the spade, duct tape and handbag – that was it. Search over. Nothing more to find except the car.

"Which brings us to George," said Shand, unsure how to phrase the rest of the question. He found it hard to reconcile Helena the calculating murderer with Helena the loving wife. But she *had* been a loving wife. However much he'd begun to doubt his instincts over the last week he was sure of that.

"Yes," said Helena, sighing deeply. "George." She brushed away a tear and took several seconds to compose herself. "I should never have involved George. That was a mistake I shall take to my grave. He said he wanted to help, but I'm sure he was only saying that to please me. He'd have done anything for me."

Helena's bottom lip quivered and she covered her face. Shand looked away.

"Sorry," she said, pulling herself together. "He never could lie. He'd start to sweat and get nervous. He was too good a man that was his problem. And you were too good a detective not to notice. Sooner or later he would have blurted something out and I couldn't." Her voice faltered. "I couldn't bear to see that dear, sweet man suffer. He couldn't have lived with the disgrace. He was too sensitive for that. Prison would have killed him."

"So you did it yourself?"

Helena nodded, her head bowed.

"I tell myself it was a kindness. Sometimes I even believe it."

Shand waited for her to continue. She stayed silent, one finger resting on her wedding ring and slowly rotating it around her third finger.

"You took the Valium from Jacintha during one of the WI meetings?"

"Yes, George and I drank the wine the night before," she said, abstractedly, still playing with the ring. "Gabe Marsh's wine. I told George we were getting rid of all the evidence. He was relieved. I don't think he noticed that I never touched the bottle."

Shand was confused. Why had they drunk the wine the night before?

Helena continued. "I wasn't sure how Valium would taste in wine so I put it in the curry."

"What?" said Shand. "But we tested the bottle."

"I mixed some of the Valium with a teaspoon of wine and

poured it back into the bottle. Then I put the bottle in the box by the door."

"And switched bottles when you came home with the Brigadess?"

"Yes, while she was in the lounge. It only took a second. Though I could barely concentrate. I thought George would have passed away quietly in his favourite chair. I didn't think..."

She broke down.

Shand could imagine the shock. She wouldn't have known if George was dead or alive. He might have rung for an ambulance and been taken to hospital.

"George probably heard the chicken crow," he said. "Lee Molland was using your stables to hide the Athelcott One."

He stopped himself speculating out loud what had happened next. Did George collapse in the dirt of the garden shed? Or come over drowsy and sit down first, slowly sinking to a peaceful death?

He changed the subject.

"What I don't understand is why? Why Annabel? Why now?"

She took a tissue from her handbag and blew her nose.

"Have you ever faced death, chief inspector?"

"No."

"It changes everything. Your perspective, how you look at your life. And it makes you ask the question – 'How shall I be remembered? Have I made a difference?'"

Shand waited, was she going to blame it on the brain tumour?

"Two months ago I asked myself that question and did not like the answer. My life is the village. I was born here, educated here, married here. We were never blessed with children, George and I. The village is all we've ever had.

"But it's dying. Bit by bit, year by year. The school's gone, the shop's gone, most of the jobs have gone. When I was a girl everyone who lived in the parish, worked in the parish. We were an agricultural community. Now we're a dormitory village, a retirement village, a repository for people who work in the cities and have a romanticised view of life in the countryside. Except as soon as they move here they want to change it to something else. A suburban park with flower boxes, and hanging baskets, and no mud on the road, or noisy animals in the yards.

"Every year more of them come. The house prices shoot up. Our families move out. We can't compete with the affluent families from the Southeast. There are no jobs or affordable accommodation for our youngsters. So they leave. In another ten years, they'll be more incomers than villagers. In another twenty, no one will care."

"So you killed Annabel and framed Gabe Marsh to even up the numbers?"

"Oh, much more than that," said Helena, spitting out the words. "I wanted them discredited. The Marchants, Marsh, Jacintha, the whole Gang of Four. I wanted them vilified in the press. I wanted them tarred as murderers and conspirators. I wanted to wake this village up to the greed that's destroying the countryside. I thought..."

She slowed down and suddenly looked tired as though drained by the outburst. She took a deep breath and continued at a slower, more considered pace.

"I thought I could give the village another fifty years. Make sure the villagers stood up against the incomers, and make the incomers think twice about living where they knew they weren't wanted."

"So you went about collecting items from the Gang of Four," said Shand. "Annabel's cardboard box from the jumble sale; the wine bottle, duct tape and match book from the garden party, and Jacintha's pills."

"Yes." She patted her handbag. "The advantage of a voluminous handbag. I collected anything I thought might be useful. Then I worked on the plan and waited for George's stag night. I didn't think the Brigadess would arrange her hunt for the same night."

Shand wondered if her plan would ever have worked. Framing Gabe Marsh certainly had. Initially. And without Lee Molland to muddy the waters, or Marius to see her moving the body...

But would it have changed people's minds? Perhaps. Even if Marsh or Marchant weren't charged, the suspicion would remain. The press would find out about the fingerprints and Gabriel's girlfriend. Conspiracy theories would abound. Was Gabe being protected by his relationship with the Chief

Constable's daughter? Were the police biased in favour of the rich and influential? There'd be a backlash which Helena could feed with well-timed stories of how Annabel and the Gang of Four had threatened her. And with only a few months to live she'd have both the sympathy of the public and the knowledge that no libel suit could ever hurt her. She could say what she wanted. And many people would believe her.

But would that save the village?

He could see it making life difficult for incomers. In the short term. But houses would still come on the market and local people would still be outbid. Athelcott was only three hours from London, well within the outer commuter belt. And affluent buyers would still dream of their rural retreat.

But maybe it would change their outlook, make them more respectful of the community they were moving to. Or fearful.

Who could tell?

Helena hadn't said a word all the time he'd been thinking. She seemed withdrawn now, her eyes unfocussed and her head slightly bowed. The strain, thought Shand.

"I'm going to have to ask you to come down the station," he said. "To make a formal statement."

"That won't be necessary," she said, staring unfocussed at the table. "I've written everything down."

"Where?"

"A letter," she said, stifling a yawn. "There are two of them on the table at home."

"Why..." He was confused. Why would Helena write out a confession? Had she suspected the meeting was a set-up?

"One's for the coroner and one's ... for you." She was having difficulty speaking. Her eyes were heavy and closing.

Shand looked down at the cup in front of him, then the empty cup opposite. Had she? He grabbed Helena's cup, picked it up, sniffed it, stared at the dregs. Then looked at the camera. Had she switched cups?

"Helena!" he shouted, reaching forward and grabbing her shoulders. "What have you done?"

Helena smiled, her eyes firmly closed, her head barely able to support itself.

"No reason concern," she said, the words slurring. "Vastly

preferable death than … cancer had in mind for me."

Shand fought with his phone – all fingers and thumbs – he rang for an ambulance. "What have you taken, Helena? Valium?"

Her head lolled against his chest as he tried to make her stand up. Inadequate medical knowledge rattled around his head. What should he do? Force her to walk? Keep her awake? What?

Marcus and Saffron appeared, breathing hard.

"I didn't see her switch cups," said Marcus. "Honest, I didn't. It's all my fault. I went to fetch Saffron."

"It's not your fault," snapped Shand. "Check her pockets for the bottle. We're taking her to hospital."

They half walked, half carried Helena out of the restaurant, through the foyer into the car park. The ambulance had to be thirty minutes away. Quicker to drive themselves. Or was he making a huge mistake? Should he try to make her vomit? Why didn't he know these things!

They got her into Saffron's car, put Helena in the back with Shand. Saffron took the front passenger seat and Marcus drove. Fast. Rubber burning, back-end swinging, tyre-squealing fast. Helena drifted in and out of lucidity. Her body swinging around the bends with the movement of the car.

She noticed Saffron and smiled. "I wouldn't have hurt you, dear," she said. "I knew something was wrong when you left. Too easy." She started to drift. "Far too easy."

Shand phoned the hospital. Cancelled the ambulance. Asked for help. "What should I do?"

The car slued and skidded. There was nothing he could do. He didn't even know what she'd taken. The bottle said 'artificial sweetener.'

He threw the phone to Saffron and grabbed Helena, trying to force her awake. "What did you take? We need to know!"

Helena didn't answer, her body hung lifeless in his hands. He felt for a pulse. It was weak and thready.

"Helena! What did you take?"

Her eyes opened and for a second focussed directly upon him.

She smiled. "I'm glad it was you," she said. And then she clutched at his hand. "Remember the second letter," she said. "Your eyes only. It's a present."

CHAPTER FIFTY-ONE

Shand watched them take her away. Doctors and nurses shouting instructions while he stood motionless. Would they stabilise her? Would she pull through? And, finally, what if she did?

She would be dead before there was time for a trial. So what had he actually achieved? Preservation of life for life's sake, or the necessity of bringing a murderer to justice?

He wasn't sure. And, somehow, he didn't think he ever would be.

And why was he so upset? That was what he couldn't understand. He felt more sympathy for Helena than he ever had for Annabel. Which was ridiculous. She was the victim not Helena. And yet...

There was still that connection, that hand around his ankle that wouldn't let go. He didn't want her to die, he didn't want her to be guilty, he didn't want...

He had to leave. This was ridiculous.

"Would you mind staying with her?" he asked Saffron, barely waiting for her answer. "Call me if there's any news."

"Come on," he said to Marcus. "We've two letters to find."

~

The first letter was propped up against a vase. It was addressed to the coroner as Helena had said. He opened it.

Inside was the confession, written in a neat blue hand - using a fountain pen by the look of it. Everything was there. Everything she'd said at the restaurant plus a few other details. Her struggle to find an explanation for George's nervousness, her confiding in the Brigadess about an invented argument between her and George about chemotherapy. And then the remorse the next day - the anger, the disgust about tarnishing his name. George had never raised his voice to her in thirty years of marriage. She should never have involved him, she should never have killed him.

Shand wondered if her brain tumour had affected her reasoning. It must have. How else could you explain a woman like Helena Benson turning to murder?

He read the note again. There was no mention of suicide or her planned meeting with Saffron.

He wondered when she'd written it. To prop it up against a vase and address it to the coroner sounded like the final act of a suicide. But nothing in the note backed that suggestion up.

And the name on the envelope was typewritten. Helena didn't have a typewriter.

"Marcus," he said. "Have a look for a typewriter."

He looked for the second letter. It was on a place mat. Chief Inspector Shand, it said, written on the envelope in that same copperplate hand. Just as he was about to open it, his phone rang. It was Taylor, his voice barely above a whisper.

"DI Morrison's arrived. Wiggins has called a press conference to announce he's taking over the case."

"When?"

"In twenty minutes."

Shand grabbed both letters and stuffed them into his pocket. "Marcus!" he shouted. "We've got to get back to Sturton!"

~

Shand had only one thought - the press conference - he had to get there. If he phoned ahead, they'd either not believe him or take all the credit.

He checked his watch, his wrist flying from one side of the car to the other as Marcus threw Saffron's car into a series of S bends. Whatever time it was, it was late.

He rang Saffron. Helena was stable, but critical. He rang the restaurant, apologised for their swift departure and asked them to lock the storeroom and secure the equipment. Then he rang Taylor.

"Are you alone?"

"No."

"Wiggins?"

"Mr. Shand's not here at the moment, sir. Would you like to speak to DI Morrison?"

Shand heard a voice in the background ask, 'Who's that?'

"Mr. Shand's informant, sir," said Taylor. "I think another asylum seeker's gone missing."

"Very funny," said Shand. "We're coming in. The case is closed. But we need someone to pick up the tapes and surveillance equipment from the restaurant. Someone you can trust."

"I'll see what I can do, sir."

~

The car park was packed – television vans, satellite dishes and lines of cables everywhere.

"Park by the door," said Shand, unbuckling his seat-belt. They were late. Even with Marcus driving they'd missed the press conference's scheduled start.

Shand burst from the car and nearly collided with a youth standing by the steps.

"'Scuse me," said the boy. "You with the press?"

Shand was about to push past when something registered. That face. He'd seen it before.

He took a second look. "Davy Perkins?" he said.

The boy's face lit up. "You recognise me?"

For some reason the expression 'Does the Pope shit in the woods?' sprung to mind. Fortunately he coaxed it to spring somewhere else.

"Of course, I do, Davy. Where have you been?"

"Ibiza," he said. "Look, are you a journalist? Only, I like got this story I want to sell. For the right price. If you're interested, like?"

"Come with me, Davy," said Shand, folding an arm around the youth's shoulder, a plan already forming in the devious left-hand side of his brain. "I'll introduce you, if you like. On one condition."

"What's that?"

"You give me a quick run-down of where you've been and why."

"Shouldn't we talk money first?"

"Think of me as your publicity agent, Davy. I don't need to

know the whole story just enough to introduce you to the press. Now what have you been doing all year?"

Shand tried to use Marcus and Davy as a shield as they swung through the foyer. But the station sergeant saw him.

"Mr. Shand?" he called.

Shand waved an acknowledgement and hurried the others along, pushing through the swing doors towards the conference extension. No doubt a phone call to DCS Wiggins was imminent.

"I worked the clubs in Spain like," said Davy as they entered the corridor. "Then I met this bloke going to Ibiza."

"Why didn't you contact your parents?"

"Nothin' to say. I wanted to like wait until I was famous and show everyone how wrong they'd been about me."

"And now you're famous."

Davy grinned from ear to sun-tanned ear. "Yeah. Cool, innit?"

~

Memories - none of them good - tormented Shand as he walked down that long corridor to the conference room. What kind of boxer was he going to be this time? One who knew the fix was in and had only to show up to win? Or a gatecrasher about to be pounced upon the moment he stepped into view?

He stopped by the door, gave Marcus and Davy their instructions, then, placing both hands upon the door, threw it open.

CHAPTER FIFTY-TWO

The room was buzzing. Wiggins and two other men were seated on the stage, but Jimmy Scott was still fussing with microphones and cables with a sound technician. Only one head turned to see who'd come in. Kevin Tresco.

Shand waved to him. A small boy somewhere in Shand's head shouted, 'Bring it on, big nose.'

Shand trotted up the steps, turned at the curtains and strode on stage. Wiggins turned in horror. There was a scrape of chair legs on floorboards as he tried to get to his feet, tried to move quickly to block his subordinate's approach...

Only to have Shand reach out, grasp his hand, shake it firmly and pull him into what could only be described as a hug.

"Don't worry, sir," Shand whispered in the DCS's ear. "I gave Satan the slip."

There was a rapid exhalation of air from the DCS and a slow and plaintive, "Oh, Shand." But Shand was no longer listening. He was concentrating on what came next.

He deftly swung his body, interposing himself between the DCS and the press, then turned to face the microphones. Wiggins made an attempt to grab him from behind, but the presence of the cameras restrained him. Shand took the nearest microphone and lifted it to his lips.

"Can I have your attention, please," he started. "I have an important announcement to make."

The hubbub subsided ... until Kevin Tresco cupped his hands to his mouth and called out. "He's arrested another chicken!"

Laughter from the floor. A groan from Wiggins and a renewed effort to wrest Shand from the stage.

Shand sat down, suddenly exposing the DCS to the glare

of the cameras and forcing him to break his grip. Shand grinned for the press and waited for the laughter to abate.

"Sorry, Kevin," he said. "No chickens this time. But I can confirm that at two o'clock this afternoon the murderer of Annabel Marchant and George Benson was apprehended by Wessex CID and has since made a full confession."

The room erupted. Later, journalists would comment upon the wide-eyed look of surprise shared by all three of DCI Shand's colleagues on stage. But, at that moment, no one had eyes for anyone other than Shand.

"Who?" someone shouted. A call echoed by others. "Can you give us their name?"

Shand teetered. Part of him was crying out for a proper denouement. He had a captive audience. Everyone wanted to know who did it, why and how? He could give it to them. A bit at a time, tantalising, teasing. There was no trial to ruin.

Only a career.

He decided to play it down. Slightly.

"I can say that she's a fifty year-old local woman whose apprehension came after an exhaustive and, at times, difficult investigation conducted by members of Wessex Constabulary."

Magnanimity, thought Shand, share the glory and let Wiggins see what a valuable team player he had in his midst.

"From the beginning," continued Shand. "This case has been complicated by a web of misinformation spun by the murderer. False evidence, false information and even planted fingerprints. At every stage, the planning behind this crime was remarkable."

More magnanimity. Not that it ever hurt a detective to build up his adversary. He wondered if he should give her a nickname. Something eye-catching for the headlines. Perhaps the Magnolia Moriarty?

"And then, of course," he continued. "There's been the wild speculation. The talk of witchcraft, druids and satanic cults. Who else would bury a person alive in the middle of an ancient stone circle and mark their grave with a corpse?"

He let the question hang. He was enjoying himself, the old confidence returning. He was 'the safe pair of hands' again. Everyone listening in respectful silence.

"Well," he said. "I can now give you the answer. Three of

them, in fact. One, a person who needs publicity. Two, a person who wants an alibi and, three, a person who desperately needs that buried woman to be found."

He paused again, then raised a finger.

"And guess what? All those people turned out to be the same person. The murderer. The woman who had herself buried beneath her victim."

Uproar. Shand was blinded by a series of camera flashes. Calls came from the floor – *How? Mrs. Benson? No!*

Shand raised his hands and the room instantly hushed.

"And before anyone asks, no, Mrs. Benson was not a witch or a member of any cult. There is no supernatural or demonic aspect to this case in any way. Although," he paused and let his eyes wander along the front row of the press. Rapt attention everywhere. Even Kevin Tresco had put away his smirk.

"I can confirm that we did receive invaluable assistance from Satan."

A long heartfelt groan of 'Oh, Shand!' came from behind as DCS Wiggins' hands once more attached themselves to Shand's shoulders.

Shand patted the hand digging into his left shoulder and surveyed the stunned expressions of the journalists.

"Who," continued Shand, milking the moment for all its worth. "Before you all question my sanity, I am relieved to say is a police dog."

Shand was not sure which was the louder, the laughter from the floor or the relieved sigh from behind.

"So, nothing paranormal there, I'm afraid, Kevin," said Shand, picking out the Echo reporter. Time to start winding him up.

"Why did she do it then?" shouted someone from the back.

This was not a question Shand wanted to answer. He didn't want to get bogged down in endless discussions of the minutia of the case. He wanted his performance to be short and spectacular.

"I have her confession here," he said, holding up Helena's letter and then handing it to Wiggins. "It explains everything in detail, but I'm sure the detective chief superintendent would agree this is not the forum to discuss such matters."

Thankfully, he did. Nodding enthusiastically as his eyes devoured the first piece of hard evidence he'd received since Shand had started speaking. His relief was obvious.

"Where is she now?" asked one of the television reporters.

Shand's smile froze. This was not a question to be answered honestly. How do you explain that the suspect tried to commit suicide whilst in police custody, and was now in hospital being guarded by a psychic?

"She's being held at a location close by."

"Where?"

"Somewhere we're not prepared to divulge at this juncture."

"What about the psychic?" asked Tresco.

Shand swung round, staring at the Echo reporter and hoping he'd been quick enough to mask his initial shock. Did Tresco know Saffron was at the hospital?

"What psychic?" he asked, feigning amused interest.

"The psychic working for the Echo."

Shand's career once more appeared on the horizon, braced for a flypast. She was working for the Echo? Had she been feeding stories to Tresco all this time?

"Do you deny you used a psychic to crack the case?" asked Tresco, his sneer growing in confidence.

Shand faltered. Which was worse? To be caught in a lie, or to become a laughing stock? There was no good way to explain his use of Saffron in an undercover operation. He could hear the obvious question – why didn't you use a trained policewoman? And how could he answer? Because people at the station thought I was having a nervous breakdown?

"I can assure you," he said, deciding to answer a slightly different question and hope no one noticed. "That no psychic powers were needed in this investigation. Good police work closed this case. Nothing else."

"Then why did you use our psychic?"

"Really, Kevin, you're becoming obsessed. Next you'll be asking me about that missing boy of yours."

Kevin's sneer widened to a breadth that few crocodiles would have attempted willingly.

"All right then," he sneered. "What about the missing boy?

Have you found his body yet?"

"No."

"Has Helena Benson owned up to killing him?"

"No."

"So how can you stand there and say the case is closed?"

Shand nodded to Marcus and made sure Tresco didn't look over his shoulder by immediately distracting him with another question.

"Do you *really* want me to answer that question?"

"My readers *demand* you answer that question."

Shand shook his head. "I don't think they do," he said, drawing Tresco farther into the trap and taking his attention away from the activity on the steps.

Tresco was on his feet by now, stabbing an accusatory finger at Shand. "You've never had a clue about this case! You've frightened some old woman into confessing and let the real murderer get away!"

"The murderer of Davy Perkins?" suggested Shand "The missing boy?"

"Exactly!"

Shand waited until Davy Perkins was in the wings, then beckoned him on stage.

"Now, Kevin," said Shand. "Either I've just coughed up a whole stomach full of ectoplasm, or your boy's been in Ibiza all year. I'll leave you to decide which to print."

~

Shand decided that that was the moment to close the conference – while the blood was still draining from the Echo reporter's face. And before anyone asked any more questions about psychics or where Helena was. He thanked the media graciously, and left.

Wiggins caught up with him by the coffee machine.

"Excellent work, Shand, but ... you could have called."

"Couldn't risk it, sir?" said Shand, wondering if hot chocolate had been the right choice.

"You couldn't?"

"The press were scanning our mobiles. Have you seen all the aerials they've got in the car park?"

"They were?"

Shand conspicuously looked up and down the corridor

before taking the DCS aside. "We have a slight problem, sir. Which I couldn't risk the press finding out."

"What?"

"Mrs. Benson took an overdose before we got to her. We had to rush her to hospital. She's stable, but critical."

"But she is guilty, isn't she, Shand? This note. It's the real thing, right?"

There was more than a hint of desperation in the DCS's voice as he waved Helena's confession at Shand.

"Every word of it. We've got it on videotape as well."

Wiggins exhaled deeply. "Thank God for that."

"But we need to get some uniforms to the hospital quick before the press find out. And do it quietly."

"I'll see to it, Shand," he said, clapping the DCI on the shoulder. "And as for that other matter ... best forgotten, don't you think?"

Shand agreed, and then saw an aftershock of doubt sweep over the DCS's face. "Satan really is a police dog, isn't he, Shand?"

"I'll get DC Ashenden to show you a picture."

~

Shand pulled himself away from the impromptu celebration that had broken out in the CID office and walked the short distance to his office. He had a call to make – something he wasn't sure he could do if he waited for his confidence to come down from the ceiling.

Her mobile was switched off so he rang her office number and waited, mapping out what he was going to say in his head, thankful that at last he had something intelligible to say, some good news to share.

The phone kept ringing.

He reorganised his opening lines, changed the emphasis on certain words, practised being bright and breezy.

"Anne Cromwell's phone, may I take a message?"

A man's voice. One he didn't recognise.

All of Shand's preparation left through his open mouth. Was this Gabriel? He sounded like a Gabriel. Educated, posh, confident. Shand swallowed, started to say 'who?' then quickly changed it to: "Is Anne going to be long?"

"She's in a meeting until five. May I take a message?"

He hesitated. "No. I'll ... I'll ring again later."

He couldn't get off the phone quick enough.

When he'd recovered his composure he rang Saffron.

"How's Helena?"

"Still critical, but the doctors are more hopeful now. She's expected to pull through."

Shand wasn't sure if he should be pleased or not. He wanted her to live. He wanted everyone to live. But he didn't want her to suffer.

"There's a celebration later," he said. "Taylor suggested it. A few drinks. Probably more than a few drinks. Maybe–"

"Shandy! Are you asking me out?"

"No! No, of course not. It's ... it's a small celebration for the team."

"You consider me one of your team?" Her voice quivered. Shand could imagine her standing there, one hand clutched to her chest, the other poised waiting to punch an unsuspecting passer-by.

"For this case, yes," he said. "We couldn't have closed the case without you. Marcus will give you instructions on how to get there. He's on the way over with your car now."

"Yay! I'll see you later then. Oh, and by the way, do I get to keep the cheque?"

~

Shand was still smiling from the news that not only was 'Sharon Sprott' Saffron's real name, but she'd actually had the nerve to use it in an undercover sting – did she really think she could walk away with a cheque for ten thousand pounds? – when he remembered Helena's second letter. The one addressed to him. He dug it out of his pocket and opened it.

Dear Chief Inspector,

Check the fingerprints on the bottle of Valium on my bedside table. As you know it was not there earlier or your forensic team would have discovered it.

A similar analysis of the bottle of artificial sweetener in my pocket would be very much recommended.

I am sure you have already remarked upon the puzzling use of a typewriter to address my 'confession' to the Coroner.

Consider this a gift from beyond the grave.

Yours conspiratorially,

Helena Benson

P.S. In case you failed to guess. I had a visit from that horrid Echo reporter this morning. It was very easy to get his fingerprints. I had just filled the sweetener bottle with crushed Valium tablets when he arrived. I wiped both bottles with a tea towel while I was making him a hot drink, then 'accidentally' dropped them both on the floor in front of him. He picked them up.

I am sure you will use this information wisely.

Shand shook his head in disbelief. She was incorrigible.

And then he read the letter again and wondered. Could he?

He rested his chin on his fist and stared into space. Images came and went.

He was still laughing when Taylor looked in from the corridor.

"You all right, sir?"

"Me? Never better."

About Chris Dolley

Chris Dolley is a *New York Times* bestselling author. He now lives in rural France with his wife and a frightening number of animals. They grow their own food and solve their own crimes. The latter out of necessity when Chris's identity was stolen along with their life savings. Abandoned by the police forces of four countries, who all insisted the crime originated in someone else's jurisdiction, he had to solve the crime himself. Which he did, and got a book out of it – the international bestseller, *French Fried: one man's move to France with too many animals and an identity thief*.

His SF novel *Resonance* was the first book to be plucked out of Baen's electronic slushpile. And his first Reeves and Worcester Steampunk Mystery – *What Ho, Automaton!* – was a WSFA Award finalist in 2012.

About Book View Cafe

Book View Café (BVC) is an author-owned cooperative of over forty professional writers, publishing in a variety of genres including fantasy, romance, mystery, and science fiction.

Our authors include *New York Times* and *USA Today* best-sellers; Nebula, Hugo, and Philip K. Dick Award winners; World Fantasy and Rita Award nominees; and winners and nominees of many other publishing awards.

BVC returns 95% of the profit on each book directly to the author.

Printed in Poland
by Amazon Fulfillment
Poland Sp. z o.o., Wrocław

59273560R00202